Secrets

Unity Hall says she has been writing for as long as she can remember. A totally undistinguished school career in Wembley was just saved by pages and pages of ill-spelt, untidy essays.

Still unable to spell, she has worked in Fleet Street as a journalist since leaving school, apart from three years of living in the United States where her jobs were more varied, including waitressing, selling and making doughnuts.

Unity Hall is woman's editor of the *News of the World*. She travels widely for her newspaper, lives in London, and spends as much time as possible at her home in the South of France.

Unity Hall

Secrets

Pan Original
Pan Books London and Sydney

for Sandie Laming –
the patient and sympathetic midwife.

And, of course for You.

First published 1981 by Pan Books Ltd,
Cavaye Place, London SW10 9PG
© Unity Hall 1981
ISBN 0 330 26339 0
Made and printed in Great Britain
by Richard Clay (The Chaucer Press) Ltd, Bungay, Suffolk

Chapter One

'This is the limit, madame,' the taxi driver said. 'I can go no further.'

Head turned, his black eyes were regarding her with curiosity from the front seat, and Anne Paradine, gathering her small soft suitcase to her side and opening her purse for francs to pay him, was amused. She realized she must seem an unlikely arrival at Les Hirondelles where the very rich swept up in their Mercedes and Ferraris to be admitted by the old *gardienne* with hairs on her chin and doglike devotion to the de Courtenay family. What was her name? Anne tried to remember, but it had gone.

The taxi had been found in Grasse after taking the bus from Nice Airport. She had little to carry, her main luggage having been sent on ahead; she had decided to go part of the way by public transport, and the Grasse bus had been the first to leave. Money was plentiful enough, but the bus was less insular than the closeted security of a taxi – more French and giving some chance to adjust to the sights, smells and sounds of a different country after the brief plasticity of an Air France airbus flight from Heathrow.

The taxi was disappearing back down the mountain, leaving behind a miasma of dust in the hot afternoon sun. Anne stood and stared out over the view. It had changed little in ten years. The crisp mountain air etched cypresses black against the sky, and far away the Mediterranean shimmered like polished silver. The sky was a blue rarely seen in England, while the snow on the tips of the mountains behind intensified its colour, like the white of a pupil around violet eyes. The burning yellow of Provence surrounded her, and swallows soared above.

The sun was hot on her bare head as Anne pushed her heavy russet hair away from her face, picked up her suitcase and limped towards the *gardienne*'s little stone house beside the barrier that went across the road and stopped cars from entering the de Courtenay domain. To each side of the barrier was a long high wall melding into a thick curtain of cypress trees, which were not needed: the mountain terrain itself was sufficient deterrent to stop most people from trespassing on de Courtenay property. At night the Dobermans discouraged those with mountaineering tendencies.

Her leg was aching a little after the journey, but she wanted to make the walk to the houses scattered on the side of the mountain as her aunt had made her do after the accident all those years ago. The houses had been the goal, with Aunt Olivia cheerleading as, aged seven, Anne walked with gritted teeth the half-mile from the *gardienne*'s stone hut to the first of the houses. Only then would her aunt let her ride in Philip de Courtenay's old gleaming Rolls-Royce the rest of the way. That was the reward for having used a leg the doctors had said would never be much good.

Now, fifteen years later, her leg would walk her to her aunt's cottage on the de Courtenay estate. It would ache for a while when she reached the house that was to be her home for the summer, but it would get her there if she took it gently.

The *gardienne* was dozing at her post, her head nodding on a thin neck.

'Madame,' Anne said quietly through the little open window from which the old lady watched who came and who went. '*C'est moi*. Anne Paradine.'

The old head jerked upright, and the tortoise eyes flickered open, darting a startled look through the window. The *gardienne* had aged even more, but the wrinkled face with the sun in it broke into a wide smile over splendid dentures, no doubt courtesy of the de Courtenays, and she was trundling for the doorway to embrace Anne.

'Berthe!' That was the name, it had suddenly come back. 'How are you, Berthe?'

'Older and older, as you can see, *chère mademoiselle*. But you? How are you? How is the leg?'

6

'You see – I am walking on it,' Anne said.

'It was a miracle. When I remember—' Berthe nodded to herself. 'Yes, a miracle. Shall I ring for the car for you, Mademoiselle Anne?'

'No, I shall walk,' Anne said.

'Like the old days?'

'Yes, like the old days. I shall come and take a coffee with you one day, Berthe. I am to be here for the whole summer.'

The old woman laughed. 'Perhaps something stronger now you are grown, eh?' she said. 'My own orange cordial. Your aunt likes my cordial very much.'

'Then I shall, too,' said Anne.

They shook hands solemnly, and Anne set off along the narrow well-kept road that wound gently upwards to the group of houses perched at the flattened top of the mountain. The land had been terraced so that there was space for a pool and tennis courts, but these were tucked away behind dark cypresses and Les Hirondelles looked at first glance like any small mountain village of Provence. The luxury was discreetly hidden. The de Courtenays were not ostentatious people.

She walked slowly, her small, slight ballet-dancer's body, with the surprisingly pronounced limp, moving carefully. To rest a little, she stopped to examine the riot of wild flowers beside the path. It was, Anne thought, as she had thought on her last visit as a thirteen-year-old to Les Hirondelles, as if the wealth of the de Courtenays encouraged even the wild flowers to bloom more luxuriantly than they would have done elsewhere.

She was pleased with herself. Her French had returned without effort; she had understood every word that Berthe had said in spite of the old girl's thick, twanging Provence accent. And her own responses had come almost without thought.

That was another thing that she owed to her Aunt Olivia. After the crash which killed her parents and crippled her leg Olivia had come to the rescue and taken over the bewildered seven-year-old's life. She had made Anne walk again. She had also taught her to swim like a fish. 'If you can't be graceful on land,' she'd said bluntly, 'you'll be graceful in water.' She had taken Anne for summers to Les Hirondelles, neglecting her own work and life to see that her niece had family and summer holidays like any other child.

Christmas had been magic, with stays in country hotels, usually in France, because Olivia had decided that Anne should speak French like a native.

'My cottage at Lés Hirondelles will be yours one day,' she had said. 'And if you can't speak the language you won't get any pleasure from it.'

Olivia Barton wrote and travelled and seemed to earn a great deal of money – enough to run a home in New York, another in London, as well as the little house in France; also enough to pay for Anne to go to art school in Florence from the time she was fifteen, encouraging her to do only what pleased her for a living.

Anne made a good living from her art. She drew a popular cartoon figure for children, and her books about Sarah Swallow and her journeys and adventures in exotic places had paid for a small but smart flat in Chelsea and an even smaller but smarter car which made her mobile. She also drew a much naughtier, sexy little cartoon about a randy rabbit called Rhoda. The two had made her very comfortably off.

The group of houses was drawing nearer, their rough stone walls stark against the sky. The view spilled itself in every direction, broken by the dowdy grey of olive trees which stood in patches near the houses while tall palms fringed and softened the big main house where Philip de Courtenay, the head of the family, lived with his American wife, Stella.

They would be quite old now, Anne thought. And the children, children no longer. Philip's eldest son, Tomas, and daughter Elisabeth must be well into their forties. De Courtenay *père* had married Stella after the death of his first wife, an English girl, and she too had given him a son and a daughter. Marion, the girl, was four years older than Anne, and they had played together as children. Peter was seven years older, an elegant, fair boy with a remote manner, but he had been sent to school in Boston, where his mother's family could keep an eye on him. Anne had barely known him. She

8

smiled ruefully as she remembered how strongly he had figured in her teenage fantasies.

Françoise and Raoul, Philip's grandchildren, both by Tomas de Courtenay, had been nearer her age – and occasionally they had let the crippled child join in their games, but not too often. As children they had not possessed the warmth of Marion.

She thought of Marion with pleasure, hoping that perhaps they would meet again. Together they had explored the fringes of growing up.

The first old *mas* was close now. The shutters were closed on the stone walls and the house had a blind look. The road widened here and was paved with soft red stone so that the thoroughfare itself formed a courtyard before the house. Geraniums were blooming in huge terracotta pots, but nothing stirred. This was the house that the de Courtenays used to house their friends from Paris in the summer, but the season had hardly begun and perhaps no one had arrived yet. Even so with the key to her summer home clutched in her hand she felt a flutter of anticipation.

Her aunt's cottage lay parallel to the biggest house; Philip de Courtenay's place, past the swimming-pool and down a gentle grassy slope. There were five houses ranged around the red paved road, all with gardens at the back. Then the rolling red, yellow and grey of mountain land which gave the de Courtenays their privacy and some of their income from the olives, the vines and the fruit. Only her aunt's house was separate. It had once been an olive mill, and Philip de Courtenay had converted it especially for Olivia. Her aunt said that there had originally been some resentment in the family, but she had managed eventually to win them over.

Anne's favourite place on the estate was nearing. She loved the huge, blue-tiled swimming pool where she had swum as a child in the clear cold water that came from the mountain streams which surrounded and converged on Les Hirondelles. As her aunt had promised, in the water she was a match for anyone. All the grace she would have had, had it not been for a crash on a wet motorway one winter night, came into play.

9

The cypress trees which protected the pool and peppered it with feathery fronds in the autumn were close now. And on impulse Anne moved towards the stone arch which led on to the patio surrounding the pool. There was a long terrace above, which had been built for non-swimmers to enjoy the view and where dressing-rooms and showers servicing the pool were hidden.

She could hear laughter and felt a little stab of pleasure at seeing some of the family again. Their glamour and their style had often left her tongue-tied as a child. That problem would no longer exist.

She put down her bag and slipped through the archway. The brilliant blue of the pool confronted her; the sunlight, diamond hard on moving water, dazzled her eyes. Two people were in the pool on an enormous red lilo, and for a moment she could not see them clearly for the harshness of the light.

She stepped back into the shadow of the arch to let her eyes adjust and then blinked, not believing what she saw. A naked girl knelt on the lilo, black hair streaming and wet, hanging down her back and ending at her waist in a dead straight line like a curtain. Below was a brown back, then white buttocks, the crease a dark line in the harsh sun. Between her legs and lying on his back was a naked man, and as the lilo rocked madly on the blue water he was thrusting into the girl's body as she moved on him. Her full breasts swung free, tantalizingly near his mouth, and one masculine brown hand pulled at a nipple while the other clasped at her back.

The girl leaned lower and let a red-tipped breast drop into his mouth, and as he raised his head to take the tight pointed nipple between his teeth Anne caught a glimpse of his face. It was Tomas de Courtenay, Philip's oldest son – still lean, brown and muscular as he had been as a young man. She knew she should move away, but there was something pagan and beautiful about the scene so that she was transfixed there in the shadow of the arch, unable to leave.

He was moving faster now, the lilo rocking dangerously. Suddenly the girl pulled her breast free and jerked her body upwards, the spine rigid, the head thrown back so that the

10

dark hair met with the white of her buttocks. Her hands, which had been pulling at Tomas's wet hair, flew to clasp and squeeze her own breasts; gasping, strangled sounds came from the mouth that Anne could not see.

Then the lilo tipped and turned, and with one supple movement the girl twisted her legs around Tomas's back without losing him from inside her. Joined together, her arms and legs clasping him, they slid underwater and surfaced, still coupled, seal-heads streaming water, mouths clasped until she pulled her head away from him and half-screamed, 'Come now. Come now.'

He was standing, his feet firmly on the blue tiles, while she was still wrapped around him, the water supporting her weight, riding on him as he thrust hard into her, his face contorted. Then he too cried out, and they stayed still in the water for a moment while her legs gradually unfolded from behind his back until she stood beside him.

She was much shorter now they were uncoupled; her head only just unsubmerged, her hair floating behind her, while his head, shoulders and brown chest with a vee of dark hair stood clear. He bent to kiss her, turning her gently so that she was in shallower water. And only then did Anne manage to see her face.

The spell was instantly broken, and the strange hot feelings that the scene had aroused in her disappeared in dismay.

The girl in the pool with Tomas de Courtenay was Marion, his half-sister.

'You're absolutely sure Father isn't in?'

Side by side, Marion and Tomas were swimming the length of the pool.

'It's a bit late to ask now,' Tomas said. 'If he is, we've given him a splendid exhibition.'

'Do him good,' Marion said. 'I don't expect he gets much of it these days. Watching's better than nothing.'

'His eyes aren't that good from his terrace. But you,' said Tomas, 'are a very vulgar young lady. I suspect it is your American education.'

11

'Probably,' Marion said, her voice smug; 'but isn't it lucky for you!'

'Very.' Tomas had swung himself up on to the edge of the pool at the shallow end. He sat, his body streaming water, legs apart, grinning down at her.

'Nice,' she said, and clinging to the rail that ran around the pool, she let her body float on the surface while she thrust her face between his legs and took his limp penis delicately into her mouth, rolling her tongue around it then gently blowing mouthfuls of water over it.

Releasing him, she looked up and said: 'Don't you like that?'

'Very much,' he said, dark eyes narrowed and glinting down at her.

'Well, I wouldn't call you very responsive,' she said and pouted.

'That water's cold.'

'No colder than five minutes ago.'

'I'm less randy than five minutes ago.'

'What does a girl have to do?' she said plaintively. 'Try imagining you're on a winning streak at the tables. I bet that gives you a charge.'

'Come up here,' he said.

She lifted herself out of the water, pressing on her arms and arching her body as her legs swung on to the warm tiles of the patio. He watched her, feeling that first tightening of the loins as the hardening began. Her body was perfect, small and rounded, the breasts almost too big above the slim waist and flat stomach, while her white buttocks curved out like cut apples so that he felt the need to clasp his hands around them. The triangle of hair at the base of her stomach was thick and black, but she cut it away between her legs to make entry easier and so that his tongue could enjoy her moistness without hindrance.

At twenty-four she had the sexual skill and experience of a much older woman, and he was curious to know who had taught her. It had to be someone in America. She'd been at school there since she was seventeen. But she would never say.

12

'None of your business,' was her response to questions.

It was not jealousy that prompted his questions, only curiosity. Tomas was not in love with his half-sister, but he was besotted by her body, her frank enjoyment of fucking. You had to call it fucking, he thought. With Marion there wasn't any love in it. If she hadn't been born rich she'd have made a great courtesan, rejuvenating old gentlemen the length and breadth of France and the USA.

Now, she had stretched herself out beside him on the tiles, her legs apart, her stomach pulled flat, and her own red-painted fingernails tweaked gently at the incredibly pink nipples. She turned her head, watching him as she played with her own body. Her eyes had a hazy look and her mouth was faintly open, her breathing shallow and her look was directed at his mouth.

'I'd rather you did this,' she said.

She was still wet, but the sun had warmed her, and the long dark hair was tangled under her head. The fixed glance of her eyes and the demand in them was almost more exciting than her mouth teasing his penis.

'You would, would you,' he said and leaning over her he took her right nipple between his teeth and bit hard. She let out a cry of pain; her body arched and she gasped. Tomas had learned in the past two months that sudden, unexpected pain, particularly to her breasts, made his half-sister climax every time.

Instantly, he thrust his fingers deep into her, rolling over so she was beneath him as he knelt above her. She lifted her head to take him into her mouth, and then after a few moments let her head fall back on the tiles, removed his fingers and with her hands guided him inside her.

'Now fuck me, please,' she said, her voice crooning. 'I want to be fucked.'

Her muscles were tightening and loosening on him with incredible strength, and as he rode her he wondered again who had taught her and then lost himself in the warmth and depth and tightness of her until, shuddering, it was all over.

He was shrinking fast, but her muscles were holding him

inside her as she lay panting underneath him, her eyelids shut over the dark brown eyes.

Suddenly a spasm ejected him from her; she had thrust him out, and at the same time as the movement, a hefty shove from her hands toppled him over and back into the swimming-pool. As he surfaced, she was standing naked, her hair over one shoulder, hands on hips, breasts jutting high and laughing at him.

'Thanks, brother,' she said, and turned to run bare as a baby back towards the house.

Christ, he thought. She takes some chances.

He himself was more cautious. He knew their father had gone into Nice, taking the chauffeur. Marion's mother, his stepmother, would be in her room at the far side of the ground floor of the house – a room she rarely left between lunchtime and dinner since she had become so enormously fat and asthmatic.

His own children, Raoul and Françoise, had gone to Antibes to look at the yacht and to try to persuade McTaggart, the skipper, to take her out. Peter, his half-brother, was in New York and not expected back for a couple more days, while his sister Elisabeth always slept in the afternoons and, hating the sun, slept in her bedroom with the shutters drawn. His own home was the nearest to the pool, his garden adjoining the cypresses which bordered it; Peter's and Elisabeth's properties were both on the other side of the courtyard.

Only an unfortunate chance would have exposed the incest in the family, he thought.

He had left a big towelling-robe over one of the chairs that were placed under the terrace. A long mirror ran along the back wall, reflecting the pool, the garden and the view of the mountains beyond. As he dried himself, he watched his own reflection, thinking idly that if the chance to lay Marion at the pool ever came again she'd probably think of some fancy things to do with that.

Instinctively he pulled in his stomach muscles. Not bad for forty-five. Not bad at all. As he dried between his legs, he thought what a pity Margaret, his elegant, frosty bitch of a

14

wife, didn't appreciate that a bit more, then maybe there wouldn't be any need for Marion. Again he considered whether Margaret ever wondered what he did for sex. She wouldn't stay in the South; hating Les Hirondelles, which she called the back of beyond, she lived most of the year in their Paris apartment.

Margaret was the thorn in his flesh, his Achilles heel. It had been pretty much a marriage arranged between their two rich and aristocratic families, but he had never been able to get through to her – hardly to get into her, he thought crudely – and she was a challenge unconquered. It was rare for a woman to repulse Tomas. Big, with broad shoulders, a strong aristocratic face and considerable charm spiced by arrogance, his successes were considerable. Maybe the appearance of money helped too, but none of what made other women so compliant interested Margaret. He often wondered if perhaps she was a lesbian. Still, she'd done her duty and given the dynasty two children. But after Raoul was born she'd never let him near her again.

There had been a lot of Marions. But the excitement and the danger of fucking one's own half-sister took a bit of beating. He wondered how it would be to crawl into bed with Françoise. Fucking your own daughter must be the ultimate and every man's most secret fantasy. The trouble was that he didn't like Françoise very much. She had her mother's blonde hair, pale blue eyes and small mean breasts. Her body was bony and birdlike. She also had her mother's cool, cold manner, but somehow he felt there was something more burning away there. At seventeen she had a very positive private life that if questioned only brought the ice-maiden stare he'd suffered so long from Margaret. Perhaps someone had already melted that particular ice-maiden though, he thought and wondered just what his frosty seeming daughter would do in bed. She, like him, was a gambler but of a different kind. As a small child she had always been one to take a chance.

He was zipping himself carefully into a pair of Fiorucci jeans, taking care to avoid the thick mass of pubic hair that covered high up his stomach. He pulled a pale-blue silk shirt

15

over his wet dark hair and, slinging the towel over his shoulder, started to walk towards the arch and then on back to his own home, opposite his father's.

Just the other side of the arch something was left on a patch of grass. He moved towards it; a brown bag, soft and squashy, not very heavy and obviously abandoned. He held it thoughtfully, the dark brows meeting above the black eyes which had suddenly darkened. Who had left the bag there? And, more important, when?

Crouching, he pulled open the zip across the top. A few books were inside, a handbag, a simple sponge bag, and a passport. He opened it.

The picture was of an oval-faced girl with direct eyes. Anne Paradine. He had a sudden memory of a small girl, face creased with determination and too-early lines of pain, trudging up the hill to the estate, one leg dragging.

Olivia Barton's niece had come, no doubt, to stay in the cottage. But why had she left her bag there? And what exactly had she seen?

Tomas stared towards Olivia's cottage and whistled softly between his teeth. He knew exactly what she had seen, and why she had left the bag behind. She ran, he thought, and forgot it. Now how the hell do I deal with that?

Chapter Two

The cottage had seemed a long way away as Anne tried to hurry, her leg aching and every now and then nearly giving way. She almost fell running down the short flight of steps from the pool entrance and on to the short springy turf, but pushed on. She still had the big iron key to the house clutched in her hand so as not to waste time when she reached shelter, but her breath was hurting in her chest and throat by the time the heavy carved door was in front of her.

She pushed the key into the lock, turned it twice and pushed the door open. Inside, she shut it behind her and leaned on the rough wooden surface, trying to breathe lightly to stop the rasp in her throat. Then she let out a long, low whistle.

The room was tranquil. A large black-and-white tiled floor, scattered with glowing rugs a huge open fireplace, ready laid with what looked like half a tree; the walls were painted white and hung with a few simple but good pictures. The furniture was covered in heavy deep-blue linen; yellow pottery decorated an old dresser. It looked deceptively simple and rustic, and the sun spilling through small deeply recessed windows threw patches of light and shade, picking up the yellow of great soft cushions and enlivening the deep blue of the upholstery. It was luxurious, and she sighed with pleasure.

After a moment or two Anne limped across the room and sank into one of the armchairs. Her leg hurt, and she sat, her eyes closed, rubbing the back of her calf through her jeans in a long, slow rhythmic movement which she knew sometimes helped to relieve the pain. She was angry with herself, appalled that she should have remained to watch a scene of such intimacy, more appalled by the knowledge her prurient curiosity had given her – knowledge she would far rather not possess.

The worst was that when she pictured the scene again with her artist's eye – the brown and white of the bodies, the blue of the water, the red of the lilo – the same hot pleasurable feelings started, deep in the pit of her stomach, that she had felt while watching. Until she had realized who Tomas's partner was, she had not been remotely offended by what she saw. The uncomplicated disporting of the two bodies in their sexual water-ballet, and their obvious enjoyment and pleasure, had a kind of innocence.

It was a pleasure that Anne had rarely felt, simply because she had met few men with whom she had felt comfortable and relaxed enough to reveal the extent of the damage to her right leg. There had been one who had hurt her; and many who had

17

made advances seemed too fascinated by her obvious disability.

The accident had shattered the bones from knee to foot, and the very best surgeons, at Aunt Olivia's behest and with Aunt Olivia's chequebook urging them on, had painstakingly put the shattered fragments back together again. Over the years, as she had grown and her leg had not, there had been more operations, and three months before there had been what should prove to be the very last: plastic surgery, grafting her own skin over the scarred skin so that one day, hopefully, her leg would not look so different from anyone else's.

Anne had never worn a short dress. Her wardrobe consisted of jeans and long-skirted garments. The plastic surgeon had promised that in a year she would be able to sunbathe in shorts. The limp? Nothing could be done about that.

Aunt Olivia had written from New York while she was in hospital, enclosing the key to the cottage and announcing that it was hers for the next six months.

'You can create Sarah Swallow there just as easily as in Chelsea, as well as your perverted, if profitable, rabbit,' she wrote, 'and send them back to London. You'll find that the French postal system is really very good.

'And I don't want any of your independent arguments. It's far too long since you've visited Les Hirondelles. A summer in France will brush up your French – if you're not already speaking with an Italian accent. Do get up to mischief, won't you? If you ring Hercules Travel you'll find they have a plane ticket ready and waiting in your name – open-dated. So when you leave hospital and you're fit enough – off you go.'

Lying there in the hospital bed, half-doped and drowsy to kill the constant pain from her leg, Anne had thought, Why not? She had weighed the key in her hand, reliving with its length and feel along the palm of her hand memories of childhood and teenage days. With the cool feel of the metal, the ward, the high beds, the few flowers and hopelessly cheerful curtains were blotted out.

She saw in her mind's eye the sere yellow and red of Provence, small lizards lazing on stone and their sudden scurry for safety, round globes of bitter oranges against glossy dark green, golden apricots dripping sweetness from the bough – all the sundrenched touches that were lost to northern children.

The pictures had run through her head like brief film-clips, sustaining her through the days of convalescence until the doctor had said she was fit enough to travel.

Now outside her window an orange tree displayed the last of the winter fruit like Japanese lanterns, and a climbing rose tapped on the glass, shaken by a light late-May breeze.

Anne had a sudden feeling of well-being and contentment as if she had come home. Her leg had ceased to ache, and she smiled sleepily at the rose nodding through the window. Her eyelids felt heavy, and the chair comfortable and deep. She sighed, a quiet little sound in the still room, and slid into sleep.

A slight noise woke her. Startled, she sat bolt upright in the chair. The room had darkened, and a large figure in shadow loomed before her. She could not control a small cry of alarm, and a voice said in accented English: 'I'm sorry. I've startled you. It's only me – Tomas de Courtenay. Shall I turn on a light?'

He had moved to switch on the tall lamp that stood beside the long sofa, and Anne instinctively pushed her fingers through her hair. As the room sprang into brilliance and the shadows fled he turned towards her, and for an instant she did not see a tall, elegant man dressed in blue, but an intent, naked man with seal-wet hair, coupled to the body of a face-less girl.

'You left your bag on the lawns near the swimming-pool,' he said, and his eyes were watching her, steady and black and all too obviously waiting to see her reaction.

Anne was thinking fast. She knew that somehow she must convince him she had seen nothing. If her stay at Les Hiron-delles was to be a success it was essential that Tomas, his father's favourite and the eldest son of the estate, should think her ignorant of what took place in his private life.

'I know,' she said calmly. 'I was going back for it later, but

19

as you see, I fell asleep. I made myself walk from the *gardienne*'s hut – just like the old days, as Berthe said – but I've just had another operation on my leg and I was getting very tired. The bag was too much.'

'I thought perhaps you'd been swimming,' he said.

She laughed. 'No. To tell you the truth I was thinking of dipping my feet in, but I could hear that someone was there. I didn't want to presume until I'd asked your father if I might use the pool, so I just trudged on.'

'It was only Marion and I swimming,' he said. 'You'd have been very welcome.'

'Marion!' Anne was pleased at how surprised she sounded. 'She's here then? How splendid. I thought she was in the States.'

'She left Vassar about a year ago. She's been living in Paris and New York and she came down here at the beginning of spring. Father said it was time she came home.'

His voice was the voice of a man imparting information, and Anne thought with secret amusement how well they were both behaving. The question was, had he believed her? She had a feeling that there had been a moment when a tiny crack in his sophistication had shown the faintest soupçon of relief.

'I am sorry,' she said quickly, 'I'm being so rude. Won't you sit down for a moment? I am sorry I can't give you a drink – I haven't had time to do any shopping yet.'

'Actually you could,' he said. 'Your aunt asked Claudine to stock the house for you. You'll find everything you need for the time being is here. Your clothes have been unpacked and hung, and Claudine tells me she has put your painting things in the little summerhouse at the back. Apparently your aunt thought you would enjoy working there.'

'My aunt is the most thoughtful of people,' Anne said, 'and in that case, can I get you a drink?'

'No thank you.' He smiled suddenly, and Anne could see exactly why his half-sister found him so attractive. 'I wasn't telling you for that – just on Claudine's instructions. She still rules us all with a – what is it you say? – rod of iron.'

There was something faintly suggestive in his use of the

phrase and again the mental picture of the naked girl impaled on him flashed for a second. Anne wondered if perhaps he was waiting for her reaction – a last small check to ensure she had seen nothing.

She laughed. 'I remember Claudine,' she said. 'My aunt says she is the best housekeeper in the world. And Berthe, down at the gate too. My aunt says the de Courtenays have a gift for finding loyal servants.'

'Because my father pays them very well,' he said drily. 'However, if you are not too tired, you are expected for dinner this evening to meet again those of the family who are here. We will expect you at seven thirty if that suits you. And I am to tell you from my stepmother that you are very welcome and that we are all happy to see you again at Les Hirondelles.'

'Thank you, and thank your stepmother,' Anne said. 'I can't tell you how happy I am to be here.'

His defensive attitude seemed to have gone.

'You like it here, no?'

She smiled at him. 'Oh, very much. All my life I've carried mind pictures of this place in my head. You probably don't know, but I'm an artist now – well, an artist of sorts. I paint for children. A character called Sarah the Swallow. It sounds so silly, I know, but all the backgrounds and all the lovely places Sarah sees are based on here.'

She stopped. She had been going on to mention Rhöda, but it seemed somehow too difficult to explain. He had been listening intently, his face serious.

'You draw Les Hirondelles and you draw an *hirondelle*?'

She nodded.

'What made you think of that?'

'Loving this place so much, I suppose.' She hesitated. Again to say how much the luxury had always attracted her would sound wrong, but he was still listening, standing relaxed, his hand on the deep mantelpiece over the fireplace, so she went on quickly: 'The last summer I was here – ten years ago now – I was sitting in this room in the spring. I'd had some operation and my aunt had brought me here to recuperate. She was out, I don't know where, and I was sitting in this chair just as I am now with my leg stuck out in front of me. I had the door open so I could watch the view, and out there on the telephone wires and the vines there were six little baby swallows, all fine-tailed and beautiful, and they were learning to fly. They were really funny, and the mama seemed to be helping them, and then suddenly they got the hang of it. They were so delighted with themselves that they started to play follow-my-leader. And somehow this room became part of the game. They swooped in through the door, swished around the room, perched on the picture over there in turn –' she pointed '– and then, one by one, flew out again.

'They made the circuit about three times, and I sat still just watching, enchanted. And that's how Sarah Swallow was born.'

She stopped, conscious of talking too much and sounding naïve, but he was watching her intently.

'And does your aunt feel the same about Les Hirondelles?' he asked.

'I think so,' Anne said. 'She's always said that one day she'll settle here and live a life of peace and quiet.'

'Has she now,' he said, and there was something odd about his tone. His face was expressionless. 'You must tell my father your story about the *hirondelles*. He feels the same way about the estate as you and your aunt do.'

'And don't you?' Anne asked.

He shrugged. 'There are other considerations. However, I must go. We'll expect you at the big house at seven thirty, no?'

'Yes,' Anne said. 'I'll be there.'

Surprising her, he bent to take her hand and kiss it, and as he rose the dark eyes seemed to inspect her face. Then he said, '*À tout à l'heure,*' and was gone.

She watched him striding across the turf towards the other houses and decided that after that she needed a drink. She had talked much more than was her habit and she knew that the words had been a cover for what she needed to hide from him. Would he guess? Her intelligence told her it was likely.

'But as long as we both play the game of pretending,' she said out loud as she took tonic and ice from the big refrigerator in the kitchen, 'no doubt all will be well.'

22

Finding the gin bottle, she poured herself a generous slug into the heavy tumbler made from Biot glass.

She enjoyed the drink while she bathed, leaving it on the edge of the deep tub that was set with traditional terracotta Provençal tiles. Someone, obviously Claudine, had seen there was hot water in the tank and large aquamarine fluffy towels waiting. Lying in the water, she watched the soft downy hairs of her body float like tiny sea-anemone fronds in the warm water, scented with Roger & Gallet's very best rose bath foam. She lifted her leg to inspect it. The skin was still red and raw, but it seemed to her that every day it became a little paler, the anger fading. Maybe the surgeon was right. Maybe in a year ...

The wall before the bath was one huge sheet of mirror glass, and as she stood to dry herself her own reflection confronted her. Anne did not enjoy full-length mirrors; the ugliness of her leg became too obvious. But now the depth of the bath cut her reflection at the thighs, and for the first time in a long time she looked at her own body.

She could not help but compare herself with Marion. When they were children they had longed for the days when they would be old enough to wear brassières, and when the grown-ups were not around they had inspected each other's breasts for the faintest signs of growth. The last time they had met as teenagers such encounters between them were not mentioned, and Marion at sixteen, to Anne's twelve, had firm apple breasts that had filled Anne with envy. She had only just lately begun to bud.

Now, inspecting herself with all the attention of an artist about to paint a nude, she thought that she had caught up with Marion. Her breasts were as full, the aureola was larger, though just as pink. But the nipples were not as firm and pointed as those that Tomas had taken between his teeth. Experimentally she rubbed the palm of her hand over her right breast, and instantly the nipple sprang upright. 'Umm!' she said, pleased.

She ran her hands down over her flat stomach and her narrow hips, and noted that the hair that covered her mound of Venus was softer, finer and less luxuriant than Marion's and that her body was altogether more delicate. It had been wasted perhaps. But her aunt had said to go carefully so as not to be hurt because of her leg. Now her leg was going to mend. Maybe things could be different.

She rubbed her hand over her left breast, and the nipple sprang to twin with its fellow. 'Teasing myself,' she thought and turned on the cold shower and, teeth gritted, got under it. Her aunt was right. It was time she got up to mischief.

Chapter Three

The light filtering through the shutters was pale grey and the sun had gone down when Claudine tapped discreetly on the door of Stella de Courtenay's ground-floor bedroom and entered without waiting for the command. A small tray holding a whisky and soda in a large balloon glass was in her hand, and she moved through the gloom to the bed deep in shadows and set in a recess in the high-ceilinged room.

'Is that you, Claudine?' The voice from the bed spoke French, but heavily accented with American. Twenty-seven years in France had not erased Boston, Massachusetts, from Stella de Courtenay's voice.

'*Oui, c'est moi, madame,*' Claudine said.

A fluffy white Persian cat leapt from the bed as Claudine placed the tray at the wide table at the side of the canopied bed and moved to open the shutters. 'Are you rested?' she asked.

'Much as I'll ever be.' Stella was pulling her bulk into an upright position, using her arms to lever herself. 'Claudine – my pillows,' she said irritably. 'And bring back Suki.'

Claudine did not answer but she was at the bedside, piling

pillows behind her mistress's short grey hair and fat back and with a deft movement helping her to sit and rest with the comfort and support that the pillows offered. Then she went to pick up the cat from the chair where it had settled, ruffled and eyes glinting green, and placed it back on the bed.

Stella de Courtenay was quiet for a moment, her breath whistling in her chest. Without instruction, Claudine handed her an asthma pump after pouring a little liquid into it from a small brown bottle.

Equally without words the woman in the bed took the pump, placing it in her mouth, and breathed in the vapour deeply before sinking back on to her pillows.

The two women were much of an age – somewhere in their early sixties – and neither had worn well. Stella de Courtenay was a huge, billowing mass of a woman. Her hair was cut short and straight and had been let turn iron-grey. Her face was blotched and swollen, but her eyes were bright and sharp, a true sea-green – so attractive still that they faded the rest of her features into insignificance.

Her servant, Claudine, was also grey but with coarse strong hair twisted into a ferocious bun at the back of her head. She was a thin, stringy woman, all angles and suppressed anger, but her eyes missed nothing; pale brown, they were deeply set above a beaky nose and a mouth that was surprisingly soft and gentle.

'Better?' asked Claudine.

'Um.'

'It's always worse when you wake up.'

The words were a ritual that, once said, could be forgotten, and the business of the evening carried on with. Stella did not let her infirmities distract her from the running of Les Hirondelles. New England to the core, Provence had never laid its languorous spell on her; she did her duty, minded her manners, and turned a blind eye to what she could not control.

'How many for dinner tonight?' The fat hand stroked the cat's white head with a slow sensuous movement.

'Nine.'

Stella mentally counted up the family.

'Is Peter back from New York? I thought he was arriving tomorrow morning.'

'No,' said Claudine, 'but I took the liberty of telling Monsieur Tomas that you had said to invite Olivia Barton's girl – the niece with the bad leg – you remember? She's here for the summer. She arrived this morning.'

'I remember,' Stella said. 'Nice child. Brave.'

'Not a child any more,' Claudine said reprovingly. 'She's only a little younger than Marion.'

'I suppose so. Where do the years go, Claudine?'

'Where they always went, madame,' Claudine said briskly.

The two women shared a curious relationship – mistress and servant and yet not quite. Philip de Courtenay said that in truth the roles were reversed. Claudine was the mistress of Les Hirondelles and always had been. Yet there was affection between the two elderly women. Claudine had come to the estate as a young girl from a village higher in the mountains. She had seen Philip de Courtenay's father die, helped at the birth of Tomas and Elisabeth, attended at the funeral of Philip's rich English first wife, and greeted the new American bride with suspicion and reluctance that eventually surprised her by turning into liking. And the years had made them friends.

The women had much in common: Claudine with her harsh peasant background where work and duty came first; Stella with her rich Boston brahmin background where the same standards applied, if for different reasons.

Stella was painfully heaving her large and swollen legs out of the huge bed. She pushed the cat from her, breathing nearly silent endearments as it moved reluctantly away.

'Get me my stick, Claudine,' she said, 'and if we have a guest I trust you have told the cook to make the meal something special.'

'Asparagus, langouste, Bresse chicken with dauphin gratiné and mousse au chocolat for desert,' Claudine said, her face expressionless.

'Too rich,' Stella said, the whistling of her breath punctuating her sentence. 'Salad with the chicken, and fresh fruit instead of the mousse.'

'Very well, madame,' Claudine said.

She was kneeling to slip shoes on to the swollen feet while Stella struggled to pull a thin silk sweater over her head. They were both engrossed in their tasks when a hesitant voice said: 'Stella – can I come in?'

Claudine's bony back stiffened, and her head remained firmly turned against the door. Stella de Courtenay gave a brief grimace that faded instantly into an expression of amiable neutrality.

'Of course, Pamela. Come in.'

The woman who came through the door hobbled on arthritic feet. Her hair was frizzed about her head and dyed skilfully red. A cigarette hung from her mouth, and she wore the most English of tweeds, sweater and sensible shoes in spite of the warmth of the day.

'Where is Philip?' she said plaintively in the English of suburban Surrey.

'He went into Nice,' Stella said.

'He didn't tell me he was going.'

'He went unexpectedly,' Stella said, her expression still neutral.

'Well, he might have mentioned it. I'd like to have gone into Nice.'

Claudine's back was speaking volumes, and Stella thought to herself, You bet your sweet life you would; but all she said was: 'I think it was business.'

'Oh well,' the woman sighed, and screwing up her face so that the heavy lines under her eyes were accentuated she said: 'Will he be home for dinner?'

'Certainly,' Stella said. 'Oh, and Pamela – we have a guest, so I'm afraid you'll be on Philip's left.'

The woman's face darkened; a heavy flush of red came up over her cheekbones.

'Who?' she asked.

'Anne Paradine.'

'You mean Olivia Barton's niece?'

'The very one,' Stella said cheerfully.

There was a long silence as Pamela Whitton fidgeted where she stood.

'Isn't she rather young to sit on the host's right?'

'Much the same age as Marion.'

'Oh.' Ash was angrily flicked into a potted cyclamen which stood on the bedside table. 'Olivia Barton's not coming, is she?'

Stella suppressed a smile. Why were mistresses always more jealous of ex-mistresses than they were of wives?

'She'll turn up sometime, I guess,' she said.

'Not too soon, I trust. Really – I can't think why Philip ever gave her that house.'

There were times when Stella enjoyed teasing Pamela Whitton.

'Darling,' she said in an exaggerated drawl, 'we both know why he gave her the house. But since it was before me—' She paused, deliberately not adding 'and before you', but her meaning was clear.

Pamela decided to ignore the innuendo.

'Well, I don't like her very much,' she said.

'Funnily,' Stella said, 'I like her quite a lot. And I like what I remember of her niece. So you won't mind sitting on the left tonight, will you?'

'I suppose not. Are we dressing?'

'When the family is here we always dress,' Stella said firmly.

'Oh, very well,' Pamela said and flounced from the room.

'She really shouldn't flounce,' Stella said out loud and in French, a language which Pamela had never quite mastered – which was something of a blessing.

Pamela had flounced beautifully ten years ago when she had been forty-five and looked ten years younger. Then she was still able to play the little girl with some success. Not any more. What had been a strong, good-looking face was now square and masculine; the willowy body had thickened with good living, and Pamela Whitton, with her own peculiar style of dressing and her round vowel sounds, would have passed as 'one of us' in any mock-Tudor stockbroker estate in England.

'Poor old Pamela,' Stella thought.

A mumbled noise came from her feet, where Claudine had stayed throughout the exchange. Stella looked down at the grey bun, grinning. 'What was that?' she asked. 'It sounded very much like *vache* to me. You mustn't be rude about the house guests, Claudine.'

Claudine's full mouth was set in a tight line over teeth that were still her own.

'It's none of my business, madame—'

'Oh, come, Claudine, when have you worried about that?'

'It's none of my business, madame,' Claudine began again, 'but it is time she went.'

'She has been in his life too long, Claudine.'

'But now there is no discretion. In and out of his room. The noises. At their age, it is disgraceful. It is,' she added firmly, 'obscene. What can they do?'

Stella sighed and looked at her servant with one raised eyebrow.

'What they always did, I suppose. She's younger than I am. Only a little, but she is. And she is taking something I don't want. Not at all. Now how could I cope with it, Claudine? I'd die trying to breathe. And I don't think it's a lovely way to go.'

'It's wrong,' Claudine said stubbornly. 'You should know what is going on. And you should stop it.'

'Come, Claudine, do you think I don't know? When you have a body like mine that won't do what is required of it any more, and appetites like mine that keep this poor old body useless –' she lifted the whisky glass and toasted her servant '– there's nothing much left to do except watch, listen and keep one's counsel. Now bring me back Suki.' She tipped the glass back and drank, taking a long breath afterwards.

'That helps,' she said, taking the cat into the cavern of her lap. 'No, there are worse things going on here, Claudine, much worse things. But in the end what is important except comfort, good health and never forgetting to behave with dignity? We all have comfort. Pamela has no dignity. My husband has no dignity. His son has no dignity, and neither does my daughter. But you and I, Claudine, we keep our dignity and therefore we are safe. They cannot touch us. Had I good health, I could conquer the world.' She finished the whisky, coughing a little as she put down the glass.

Claudine shook her head.

'Perhaps it would be better if you didn't know these things after all. Come, *chère madame*,' she said, almost tenderly, 'I shall help you to dress, and you can still conquer the world, if you wish to.'

It was a very correct young maid in black dress and white apron who took Anne's wrap as she went through the double carved-wood doors that led into the open hallway of Philip de Courtenay's home that evening.

Anne was feeling a sense of anticipation. It was her first dinner party at the de Courtenays'. Before, she had always been too young. While her aunt ate in the big dining-room at the rear of the house she had been put to bed in the nursery quarters on the top floor with the other children, and a very strict nanny had seen they stayed there.

Therefore the invitation had given her some pleasure – like a barrier passed in life. She had dressed with considerable care, remembering how her aunt had always taken trouble to look and smell delicious before leaving for the big house.

She had washed and dried her hair, and its dark russet tones shone as she brushed the thick mass into a full fringe and a long dipping pageboy which suited her small pointed face. She used some colour on her cheeks – her skin was always porcelain pale – and patted on a green eyeshadow which brought out the emerald tones in her speckled hazel eyes.

Her dress had long tight sleeves, coming from a wide neckline which dipped low to push up her full breasts. It was black, narrow-waisted and full-skirted, chosen to accentuate her womanly figure and take away attention from her legs.

She had dipped extravagantly into her aunt's Chanel No. 19, deciding after a long sniff it had more class than the No. 5 which was also on the dressing-table along with a dozen other bottles. Lipstick she stroked on with a brush and an artist's hand, and one look in the mirror pleased her. She looked right for the evening ahead. She looked good, indeed. All she needed now was to behave correctly for the formal French. And that meant being spot on time.

The maid had directed her towards the drawing-room, and as she arrived at the doorway, deliberately pausing, Tomas rose from his seat and came towards her.

If he had looked handsome in the blue jeans and shirt that afternoon, the deeper-blue dinner jacket suited him even more. His shirt was simple, dazzling white, and the deep-blue bowtie a conservative one. The lean face was smiling as he came towards her, his dark hair slightly curly and casual looking. The wet, straight look of the pool had gone. Again came the dizzying flash of memory of white and brown, blue and red, but that picture seemed to have nothing to do with the elegant man who took her hand and kissed it. Then he was leading her across a Persian carpet to where a fat old woman sat in a solid leather armchair, a stick at her side; a woman with piercingly green eyes which watched without blinking as Anne came nearer. It had to be Stella de Courtenay, but the size of her hostess was a shock. What had happened to the admittedly large but elegant woman of ten years before?

'My dear.' The voice was husky, American and whisky-toned, but as compelling as the eyes. 'Forgive me for remaining seated. It is a great pleasure to have you with us again. And to see you looking so well.'

Anne took the proffered podgy hand, bejangled with rings embedded in the flesh.

'It is very exciting for me to be here, Madame de Courtenay,' she said. 'And thank you for inviting me to dinner.'

'You have hardly changed,' the woman said. 'I would have known you instantly. But what about us?' The movement of waving her arm to take in the room seemed to make her breath bubble somewhere in her chest, and she reached for the glass of whisky at her side.

Anne had been so mesmerized by the elegance of Tomas and her hostess's extraordinary eyes that she had been unaware of the others in the room. Now she turned, Tomas's hand at her elbow, as Philip de Courtenay came towards her, his hand outstretched.

His English was not as good as Tomas's, but he said: 'My dear. Welcome.'

He had aged, but not very much, Anne thought as he stood smiling at her. He did not seem as tall as she remembered but he was still well over six feet; a big, bulky man with broad shoulders wearing a dinner jacket that sat on him uneasily. She had a sudden vivid memory of him working about the estate, moving rocks, creating gardens, laying terraces. He worked stripped to the waist, she recalled, an old sun-hat covering his thinning hair, whistling snatches from operas as he laboured.

'He's a peasant at heart,' her aunt would say, watching him with affection.

The strength still seemed to be there, but the face had lined and the squirrel eyes that never wore sunglasses seemed deeper set in his face. And Anne noticed with her adult eye something she had not seen before – the full, thick lower lip under the neat military moustache, a lip that was downright self-indulgent in what was predominantly an austere face.

'My eldest daughter, Elisabeth,' he said, and a sear woman in her mid forties gave a thin smile. 'And you remember Marion, my daughter?' he was saying. 'You were friends, you two, as children.'

She was seeing Marion's face properly now – brown eyes, narrow in a broad tanned face; a small flattish nose and full lips. She had grown to look Moroccan, or perhaps Southern Spanish. The body was covered in a long, slim, flame-coloured gown. High to the neck and tight to the wrists, its cut nevertheless left very little to the imagination.

'Of course we were friends,' Marion was saying, in an accent most definitely American. 'Good friends. And it's great to see you again. How's that leg?'

'I'm still a hop-along,' Anne said. 'Remember – you called me that. But plastic surgery might have made it nicer to look at. Not yet – but soon.'

'You were always too self-conscious about it,' Marion said easily. 'You did all right, even hopping along.'

She had the grin of an all-American girl; nothing to do with the naked siren who had wallowed in the pool, riding her man like a mating dolphin. Anne remembered how easy and cheerful she had been as a child; much more direct and friendly than her totally French cousins, Françoise and Raoul. Marion had never played the aristocrat, though the others even as small children had had a chilling air about them when things did not go their way.

Nothing had changed, she thought. Françoise de Courtenay was lounging in a chair and made no move to greet her. The child's face had not been lost over the years; Anne would have recognized her instantly. Pale blue eyes, pink and white skin, a thin pointed nose with flaring nostrils. A pretty face, but with a coldness about it. Anne had never met Tomas's wife, but her aunt had told her that Françoise resembled her mother, who came from Alsace-Lorraine, and who therefore had none of the darkness of the South.

Raoul had risen, a tall muscular boy of about sixteen with his father's dark hair and high-bridged nose. His skin was tanned and dark, but sparked by pale blue eyes. His deceptively lean body bent over her hand briefly and sprang upright after a token kiss.

'Enchanté,' he said, but his eyes were without warmth.

'Raoul, get Anne a drink,' Tomas said. 'What will it be?'

'Gin and tonic, if you please.' Anne was inwardly amused. It seemed strange to be drinking grown-up drinks with these people from her childhood.

'Fine,' Tomas said and nodded to his son who moved to an enormous silver tray which was laden with bottles. 'And now,' he said, 'I don't think you will remember Pamela Whitton.'

There was something in his voice that Anne could not quite place. It was as if he were saying that no one would remember Pamela Whitton or even that no one could ever forget Pamela Whitton. And Pamela Whitton seemed to sense something too. She threw Tomas a look that could only be described as malevolent.

Her appearance bewildered Anne even more. The woman was wearing a long plaid skirt and a black knitted sweater cut to a deep vee both front and back. The plunging front revealed an ample bosom and a prune-wrinkled expanse of cleavage. Her hair was in small red curls over the head, and her eyes were fringed with tarantula-like false eyelashes.

'No,' she said, 'we've never met.'

'You're English,' Anne said.

'I am.'

'How did I guess?' Anne said, smiling.

The woman was not amused, and Anne realized that maybe the ultra-suburban accent had been commented on too many times before.

'It's so nice,' she said quickly, 'to hear an English voice. Isn't it funny how the minute one is abroad, to hear someone from home makes everything seem cosy—?' She stopped abruptly as she realized that this particular attempt to soothe Pamela Whitton could be misconstrued by her hosts.

But Stella de Courtenay's green eyes were watching her with amusement. She understands, Anne thought.

'That's exactly how I feel when I hear a Bostonian voice,' she was saying, her face totally expressionless. 'Cosy.'

Pamela Whitton looked at her and sniffed.

'I'm astonished that a Bostonian accent could have that effect.'

'Ah well,' said Stella. 'I guess you have to be Bostonian.'

Anne had a distinct feeling that she was the cause of what seemed to be a barbed exchange between the two women, and prickling with curiosity she took the glass that Raoul was handing her. She then let herself be led to a long sofa near the window where Marion already sprawled.

'Sit down, pal,' Marion said. 'Hey, it is good to see you again.'

'You too,' Anne said, meaning it. Somehow the memory of the afternoon had been wiped away.

They were deep into catching up with the last ten years when a bell rang. Stella de Courtenay reached for her stick, and with her husband's assistance got to her feet.

'Raoul,' she said. 'You may lead me in. Philip, take care of Anne. The rest of you can sort yourselves out.'

Philip de Courtenay moved to take Anne's arm. He smelt very expensively of lemony toilet water and his thin grey hair was pomaded with something that gave it a silvery tint. Towering over her, he smiled down and said: 'You didn't grow that much, did you?'

'No.' It was a subject she disliked. 'I suppose because of my leg.'

'But your aunt is a little lady. Perhaps it is in the family?'

'I don't know. I hardly remember my parents.'

'I like little ladies,' he said, and the squirrel eyes twinkled down at her as Anne found herself thinking that the de Courtenay men had too much charm for both their own and any woman's good.

The dining-room as they entered almost stopped Anne in her tracks. It was the one room in the de Courtenays' house that she had never seen before. It was lit with four huge candelabra, with silver and fine glass gleaming on a long polished table; a great log fire burned in a fireplace, wide enough to roast the proverbial ox. The red and yellow flames helped add to the dancing white candlelight and created a sparkle which bounced off the white ceiling and walls. It was a rustic room with superbly rich accoutrements, a mixture which had worked better than could have been expected. I like it! she thought.

Philip was seating her at his right hand, and the woman, Pamela Whitton, settled herself at his left. She glared across at Anne who, uncertain of what she had done to offend, half-nodded. The woman was arranging her plaid skirt with a great deal of fuss.

'Philip,' she said, her voice overloud and bad-tempered, 'I have no napkin. I swear Claudine does it deliberately.'

The same maid who had taken Anne's wrap was waiting at table. Philip de Courtenay gave her a small signal, and without a word she melted away to return with a heavy white linen napkin.

'There you are, my *chérie*,' he said. 'Just a small error.'

'Claudine makes too many errors,' Pamela Whitton said.

Anne could not understand why, but she felt sure that she was responsible for the woman's ill humour. She would, she decided, try to lighten the atmosphere.

'Do you live in the South of France, Miss – Mrs—' She hesitated, aware that she had no idea of whether the woman was married or not.

'Mrs Whitton.' The little-girl curls looked hennaed in the candlelight and were ludicrous above the hostile ageing face. 'And I live here. At Les Hirondelles.'

'Oh. Which is your cottage?' Anne asked politely.

'I live here. In this house.'

The conversation was not going well.

'Asparagus?' Smoothly Philip de Courtenay came to her rescue. 'Take as much as you wish. There is a great deal. We grow it ourselves.'

Thankfully, Anne busied herself with the silver plate proffered by the maid.

'I always think it unfair to be served first,' Philip said lightly. 'One has to be so polite, whereas those at the end can be gourmand. Come, come. Take more.'

'All right,' Anne said. 'I will.'

Tomas, who was seated on her right, was equally greedy, and as they ate the greyish green stalks, sliding them carefully between teeth to avoid a downpour of butter, Anne saw that Tomas was regarding her with amusement.

'You look very sexy eating that,' he said.

She was startled. 'Sexy? I don't understand.'

'You don't?'

'I don't.'

His black eyes considered her, undressed her.

'Do you know, I believe you don't.' The large mouth broke into a smile, but the eyes still speculated. Suddenly Anne knew what he meant and burst out laughing. She had not expected such vulgarity at this elegant dining-table. 'Really, monsieur,' she said sternly, and interrupting Pamela Whitton's whispers turned to Philip and asked: 'Who will be in the visitors' cottage this summer, Monsieur de Courtenay?'

He turned to her instantly, and if it had made any sense at all Anne would have thought him grateful for the question.

'Stella,' he called down the length of the table. 'Anne wants to know who will be in the visitors' cottage this summer. 1

had forgotten to tell you, but I have decided to let it.'

'Let it?' Tomas looked suspicious. 'To whom?'

'Well,' Philip said, and his voice seemed overhearty. 'I'd put it in the hands of a Nice agent, and he seems to have come up with a pleasant young couple as *locataires*. They're arriving tomorrow.'

All talk around the table had ceased, and everyone was intent on Philip. Even Raoul, who had been lounging, bored at his step-grandmother's side, had straightened up, and the language had switched from English to French.

'What made you decide to do that, Philip?' Stella asked, pushing her asparagus plate away from her slightly. Her face was blank, and in the wavering light of the candles her eyes glowed as if through a mask.

'Time we made the place pay a bit more,' Philip said, his food neglected on his plate. 'The running costs are astronomical these days.'

'And how much are you charging this young couple?' Elisabeth was speaking for the first time that evening and her harsh voice sounded angry.

'Not a lot,' Philip said evasively, 'but they'll keep the place in trim – do repairs, that sort of thing.'

'Who are they exactly?' Marion asked.

'I don't really know,' Philip said. 'The man is some kind of croupier and she's a masseuse.'

'A masseuse,' Marion said. 'Really? You seem very sure of that.'

'I'm not sure of anything,' Philip snapped. 'I'm merely repeating what the house agent said. And any further discussion is unnecessary. They move in tomorrow.'

His voice was authoritarian, and Stella signalled the maid to take away the plates. The brief clatter covered an awkward silence, but the air of tension remained. Tomas's and Marion's eyes met across the table, and she made a small grimace. Françoise was staring angrily at her grandfather, and Elisabeth looked down at her plate. Anne sat quietly in her place, her hands in her lap. The de Courtenay family were so concerned with Philip's news, she felt they had forgotten her presence and it seemed sensible to melt into the background if she were to learn more of what was going on.

The atmosphere in the room had changed. The candlelight which had been so pretty and pleasing when she came into the dining-room now lit the faces of the family to show their weaknesses. Tomas's nose seemed hooked, and the mouth too deeply set in the shadow; Stella's face grotesque; Marion's more African. The candelabra, branching in a military line down the centre of the long table, turned the rest of the room into a cavern; the fire had dimmed, and the diners seemed isolated by darkness.

The spell was broken by Pamela Whitton saying plaintively: 'What was all that about, Philip? Really, it's too bad the way you all gabble away. I can't understand a word.'

'Nothing that would interest you, my dear.'

'Oh, I don't know,' Stella said. 'Philip has let the summer cottage, Pamela. To a young couple. The man is a croupier and the girl a masseuse.'

'A croupier and a masseuse! Good heavens, what an extraordinary thing to do.' Mrs Whitton gave an audible sniff. 'How on earth can he be a croupier right up here?'

'I gather he'll only be here at weekends,' Philip said. 'Ah – here's the langouste. You'll enjoy these, Anne, my dear. We keep our own tank, so they couldn't be more fresh.'

Drawing her back into the conversation seemed to have reminded the family that there was a stranger in their midst, and the meal went on with a semblance, but only a semblance, Anne thought, of normality. The undercurrents were still there, and as she made polite conversation the civilized behaviour of the family did nothing to dispel her impression that all was not well at Les Hirondelles.

Chapter Four

It had been about ten o'clock when the family had left the dining-table and moved back into the drawing-room for brandies and liqueurs, and Tomas had decided he could decently leave for his own home at about ten thirty. Raoul and Françoise had already gone, pleading tiredness after the day at the coast, and Elisabeth had moved straight to her room after the meal ended. She drank very little.

Philip had walked Anne Paradine home, and insisted on doing so himself – to avoid any awkward questions about the new *locataires*, thought Tomas. His departure with Olivia Barton's niece, whom he had to admit was remarkably pretty apart from the leg and the limp, had put poor Pamela Whitton into something of a twist.

Back in his own home, he went to the library and poured himself another brandy and, as he sat staring into the amber depths as if it could tell him something, he heard someone clattering down the stone stairs of the *mas*.

He recognized his daughter's footsteps. She was wearing the highly expensive high-heeled clogs she always picked to go with tight jeans, so she obviously wasn't ready for bed. He looked at his watch. Eleven o'clock. Where the hell was she going?

She was in the hallway, pulling on an oversized cardigan over straight-legged blue jeans and a high-necked navy silk sweater. Her blonde hair hung in a thick fuzz down her cheeks.

'What are you doing?' Tomas asked.

'Going to the yacht,' she said.

'At this time of night?'

'Why not? I want to make an early start in the morning. McTaggart is taking her out.'

'Well, you're not going to the yacht,' he said. 'You can drive down in the morning. You've been drinking; it's a good hour's drive and it's time you were in bed and asleep.'

Françoise's cold blue eyes looked at him, and the corner

39

of her mouth quirked into what passed as a smile for her. Christ, he thought, she was like her mother.

'I'm going to the yacht,' she said. 'Sorry, Father. But you really should be delighted. You know how soundly Raoul sleeps. A quick *coup de fil* could bring a certain young lady over here with no one the wiser.' She paused and added silkily, 'Don't you think it would be better if you don't interfere in my life and then I won't interfere in yours?'

She left him staring at her as with a small backward wave she slipped out through the front door, closing it ever so gently behind her. He shrugged his shoulders, defeated, and went back to his brandy.

The night was crisp and starlit, and her father was instantly dismissed from Françoise's mind. She was randy. She ran, heels clacking, to the other side of the courtyard where the Les Hirondelles parking space and garage housed her small Porsche. With luck, she thought, she would be in Antibes before midnight. It had been bad luck meeting her father, but not too difficult. People who lived in glass houses were always simple enough to deal with.

She set off with a roar of engine and switchbacked down the mountain, glimpsing here and there the amber necklace of the coast road; between, there was nothing but velvet blackness and the chirp of the cicadas, louder than the quiet purr of her car. Her headlights, piercing the darkness, transfixed small animals, but she made no attempt to cut her speed. Their survival was their own luck and the luck of where the wheels rolled.

Françoise enjoyed night driving; the privacy of the roads and the speeds that were possible suited her temperament. She drove skilfully, not really taking chances, but at speeds many good drivers would have hesitated to sustain on the dipping, winding road to the coast.

She reached the long straight stretch of the sea road, where more cars were about. She manoeuvred her way in and out of them with bursts of speed, the oily metallic water to her left, the railway line to her right.

There were no problems parking at the new Antibes marina

where *Hirondelles III* was moored. A light was burning on the main deck in the big main saloon, and other lights glowed through the lower deck portholes. But she could see no one. Her clogs clacked impatiently up the gangway, and as she came on board she gave a soft whistle.

'Here.' The voice came from a tall-backed leather armchair in the saloon. The chair was turned away from her; as she moved to stand in front of it, she saw that Andrew McTaggart was comfortable in its depth, his feet on a leather stool, a whisky at his side, a long thin cigar in his mouth.

She stood in front of him, arms akimbo and his blue eyes wrinkled into a grin as he stared up at her.

'Hello,' he said softly.

She did not respond. 'Drinking the boss's whisky and smoking his cigars again, I see,' she said, her voice severe.

'Umm,' he very deliberately stubbed out the cigar, 'and I'm about to fuck his daughter.'

'Who says so?'

'I say so,' he said quietly. 'Where do you prefer, bed or bunk?'

'Bunk for me, then bed for you?' she said. Her pale eyes seemed to have glazed as she looked at him. She moved to pull down the blinds in the saloon, every move deliberate and provocative; hips swaying in the tight jeans, nipples obvious through the silk of her sweater.

'You're a very naughty little lassie, you are.' Andrew McTaggart's voice was still soft, but there was an undercurrent there. 'I might have to punish you a little. I might have to make you wait a while.'

'Maybe I'll make you wait a while,' she was smiling at him, and very deliberately she moved to the middle of the saloon and, lifting her arms, slid her sweater over her head.

He caught his breath. Beneath she was wearing a thin black brassiére which clung to her small flat breasts. In the centre of the two cups, a hole had been cut away and bound with red satin – a hole that fitted exactly around two deep red, broad and spreading nipples which came into sharp points standing proud from the bra.

She put her hands on her hips and pushed her breasts towards him as he sat in the chair watching her. She wriggled her hips derisively and very, very slowly slid the zip fastener at the centre front of her jeans down and down. Under her navel, the first sign of a sheer black fabric appeared. Then, turning her back, she slid out of the jeans, her behind aimed at where he sat. Below the small transparent panties, tied on with red satin ribbons, was a suspender belt, and then sheer black seamed stockings vanishing into the black clogs. She kicked the jeans off, hoisted them with her toe to throw in his face, and then paraded around the room, until he rose, a hard upright line along the front of his own jeans. Deliberately he advanced towards her.

'Come here, you randy little bitch,' he said huskily.

'Come and get me,' she said. She kicked off her clogs and ran for the entrance at the back of the saloon. She sped lightly down the cabinway, down a flight of stairs into the crew's quarters and then to his cabin. He was close behind her, and as he came in she was standing panting with her back to the two bunks which almost filled the room.

'Get those pants off,' he said.

'No need.' Her eyes challenged him.

'Get them off.'

'I told you – no need.'

He was a big man, in his late thirties, broad-shouldered with a lion head of blond hair. He grabbed at her, picked her up and not too gently laid her on the top bunk, her legs hanging over the end. As he went to grab and tear at the black briefs, her legs flew open, and he saw that the pants had no crotch.

Instantly his face vanished between her open legs and the silky blond hair there, one hand squeezing her buttocks, while the other undid the zip on his own trousers. She lay groaning as his tongue probed and gorged into her, but her feet found his erection, released and strong from the confinement of the tough jean fabric, and caressed and stroked and captured it between her legs, then squeezing and rolling it between her feet.

His face was wet when he stood up again, and she lay, her

hips moving up and down, thrusting towards him, while small sobbing sounds came from her. He swiftly slid out of his jeans and shirt and then plucked her from the top bunk, holding her in his arms, and slid her down on her back on to the lower bunk, leaving her head hanging over the end. Then kneeling before her, he pushed himself into her open, waiting mouth. She took the full length of him, and then her head rose and fell as his hands pulled at her nipples in the same rhythm and pattern.

She sensed he was near to coming and pulled her head away, grasping the head of his erection firmly between her teeth. 'Not yet,' she said, letting go. He climbed on to the narrow bunk beside her, pulling her so that her head rested at the foot, and then knelt across her again, pushing his head between her legs while she took him into her mouth.

It was she who finally turned, twisting from under him, to push him inside her. Gasping, they rode together side by side, her legs scissored across his until both came in concentrated silence. Only after the final spasm did she gasp, and instantly he slid out of her, and her hands went to grasp at his small slack penis, gently tugging and pulling as she lay with her eyes tight shut.

'Give me time,' he said. He was breathing deep and hard, and his eyes, too, were shut.

'I need a younger lover,' she said.

He breathed deeply again. 'A younger lover couldn't wait for you,' he said. 'It takes you a while. Maybe I need an older mistress.'

'*Pouf!*' she was sitting up and leaning to lick at him. 'Flabby body; drooping tits. Like Pamela Whitton.'

'At least she's got tits,' he said.

'Bouncing about on her belly! Mine won't sag.'

'Nothing much to sag.'

'What about this?' She had his small, shrunken penis hanging over her index finger. 'I've never seen anything so saggy.'

Her long red fingernails found the tiny thread of string on its foreside and she scratched gently and persuasively until he began to harden under her fingers.

'And –,' she had her mouth close to his ear now and was breathing warm breath into him '– now it's your turn. On the bed? I please you anyway you like. What shall I do to you? What would you like today, monsieur? Shall I tease you with my tongue? Suck at you? Lie back and let you play with your toys? Or shall I play with my toys? The choice is yours, monsieur.'

The breathless, whispered words played their role. He was hard again. And laughing, she jumped up off the bunk.

'Shall we have a change of costume?' she said. She twisted her arms up behind her back and unhooked the small brassiére and flung it at him. Then she stood in the doorway, crooking her finger at him. 'Come follow, come follow, come follow,' she said.

Naked, he followed; a tall, smooth-bodied man with ginger curls of pubic hair and a very slight pot-belly. He was at ease, nude, and moved behind her along the cabinway, deliberately making no effort to catch her. She, as she moved, untied the tiny strings that held the black *cache-sexe*, and stopped to remove the black stockings and the suspender belt so that by the time they had reached the state room she was naked. And he was flaccid again.

He flung himself on the great bed that filled the centre of the room and she settled herself next to him.

'All your games,' he said grumpily. 'Françoise, a fuck is a fuck. I don't need all that jazz.'

'I enjoy the jazz,' she said.

'Aye, there's a frosty lady hiding somewhere in you,' he said. 'You're like a whore. Why won't you ever kiss me?'

'I don't like kissing,' she said.

'No, just fucking. I'd noticed,' he said. 'The hell with you.'

'No need to be nasty just because you can't get hard.'

'Listen,' he said. 'It's one o'clock in the morning. I've been getting this damn boat seaworthy all day, I'm nearly forty years old, and tonight I feel it. What about you? You've laid yourself out on that deck, damn nearly naked with your fucking brother for a chaperon and done sweet fanny adams all day.'

'What is sweet fanny adams?' she asked.

'This,' he said, plunging his hand between her legs, his thumb entering her.

Instantly her body arched. 'That's nice,' she murmured.

'Och, hell.' The Scottish accent was more obvious in his irritation. 'Do you ever think of anything else?'

'Umm,' she said, eyes closed. 'I think a lot about money.'

'I think more about money,' he said. 'What's the situation?'

'Not good. Darling Grandpapa has let the summer cottage to strangers.'

'What's that got to do with anything?'

'Nothing to do with our operation; a lot to do with Father's. I suspect Grandfather has guessed what Father's trying to do, and these *locataires* are going to be a hazard to the sale. So now there are two hazards. Olivia Barton and whoever these new people are. My guess is he's done it deliberately. He doesn't want to break the trust and doesn't want to sell Les Hirondelles and he suspects we all do. So if we're going to get rich quick it's going to have to be the yacht and Achmid. But at least it'll be exciting – as well as profitable.'

'And extremely dangerous,' McTaggart said. 'How's your grandfather's health?'

The question was ironic, but Françoise took it seriously. 'For sixty-five, remarkably good,' she said. 'He still seems to be laying his hideous mistress. Or maybe she's laying him.' She grimaced. 'But – a thought. The new tenant of the summer cottage is a masseuse. Ideal to give an elderly gentleman a hand-job.'

Andrew McTaggart winced. 'How the hell did a kid your age learn all this stuff you come out with?'

'Two years in a posh English school, followed by a year in Paris with Mama, was something of an education,' she said. 'Not that Mama knew what I was learning. Mama was too busy in quite different directions. British public schoolboys who aren't queer can be very dirty, and leather-jacketed lads on motorbikes coming in from St Denis can be quite an education. I think,' she added thoughtfully, 'it's because they never had toys when they were children.'

'Did you?'

'Too many. I prefer this.' Again her hand was stroking his penis, and the slow hardening began. 'Wouldn't you like to screw me, darling?' she whispered in his ear. 'This one's for you, remember. Anything you like.'

The whites of his eyes were faintly shot with blood, and he groaned. Then without speaking he knelt and put his hands under her buttocks. Her small slight body rose easily under his grip, and then he rammed into her as hard as he possibly could.

'Just take that, you bitch! Just take that,' he said angrily, 'and think yourself bloody lucky.'

But he could not hide the expression of anguish on his face, and Françoise smiled to herself, pleased, as her hips rose and fell with him and then the smile faded as she gasped and clutched at him as he seemed to swell inside her, and her body grew hot and her entire attention riveted itself on the need for relief from the itch between her legs ...

At their collapse he slept. But she was watchful and awake. She had a morning appointment in Cannes and when he awoke to the morning sun streaming through the porthole she was gone.

Chapter Five

Peter de Courtenay got off the New York–Paris–Nice night plane with sand in his eyes, a bad taste in his mouth and the beginning of a hangover from too much whisky taken to sustain him through the long trip. It was far too early in the morning, and the flight had been the usual bore, except for the spectacular moment when with blue darkness and the yellow moon behind, and red sun and the azure daylight in front, the big airbus had flown from night into day.

The sea behind him looked opaque and still as he walked

up the tarmac to the Nice Airport buildings, and a white glare came from the walls, flittering off the wide expanse of windows. It was going to be a hot June Riviera day. The customs men recognized him, saluted, and he was through into the elegant hall, dotted with shops to catch the unaware and unwise, out through the automatic doors and into the palm-fringed forecourt while most of his fellow passengers were still behind official barriers.

On cue, his father's Rolls glided up, Dupré impassive at the wheel. The chauffeur started to get out of the car to open doors for Peter who waved impatiently, opened the front nearside door himself and climbed in, throwing his briefcase on to the back seat.

'Straight home,' he said. 'I need a bath and some sleep.'

It was nearly an hour later when the black Rolls purred in through the Les Hirondelles road barrier. Berthe, at her post even so early in the morning, waved a salute as Peter passed. He waved back sleepily. He had been dozing as the Rolls smoothly climbed into the Alpes Maritimes and now he sat up, pushed a hand through his crisp fair hair, yawned and reached over the back seat for his briefcase.

Within seconds, Dupré was pulling up outside the small villa that was Peter's own property and which had been his for the past four years, since his twenty-fifth birthday.

Tomas had had first pick of the property and as a married man with children had taken the largest house after Philip's, but the smaller cottage at the west side of the estate and next to the big house suited Peter very well. There were three bedrooms and a large living-room with a superb view of the mountains beyond and a perfect picture of the whole west side of the de Courtenay estate. The sunsets from his living-room were spectacular.

He stood in his own living-room, looking out on the view with pleasure. The mountain that looked like a crouching lion and which formed the edge of a huge gorge was clear in the morning sunlight. Above, the mountains were still white-tipped; they were so high that the sun rarely melted the winter's snow.

He gave a long sigh of satisfaction. New York exhilarated him and pleased him, but he needed Les Hirondelles. New York was necessary for his work; at twenty-nine he was already a well-regarded international lawyer, but the wealth of the de Courtenays meant he could work when and where he chose and only on cases that interested him. It was astonishing that he worked at all. The de Courtenays thought work vulgar, but Stella had seen that her eldest son had too much of the American in him to live the lotus-eating life, and it was she who had persuaded Philip to send Peter to Harvard Law School.

His problem as a man who needed an occupation was a deep-seated passion for Les Hirondelles and all it stood for. He loved the land; he loved the estate, the mountains beyond and the whole conception of what was truly a feudal state. It was his secret grief that it would all go eventually to Tomas. Though he would be allowed his share of the inheritance in money, he would have rather had the estate itself, running it as a business, and improving it so that he and his children and his children's children would always have a stake and a home in the incredible beauty of what he felt was a totally incomparable part of the world.

The sleepiness was passing now, and the idea of a swim seemed attractive. The pool was hidden behind its side barrier of cypresses but he knew that the sun would be lighting it from the far end where the trees stopped to allow a view of the mountains.

In his bedroom he took off and hung up his New York suit, stripped off his tie, shirt and shorts, and took a brief blue bathing slip from a drawer. He looked at himself critically in the mirror which ran the length of his wardrobe. Too white. That was New York; and the weekend on Martha's Vineyard hadn't helped. A cold Atlantic wind had kept the boats in harbour and the sailors in bars.

It had kept him in bed with Evelyn Grenville. A not unpleasant pastime, nor a memorable one. Evelyn was the daughter of his mother's old schoolfriend who, like Stella, had married well. Evelyn, her family had indicated, would be an ideal wife for him. His own mother was less enthusiastic, she had said drily that she hoped Evelyn had not turned out as stuffy as the rest of the Grenvilles.

However, there was money on either side, similar education and background, and also Evelyn was undoubtedly very much in love with him, which he could have done without. He had no intention of marrying Evelyn or anyone else for the moment. Evelyn might indeed do, if he decided to make a practical, French-type marriage, but the American in him balked at the idea, even though Evelyn quite pleased him. She played tennis well and was athletic if not erotic in bed. She'd probably become pregnant without much problem once off the pill, as she was exceedingly healthy. She liked to sail and she liked expensive clothes and grand restaurants. She was as arrogant as any of the de Courtenays, but whether she would like Les Hirondelles remained to be seen; to be seen, in fact, in three weeks' time when she was coming to join him.

Walking towards the pool, he decided that it might be wise to put her in the visitors' cottage if no one else were about – more proper, less open to misinterpretation. She might get quite the wrong idea if he took her to share the bed and board in his own home. He did not intend her to get any ideas – not yet. And she might well feel sleeping with him with his parents at hand must lead to a proposal.

As he rounded the arched entrance to the pool he stopped short. Someone was swimming, a girl. Russet hair floated on the water, and she wore an aquamarine bikini which blended with the blue of the pool. Whoever it was swam joyously, her body twisting to dive beneath the water and swim along the blue tiled floor. He was too tired to find the performance sexual, and after his momentary irritation at finding the pool occupied he stood for a moment to watch this human dolphin enjoying herself. And then his sense of ownership returned. *He* wanted the pool; he wanted his swim and he wanted the pool to himself.

He moved to stand at the pool's edge, a towel over his shoulder, and curling his toes over the side stared down at where the girl swam. She came up from one of her explorations of the depths, saw him standing there and, her face streaming, trod water, staring at him in surprise.

'Who are you?' he asked crisply.

She did not reply, but swam a few yards until she was able to stand. Her body, what he could see of it, he noted, was graceful, as would be expected from anyone who swam so well. Her face was unimpressive. A pleasant enough ordinary face, with large eyes, now decorated by black, spiky, wet eyelashes, which held tiny droplets of water at their tips.

'I'm so sorry,' she said. 'It was so early that I didn't expect anyone to be around. I'll get out now.'

The bikini was an expensive one, he saw, but his father's guests most certainly did not get their hair wet when they swam. Therefore, she must be one of the servants' relatives, trespassing in the pool at a time when she thought no one would catch her.

'Yes, but who are you?' he said impatiently.

'I'm Anne Paradine,' she said. 'Olivia Barton's niece. I'm staying at Miss Barton's cottage. You're Peter de Courtenay, aren't you? I remember you from years ago.'

A faint flush of anger had risen on her cheeks at his abrupt manner, but she spoke with composure, her voice low and modulated. She spoke good French, her accent only faintly English – enough so to be pleasing.

She was lifting herself on to the pool's edge, turning her back to him, and suddenly she seemed ill at ease. He knew why. She was trying to hide her right leg and a mass of ugly red scarring from him, but seeing it was not possible she seemed to shrug, and stood up facing him.

The scars were so bad and the flesh so crimson that he could not drag his eyes from her leg, and he felt ashamed of his arrogance with her and yet irritated that she had been able to shame him.

'I remember you,' he said abruptly in English. 'You're the one who had the accident as a little girl. Your aunt used to make you walk the last bit of the journey. We always thought she was cruel to make you do it.'

Anne laughed and she had, he noted, neat, even teeth and a

50

smile that lifted the corners of her mouth in what seemed to be genuine amusement.

'If she hadn't,' she said, 'I'd probably be walking on crutches or not at all today.' She drew breath and said: 'I'm sorry my leg is so hideous now. But I've just had plastic surgery on it. When it heals they promise me it will look reasonably normal.'

Her direct eyes were looking at him with a sort of defiance, and he remembered back over the years to the plucky little girl who even then tried to hide the damage to her body.

'I wouldn't have recognized you,' he said.

She laughed again.

'I recognized you. I had a crush on you when I was little – mainly because you never took the slightest bit of notice of me or Marion. You were,' she said thoughtfully, 'a very manly little boy. Then you went off to America, and I never saw you the last time I was here.'

'When was that?' he asked.

'Eight years ago. I was twelve.'

Yes, he thought – my third year in Boston.

She was shivering a little, he noticed.

'Don't you have a wrap?' he asked abruptly.

'No.'

'Dry yourself off with this.' He flung the heavy, deep-blue towel he was carrying towards her, and she deftly caught it.

'Dry yourself,' he said authoritatively. 'How long are you here for?'

Her face brightened.

'The whole summer.'

'You don't work?'

'Of course,' she said, as if it were a ridiculous question. 'But I'm fortunate. I draw, and I can do my job anywhere really. My aunt thought it would be a good place to let my leg heal.'

He grunted, wondering about how antiseptic the pool was, and making a mental note to tell Dupré that the filter must be kept working all the time. If the girl caught septicaemia it could only be a nuisance.

'You were going to swim,' she said. 'I'll go now. And it was nice to meet you again.'

He said: 'No hurry. I've got all day to swim.'

'Don't you work?' she said, mockingly.

'When I feel like it,' he said. 'I've just got in from my office in New York.'

She looked guilty, and he found himself thinking how transparent she was as she laid the towel carefully over one of the lounging chairs.

'You need a swim, and thanks for the loan of the towel,' she said. 'I'll leave you in peace now.'

She smiled, waved and went, and he could tell that she was doing her damnedest to walk without limping – and not succeeding.

When she was out of sight he dived neatly into the pool, skating along the bottom on his belly and coming up only at the shallow end. The cold of the water cleared his head instantly, and he began the purposeful twenty lengths that he did every summer morning when he was at Les Hirondelles and which kept his body lean and muscular. A lot of eating and drinking went on in his life. Exercise had to have an important place.

He found himself thinking about Anne Paradine as he swam and her incredible ease in the water, and he thought how pathetic she was – her instant acceptance that the pool was not hers to play in, her disappearance. Evelyn would not have left until she was good and ready, but then Evelyn, like himself, was a product of privilege. It even showed in appearance, he thought – Evelyn, tall and slim with the kind of glossy nut complexion from a lifetime of sun cosseting and the best of food. Rich people definitely had better skins; the girl in the pool had been pale, too pale, and though her skin was good it did not have the kind of rich underglow as if the sun had been captured and stored. Evelyn's skin was like that – a privileged skin. Nevertheless, he had to admit she was sexually more attractive than Evelyn. Full-breasted and bright-eyed with a sort of secret sensuality in spite of the leg.

Also, he thought, as he swam on, breathing deeply, enjoying

the feel of the water resisting him and then parting to let him pass, she had good manners. Perhaps sometimes his manners were not so good. Only with his own kind, or with servants. It's to the people in the middle that the rich show arrogance, he decided, rather guiltily.

The twenty lengths were completed, and as he lifted himself out of the water and sat panting lightly on the side he used the view of the far distance as an excuse to relax and catch his breath. And he felt for an instant the surge of anger that always gripped his guts when he knew this place could never in all its entirety be his. He lusted after the land, the old stone, the dowdy olives, the witch-armed vines. He wanted all of it for himself; wanted to keep it intact.

'There's time,' he told himself. 'Anything could happen. Father has a long way to go yet.'

Suddenly, very tired, he used his already damp towel to dry himself and went back to his villa where he fell naked into bed, his bathing slip making a wet patch on the cedar floor of his bedroom, and slept.

Philip de Courtenay was up early too. On the occasions when he managed to avoid Pamela Whitton creeping into his bedroom at night – so simple for her with Stella safely marooned on the ground floor – she had the habit of slipping in to see him in the morning. Sometimes this way she caught the early-morning erection, and though it did not last long she made the best of it. Normally he could no longer stand up for her any more, and he was bored with the hand-jobs, the mouth-jobs and her frantic efforts to please him.

Pamela Whitton had been a sexy, exciting woman ten years ago. Now, in her desperate efforts to keep him – and her meal ticket – what had been erotic seemed lascivious. It had been all right while her husband had been alive, Philip thought, though the old boy had probably suspected what was going on. Pamela had been determined he should not know about her extramarital activities with his best friend, but Philip was fairly sure he did. For himself, the affair was already fading when Paul Whitton died. He had intended to let the whole thing gently end, but Stella had said that he could not leave the wife of his dear friend to live alone, and she had invited her to stay with them.

He was pretty sure that this was Stella's revenge on them both – he still having to prove an interest he did not feel, and Pamela, daily more anxious and eccentric, was having to try to arouse an interest she must realize no longer existed. He wished to God he had the courage to say 'let's call it a day', but then he'd never been noted for his moral courage. Stella, without rancour, called him a vain, silly man and maybe she was right.

But he was a happy man on this particular morning. He wore an old torn shirt, ancient corduroy trousers tied at the waist with a leather strap, and a battered straw hat on his head. The sun was not yet high, and he was hoeing along the rows of vines that bordered the road from the entrance of the property to where the houses began. There were plenty of employees, mostly Algerians, to do exactly what he was enjoying, but Philip de Courtenay's greatest pleasure was to be near his own land; to feel the rich red earth under his feet and between his fingers. His greatest satisfactions were wine from his own vines, fruit from his own trees, meat from his own beasts and fish from his own streams. It seemed to him that, whenever his own land produced for him, he was beating the system; therefore nothing on Les Hirondelles went to waste. It was his proud boast that they had not had to buy a log for the huge fireplaces in the houses for forty-five years, not since he took over the running of the estate – an estate that had belonged to his family since Napoleonic days. And fortuitous marriages by de Courtenay men to rich women had increased the estate's wealth.

It was a sorrow to him that only one of his children, Peter, showed the same interest in the land. This would make the inheritance a problem, but he figured he knew how to deal with it and he had no intention of dying yet a while. Nor had he any intention of selling the place, however much they pushed him, nor any intention of handing out the vast sums of money which his children seemed to think were their due.

While they lived on his land and under his roofs, with even smart and expensive motorcars provided, he saw no necessity to indulge their extravagances – particularly Tomas, who was too fond by far of the casinos along the coast. And it wouldn't have hurt any of them to do a day's work, he thought. Drones, all of them.

As he worked his hoe cheerfully along the rows, taking care not to disturb the fresh young leaves, he heard a car, gears complaining, driving up the mountain.

He looked at his watch. It would be the new *locataire* from Nice, and he felt the sort of excitement he had not felt for a long time.

His story to the family that a house agent had found the new lodgers for the summerhouse had not been quite true. He had met the girl, Martine, at his club in Nice. She was the masseuse, and a very good one. The club was respectable, but she managed to give the impression that outside of its sober walls anything was possible.

He had had a Wednesday afternoon appointment with her for the past six months, and it had not been his imagination that the towel over his private parts had become more and more carelessly placed, and that her strong fingers had ever-so-lightly brushed against him in the forbidden places so that he had been aware of a response he had not been able to find for a long time. She was a funny little thing, small and pale; her teeth were not perfect, and her colourless hair was always tied back into a ponytail. She had told him she came from a *pied noir* family in Algeria and that, when the French had had to leave, her family had settled first in Nîmes. Her father was a peach farmer, and Philip gathered that they were peasant *pieds noirs*. Now the father worked on a peach farm in the Languedoc, somewhere near Nîmes, but she had decided to seek her fortune in Nice.

She had told him about her marriage to a young man of Corsican descent, and their problems in finding somewhere to live. They existed in one room somewhere at the back of Nice in an area he did not know. She had also made it clear, as the fingers brushed tantalizingly about his groin, that of course if she found somewhere to live her husband would have to stay in Nice for the week, and the one room would be quite adequate for him. If they had a proper home she would give up her work. Or she was sure she could find something to do in the country.

And it was then he suggested that they take over the summer cottage. He knew exactly what he had in mind and he was fairly sure that she did too. It was dangerous and difficult, but when it came to women his life had always been absurdly complicated; he had got away with murder in the past.

He could see the girl arguing with Berthe at the gate, and he remembered that he had forgotten to warn the old girl that there would be new arrivals this morning.

The hoe over his shoulder, he ambled down towards the barrier, and as he neared, Martine looked up, her sharp little face petulant.

'Excuse me, monsieur,' she said. 'But I have an appointment with Monsieur de Courtenay. Do you know where—?' she stopped dead as she looked beyond the old clothes to his face under the beat-up hat. 'Excuse me, monsieur,' she said again. 'It is you. I thought—'

'You thought I was a farm worker?' he said. 'Don't worry – everyone does. It's all right, Berthe – I am expecting madame. She is to move into the summer cottage.'

Berthe's face looking the girl up and down mirrored disapproval. This was not the usual Les Hirondelles style of visitor; Berthe knew a peasant when she saw one. She lifted the barrier so that the girl's old Volkswagen could come through, and went muttering back to her hidey-hole.

'I'll come to the house with you,' he said, getting into the passenger seat.

'You are very kind, monsieur,' she said. She drove efficiently, he noticed, her hands strong on the wheel. Her hands were big compared to the rest of her small wiry body. The nails were cut straight and unvarnished, but their competent look made them attractive, and he could hardly take his eyes off her fingers as she drove the short distance to where he pointed out the summer cottage.

She had very little luggage. Her husband, Jacques, was bringing the rest at the weekend, she said. She just had her own things with her, and he had said that the house was adequately furnished.

'It is,' he assured her. 'It is.'

He helped carry in her cheap leather suitcases and she fussed and told him it was not necessary and that he was too kind. She kept her head slightly bent and hardly smiled, trying not to show her bad teeth, he supposed, but her teeth did not bother him. When all her things were in the wide stone-flagged hallway of the cottage he showed her where to park the car and sat smoking, waiting for her to return.

'Now,' he said. 'Which of this luggage goes to the bedroom?'

She looked at him, and he saw how grey and calculating her eyes were. But her voice was low and polite, servant to master.

'The red valise and the blue, monsieur,' she said, 'but there is no need.'

He did not answer her, but picked up the two cases easily and swung up the stairs.

'You'd better follow,' he said. 'You don't know where the bedroom is.'

Like a small grey mouse she came up the stairs behind him and followed him into the big master bedroom. The shutters were closed and the morning sun filtered through, striping the heavy fabric bedspread and the rag rugs which were scattered over the cedarwood floors.

He opened the doors of the fitted cupboard and put the bags inside. She was standing, her hands clasped before her, her back to the oversized bed, watching him.

'You are too kind, monsieur,' she said. 'Much too kind. Is there anything I can do for you?'

She wasn't sure, he realized. The estate had impressed her and perhaps thrown her. The ball was now in his court.

'As a matter of fact,' he said, 'there is.'

'Oh?'

The ball was still in his court.

'A free massage?' he said, making a joke of it.

'But of course,' she said. 'It is the – the least I can do.'

She went to the cupboard and from the red valise took out a large sponge bag. Without wasting time, he slid out of his trousers and shirt, letting them drop to the floor. He was not wearing underpants and he was pleased that his body was still firm and tanned.

He could see how her eyes went to his crotch and then slid away. Nothing was happening there at the moment, but when those capable hands got going ... He grunted and threw back the bed covers, settling himself on the crisp white sheets.

She was very deliberately taking off rings, watch and, oddly, her necklace. Then she slipped off her shoes. She was wearing a jean skirt and her legs were bare. She rolled up the sleeves of her cotton blouse and opened it lower at the neck.

'You must forgive me, monsieur,' she said, 'but the bed is too low and too wide for a normal massage. Will you permit me to improvise?'

He felt a growing excitement.

'By all means,' he said.

'I think my skirt is too tight,' she said, frowning a little. 'It will be better perhaps if I remove it.'

She unzipped the skirt in a businesslike manner, and with a small wriggle of her hips let it slide down to the ground. Then she picked it up, folded it neatly and laid it over a chair. He watched her, half amused and very expectant. She was wearing very small pink and white striped cotton pants, and her shirt ended just above her navel. Her legs were thin but well shaped, the blond pubic hair strayed from the side of the briefs. She looked totally unerotic, like a small boy, and he wondered if he was going to be disappointed.

She took a large bottle of oil from the sponge bag and said: 'Perhaps it will be better if you lie on your stomach, monsieur. Will you roll over, please.'

He rolled over, burying his face in the pillow, and waited. He felt her climb on to the bed, one leg sliding over him, and then her weight resting lightly on his buttocks and her knees tucked in to his waist.

He jumped as the oil fell cold on his shoulders, and then he felt her capable hands rubbing and pulling at the muscles of his neck and shoulders, smoothing the oil along the length of his arms and tugging gently at each finger. She was concentrating on his back and waist now, pushing deeply, rubbing the flesh and loosening each muscle. It was a tougher massage than she had ever given him before, and he found himself resisting her hands.

'Relax, monsieur,' she said. 'You must not fight me.'

She had reached his buttocks now, and was slapping them hard with strong, stinging movements, and he could feel himself growing, pressing into the rough linen of the sheet under him. And then she paused for a moment to pour more oil over his buttocks, letting it drip into the crease, and suddenly her finger was inside him, stroking and teasing at just the right place, and his long dormant penis sprang to full life. As her finger left him, he rolled over. Somehow she had slipped off her briefs, and the shirt was hanging open. She wore no bra, and her breasts fell like small pointed triangles near his face. Without a word she settled herself on his erection, letting him sink deep into her, and calmly continued to massage his neck and chest, using the massage movements to move herself on him and stimulate him.

'I can't come like this any more,' he said, his voice thick.

'Of course not,' she said. 'It's not time. The massage is not finished.'

She worked on, rolling his flesh between her hands, pouring the oil over his testicles and, hands behind her, rubbing and gently squeezing them, separating each loose bag from the other and gently pressing so that there was no pain, only pleasure, to each small nut inside.

Then without releasing him her inner muscles clamped tight on him; she turned on him with one fluid movement, so that he saw her back, and she was leaning forward, pulling his erection with her, to stroke at his feet and legs.

He knew he was groaning with the pleasure of it and he wanted to come, but she would not let him move on her. All movement came from her.

'Not yet, monsieur,' she was saying sternly. 'I have not finished my work.'

She had reached his thighs, and again delivered the stinging little slaps with the edge of her hand. And then her fingers were tracing a delicate movement, butterfly light, inside of his groin.

She paused.

'Now, monsieur,' she said, and twisted on him again, turning him with her without releasing him, and lay on her side, her back to him, her legs intertwined with his.

'I think you can come this way, no?' she said. 'Please do, monsieur.'

She was small and light and very tight on him, and he rode her furiously, grabbing at her small soft breasts, able from the angle she had chosen to get deep inside her. Then he could not wait a moment longer. It was like floodgates. It had been so long since it had worked properly. He strained once more, gasped, sank back and fell instantly asleep.

Martine slid carefully away from him, and giving him a long slow look she walked to the bathroom where she washed herself carefully, drying between her legs with the large deep-blue bath towels. Then she dressed. De Courtenay had not stirred. He slept with his mouth slightly open, his penis small and shrunk above his large scrotum.

She was bringing him a cup of tea when he awoke, to find her standing by the bed like a lady's maid, the cup and saucer on a small tray.

'I thought you might like this, monsieur,' she said.

'How kind, madame,' he said and took it. Without a word she left the room, leaving him alone; Philip de Courtenay congratulated himself as he sipped the well-made tea on his instincts being absolutely correct.

Chapter Six

It was early when Tomas woke in his lofty bedroom. From the high pillows that he favoured, he could see through the narrow windows out over the mountains, and the light flooding in had disturbed him. He had left one shutter opened by mistake, for Tomas rarely opened his windows. He liked the dark, deep, cavelike atmosphere of his room – an atmosphere he enhanced with a heavy fur bedcover and large, looming pieces of furniture.

The sun seemed to be high, and when he looked at the small ormolu clock beside his bed he realized it was already late. Nine thirty. And he lay there, eyes closed, reluctant to get up and thinking over the events of the evening before.

Now there was another problem. Françoise either knew or had guessed about Marion. He was aware that he should be more anxious than he was. He ought to be appalled that his only daughter had discovered that her father was dallying with his own halfsister, if dallying were the correct word. But somehow it didn't seem to matter very much except as a piece of information that could be used in evidence against him, and he had no doubts that his frosty-faced daughter would do just that if it suited her.

But there wasn't too much she could blackmail him for. To get her own way? But she always did. More money? Not a hope. Philip handed out all the money to the family, and Françoise got much the same share as anyone else. He could not think of one way in which she could use the information. And he knew it was unlikely she would be shocked in any way. The cold core of Françoise was pretty unshockable. He was certain of that. Even as a child she had been odd. The pale blue eyes would look sideways in an adult, calculating manner that had been unnerving from a four-year-old.

Could she blackmail Marion? Not much chance, he decided. Marion simply wouldn't care. And Marion was as hard up as the rest of them. She'd always been favourite, but as she wasn't all that interested in money she asked for less and made what she got her hands on last longer.

Money ... the other problem ... but he had made up his mind not to think about it until he had been into Cannes. So stop thinking about it, he told himself, toying with the idea of ringing Marion to come over to his house. She would take his mind off his problems.

He found himself thinking about her, mentally dwelling on the ripe breasts, round belly and full buttocks, and the way she felt when she closed herself over him, and his hand slid down over his stomach to cover the tumult growing there.

He looked at the telephone, tempted, and decided no. He could comfort himself. He hadn't had to do that since the affair had begun, and it wouldn't hurt for once. And it would take his mind off his money worries with less problems. Marion would leave him and the morning exhausted. He took a copy of *Lui* from the bedside table, one hand caressing himself as he viewed the naked girlie pictures, comparing them with Marion. It was only gentle comfort he needed and, desire eased, the evidence washed away in his *en suite* bathroom, he rang for his breakfast to be brought to him in bed.

Afterwards he showered and shaved carefully, inspecting himself in the full-length wall mirror for any signs of surplus weight or ageing. He still looked pretty good, he thought. Something at least to be complacent about. There wasn't much else. His face seemed smooth and rested despite his worries, and he decided to wear a heavy silk suit that he had had made in Savile Row when things were better. He needed confidence. He chose a shirt and tie with care, flicked dust from the shoes that Dupré polished so perfectly, and putting a thousand francs in hundreds in a gold note-clip so they did not bulk out the cut of his suit he felt himself ready to face the problems of the day.

His appointment in Cannes was not until one o'clock – a bad time and one he was sure that Achmid had chosen deliberately to ruin his lunch hour. Achmid had ulcer trouble and ate very little, which meant that he, Tomas, would have to find his food either very early or very late. He was accustomed to taking his lunch at just the time Achmid had asked to see him, and Achmid knew it very well.

He had just an hour and a half to use profitably before he left for Cannes. He might, he thought, take a coffee with his sister, Elisabeth, to see how much of an ally she would be if he could somehow force the sale through. Then he might try again to speak to his father. Achmid would want more than promises this time.

Elisabeth's maid let him into the house that in size and shape was almost a replica of his own on the other side of the courtyard. But there any resemblance ended. Like a hibernating animal, Elisabeth had squirrelled most of the finer pieces of family furniture into her home. It was choking with elegant desks, period chairs, wardrobes, small and large tables, rugs from the Orient, some superb and some from Moroccan bazaars, fine paintings, and an incredible selection of glass and china. To move through Elisabeth's home was to complete an obstacle course.

She was in her drawing-room; the shutters were drawn so that even though the sun shone brightly outside the room was in half-darkness apart from the leaping flames of a log fire burning in the grate. Elisabeth hated the sun with passionate intensity and yet was always cold. She sat in a regal Louis XIV chair at the side of the fire, a snorting pug-dog at her feet, a *boule* cabinet worth a fortune at her back, and with rows and rows of bookshelves filled with rotting leather-bound books that had probably not been touched in twenty years. She was working on a piece of tapestry in a heraldic design and barely looked up as the maid ushered him into the room. It smelt, he noticed, strongly of musk, dust and the enormous bowl of roses placed on her desk.

He collapsed into a chair opposite her, drawing his silk-covered legs away from the heat of the burning logs.

'Really, Elisabeth,' he said irritably, 'how can you stand a fire in this weather?'

'This house is cold,' she said. 'Yours is in the far better position.'

It was a grumble she never failed to find an excuse to air,

63

and Tomas sighed impatiently. His sister had the family looks of dark eyes, high-bridged nose and fine features, but her mouth was too wide and too narrow at the same time. The nose was too hawked and the bones too prominent. She looked uncomfortably like a death's head; even her teeth seemed long at the roots, though she had been a good-looking young woman before age and disappointments had sharpened every feature.

'And what do you want, dear brother?' Her voice was heavy with sarcasm.

'Why should you think I want anything?' he asked uneasily. This austere sister had always had the gift of making him uncomfortable.

She twitched the neckline of her black shirt-waisted dress impatiently.

'When else do you come to see me? Do you want coffee? Or I suppose you would prefer a drink. I believe there is only brandy.'

'Coffee will do,' he said as she leaned to ring the bell at the side of the fireplace.

'And where is our half-sister this morning?' she asked, her dark eyes glinting malice. 'Her company is generally preferable to mine.'

Resignedly Tomas thought that it seemed as if everyone knew about him and Marion – or at least suspected. He decided to ignore the question. Instead he said abruptly:

'Elisabeth – do you really like living here? Wouldn't you like to get away?'

She put down her tapestry and stared at him.

'Tomas,' she said, 'you know perfectly well that I have always loathed living here. My one attempt to have a life of my own failed; Father has always had us too firmly under his thumb. He sees himself and has always seen himself as the patriarch, the *seigneur*, and he will not change now.

'Of course I would like to get away from here. Mostly I would like to get away from him and our disgusting stepmother, wheezing and heaving her hideous bulk about the estate. And I would like to get away from his ludicrous mistress and her pretensions and their disgusting encounters under his wife's roof. I would like also to get away from you and your squalid little affair with our half-sister. But where do you suggest I go? And if you are asking me what I would really like to do with my life, I have no intention of telling you, for you do not ask out of interest in me. You ask because you have some fish of your own to fry. Some scheme to benefit yourself.

'What is it, dear brother? Has your gambling landed you into really deep trouble? What plans have you to get yourself out of the mess you have created? How could they involve me? And if you have come here for my support it is not forth-coming.'

She was sitting upright in her chair, her bony shoulders aggressively thrust forward, her hands clenching and unclench-ing in her lap. It was the longest speech that Tomas could remember her having made in years, and he was shaken for the moment by her bitterness and her obvious hate and contempt for them all. And then he was angry.

'All right,' he said impatiently. 'You hate us all. You always were a superior bitch, thinking you had more style, more intelligence and a double ration of all the graces compared with the rest of us. But it didn't stop you getting yourself pregnant by an Algerian gardener, did it? I've often won-dered how you managed to let yourself go that far. Did it have to be someone socially inferior so that you could retain your superiority even when he was fucking you? Were you the *grande dame* dispensing largesse with your legs wide open? Or do you really appreciate that you're such a nothing that in your heart you know you're only worthy to lie down for the hired help?'

He stopped, his anger evaporating, and she sat rock still, her crêpe eyelids closed over the black eyes.

'You always were coarse,' she said with her unerring ability to make him feel inferior.

'Oh, shit,' he said. 'I'm sorry. There's no point throwing insults at each other. The fact is that I want to get away from here and you want to get away from here and neither of us can do it without money. And we're not likely to get any more

65

money from Father unless we can persuade him to sell the place and pay us all off our share. If we all brought pressure to bear he might just do it.'

'You're insane.' The eyes were opened now, regarding him steadily. 'Father will never sell. And, you'll never get Peter to agree. He wants the place for himself. And besides, who'd buy it? A mountain in the middle of nowhere with half a dozen houses marooned on the top. The houses would sell easily enough, but I doubt if the share-out would bring in enough to get you out of your troubles, dear brother. This place is only profitable being worked as a single unit off which we all live. And Father is not ready to share out his personal fortune.'

'I know someone who wants to buy it,' Tomas said abruptly, 'and he's prepared to pay a great deal.'

'That makes me suspicious.' As if to dismiss what he was saying as nonsense, she had picked up the tapestry again. 'Who is it?'

'An Arab.'

'From Arabia, presumably?'

'Not an Algerian or a Moroccan,' he said, impatient.

'Arabs have more money than sense these days,' Elisabeth said. 'And why does he want Les Hirondelles?'

'He wants to turn it into a millionaire's retreat. He would add to the houses, copying them, so that the place looked like a natural Provence village. He'd create a golf course—'

'He'd have a problem,' Elisabeth interrupted, 'with this terrain.'

'Money can do anything. There'd be more swimming-pools, a club house, tennis courts, all superb and all absolutely exclusive to the people who'd pay a fortune for the houses and for the privilege of escaping the vulgarity of the coast.'

'The alternative sounds very vulgar to me,' Elisabeth said.

Tomas looked as if he could hit her, but said: 'His idea is that it should be discreet and perfect.' He was pacing around the room, dodging pieces of furniture, sweating from the heat of the fire and his anxiety to convince his sister. 'You know – similar to, but much, much better than, Castelleras.'

'You mean that artificial village outside Mougins, full of

artificial *mas* and artificial people?' Elisabeth said. 'That *is* my idea of vulgarity. Rich fat Americans in the film business wearing South Sea Island shirts, sniffing cocaine and drinking themselves into a stupor.'

'Christ, you're a snob, Elisabeth.' He sat down. 'Now listen, what does it matter? He'll pay twenty million francs.'

'Madness,' said Elisabeth.

'Listen. I didn't mean to tell you this, but he's already loaned me a million and a bit more against the sale. He wouldn't loan me that much if he didn't intend buying.'

'That should rather comfortably take care of your share then, dear brother.'

He hesitated, and the sharp black eyes watching him opened wider.

'I see,' she said, 'I suppose you get an extra payment for your assistance in persuading us all. Well, should that happen and should I decide to back you, I shall require a share of that.'

He felt the sweat pouring down his forehead and he was angry. Sweat denoted anxiety and Tomas hated to show his feelings. It was necessary to remain cool in all situations, but how to remain cool with a great log fire burning on the hottest day of summer and the cold black eyes of his sister watching him?

'That damned fire!' Then he said, hoping the lie did not show, 'You're wrong. There's no extra payment. But I'll be out of trouble and with some money in hand. And you'll be able to do exactly what you like.'

The maid had brought in the coffee and poured him a cup. Neither of the de Courtenays had taken the slightest notice of her presence, and as she left the room Tomas pushed the cup away, slopping the liquid in the saucer.

'It's far too hot in here to drink that,' he said. 'Can I count on your support or not?'

'For what it's worth, I suppose so,' she said, 'but it is worth absolutely nothing. There is no possibility of Papa selling. None at all. And you know it. You may have something of a problem placating your Arab friend when he realizes the situation.'

Yet Tomas, partly knowing she was right, was not displeased when he left Elisabeth's mausoleum. The gambler in him told him that with her even reluctantly and unbelievingly on his side the odds were shortened. He had no doubts about Raoul and Françoise. Raoul would do as he was told; Françoise would be happy to get her hands on the money and shake the red dust of Les Hirondelles from her expensive shoes.

His stepmother would be a problem, but he wasn't sure how much notice his father took of her wishes these days, nor was he sure whether or not she was happy at Les Hirondelles. She had little to gain from the estate anyway. As the second wife, she could only keep it as her home until she died. She had no rights to the capital; that would be shared among her and the children. But if she were difficult, some extra financial arrangement would have to be made in order to persuade her. It had occurred to Tomas that she was not long for this world, which could mean she would want to end her days exactly where she was or, on the other hand, perhaps she would welcome getting away from the humiliations of living with his father.

Tomas had an uneasy feeling that she did not particularly care what her husband did and quite liked her life as the mistress of Les Hirondelles. In which case she would have to go on the debit side.

Marion? Marion he thought he could persuade. He had already told her a little of what was in his mind, and she had not seemed to care one way or the other. Her mind had been on fucking at the time and while he had been talking she had been gently blowing in his ear, licking his neck, scratching with her fingers along the zip of his trousers, and had become annoyed when she had been unable to arouse him. Sex and money were in totally different compartments in Tomas's psyche, and he could only cope with one at a time.

But there had been that little *moue* from her over the dinner table last night when his father had spoken of the new *locataire*. Was that because it was a blow to his plans? Or was it because she thought their privacy to continue the affair would be lessened?

The *locataires* were a nuisance – he had no idea what kind

of lease his father had given them. So was Olivia Barton – she owned her house outright. It had been a gift. The niece's remark that she intended settling there had not filled him with confidence. How to sway Olivia Barton? Through the peg-legged niece, maybe?

But Peter was undoubtedly the stumbling-block to end all stumbling-blocks. His obsession with Les Hirondelles was obvious, as was his disappointment that it was unlikely that he could inherit. But he loved the life of the estate and would not part with it easily. The only chance was that, as it had always been made clear that the inheritance must be shared, he would be willing to cut his losses and take the sort of profit that the family would never receive from an ordinary sale. The businessman in Peter might be attracted by that thought, as the gambler in Tomas was attracted by it too.

He still had time to see his father. As he walked across from Elisabeth's to the big house, he debated whether to actually bring up the subject or whether to just make his mark a little with the old boy. He made a decision. The subject had to be brought up at some time, and perhaps today was the day. He could plant the seed of the idea in his father's mind, and he would have every excuse not to go too deeply into the matter as he had the appointment in Cannes. Surely his father must be attracted by the idea of twenty million francs? It was an incredible sum of money by anyone's standards, and only an Arab would be able to put his hands on that much in this day and age.

Claudine was in the hall as he entered and she looked up at him disapprovingly.

'Your father is not here,' she said. 'He said he would be working at the vines.'

Doing his peasant act again, Tomas thought, but nodded his thanks to the stiff-backed Claudine, thinking that no one seemed very pleased to see him this morning.

But his father was not working at the vines. Shrugging, Tomas decided he would be messing about on the estate some-where, though there was no sound on the still air of his father's expensive toys. His father had a collection of miniature farm machinery from which he gained enormous pleasure. There was a blue tractor with thick wheels; something large and red which seemed to carve up and dispose of grass in seconds while his father sat like an admiral on the bridge, propelling the thing along. He also had a mechanical digger and stone-lifter. He would ruin the peace of a somnolent afternoon without regard for others, playing at farmers with his noisy, buzzing machinery, just as he played at peasants. But at least that was quiet.

There was no sound of the toys, and his father's Rolls was in the parking-lot alongside his own Ferrari. There was also an incredibly old Volkswagen which made Tomas stop and think.

He put his car keys back into his pocket and went back into the main courtyard and down the hill to the guest house, now the *locataires'* house.

The front door was wide open, and a woman's handbag had been left on the long wooden settle in the hall. He moved quietly, almost on tiptoe, slid into the hall and stood in the shadow at the foot of the stairs, listening.

All was quiet at first, and then he heard a curious slapping noise, the noise of a hand on bare flesh, then a faint groan and more silence until the slapping noise came again.

A massage, he thought. He said she was a masseuse. The cunning bastard! He was creeping out of the house when he heard his father's cry of relief – a cry remembered from when as a small boy he had stood outside other doors listening and curious.

He knew now why his father had let the guest house. It very clear. But how would it be possible to use the knowledge? That was the question.

Chapter Seven

Anne had showered, rinsed her hair through after her swim and was dressed in light trousers and a shirt; it was still only ten o'clock in the morning. She was putting on the kettle in her aunt's big country kitchen and thinking about Peter de Courtenay when there was a tap at the back door, a 'coo-ee', and Marion's dark head, nose pressed to the pane, looked in, grinning a wide African grin at her.

'Can I come in?' she mouthed as if Anne were lipreading, and Anne unlocked the door and let her in.

'You're just in time for coffee,' she said.

'Great.' Marion stretched, sighed, took a packet of Gauloises from the back pocket of her jeans and offered them to Anne, who refused. Marion then settled herself on the corner of the big olive-wood table, cigarette drooping from her full mouth, and for a moment stared into space.

'Sorry about that God-awful dinner party last night,' she said eventually. 'It wasn't much of a reintroduction to the old place, was it?'

Anne was pouring boiling water over fine-ground coffee in a Melita pot.

'Well,' she said briskly, 'the atmosphere did seem a bit odd; I didn't quite understand what it was all about.'

'Money and freedom is what it is all about,' Marion said, screwing up her face against the cigarette smoke. 'Most of my little pals around here would like to sell up the place and scamper off into the wide blue yonder with their share of the loot and away from under Father's thumb. The only one who isn't too keen naturally enough is Papa; Mama is not interested one way or the other, but I'm pretty sure the rest of them – well, Elisabeth, Tomas, Raoul and Françoise – can't wait to grab their share. They all have all sorts of other fish to fry, but no courage to try life without a pocketful of Father's money.'

'Not Peter?' Anne asked.

'My darling brother? No, he sees himself as a sort of *seigneur* around the place, *droit* and all. If Peter's concerned with anything it's to work out a way to get the place for himself. He's obsessed with Les Hirondelles. He's also the nicest of them all. The only worker amongst a load of drones.'

It didn't seem politic to say that she too felt Peter to be not only the nicest but the most attractive member of the family; silently Anne poured the coffee into big bowls from the kitchen dresser and sat at an upright chair pulled up to the table. She passed a bowl to Marion, who also settled herself in a chair after finding an ashtray to place in front of where she sat.

'And you?' Anne asked.

The other girl shrugged. 'I don't really care one way or the other. I'm not into money. Actually, I can always get what I want out of Papa, whereas for reasons of his own he does keep the others pretty short. I don't want that much, and he gives me what I need. There's never a problem, so I'm happy. Lazy, enjoying life and happy.'

She laughed, stretched, teeth white in her dark, tanned face.

'And how's your attitude to money? Are you into it, I mean?'

Anne considered.

'I think I am. I like it. I like what it does. And I make rather a lot of it.'

'Make it! Clever you. How?'

Anne laughed. 'Well, I draw a comic strip for small children about an innocent swallow called Sarah who has marvellous adventures, and another one about a rather nasty lady rabbit called Rhoda who does unspeakable things with a carrot.'

Marion's happy grin spread again over her face.

'Which one makes the most money? No, don't tell. Let me guess – Rhoda.'

'Right,' said Anne.

'And apart from that,' Marion said, 'are you still the deep one, like you used to be? I can remember you, never saying too much but watching us all the time. Observing us and tucking us away for future reference. Quiet as a mouse you were.'

'I'm not always quiet,' Anne said, thinking how easily she and Marion had slipped back into a relationship that she had almost forgotten over the past years; thinking too that the Marion in old jeans, a teeshirt that had seen better days and long black hair tugged back in a ponytail bore little resemblance to the exotic girl of the pool she had seen the day before.

'I think you *are* still quiet,' Marion said abruptly. She picked up her coffee cup and took a long sip. 'Tomas has a feeling – an uneasy feeling – that you saw us in the pool yesterday.'

Completely taken off guard, Anne could not help momentarily stiffening.

'Ah, yes – you did. He said he thought you were a pretty good liar. Congratulations. You almost fooled him. Hope you enjoyed the exhibition.'

Marion's manner was flip, but her eyes were watchful, and Anne took a deep breath and said: 'I'm sorry I watched. It wasn't exactly well mannered. But –' she hesitated '– well, somehow it was rather beautiful.'

'Yes,' Marion said complacently. 'We are both pretty people. But I'd have thought you'd have been shocked to the core—' her voice dropped to a deep whisper.

The only way to deal with the situation seemed to be with honesty.

'Not to the core,' Anne said, 'but definitely startled once I realized it was you.'

'And that's why you left your bag behind?'

Anne nodded.

'It's not really all that shocking,' Marion said, staring into her coffee. 'We're only half-brother and sister. I can't get pregnant thanks to the pill and there's a lot more incest about than you'd think.'

'I suppose so,' Anne said. 'But you're so attractive, I can't think why you have to pick on your half-brother.'

Marion laughed.

'Well, he's a super fuck—' Anne's eyebrows arched a little, and Marion laughed again. 'Well, he is. Also it's the forbidden bit that gets me. All through college in Boston I had black guys. Not because they're any better than white guys – they aren't, but it still shocks a bit. People think you're very daring, and it all adds a bit of excitement. I suppose I like shocking people. You're the first person I've been able to shock with Tomas, though. He won't let me tell anybody, miserable sod.'

'Aren't there any black men here?' Anne asked.

'Darling, there are black guys and black guys. My American black guys were r-a-t-h-e-r special. College-educated, rich and smooth—' she let the word roll. 'Around here what have you got? A load of road-digging Algerians or smelly students from Sierra Leone. Not the same thing at all. So Tomas will do me fine for the moment, if you know what I mean.'

The conversation was fascinating Anne, but she was puzzled as to why Marion was being so open with her. As the thought came, the question was answered.

'You know, it's marvellous you're here for the summer,' Marion was saying. 'Everyone is so Goddamn old. I mean, Tomas is forty-five, right? Françoise and Raoul, my dear little niece and nephew, I cannot stand. What a couple of arrogant pigs, and into God knows what! You and I could have a lot of fun. Say, have you got a fellow?'

Anne shook her head.

'No one?'

She shook her head again.

'Ever had one?'

'Not for a long time.'

Marion whistled through her teeth.

'Almost a virgin, are you?'

Anne laughed. 'You can't be almost a virgin. There have been the odd encounters.' She hesitated, not wanting to explain further, then said lightly: 'But you'd be surprised how many kinks fancy a girl with a heavy limp. Who'd fancy a kink?'

Marion pulled a face. 'Not me. But how on earth do you draw a rude rabbit? You're going to be someone's prize possession for sure. But watch out who you choose for the big scene – the wrong person can put you off for life.'

Anne laughed out loud. 'I'd say you must have found the right person,' she said. 'Judging by your performance yesterday, nothing's put you off. You made me quite keen to have another go myself.'

'I did?' Marion said, ignoring Anne's first sentence. 'But who can we find for you? Hey, there's always my brother Peter, but he's meant to have some socialite New England broad lined up. You know, I've had quite a yen to try him myself, but he's such an old sobersides he'd have kittens at the thought. If you have him I want a blow-by-blow description.'

This time it was Anne who evaded the subject. It was too near to reality. And the idea of him having a woman already caused a pang. As soon as she had seen him standing arrogant and demanding at the side of the pool that morning she knew exactly why he had spiced her teenage fantasies and realized he would do a lot for her adult fantasies too. In fact she was determined that he'd do more than figure in fantasies. She wanted Peter de Courtenay. The news of a possible rival was bad news.

'I think you fancy him,' Marion was saying, her eyes shrewd again. 'But really Tomas would be better. He's so experienced. He'd really get you going. How would you feel about a threesome?'

Surprised, Anne put down her coffee cup and then realized that Marion was teasing, but perhaps not entirely teasing. 'It's OK,' she was saying. 'Two fellows maybe, but other ladies aren't my bag. I leave that to Tomas's wife. No wonder her two kids are such creeps.'

'Tomas's wife is a lesbian?' Anne asked.

'Yeah. And with fairly exotic tastes.'

'Does Tomas know?'

'I'm not sure. Probably. He hardly ever talks about her. She's coming down for a couple of weeks soon, so that will spoil my scene for a while. She might cut up rough if she thought her husband was laying his half-sister. Not for any truly moral reason though. She'd think it was expected of her to protest.'

'What would your father think?' Anne asked.

Marion's face shadowed.

'Don't mention it. But he has his hands full with Pamela Whitton so he doesn't worry too much about us.'

'Pamela Whitton!' Anne was genuinely startled. 'That funny looking woman at dinner last night?'

'Umm – she's been around for yonks. He can't get rid of her. But she's still in and out of his bedroom. They must be doing something.'

'Doesn't your mother object?'

'Mother hasn't the health or the strength to object to anything. She keeps alive by existing on a very low key. You must have seen she's asthmatic; she also has heart trouble. One day she'll just pop off and then Papa will have problems with Pamela Whitton. Imagine *that* as a step-ma.' Marion grimaced. 'Anyway, enough of the sexual confusions of the de Courtenays. How would you feel about coming down to Nice tomorrow morning to do a bit of shopping and have a light meal there before it gets too hot? I won't make you walk too far. We could even take the Rolls and make Dupré follow us.'

'I'd like that,' Anne said.

'Right. You're on. And I'm off for a swim –' she put down her cup and grinned at Anne '– don't worry, all on my own. You won't interrupt a thing if you're down that way. Pick you up about nine thirty, eh? Oh, and if you want any food shopping done just leave a list in the kitchen and Claudine will arrange it all. You can't go carrying stuff with that leg. In fact we'd better loan you one of the family cars or you'll be marooned here for ever. There's a *deux chevaux* knocking about that nobody uses. You do drive? Yes, of course you do.'

With a cheerful wave she made for the kitchen door and then spun on her heel. 'I forgot what I really came to say,' she said. 'Mother says will you join her for coffee on the lawn in her own garden this morning if you've time? Doesn't matter if you're doing something else, but I guess she's taken a fancy to you. The trouble with living up here is that we're all inclined to pounce on new people who come, like a lot of conversational leeches.'

'I'd like to,' Anne said. She should be drawing but perhaps a little holiday was in order. 'What time?'

'Anytime. She'll be out there by now. It's cooler than in the house in the mornings.'

'About half an hour?' Anne suggested.

Marion nodded. 'I won't join you – you going gives me a let-out and I get a bit fed up with the family.'

She waved again and went back out through the kitchen door, and Anne, washing up the coffee cups, found herself shaking her head and smiling at the same time. Any sense of shock from the day before's accidental viewing had gone; the other girl's open attitude had relieved the situation of any drama.

Well, well, well, Anne thought, I wasn't even shaken when she said she'd like to try Peter. All I thought was I wouldn't mind trying him myself, and then added out loud: 'Chance would be a fine thing.'

She wasn't sure what one wore for coffee in the garden with the *châtelaine* of a huge French estate and so settled for a short-sleeved cotton dress with a longish skirt with a ruffle that covered most of her leg. It was the first time she had worn it, and she was rewarded by Stella de Courtenay saying: 'You look very pretty, my dear. Such a change from those endless jeans that the young wear today.'

The old woman was sitting under the shade of a broad oak tree settled into a complicated garden chair, deeply cushioned, and with a foot stool on which rested two enormously fat and swollen legs. Her white cat, Suki, was curled into the vast lap and stared at Anne with hostile bright-green eyes not unlike her mistress's. Anne took Stella de Courtenay's outstretched hand and leaned to kiss her on the cheek.

A cool breeze stirred the leaves of the oak and the white linen cloth covering a heavy white wrought-iron table set with cups and saucers. There were half a dozen chairs placed around the table, but no one else was about.

'Claudine accuses me of holding court here every morning,' Stella was saying, 'but I love the view, and it is cool here until nearly lunchtime. As you see, the sun is behind the house but it still lights the view.'

The view was spectacular, dominated by the misty mountain shaped like a crouching beast to the west, and the sweep down to the valley, created by the mountain of Les Hirondelles itself to the east. Philip de Courtenay's house stood centre of the courtyard, the front windows looking down to the gate-house, while the garden at the back had no buildings other than the house itself to break the view.

'How is your aunt?' Stella de Courtenay was asking. It seemed to Anne that she was breathing better this morning; perhaps the light breeze helped.

'She's well,' Anne said. 'I haven't seen her for a long time. She's been finishing a book in New York. She likes the atmosphere there when she's writing. She says it exhilarates her and gets her going.'

'She's a clever woman, your aunt,' Stella said reflectively. 'We're all so useless up here. We do nothing except complain about our lot. Apart from Peter, that is. He is a top lawyer now, but at heart I think he prefers to be here. It's a very special place, Les Hirondelles.'

'I know,' Anne said. 'I've always loved it.'

Claudine had arrived with coffee, and was pouring from a large pot-bellied earthenware pot.

'Mr Peter is on the way, madame,' she said. 'He is back from New York.'

'That's good news,' Stella said. 'You'll meet him, Anne.'

'I already have. At the pool this morning. He'd just got off the plane,' Anne said. 'He's very charming.'

'Was he? That's also good news. He can be like a bear with a sore head when he's tired.'

'W-e-l-l,' Anne said, and they both laughed.

He was coming across the lawn now in white trousers and a dark blue shirt. He had a faint look of his stepbrother, Tomas – but his hair was much fairer, and his eyes were blue-green. He had the de Courtenay height and lean body, though his features were not as bony. She thought him better looking than Tomas, and where Tomas spoke English with an English accent he had the Bostonian tones of his mother.

'Good morning, Mama,' he said, bending to take his mother's hand and kiss it before kissing her on both cheeks. 'Are you any better?'

'I think perhaps I am this morning,' she said. 'It's the breeze. And you?'

'I was tired, but a swim and a nap have helped. Good morning again,' he said, turning to Anne. 'I'm sorry if I was abrupt this morning.'

Both she and his mother laughed and he looked inquiringly at them both.

'I told Anne you were a bear with a sore head in the morning,' Stella said, 'and though she didn't exactly agree with me she got her message over.'

'Well, I'm sorry,' he said, eyes glinting at her. 'Am I forgiven?'

'You were never in disgrace,' Anne said.

'Thank you,' he said.

Claudine was handing around the coffee, and he took a cup from her and handed it to Anne.

'Pour for Elisabeth,' Stella said. 'She'll be here any moment.'

'To what do we owe that honour?' Peter said.

'Not sure,' Stella said. 'She phoned in a twitch about something. It'll be the first time she's faced the morning sun for years.'

Elisabeth was coming across the lawn wearing a dark shirt-waisted dress with a shawl over her shoulders. She was also wearing stockings and lace-up shoes. Anne tried to work out her age. She couldn't have been more than forty-three, but she looked ten years older.

Without speaking she sank into one of the more upright garden chairs and took the cup of coffee that Claudine handed her.

'How nice to see you, Elisabeth,' Stella said, 'are you well?'

'Very well, thank you,' Elisabeth said. She was speaking in French and had not seemed to notice Anne's presence. 'I thought I had better come and see you. Has Tomas spoken to you of this nonsense of selling Les Hirondelles?'

'Selling Les Hirondelles?' Stella showed no sign of surprise or emotion of any kind. Elisabeth could have been speaking of the weather. 'No, but I'm sure it's been in his mind. After all, Elisabeth, it's been in all of your minds, now hasn't it?' Stella's tone was equable, but Peter shifted uneasily.

'It hasn't been in my mind,' he said.

'No, along with your father, you're the exception. But the

rest of you would like to get out, now wouldn't you, Elisabeth?'

'That's beside the point,' Elisabeth said, 'but you must speak to Father of this. Tomas is into some of his mischief again. He says some Arab wants to buy the estate for twenty million francs.'

A hush fell over the group. They were all so still for the moment that to Anne it seemed a tableau. She herself was startled. Twenty million francs was more than two million pounds sterling. Les Hirondelles was beautiful – but two million pounds?

Peter let out a long whistle.

'Twenty million. It's madness. Whatever for?'

'That's exactly what I said.' Elisabeth's head nodded on the long neck, and the long teeth were hidden as her lips pursed. 'Madness. That's what I said. But he says it's some plan to turn Les Hirondelles into a millionaires' playground. I know Arabs have more money than sense, but really!'

'A millionaires' playground? Up here?' Stella said. 'I don't get it.'

'Apparently there will be more swimming-pools, and tennis courts and a golf course.'

'On this terrain?' Peter said.

'That's exactly what I said. According to Tomas it is going to be the most exclusive place in the South, and millionaires will pay fortunes for our houses and the privilege of staying here to get away from the coast.'

'It doesn't make sense,' Peter said. 'Arabs aren't *that* spendthrift. They'll pay over the odds for what they want, but they know the price of things as well as anyone else. It's extraordinary.'

Anne was not sure whether or not she should be listening to the conversation, or if they realized that her French was quite adequate enough to understand what they were saying. She made a little move as if to go, and instantly Stella de Courtenay turned and said: 'It's all right, my dear. After all, your aunt's cottage would be involved in all this and she has always said that she intends to will it to you. What do you think?'

Anne still hesitated. It didn't seem to be her business, but they were all waiting for her to reply.

'I think it's an awful lot of money,' she said finally, 'and I think it would be a shame to turn the place into a millionaires' playground. It's so beautiful as it is.'

'I have no objection to selling the place,' Elisabeth said, 'but Tomas is up to something, and it's something that's going to benefit him in the end – not us. You know what he's always been like.'

'I'd better make some inquiries,' Peter said. 'Who is this Arab?'

'I've no idea,' Elisabeth said.

'I think I know,' Stella said. 'Do you remember – no, you were in New York, Peter – Tomas took the visitors' cottage for a man called Achmid something? He'd met him at the casino. He was here for about three days. He signed the visitors' book. You'll find his name there. I think he lives in Cannes.' She signalled to Claudine to refill the coffee cups. 'But really there is no point in fussing, Peter. Find out about this Arab by all means if you wish, but your father will never sell. Not in his lifetime. So the whole thing is academic. A hare-brained scheme of Thomas'. I'm afraid that you're all stuck here – for as long as your father and I am around, that is. Sorry, Elisabeth.'

'I'm not a fool,' Elisabeth said stiffly. 'I realized that. But there is one thing I haven't told you. This Arab has already loaned Tomas over a million francs against the day of the sale. I'm afraid that Tomas really is in trouble.'

'And he'll have gambled the lot,' Stella said. 'I see what you mean, Elisabeth. No, it's not straightforward at all.'

Her breath had begun to wheeze in her chest, and Claudine was at hand quickly with the asthma pump.

Elisabeth and Peter looked at each other.

'I'll see what I can do,' Peter said. 'But a million francs ...'

Chapter Eight

Françoise arrived in Cannes and was driving along the Croisette at about ten. The sun was already high, the beach crowded with prone browning bodies stretched on thick mattresses and turning themselves as if on a spit. Brightly coloured umbrellas marshalled in the shade, and the waiters were busy with their white clothes and trays of frosted drinks. The once-a-year people were all grabbing at a little luxury to sustain them for desk and kitchen sink for the next eleven months. She felt a little glow of superiority that she was not one of them, coupled with a touch of momentary anxiety that she might become one.

Cannes sparkled like a wedding cake. The sweep of the sea bounced back the sun's rays on to the well-kept gardens that bordered the road and the beach. Palms swayed exotically in a light morning breeze and the buildings were icing clean. It all looked so normal, so open, civilized and safe that Françoise found herself driving more and more slowly, ignoring the impatient drivers behind her. She was curiously reluctant to arrive for her appointment with Achmid Fouezanne and immerse herself in his dark and perverse world.

She decided to have coffee at the Royal and sat on the wicker chair watching the passing parade while plotting her moves with Achmid. There was no point in being anything but straightforward. His sources of information were too widespread and his lines of communication as precisely complex as a spider's web.

Which would come first, she wondered? The business or the sex. Neither was pleasure, but she found herself hoping it was business first. Sex with Achmid could only be described as hard work. She had learned a tart's trick of switching most of her mind away from what went on, but it was not as easy as it would have been had the sex been straightforward. The play-acting was so absurd. Her contempt for him when the silk suits were stripped away, the silk underpants pulled down revealing his flaccidity, was as great as her half-fearful respect for him when, wearing the trappings of his money and power, the blind-seeming eyes behind the dark glasses stripped her mind of any attempt to mislead him.

By quarter to eleven she had parked her car, entered the hotel where he kept a permanent private suite and had been escorted to his door by a grey-clad pageboy. The room was the same as always – blinds drawn, with Achmid in his dark glasses sitting behind the huge green leather-topped desk, one lamp throwing a pool of light on to the papers before him. If he was at his desk, she thought, it was liable to be business first.

'Good morning, Françoise,' he said in the accent of a French academician. 'You are late.'

'The traffic was heavy,' she said.

'That was why you stopped at the Royal for coffee?' he said.

'I stopped at the Royal because I felt like it.'

'Then you won't be wanting coffee here, will you,' he said. 'It will save the time you have wasted. I have an appointment with your father at one o'clock and I am sure he will not keep me waiting.'

'At the moment,' Françoise said, lighting a cigarette with studied rudeness, 'he needs you more than I do. Has he persuaded Grandfather yet to let you have Les Hirondelles?'

'I shall find that out today,' he said.

She wished he would take off the dark glasses, but the moment to demand he did so had not yet come. Instead, she blew smoke across the desk, only just missing his face. He took no notice.

'And what is the news?'

'McTaggart has agreed,' she said.

'What did you promise him?'

'Myself, and a better boat than *Les Hirondelles III* all for himself. If we do it, it's going to cost you, Achmid.'

'Yourself? I thought he already was having you.'

'Permanently,' she said abruptly.

'And of course you will – what is the phrase – welsh on the deal.'

'Yes. But he'll get his boat. And me until I'm fed up with him.'

'And when will you be ready?'

'I don't know.' She hesitated. 'My grandfather hasn't agreed to let me use the boat.'

'Hasn't agreed.' The hawk-face pushed itself into the patch of light, threateningly. 'Are you wasting my time again?'

'No, because McTaggart has worked out a plan, and he won't do it unless you agree. So we're going to need a lot of money from you and then if Father says no to the cruise we'll just go anyway. Once it's a *fait accompli*, and if it's not costing him money, he'll shrug his shoulders and give up.'

She stubbed out the cigarette in a large cut-glass ashtray and took a deep breath.

'McTaggart says Kenitra is out. He won't load the stuff from there. It's the most dangerous port in Morocco. Since the clean-up in the Riff, he says the King's police watch the port like hawks. The Riffians were getting too big for their boots with all the hash they were able to produce. Hassan thought they were planning their own take-over bid and put the boot in.'

'I know all this,' Achmid said impatiently.

'In that case you'll understand why McTaggart wants to know where you're getting the stuff from and why you suggested Kenitra. He thinks you may be double-crossing us and using us as a decoy while you get a much larger load out a safer way.'

'My dear girl,' Achmid said, 'the load you are to take out is worth two and a quarter million English pounds on the market. I'm hardly likely to sacrifice that much money deliberately.'

Françoise's eyes were steely blue, she had a feeling that the ball was in her court and that she could be winning.

'Right then – where does the stuff come from?'

He tapped impatiently with a pencil on the desk, shrugged and said: 'The Riffians moved their centre of operations. They're growing it somewhere deeper in the mountains and they've replaced all the processing equipment that was destroyed. The King will find it eventually. But there is a conspiracy of silence in the mountains that will last for a while yet. But not much longer, which is why you and McTaggart must move quickly.'

Françoise lit herself another cigarette.

'Right. Where is the stuff? In Kenitra?'

'No.'

'Where?'

'That is nothing to do with you.'

'Then why pick Kenitra?'

'Because I have a network there that survived the last purge.'

She shook her head. 'McTaggart won't have it. Remember he's a professional skipper. He talks to other skippers. They all know what's going on in every port in the Med. He says Kenitra is shut up like Pandora's box, and he's not putting foot – or rather anchor – there. He says he hasn't seen the inside of a Spanish jail yet, and he doesn't intend finding out about them at his age. And jail, Spanish or otherwise, would not suit my style.'

'So where do you suggest I send the stuff?' Achmid said sarcastically. 'Cueta? Right under the Spaniards' noses.'

Françoise shook her head.

'McTaggart says you'll have to get it to Tangier. He's clean; he's never been involved with anything, and he's well known at Tangier. He's got friends, Moroccan friends and Spanish friends who know he's straight and he says there's a lot more chance of getting it aboard there with him as skipper than anywhere else on the Moroccan coast. We know it's still the centre of the drug trade and swarming with agents, but McTaggart thinks it'll work because he's clean.'

'And how does McTaggart suggest I get it to Tangier?'

'That's your problem.'

Achmid got up from the desk, walked across to the window and switched the blind back briefly to look out over the sea.

'What else?' he said.

'McTaggart wants a decoy. In fact, he wants two decoys. A small-time smuggler of your own choosing coming out of Kenitra with a load and landing at Algeciras and a greedy amateur tourist coming out of Tangier with a load heading for Gib. Both at the same time as we go. The Spanish police are to be tipped off, and we reckon you're going to have to lose about at least £50,000 worth of the stuff to make it look genuine.'

'There would have been a decoy anyway,' Achmid said.

'Another thing,' Françoise said. She crossed her legs and smoothed her jeans over the knees. 'You're going to have to wait for the stuff. We've got to make it look like a proper cruise. And McTaggart won't unload in Marseilles. He suggests St Tropez and other playtime ports along the coast. We'll literally unload it on the beach in beach bags. And we're going to be calling in at a lot of glamorous places on the way, with a boat full of guests whom you'll be paying for, dear Achmid.'

'That's madness.' Achmid's voice was cold. 'The longer you keep the stuff on board, the more chance you have of being caught.'

'McTaggart doesn't think so, and neither do I.'

'It's too amateur,' Achmid said. He had paced to the window again and was standing with his back to her, one gleam of sunlight striking across the very black hair.

'Listen,' Françoise said. 'I've agreed to go into this for the hell of it, to relieve the boredom and for a great deal of money. McTaggart wants his own boat. He's sick of skippering for people like my father who hardly use their expensive toys. We've both got ulterior motives – mostly to do with money – but we're not stupid. We know you're using us because we *are* amateurs and all the pros are frightened of the Spanish clean-up at the moment. The pros are mostly known, or at least suspected. We're not.

'It has to look like an ordinary cruise. Rich French girl on daddy's yacht with her equally rich friends, all screwing each other across the Mediterranean and worrying about their tans. If we start rushing about, particularly back to Marseilles, people, especially policemen and customs men, are going to wonder. The idle rich don't hurry. Christ, you should know that.

'The hash stays on board while we stop off at Marbella, Malaga, Ibiza and all points to St Trop. We shall definitely bypass Marseilles. We'll be having a lovely time, whooping it up on your champagne.'

Her voice had become more authoritative as she spoke. She was watching Achmid through narrowed eyes. From the way he fidgeted, less still and watchful as he was when only business was on his mind, she judged that the moment was near.

'So you can take it or leave it. We go on our terms or we don't go at all, and if you don't agree you can get stuffed.'

She made her voice as rude and as hectoring as possible. He nodded and moved to press a bell on the wall beside what had once been an open fireplace.

'Shall we have elevenses now?' he said in English, asking it as a question.

Here we go, Françoise thought, but nodded and said: 'If you wish.'

Achmid's servants were well trained. It was no more than a second before the door opened and a white-coated Arab entered with a tray of coffee and English biscuits.

'Now, Achmid,' Françoise said, 'I shall be mother and you must speak English, and then we shall have our other lesson.'

She had placed herself on a high chair by the low coffee table so that she had to lean to pour the coffee, and Achmid had settled himself on a large red leather pouffe so that his head was below hers and he had to look up at her.

'Now what are you going to do today?' Françoise asked him.

Achmid took one of the chocolate biscuits having made a careful selection first.

'I'm seeing your father at one o'clock. After that I shall take a little light lunch and a siesta—'

'Not a siesta,' Françoise said sternly.

'An afternoon nap,' he corrected himself, 'and then in the early evening I shall do a little more business and have dinner with some friends from Beirut tonight at La Réserve.'

'All the way to Beaulieu for dinner?' Françoise said. 'With the coast so crowded?'

'It is easier with the *autoroute* opened now,' he said, 'and besides, I shall take the chauffeur.'

He had been drinking his coffee in short sharp sips, his eyes on her face as he spoke. His English was impeccable. Whoever had trained him had done a good job in that direction at least, Françoise thought. The other lessons had taken well too, but perhaps not for the best.

She had been drinking her coffee and eating her plain digestive biscuit with deliberate slowness, and his fingers crumbled another biscuit that he did not want to swallow.

'Achmid,' she said. 'You've got chocolate all over your fingers. Go and wash. And take those ridiculous dark glasses off immediately.'

He took off the glasses, and the eyes behind were dark and narrow with a little hot glow of red in the gloom of the room.

'I shall change,' she said, 'while you wash. And you are not to come in until I tell you.'

She rose from the high chair and moved towards the bedroom, wondering how long it would take today. It had been known to take two hours, and after her late night with McTaggart she wasn't in the mood. Regard it as a means to an end, she told herself as she always did, and get on with it. The bank balance was building in a most satisfactory way. Besides there were bits she enjoyed. Really enjoyed. The bits with the cane. Achmid probably thought she was feeling the same sort of passions that he was, but those satisfying, stinging slaps that so excited him made her feel better for the stupid long-winded play-acting that he put her through. She wished to heavens he could just climb on top and fuck her. But nothing so simple.

The bedroom was austere and as plain as the big living-room was exotically Oriental. There was a neat narrow bed – probably the most simple the hotel had been able to provide, unless Achmid had moved it in himself. Basic furniture and very little decoration. It was still a typical hotel bedroom but stripped down to essentials to look like the room of a school-boy.

Here light flooded in through the plain curtains, and Françoise opened the bottom drawer of a chest of drawers and took out a grey dress that buttoned down the front with a neat white collar, and white cuffs on the long sleeves. She looked at it with distaste. Far too hot for the weather; what a pity Achmid's kink was such a dreary one. Why couldn't he have been seduced at an early age by a sexy French maid instead of a severe English nanny?

She stripped rapidly and when she was naked pushed the clothes that had so excited McTaggart into the drawer out of sight, and put on the nanny dress, belting it with a webbing belt, and slipping her feet into sensible shoes. The cane was in its usual place at the back of the drawer and she took it out and swished it through the air, liking the singing noise that it made. She then bundled her hair back in an elastic band into a plain ponytail.

Now she was ready. She went to the bedroom door, opened it to find Achmid lurking outside.

'What are you doing, Achmid?' she said. 'Come in here immediately.'

He only joined in the fantasy to obey. He would never speak until it was all over. He was dumbly obedient to all she ordered. At the beginning, after Achmid's personal physician had explained his needs, she had tried to vary the routine a bit to make it more interesting, but after three months she had decided it was not worth the effort of invention. He seemed to be quite happy with the same old thing over and over again.

'You have chocolate on your shirt,' she said. 'You are a dirty boy. Take it off.'

She stood watching him while he unbuttoned the shirt, sliding it off over narrow brown shoulders and a lean brown chest.

'You have got to learn to be clean,' she said. 'Into the bath with you. But get those trousers off and hang them up neatly first.'

Silent, he unbelted and unzipped his trousers, stepping out of them, hanging them on a hanger from the wardrobe and carefully putting them away.

'Right, come along.' She had always had the urge to pull

him along by the ear, but as he was a good eight inches taller than her she felt it would look so ridiculous that she would probably laugh herself sick. And the physician had warned her of the dangers of laughing at Achmid.

So, she took him by the elbow, dressed in his silk underpants, silk socks and loafer shoes, and pinching the flesh of his arm marched him into the bathroom.

All was prepared. A warm bath waited, a large block of Pears soap and a back brush.

'Shoes and socks off,' she said. He kicked off his shoes and bent to pull off his socks. His feet, like the rest of him, were very long and thin and sinewy. His body, Françoise thought, with a little more weight on it would be more attractive than McTaggart's.

He stood meekly in his underpants, and Françoise moved to pull them down. She exposed him in a neat and tidy well-practised movement, so that the pants slid to his feet. She then stood for a moment staring at his crotch. His penis was long and thin and very limp, protected by thick dark hair.

'Right,' she said, 'into the bath,' flicking her finger under it, so that it jumped and fell again.

She stood there without moving as he picked up the Pears soap and began rubbing it over his chest and stomach.

'Underarms,' she said.

He soaped under his arms obediently.

'And don't forget there—' One finger pointed to his crotch. 'Look at you. You're hopeless. I'll do it.'

She rolled up her sleeves, grabbed the soap, briskly lathered it between her hands, and plunged her arms into the water to find his scrotum which she squeezed in her hands and rubbed hard until he winced. Then she washed his penis, thinking as she always thought at this stage of the game, what a pity it was he was circumcized; had he not been, she could have made a lot more play of the washing scene.

His back was then scrubbed with the rough scrubbing brush, viciously until his skin was red above the brown, and then she ordered him out of the bath into the heavy towelling bathrobe and back into the bedroom.

He did exactly what he was told, and Françoise felt the laughter bubbling inside her. The fierce moustache and the hangdog expression were so at variance. One day she was afraid she would laugh, but the penalty might be too unpleasant.

There were times when she was afraid of him. Sometimes when she dug her nails too deeply into his flesh, his eyes would look at her with a glow that was not sexual, but of hatred. When she beat him with the cane she could not see his face, so she never knew his expression then, or even if he were erect. Had he really hated the nanny who had taught him to be a masochist? She longed to ask, but the subject once the sessions were over was taboo.

'Are you dry?' she said. 'Take off that bathrobe.' He dropped it on to the floor. 'Not like that. What an untidy thing to do. Pick it up.' He stood holding it as she said : 'Now you're going to learn how to pleasure and please me. I shall teach you, but it's a secret between us. You must never, never tell anyone what we do.'

The ridiculousness of it all seemed to be striking her with more force than usual today. Françoise knew she had a low boredom threshold, and she was becoming extremely bored with all this. Think of the money, she told herself.

She seated herself on the bed, the cane to hand.

'Kneel down,' she said, and before he had started to move, she had swished the cane across his shins. 'Quickly,' she said.

He dropped on his knees in front of her.

'Undo the buttons of my dress—' The cane swished across his bare back this time, and he moved to clumsily open the grey dress starting from the hem. When he reached the belt, she commanded him to stop and then opened her legs very wide.

'That's the place that pleases ladies,' she said, pointing at herself with the cane. 'Now please me.'

He looked at her dumbly, and she brought the cane down on his bare buttocks with genuine feeling.

'With your tongue,' she said.

He thrust his head between her legs, and his tongue was

groping, achieving little. Looking down all she could see was dark hair, thinning faintly at the crown. She stared across the room at the wall opposite, wondering if she and McTaggart could pull off the hash deal. Achmid had promised them a third of the value if they did. He'd probably only give them a quarter, but that wouldn't be bad, and she'd had a lot of money off Achmid already. McTaggart would have a fit if he knew how.

'Deeper,' she said, remembering her duties, and brought the cane down again. She felt his tongue enter her, and then he pulled away and his face looked up at her, with an expression of loathing on it.

'Do as you're told,' she said. 'And if you're very good, I'll do it to you.'

He made no move, and Françoise thought, Christ, he really does hate women's pussies. She brought the cane down in a stinging slap over his shoulders.

'Get on with it,' she said. He got on with it and she wondered if Achmid was right – if McTaggart's plan was too amateur. But it seemed the only way.

His tonguing of her was actually about to have some effect, Françoise discovered with surprise. It was time for the next move.

'You didn't do that very well,' she said to the buried head, viciously squeezing her thighs against his ears. 'Stop now and see if you can do better.' He pulled back from her and she stared down at him kneeling there, and thinking how sex could make such fools of people. There he was, rich, powerful, *someone*, and he let her order him about, beat him with a cane, just because it was the only way he could come.

'Right,' she said. 'Take my dress off.'

With reluctant fingers he untwisted the clasp of the webbing belt and finished unbuttoning the rest. She let him help her out of the dress, relieved to get the coarse fabric away from her body and noticing that she had been sweating.

'Hang it up,' she commanded him. He did.

She was standing naked in front of him when he turned back from the wardrobe but there was no erection on his naked body; no sign even of the beginnings of one.

'On the bed,' she said. He lay down and she kneeled over him, dropping her small breasts close to his mouth. 'Suck my tits,' she said. Obediently, he did so and deliberately she lay so heavily against him that she could hear he had difficulty breathing. 'Now the other one,' she said. She snatched the one nipple from his mouth and pushed the other towards him. Automatically his mouth closed over it.

He was almost snorting as she pushed her bony breast into his face. Her knees were uncomfortable on the hard bed, and she was very bored with the whole scene, she decided, though it had seemed like something to relieve the boredom when she first got into it. 'Why me?' she had asked the physician. 'Because you look very English,' he had said, 'because an ordinary girl could blackmail Achmid, but as the daughter of Philip de Courtenay, Achmid could blackmail you if he wanted. Besides, Achmid had the impression it was something that you would enjoy.'

'I'm no sadist,' she said.

'Exactly,' he had said. 'True sadists are very dangerous. We wouldn't want any accidents. But you might still enjoy it.'

She wondered if Achmid was perhaps blackmailing her by involving her in his smuggling activities, but there was no blackmail involved from her point of view. It would be exciting. She wanted to do it. McTaggart wasn't so certain, but he was a first-class skipper and his reputation was impeccable. With him in charge, they might well get away with it.

Achmid was still sucking away like a hungry baby and she was definitely uncomfortable. Impatiently she pulled her breast away from Achmid's mouth and decided to press on with the next scene in the play. Now she had to try to make him hard. She had never managed it yet. For a while it had been a challenge, then a frustration and now her failure to arouse him had become a nagging irritation. She felt she was failing – not him. And that had made her hate the charade more.

'Your turn now as you've been a good boy,' she told him, and set to work on the long, thin, unresponsive penis. She tried every trick her English public schoolboys, with their leanings to the anal, had taught her; every trick from the St Denis motorbike boys with their leaning to the oral, and all the more sophisticated tricks that the well-travelled McTaggart had taught her. But he remained limp in her hands, limp in her mouth, and limp between her legs.

She knew the signs now of when he had had enough. His fingers plucked and pulled at the coarse linen sheets. Thank God, she thought, lifting her face from his thighs. Though it could have been worse. It was nice that the long-ago nanny, governess or whatever she had been had insisted on the bath, and nice really that he never did get hard. At least it made breathing simpler when she had him in her mouth. And at least he never did actually screw her.

She got off the bed and stood, arms akimbo, looking down at him.

'You are useless,' she said. 'What good will you ever be to a woman? Useless. I shall have to punish you for not pleasing me.'

His hawk face looked up at her from the pillow, somehow vulnerable without the dark glasses.

'Lie on your stomach,' she said. He rolled over so that the long length of his brown back, still a little pink from the scrubbing, was exposed to her. His fingers were clutching at the pillow, and he was pressed into the bed, his toes curled down the side of the mattress.

Very deliberately she picked up the cane and began to beat him with it. The physician had said she must never draw blood, so it took some judging. If she did not hit him quite hard enough it took such a long time; she had to work up to what she thought was the right pressure – and pain.

He was slow today. Her arm was aching, and she began to feel resentful. His buttocks were a mass of bright red weals, which she knew faded quickly on his dark skin. She changed arms and brought the cane down with her left hand, but she couldn't exert so much force. She reluctantly went back to the right arm.

Tentatively, to get it over with, she tried a little harder, and she saw his back begin to arch like a salmon, and she knew he was nearly there. Suddenly he gasped, raised himself from the bed in a curving movement and collapsed flat, his face buried in the pillow. There were some convulsive pumping movements of the hips, and she knew he was through. She stared at him with anger and contempt and, unable to help herself, lifted the cane well back behind her shoulder and brought it down across his buttocks with all the force she could find.

A line of blood appeared instantly, and he screamed and leapt to his feet, his movements as fluid as a cat. Naked, he stood facing her and his expression was murderous. Terrified, Françoise backed away from him.

'I'm sorry,' she said. 'I'm sorry.'

She thought he would attack her, but he regained control of himself and said: 'Bring me my clothes. And dress yourself.'

His voice was harsh.

He had the upper hand, Françoise realized. She had somehow changed the pattern with that angry blow. And she did as she was bidden without argument.

He had vanished into the bathroom, presumably to bathe the wound, and Françoise wondered whether or not she should volunteer to dress it. But how? It was a long weal. It would need a lot of sticking plaster. Again she had the ever constant urge to giggle, but every instinct told her that this was not the moment.

As he came out of the bathroom, the phone rang. He looked at the living-room clock and frowned.

'Your father,' he said. 'Stay here – I'll see him downstairs. I don't want you meeting him.'

He answered the phone, gave his instructions and dressed swiftly.

'I'll see you when I get back,' he said. 'Wait.' And it seemed to Françoise that there was an ominous undercurrent to his words. She felt very strongly out of control and not a little afraid.

Anne had cooked and eaten an omelette with a green salad and forcing herself to ignore the seductive sun had gone to work in the little summerhouse which her aunt had had turned into a small studio.

Once the summerhouse had been a conservatory. Where the frames for plants had been there was a workbench and a high stool. Along the back wall facing the door was a long overstuffed sofa which had seen better days and come to rest in the summerhouse.

As engrossed as she was in her work, Anne sensed and then saw that Peter de Courtenay was walking to the back door of her aunt's cottage. He knocked, and receiving no reply stood hesitant for a moment until Anne rapped on the window, caught his attention and then waved and beckoned.

He smiled, waved back and headed purposefully towards the summerhouse as she opened the door to let him in.

'Working?' he asked, peering round the room. 'That's unusual around here.'

'I have to earn a living,' she told him, her voice serious.

He stood looking at her quizzically, one fair eyebrow raised, his hands in the pockets of blue velour slacks. He was wearing a matching jacket that zipped up the front, and its colour brought out the blue of his eyes and made his crisp hair seem fairer. He looked more American than French – athletic and wiry.

She stood quietly waiting for him to tell her why he had come, noting with almost academic interest that she could feel a pulse throbbing in her throat and that she felt absurdly shy.

'Mother said I should check you have everything you need,' he said abruptly, 'and apologize properly for being so offhand this morning. I didn't recognize you, to tell you the truth. You've changed a lot.'

For the better or worse? she wondered, but said: 'You haven't. And thank you – I've everything I need, and more.'

'Good.' He was moving to look at the work on the drawing board.

'That looks like the local mountain there,' he said. 'And what's with this bird?'

'That bird is Sarah Swallow,' Anne told him, her voice mock-severe.

'And who is Sarah Swallow?' he asked.

'My livelihood,' she said and went on to explain as she had explained to Tomas the day before. This time the reaction was different.

He listened, nodding agreement, and said: 'I know how you feel. Les Hirondelles has the same effect on me. I love this place.'

He had settled himself on the sofa, leaning back, while she perched on the stool, looking down at him.

'So what's been happening to you all these years?' he asked.

'Not a lot,' she said. 'Endless operations. Art school in Florence, at fifteen. And now I make my own living with Sarah and another cartoon character – a rabbit called Rhoda. I live in my own flat in London, run my own car, and generally I'm pretty lucky. End of story.'

He was silent for a moment.

'I always felt terribly sorry for you as a child,' he said thoughtfully. 'You were such a solitary little thing. I used to wonder what sort of life you had without parents and a proper home.'

She considered. 'It was all right,' she said. 'My aunt was always there in the background and she had me for all my holidays. The rest of the time it was boarding-schools. I got used to them.' She paused. 'I suppose I'm still solitary in a way, but I don't mind. I think that if you can be alone and not be lonely you're better equipped for life than most.' She flushed, not wanting to say anything that could spoil what might be the beginnings of an interest in her. 'That sounds terribly corny and rather smug, but I mean it.'

He took out a cigarette, offered her one which she refused, then said: 'Boarding-schools should have made you used to a lot of people around. I'd have thought you'd have found it hard to be alone.'

'Not really. My leg made it difficult for me to join in. And then there were all those long periods in hospitals. And you can be very alone with an awful lot of people around.' She laughed. 'Oh, God! I keep sounding like Patience Strong. But those clichés are true – yuk! Another one.'

'Oh, yes,' he said in a nasal, drawling comic's voice, 'clichés have become clichés because they're all true, that's what I always say.'

They both laughed and then there was a small silence that seemed to Anne charged with electricity. She knew why she was talking in such a fatuous way. It was him. She was finding it difficult to be natural. She wanted so much to make a good impression on him.

'Did you miss your parents?' he asked suddenly. 'I used to wonder about that too. I couldn't imagine life without parents and I'm afraid I missed mine in a way small boys are not meant to when I was sent off to school. As old as I was, I was thoroughly homesick and miserable. There were a few secret tears, I tell you.'

He was making her think again for the first time in many years about those days after the accident.

'At first I missed them dreadfully,' she said slowly. 'Particularly in hospital, immediately after the accident. It was a long time before they told me they were dead. That was the worst thing. I just thought they'd abandoned me. They said they were hurt, but it seemed to me that however badly hurt they were they ought to come to me – I was so sick and, being only little, selfish. But them not being there – that was the worst thing about it.'

She stopped abruptly, realizing this was something she had never before voiced.

He nodded.

'And you're obviously not married.'

'Nope.'

'Living with anyone?'

'Nope.'

'Anyone in mind?'

'Nope.'

'So you're still solitary?'

'Not solitary,' she protested. 'I'm just not afraid of my own company. Anyway, what about you? You're not married?'

'Nope!' he mimicked.

'Living with anyone?'

'Nope.'

'Anyone in mind?'

He hesitated.

'There's a girl in the States,' he said. 'An old friend of the family, name Evelyn Grenville.'

Anne felt a sinking sensation of disappointment.

'Is she nice?' she asked lightly.

'Very,' he said. 'You'll meet her. She's coming here in a few weeks' time.'

'Great,' Anne heard herself saying, and turned to pick up a paintbrush, afraid her expression might give her away. 'Does she like it here too?'

'She's never seen it yet, but I'm sure she will,' Peter said. 'She's an athletic outdoor girl – likes tennis, walking, riding, swimming, all those things.'

'And you like those things?' Anne asked, miserably conscious of her own disadvantages.

'I guess so,' he said. 'When there's time.' But she thought he sounded a little indifferent.

She had put a tentative stroke on the artist's board in front of her to hide her feelings a moment longer.

'Hey, listen,' he said. 'I'm sorry. I'm stopping you working. I'll get out of your way.'

She wanted to say 'no, stay', but instead she managed a grin and said: 'Deadlines and all that. You know how it is. But it was nice to chat.'

'Oh, we'll chat some more,' he said easily. 'Got to stop you being so solitary.'

He waved, nodded and went out of the door, striding back past her house; she watched him until he had rounded the corner and was out of sight.

'Evelyn bloody Grenville!' she muttered as she dipped her brush viciously into the black paint. 'Damn! Damn! Damn!'

Chapter Nine

Tomas was racing along the dual carriageway that ran from Golfe Juan and into Cannes. The Ferrari was running perfectly, purringly eating up the miles, and he felt a strong sense of optimism and of well-being. He had a feeling that things were going right; his life was on an upgrade. Achmid would almost certainly create the miracle in the end. Achmid was determined to have Les Hirondelles and would think of the right persuader that would convince his father to agree to the sale.

The road was running out as Cannes neared, and Tomas was reaching a point of decision. To turn left, go under the bridge and take the coast road to the Palm Beach Casino, or to carry straight on into the town and avoid temptation.

He felt so good that he was certain his luck would be too. Just time for perhaps six – or lucky seven – spins of the wheel, and then on to face Achmid, probably with a little more cash in his pocket.

He turned left.

The coast sparkled in the high sun of midmorning, but it was already quieter as holidaymakers drifted off the beaches and the rocks and into town for their lunch. There were picnics taking place on rocky promontories and on the decks of small boats, and Tomas thought of food. Damn Achmid for making the appointment at one. He rounded the bend and the Palm Beach Casino was confronting him, exotic with its Moorish curves and modern with the huge glass entrance. It was familiar, and he felt that buoyant lift of the spirits that always accompanied entering a casino. Today might be the really lucky day.

He managed to park with ease – another omen that the day was right – and hurried in through the glass doors. He was just signing himself in when he felt a light touch on the arm.

Ten minutes later he was back in the Ferrari, staring blindly out over the palm trees, the perfect flowerbeds of the Croisette and the sea, haphazardly decorated with the white wings of sailing boats.

Achmid had stopped his credit.

After the initial shock had passed he began to be very angry. Achmid would pay for this humiliation. The price for Les Hirondelles would mount higher, and he was certain that Achmid would pay. The man's fingers itched to get on the title deeds. Well, for this the title deeds would cost him more.

He put the car into gear and roared backwards out of the parking place, causing a *deux chevaux* to brake noisily, and swung himself back on to the Croisette. The traffic was in a snarled, snail-paced knot but he still was in time and as he nosed and inched his way, oblivious to the beauty of the carefully nurtured gardens at the roadside, he thought vengeful thoughts about Achmid Fouezanne.

He would win in the end. He knew it, and laughed out loud at the thought. The winning would be expensive, but a bird in the hand ... and in his present situation he had no choice. Ten million all to himself plus his share of the twenty million would end his problems.

The twin cupolas of Achmid's hotel were nearing and he roared the Ferrari to the front of the hotel, throwing the keys and a ten-franc piece to the doorman for him to deal with the car. He phoned up from the concierge's desk. His instructions were always to phone up. Achmid did not like unexpected visitors. The concierge put down the phone and said that he was to wait in the small bar across the entrance hall.

Tomas felt a momentary sense of unease. Achmid always saw him in the hotel room, the blinds drawn, the desk lamp lit. He saw the Arab as a creature of the dark. That time at Les Hirondelles in the brilliant light of the mountains he had seemed exposed, and Tomas, sensing this, had had Claudine keep the blinds drawn and shutters closed at the guest house. It had been interesting, though, that when Achmid had insisted on walking over a great deal of the land in his highly unsuitable crocodile shoes his skin had noticeably darkened almost minute by minute. The rather yellow tinge of his face had gradually turned to brown. He had looked so much improved that Tomas couldn't imagine why he shut himself up in the dark all the time – unless of course he wanted to look more European. And there wasn't much chance of that.

Achmid had the most Semitic cast of features possible, and for anyone who liked that sort of thing, Tomas thought, he'd be rather attractive ...

Why was Achmid meeting him downstairs? The change of routine disturbed Tomas with his gambler's superstitious preference for patterns remaining the same. He had never seen Achmid in the public part of the hotel. Sometimes he thought that Achmid never left his darkened, secret rooms. So why today? Why now were they to meet in the bar when, so far as he knew, the Arab did not even drink?

He ordered himself a gin and tonic and sat moodily staring at the spitting bubbles while he waited. Then he decided that perhaps it could be a good thing. Achmid was meeting him socially; it was less of a business confrontation. But then if that was the case, why had his credit at the casino been stopped? And had his credit at all the other casinos been stopped too?

'Good morning. Or is it afternoon now?' Achmid was standing over him, eyes behind dark glasses, moustache hiding the thin upper lip, and the lean, bony body covered with a silk suit not dissimilar to his own. The Arab's shirt was very white, and his tie that of a famous English public school, though Tomas for the life of him couldn't remember which.

'Afternoon, technically, I suppose,' Tomas said, getting to his feet. 'What will you take?'

'Merely a Perrier water,' Achmid said. Tomas waved to the waiter who ignored him. He waved again, angrily, with no result. It was not going to be his day.

Achmid seemed only to lift a finger, and the waiter was there.

'Perrier,' he said, 'and whatever monsieur is drinking. Now,' he turned back to Tomas, letting the one word hang in the air. He crossed his legs, arranged his tie and let his hands fall neatly on the table. He was so boringly British in all his mannerisms. Tomas thought the public school would have done it. But he was Semitic all right in his business dealings.

'Achmid,' Tomas heard himself saying, unable to refrain from the subject for a moment longer, 'there seems to be some

102

mistake. The manager at the casino says you have stopped my credit. I told him I was sure he had misunderstood, but he was adamant.'

'There was no misunderstanding.' Achmid stroked his moustache lightly with a long forefinger. 'It is for your own good, my dear chap. If you go on losing at the rate you are losing, when the sale is complete there will be nothing in it for you. As it is, there will be very little. I will pay all the outstanding debts and the ten million I have promised you for yourself, but after that – no more. Even oil wells have their limits. And it is time you persuaded your father. I cannot wait indefinitely. You must arrange the sale.'

Tomas thought, and then in unconscious parody of Achmid, crossed his legs, fingered his tie and took a cigarette from his case and lit it. Achmid, he knew, did not smoke.

'Oh yes,' he said, 'the sale. I'm afraid I have bad news. I think my father might be persuaded to sell, but the price would be considerably higher. Twenty million simply will not do.'

The dark glasses seemed aimed at him like two round barrels ready to fire. Tomas forced himself to sit still and relaxed.

'Twenty million will not do?' Achmid said softly. 'Perhaps your father thinks that he too is sitting on an oil well, but to my knowledge oil does not flow in the South of France. I must say I am surprised and not a little hurt, my dear Tomas. We both know that Les Hirondelles as it is now is not worth the twenty million that I have offered, let alone the ten million to you personally. You can tell your father that as it is my dream to own it, and to create the kind of world for the rich that I have described to you, I am willing to pay so much. Tell him also the offer is high because I appreciate that selling in many ways would be a great sacrifice to some of your family.

'But more than twenty million – no. That is the offer to him and it stands. It would be unfortunate if it fell through and you were suddenly responsible for your debts and with no chance of receiving your own little extra for making the arrangement.'

Tomas had been sipping his drink, and he put it back on to the round table with a slap that caused it to spill.

'What do you mean?' he said.

'Well, I will pay your debts at the casinos, and then of course there is the money you have already had from me. About a million and some, I believe. But if I cannot buy Les Hirondelles, you of course will owe me all this money. It is perfectly simple.'

He had his hands cupped around the glass of Perrier and still stared at Tomas. It was impossible to tell what was going on in his head. He wore the dark glasses for a very good reason, Tomas thought, wondering whether or not he was bluffing. Achmid would pay more – he was absolutely certain of it. But how to create the double bluff? He needed time to think. This was not his day after all. It was a bad day, and therefore a day to do and say as little as possible. He could deal with Achmid better when things were on the up and up.

'Let's not talk about it any more,' he said. 'I'll have to see what I can do with the old man. Incidentally, don't worry – your million is safe. It will cost me, but I can always get my hands on that much ... the estate, you know.'

'Really? Your father would have to die first, surely?'

'No, no,' Tomas said. 'We wouldn't need anything so dramatic.'

'I think perhaps you would,' Achmid said. He was about to say something more when he stiffened in his chair, eyes towards the door. Tomas turned to see what had caught his eye and was confronted by Françoise in her tight jeans and silk sweater of the night before, nipples prominent, about to put her hand on his shoulder.

'Hello, Father,' she said. 'Fancy meeting you. And it's Mr Fouezanne, isn't it? We met at Les Hirondelles.'

Achmid had risen to his feet, and it seemed to Tomas that he was not at ease. He seemed almost angry. The thin mouth was drawn in a tight line, and a small tic pulled it downwards on the right side of his face. Françoise, on the other hand, seemed almost cocky. Her blue eyes held more animation than he had seen in a long time, and she was smiling broadly, and astonishingly leaned to kiss him on the cheeks giving his shoulder an affectionate little squeeze.

'Are you going to buy me a drink, Papa?' she said.

Achmid had sat again and was very silent; his stillness was almost threatening, and Tomas's sense that something was wrong persisted. But what? Could it be that the Arab fancied his daughter and was disturbed by the sight of her? It was possible, with her so fair and him so dark, but if that were the case surely he would be falling over backwards to charm her, rather than sitting staring like a stone rabbit.

This time the waiter came, probably courtesy of Françoise's nipples, Tomas thought, noticing the sly look they got from the young white-coated barboy. She said she thought she would like a glass of champagne.

'Just because it's such a beautiful day,' she said. 'Don't you think so, Mr Fouezanne? I think it's one of the most beautiful days I can remember.'

What the hell was going on, Tomas thought. There was definitely some kind of strange signalling between the two of them, and it wasn't a signalling of attraction. There was hostility there. A lot of hostility. He knew he could ask Françoise for explanations until the cows came home, but if she didn't want to tell him, nothing would budge her. For all his faint dislike of his daughter, he felt a moment of anxiety. If Françoise were up to something, and she might well be as it seemed to be a family failing, he hoped she realized that she was playing in very dangerous grounds. He had a very strong feeling that she was mocking Achmid in some subtle way that he understood and disliked very much.

He decided his instincts were correct when Achmid abruptly rose to his feet before the champagne had arrived and said: 'Well, I must be off. I have an appointment. It was good seeing you, Tomas. We must meet again. Perhaps you'll ask me to Les Hirondelles ...'

'Of course,' Tomas said automatically. 'Any time.'

'Any time?' The Arab's voice was jovial. 'Why don't we make a date right now then?'

Why don't I keep my big mouth shut, Tomas thought. In

every move of the game between him and Achmid since he had met the man at the casino at Monte six months previously he had been drawn in deeper by making some automatic, polite response which Achmid had seized upon. Now he had let it happen again.

'When are you free?' he heard himself saying feebly, and it seemed that some of Françoise's buoyancy had fizzled too.

'Any time, any time,' Achmid said. 'Supposing I come up for the weekend? No, that's not possible. The weekend after next. Will that do?'

'Great.' Tomas's head was searching for a way out while he smiled and nodded. 'It'll be a bit crowded. Father's let out the guest cottage to some people from Nice, so you'll have to stay in my place. Is that OK?'

'Your father has let the guest cottage?' Achmid frowned, and Tomas thought, Oh, shit – he's picked up the significance of that!

'Only for a week or two,' he said quickly. 'But my place is pretty comfortable.'

'I shall look forward to it,' Achmid said. 'You may expect me at about six on Friday evening week, if that will be convenient.'

'Great. You'll take dinner with the family of course,' Tomas said again, and stood to shake his hand. Achmid then stared down at Françoise.

'*Au revoir, mademoiselle,*' he said. 'No doubt we will meet again.'

'I do hope so,' Françoise said.

He bowed again to them both and then strode towards the foyer, throwing the waiter a note on the way.

'Good,' Tomas said, 'he's paid the bill. That's something.'

'Don't you like him?' Françoise asked, eyes big over the rim of the champagne glass.

'Not much,' Tomas said. 'But he's useful.'

'In what way?'

'Oh, I don't know.' He changed the subject. 'He seemed very interested in you.'

'I thought so too,' she said, using the swizzle stick that the

106

waiter had provided with studied nonchalance. 'Think he fancies me?'

'God knows,' Tomas said irritably, 'but don't mess about with him. He's dangerous.'

'How dangerous?'

'Well, he's not straight. He's into all sorts of things.'

'What sort of things?'

'All sorts of things.'

'You mean he's a criminal?'

Tomas shook his head.

'Not quite. He doesn't do any of the dirty work himself. He gets others to do it. He's rich enough. He's very rich. And he's greedy.'

'How do you know all this, Papa?' Françoise said, her head tipped to one side inquisitively. She looked very young and very pretty, he thought.

'Because after I first met him I had someone, well – look into him. I like to know who I'm dealing with.'

'And you are dealing with him?'

'Yes. He wants to buy Les Hirondelles. For a packet. You'd get your share like everyone else if you agree, and if you can help me persuade your grandfather.'

Her eyes were shrewd.

'Grandfather won't sell. Neither will Grandmother.'

'Don't you start that. He can be persuaded, surely – for twenty million? Maybe more.'

She laughed showing sharp little white teeth.

'For that much money, I'll help persuade too.'

He looked at her curiously, aware that he hardly knew his daughter.

'What would you do if you had that much money, Françoise?' he asked.

'Get away from here,' she said promptly. 'Go where I wanted when I wanted. Be free, with lots of money to do it in comfort. I hate Les Hirondelles. The boredom!'

'Why don't you stay with your mother in Paris?'

'Because I hate my mother too,' she said flatly.

He found himself uncomfortable and a little embarrassed.

'So you prefer me?' he said.

'I suppose so,' she said indifferently. 'We're really quite alike, we two.'

'We are?' he said, surprised. He saw nothing of him in Françoise at all.

'Oh yes,' she said. 'We are.' Her voice was enigmatic, and he decided to let the subject drop.

'What are you doing here, anyway?' he asked.

'I'm meeting Raoul at the Voile au Vent, but I suddenly had the urge for a glass of champagne in the most civilized of circumstances. It was lucky that Mr Fouezanne was here to buy it for me. Grandad's allowance really doesn't run to much champagne in glamorous places. Which reminds me,' she swallowed the last of her champagne and said: 'I'll help you about the sale, if you'll help me. I want to take Les Hirondelles III out – for a cruise. A long cruise. And I'd like particularly to be away when Mother comes down.'

She really does hate her mother, he thought with a little glow of satisfaction which surprised him.

'Difficult,' he said. 'A long cruise is expensive. Your grandfather will never agree.'

'Not even if it doesn't cost him anything?'

'What do you mean?'

Her eyelids dropped over the pale blue eyes.

'Well,' she said, 'I have this very rich boyfriend. Very rich, but he doesn't own a yacht. He'd pay all the expenses, and we'd take along a few friends to make it look all right.'

Tomas shook his head.

'I can't see your grandfather agreeing, but he might just be persuaded to charter it to this friend of yours. Who is he, by the way?'

'No one you'd know,' she said, so flatly that he knew she would never tell. Though she'd have to tell if the fellow did charter the yacht. 'Charter?' she was saying, almost to herself. 'I hadn't thought of that. Do you think that might work?'

'Your grandfather has never been known to turn down money,' Tomas said, 'just as he has never been known to part with it willingly. In fact, I've often wondered why he hasn't chartered Hirondelles III before.'

'Because it's his,' she said shrewdly. 'It's like the estate. It's his. He doesn't really like strangers about at Les Hirondelles at all. He's very possessive.'

'You can say that again,' Tomas said with feeling. 'But he might just agree if you took Raoul and made it a family cruise that someone else was paying for.' And, he was thinking, leaving me free in my own home without the pair of you around. Easier, much easier, with Marion. And at the thought of Marion he wanted to get out of the bar and back home and into bed with her.

'Listen,' he said, 'I have to be off. Are you and Raoul in for supper?'

'Don't think so,' she said. 'We'll be out all afternoon and early evening, if the information's any good to you.' She smiled the sharp little smile again, and he could have hit her.

'Right then, see you later,' he said, and got to his feet. 'Where's your car?'

'The doorman put it somewhere.'

'Mine, too. Do you want to stay here?'

'Just for a minute – you go on.'

'Right,' he said, and bent to kiss her cool cheek. He left, realizing that the last five or ten minutes had probably been one of the only conversations he had ever had with his daughter that had any meaning of any kind.

But his mind was on Marion. He was forcing his mind to be on Marion. Otherwise his mind was skittering between the million francs he owed Achmid, the necessity of persuading his father to sell, the need to gamble to perhaps make the means to put everything straight – a method which he knew was not the answer. He could not reconcile his feeling about Achmid cancelling his credit arrangements. There was anger, there was anxiety, but somewhere there was relief. And then he wondered if perhaps it was only at Cannes the credit had been cancelled, and for a moment his spirits rose until he realized that if Achmid had cancelled Cannes, Achmid had cancelled Monte, Juan and Beaulieu.

Think of Marion, he told himself, as his mind seethed with all the problems. Think about her. He went to the concierge and put through a call to Les Hirondelles. The maid answered

in his father's house, and after a short delay while he sweated –
angry with himself for sweating – she came to the phone.

'I'm on my way back,' he said, conscious that his voice was
tense. 'I want you. The kids are away. Be in my bedroom. I'll
be there in just over an hour.'

She laughed, and said lightly: 'What a greedy-guts you
are!'

It didn't match his mood, and he said tersely: 'In an hour
then.'

His car was waiting; at least he retained some of his authority, and at least the servants knew who they were dealing
with, he thought. He threw a ten-franc piece from the collection
of ten-franc pieces that he kept for tipping in his pocket, and
sped off. No point in taking the Croisette. No point in passing
the casino. He turned into the town and took the short way
home. And she was there – waiting for him. Without wasting
time on words or explanations, he laid her, quickly and almost
brutally – his appetite matched by hers.

And then they slept.

When he woke it was cool and dark in the bedroom. The
fur bedcover lay on the floor, covering a Persian rug, and
stray beams of light from the late-afternoon sun teased their
way into the soft gloom behind the shutters.

Tomas felt temporarily at peace. He knew it would not
last, but for the present he was totally relaxed as he lay on
his wide bed, Marion at his side, the two of them covered by
a light sheet. Her body was softly damp, and his hand ran
over her, almost with love for the pleasure she had given him.
The curls of her body hair were tight and wet, and her skin
felt soft and slippery from the heat of their lovemaking.

He rested his hand over her breast and sighed deeply, and
she stirred under his hand.

'Not yet, darling,' she said, her voice sleepy.

'No, not yet. Did I wake you?'

'No. No. I was just dozing.'

She turned to nuzzle her head into his shoulder, and he
could feel her wet lips finding the hollows of his body.

'That was very nice,' she said, her voice coming out as a small drowsy croak. 'Very nice indeed.'

'I thought so,' he said. He had thought so. Her ardour, her skill had calmed him. With Marion's hands, Marion's mouth and Marion's sexual accomplishments, there was no way that a man could fret about gambling debts, plots, plans or the future. The only thing to do was to sink into her warmth, moisture and closeness and think of nothing else.

The room went quiet again, and he too dozed a little. The sound of his own breathing eventually wakened him, and he found himself turning to wrap himself around her body as if they were more than just casual and guilty lovers. She had been asleep, and as he moved, her breathing quickened, she lay still for a moment and then sat upright, reaching to the side of the bed for her packet of Gauloises. She lit one, put it between his lips as he lay staring up at the ceiling and then lit another for herself before settling back beside him.

'I think we had better be careful,' she said, 'or we are going to find ourselves in an embarrassing situation.'

Her voice was sombre and he knew exactly what she meant; there was a dependence growing between them and that must not happen. He did not reply, mostly because he could think of nothing to say. The balance between them was too precarious. Someone might have mentioned love, and then they would be lost.

He needed to keep the moment light.

'You,' he said, stroking her full breast, and tracing round the nipple with the forefinger of his left hand, 'are quite, quite incredible in bed.'

'Lots of practice,' she said. He recognized it as her own way of lessening herself and therefore their relationship. 'Some would say too much practice,' she added.

'And which of them taught you to be so spectacular?' he asked and felt under his hand the slight stiffening of her body that specific questions about her lovers always brought.

He leaned up on one elbow to look down at her. Her eyes were tight shut in the grey light of the room, and she lay very still, the smoke from her cigarette spiralling upwards in a

111

light haze. He stroked her breast again, and she shifted impatiently.

'Hey,' he said, 'what is it? What's the guilty secret?'

'Questions!' Her voice was irritable. Marion was rarely irritable.

'I would have said there was a problem,' he said, 'and problems are best talked about.' He was being gentle, surprised himself by his feeling of tenderness towards the girl lying beside him.

'It's not a problem,' she said abruptly. 'Nor even really a guilty secret. Well, not my guilty secret anyway, because it wasn't my fault.' She stopped. 'Or was it? Yes, I suppose I was as much to blame in that I knew exactly what was happening.'

'And what was happening?' he asked to encourage her to go on.

'I was being seduced. Aged not quite fifteen. For the first time. By Father.'

'Father!' He sat upright, to stare down at her, astonished at his own deep sense of shock. He had not thought he could ever have been shocked by anything again. 'Father!'

'Yes, Father!' She imitated his shock and amazement, still resting with eyes closed and cigarette in hand. 'Our father. Yours and mine. Not the one in heaven.'

He was sitting fully upright, putting out his cigarette. It seemed too much to cope with.

'But what happened?'

'You'd like the grisly details? I'll tell you. Perhaps you're right; one should talk about these things. I never have. For his sake, really. You see, I've never felt badly about it. He did it so well. It was probably the best introduction to sex that I could have had. I don't know how I feel about it really. I sometimes wonder if most of my outrageous behaviour stems from that, or if I was going to behave outrageously anyway, and Father recognized it and realized he could get away with laying his daughter and she wouldn't complain but would definitely lie back and enjoy it. Maybe he felt he was genuinely the best person to introduce me to what was in my nature.

112

'It's very confusing. I suppose a psychiatrist could sort it out, but I'm really not all that concerned about my emotions on the subject to want them sorted out.'

She had been speaking very quickly, then was silent for a moment, still lying on her back. She had opened her eyes and was staring at the ceiling, and he remained silent, breathing quietly and trying not to do anything that would disturb her. She was speaking now as if he were not there.

'I was fifteen – almost. I told everyone I was fifteen anyway, even if there were a few months to go, and I was what you might call a big girl for my age. Seeing Anne again reminded me. We were always comparing the size of our tits, and mine were always far in advance of hers. I was quite proud of them.

'It was the first summer that Mother got ill and had to go to that place in the Swiss mountains for her chest. Peter was in the States, and you were on the boat with Margaret and the children. I was only here for a month of the summer myself. Do you remember – I joined you later on the boat, and Margaret was none too pleased about it.

'Anyway, Father was very much about and was wonderful about keeping me company. He showed me all over the land, explaining things and saying I was grown up enough now to know how the estate worked. He'd swim with me – he actually got into the pool – and he took me for a lot of long drives around the countryside, so I really got to know it very well. I was perfectly happy with him. I'd read in the evenings, or watch the television, while he pottered and did his peasant act about the place.

'And that's how it was for about a week. And then one morning I had just got up and I was taking a shower in his bathroom. I always liked showers best, and my bathroom only had a bath at that time. He'd said I could use his shower anytime I wanted.

'Well, this morning he came into the bathroom. I wasn't particularly embarrassed. I mean, he was my father and he had seen me nude before, but I was aware that he was looking at me very differently.

113

'And I rather liked it. I was stretching my arms up under the water because I knew from looking in the mirror that my tits looked more pointed like that, and he just stood watching. Then he said: "I haven't bathed you since you were a baby, have I?" Now actually I doubt very much if Father ever bathed any of us when we were babies, but I never thought of that at the time. He took the soap from me and lathered his hands and turned me around so my back was to him, and then started sliding his hands up and down my body, washing me. At first, he just ran over my breasts and then he started to concentrate on them, rubbing the nipples with the palm of his hand and it felt lovely. I just stood there and let him do it, and it was easy because I couldn't see his face and he couldn't see mine.

'Then he stopped doing that, and he turned me back to face him, and made me give him a foot, one by one, and he soaped and washed my feet, then running his hands up my legs, but stopping just at my thighs. He'd turned the water so that it was barely running – I suppose he thought it would be ridiculous if he got soaking wet too, so he was sponging the soap off me with his hands. He'd washed me everywhere, and then he slid his hands between my legs and soaped me there.

'We hadn't said a word while all this was going on, and I was loving it. It all felt so nice. Would you believe, I felt very safe and protected – loved, too, I suppose.

'It took him a while washing there, he didn't hurry anything, and then he got to what the Americans call the hot button. Revolting expression! Anyway, he was very skilful manipulating that particular button, though funnily I wasn't as surprised by those lovely feelings as I had been with some of the other things he did. Peter and I had done quite a bit of playing at mothers and fathers when we had been smaller and no one was around, and I knew how it felt being fondled there, though Peter never had done it so well.' She stopped to stub out the end of her cigarette and light another, offering one to him. He shook his head.

'He stopped doing that and I really felt as if I was about to melt into a puddle in the shower, right then and there. I

114

wanted something and even at that age I had a pretty good idea of what it was. He got a big bath towel and wrapped me in it, picked me up and carried me through into his bedroom. All very romantic stuff as you can see, and designed to appeal to a fourteen-year-old who'd always had something of a crush on daddy anyway. He laid me on the bed and dried me very carefully, between the toes, under the arms, all the bits that nannies go on about. Then he said: "I want to show you something."

'I don't think I said anything. I think I nodded dumbly. I was having a lovely time, and I knew I shouldn't be, and I was pretty sure that he shouldn't be either.

'He sat me on the edge of the bed so I could see into that long mirror that goes the length of his wardrobe, and he very gently opened my legs. "I want you to see something very pretty," he said. "A very special rose."

'He sat beside me, staring at me in the mirror, and he pulled my legs even wider open and pulled back the lips, smoothing away what hair was there and then proceeded to explain how this pretty thing with all its complicated layers would give me and others so much pleasure when I was grown up. All the time he was fingering me sometimes his finger disappearing into me, and I was watching fascinated as he did it; I could see myself getting wetter and wetter, and little white creamy patches oozing on to the red, which didn't look like a rose to me at all. I thought it looked hideous. But it felt great.

'He asked me if I liked what he was doing, and again I don't remember saying anything. Then he lifted my legs back on to the bed, and he leaned over me and started on my breasts. I mean, this was my father, and yet I was loving every minute of it. I knew my father wasn't going to hurt me, and I just liked what he was doing.'

Tomas was lighting himself a cigarette and trying to keep his hands steady.

'I'm not sure that I want to hear any more,' he heard himself saying. He was still astonished at his sense of shock, and furious with himself because as she spoke, her voice a reflective monotone, with no attempt at titillation, he found he was growing hard again, and as she described what their father had done to her he wanted to do the same. And somehow that disgusted him.

'No, I want to tell it now I've begun,' she said, her eyes very bright, almost as if she were tearful as she turned to look at him. 'It's your fault. You've always been curious. I sometimes thought that you might have guessed.'

'No, I hadn't guessed,' he said.

'You know, the funny thing was, he never kissed me, except afterwards, and then it was on the cheek – just like dear old daddy again. But that all took a while. Was pushing his tongue in my mouth more wicked than what he was doing? Funny that.

'I was naked, of course, and he had his clothes on, and I think as young as I was I wondered how he was going to get around that problem. He solved it quite nicely by telling me to wait like a good girl and he'd be back. He was going to have a shower too. He was very quick, just long enough so that the hot feelings didn't go away, and I was still definitely wanting more. Quite impatient I was. Then he came back with just a towel around his waist. He looked much the same as always. You know how he's always worked without a shirt, so it was all reassuringly familiar. Then he lay down on the bed and let the towel fall away, but I couldn't see anything with him beside me like that, and he was careful not to let anything alarming touch me.

'He just went on stroking me, and then he nearly made me jump out of my skin. He'd bought in a jar of cream from the bathroom and he put a huge dollop of it on my nipples. It felt ice cold, but exciting, and then he proceeded to massage it into me, eventually getting back down to my cunt, so that I was all covered in this white, pleasant smelling cream. I'm pretty sure it was nothing more glamorous than Nivea.

'I was really beginning to feel as if the top of my head was coming off. And then he asked me if I'd ever seen a man naked. Well, I wasn't about to tell him about my little explorations with Peter, so I just did the dumb head-shaking bit again.

116

Then he took my hand and guided it down. He was like a rock and I must say I didn't have any experience of that.

' "Would you like me to put it in your rose?" he said. "That's what it's for, and what your rose is for."

'Well, the girls at school had always said it was agony first time and that you were bound to get pregnant, and that men had all the fun. But I had the feeling that it wouldn't be agony – not with my father – and I couldn't imagine him letting me get pregnant and I was having a lot of fun, so I nodded yet again, and he was very gently, very cautiously, easing about in all the Nivea which really, the way I felt, I didn't need. He just put the tip in, and took it away much to my chagrin, and then I felt him put his finger in – deeply and as slowly as possible. It didn't hurt a bit, and I decided then I definitely wanted the real thing.

'I can remember clinging to him, biting at his shoulder and saying, "Do it! Do it!" over and over again. So he did it. Very quickly, and for a moment it hurt like hell, but then he was stroking and petting me again and moving in me very gently and I well, just lay back and enjoyed it. It was a very good first fuck, I tell you. Not many girls climax first go.

'Now, I knew perfectly well that we shouldn't have done it. And I suppose he must have known that too. But it didn't stop us fucking everywhere possible and anywhere possible over the next three weeks. I had an education the like of which you wouldn't believe. At fourteen I was fucked on fur rugs, in armchairs, in the shower, in the bath, in the open, under an olive tree, perched on the edge of a table with him standing, in the back of the Rolls. There was a certain amount of gymnastics, but he wasn't much of a one for exotic positions. He liked exotic places. And he was honestly more interested in playing with me than wanting me to play with him. Maybe he felt that getting his daughter to go down on him was a bit much, though I did get the idea of my own accord. Nor did he go down on me. I learned *soixante neuf* elsewhere.

'Actually, it was all straightforward fun sex. Generally speaking, oral was out. We had the sort of fucks that the young generally indulge in between themselves, before they've learned a bit. Nothing what you might call offbeat or re-motely kinky. I've often wondered if that's how he likes his sex, or if he was just being a bit delicate on account of the fact he was fucking his daughter. He was careful, incidentally. Sorted out when my periods were – and that did embarrass me – and used a rubber most of the time.'

She was lighting another cigarette and he was still silent.

'Anyway, we got word that Mummy was coming home, and I was packed off to the boat to you. You may recall I was moody and not exactly the life and soul of the party. Not surprisingly. I'd found a lovely new source of fun that beat playing tennis every time, and there it was gone. And I couldn't see much chance of ever getting it back again. Not in that particular direction anyway, as I was to be sent to board-ing-school after the holidays, and it was all planned for me to go to the States as soon as I was sixteen. Who was going to fuck me at a boarding-school? It was lucky I'd always enjoyed masturbation.

'The curious thing is that Father and I have never ever discussed those three weeks. He never told me not to tell Mother. He never told me to keep my mouth shut. I think he just knew that I would. I suppose he must have spotted my sexuality all pushing through there and thought, why not? And really, why not? He was a marvellous lover.' She paused, laughed out loud and added: 'Do you think he did it to Elisabeth too?'

'Christ, what a thought,' Tomas said. He was trying to hide from her the fact that he had an erection that was lifting the sheets. He didn't want to be roused by the tales of his father's fucks and he found he didn't know what to think or feel about any of it. He moved a little further away from her, but her hand had found the telltale bulge under the sheets, and she was caressing him gently.

'It's all right,' she said matter-of-factly. 'Telling it had the same effect on me.'

Tentatively he touched her. Her nipples were rigid, and she was wet and open for him. With a groan, he rolled over on to her, riding her furiously with no affection, only anger,

'Well, suddenly the boot was on the other foot. I know what he's up to, Raoul. You know he told me he wants to buy Les Hirondelles and that he's offered Father twenty million.' Raoul nodded. 'Now,' Françoise said, 'I know why he's prepared to offer that ridiculous sum for the estate.' She paused again and dropping her voice even lower: 'Because it's worth millions and millions more.'

She settled back on the banquette, smiling, and waited for his reaction.

'Don't be bloody ridiculous,' Raoul said flatly.

'No.' Her voice had dropped to a whisper. 'It's true. Do you remember that time when Achmid came for the weekend – about the second time we met him – and he stayed at the guest house? Remember there were two men who arrived unexpectedly just for the day – a German and a Frenchman from Paris?'

'I remember. The ones that did so much walking?'

'That's right. Well, it appears they are geologists – not friends at all. And they've discovered that Les Hirondelles is a mountain of bauxite.'

Raoul looked bewildered. 'A mountain of what?' he asked.

'Bauxite. To tell you the truth, I'm not sure what it is either. But it seems from the reports these two had written out for Achmid that it's the basic ingredient of aluminium and worth a fortune. Achmid had written two hundred and fifty thousand million pounds sterling down as the possible value of the deposit and also that the operating costs would be twelve million. Imagine all that money, and we're actually sitting on it. No wonder Achmid is so eager to get his hands on the place.'

Raoul's bony shoulders were hunched forward, and the fair and the dark heads together made a conspiratorial pattern in the dark corner of the bar.

'Then why's he interested in our thing? I mean comparatively it's peanuts.'

She shrugged. 'I suppose he likes to have a lot of things going, but we'll have to watch that he's not thinking of blackmailing us in some way about Les Hirondelles.'

'How could he do that?'

'I don't know. Maybe if Father won't sell, and if we do

the job for him, he'll threaten to tip the police off that we're smugglers or something if Grandfather remains stubborn.'

'But that wouldn't work any more now that we know why he wants Les Hirondelles,' Raoul pointed out. 'It's us that could spill the beans on him.'

'Good thinking,' Françoise said. 'You're right. We're in charge now, and I think I sort of knew it before I'd even had time to think it out. I walked out of that hotel room, sailed into the bar downstairs and met up with him and Father and made them buy me a glass of champagne. I felt great. Achmid was furious, I could see. He couldn't work out why I'd disobeyed him, and I'm sure he was thinking up dreadful punishments for me behind his horrible dark glasses.'

For a moment, brother and sister stared at each other, weighing the enormity of the knowledge they had acquired.

'Do we tell McTaggart?' Raoul asked.

'I don't think so,' Françoise said. 'Let's just keep it to ourselves for the moment until we decide what we're going to do.'

'What are we going to do?'

Françoise was silent. She still felt exhilarated, but there was a tense, worried feeling dampening her euphoria. Achmid Fouezanne was not one to cross, she was certain. For one moment this morning she had already seen his dark side and she was certain that she did not want to see it again in a hurry.

'I'm not sure,' she said slowly. 'We must think it out, and we must be very careful. We may in the end just tell Grandfather, but I'd like to make a little capital for us first. I'd like to make a lot of capital for us first, come to think of it.'

'Are you a bit scared?' Raoul asked.

Françoise had no secrets from her brother. He was almost the only person for whom she felt any kind of affection at all.

'I'm a bit scared,' she said.

'Then maybe we should tell McTaggart.'

She shook her head.

'No – this information is ours. He'll want a cut.'

'Well, in that case we'd better stop talking about it,' Raoul said. 'He's coming in now.'

McTaggart, solid in jeans and a navy blue teeshirt, his sandy hair combed neatly, stopped at the bar, bought himself a beer and then came to sit with Françoise and Raoul. He eased himself into the banquette next to Françoise and settled himself so that his knee was pressing against hers.

'Sorry I'm late,' he said and took a long gulp of beer, wiping the froth from his upper lip with the back of his hand. 'What did Achmid say this morning?'

Françoise stared into her whisky.

'He's not sure about your plan. Says it's amateur. The thing that really makes him nervous is that we want to keep the stuff on board while we cruise.'

'Well,' said McTaggart, his voice belligerent. 'If I'm getting into this at all, I'm getting into it on my terms. Why won't you let me meet this Achmid? I prefer to know who I'm dealing with.'

Françoise sighed exaggeratedly.

'It's not that I won't let you meet him, it's that he doesn't want to meet you. I suppose he thinks the least number of people who actually have contact with him, the better.'

McTaggart was bad tempered this morning. He said: 'Well, it's ludicrous, dealing with a seventeen-year-old girl on a thing of this kind. Ludicrous.'

'Don't you think I'm intelligent enough to cope, Andrew?' Her voice was dangerously silky.

'I think you're highly intelligent, but I also know that you're in it for the kicks. That's more important to you than the money. Now I am in it for strictly business reasons, and the duller and more boring the whole operation becomes the happier I shall be.' He poured the beer down his throat and slapped the glass back down on the table. 'As far as I'm concerned, it is not a lark. It's a very dangerous job of work and I want to come out of it intact, with money and, more important, with my freedom. Therefore I would prefer to be a lot more in charge than I am.'

'You are in charge, Andrew darling,' Françoise said. 'I'm just the go-between – that's all.'

She sensed he was on edge, and still not totally convinced

of the wisdom of what he had agreed. It wouldn't take a lot to make him change his mind and back out of the whole deal. And they needed McTaggart. Or did they with this new knowledge about Les Hirondelles?

Yes, they did need McTaggart, she decided without hesitation. She was looking forward to the adventure of the so-called cruise. She'd set her heart on it. McTaggart was right – she was basically in it for the excitement.

Raoul was slumped low over the table, looking bored.

'I don't know why you all keep going on,' he said. 'You know we're going to do it. All for our own different reasons. Provided Grandfather ever agrees.'

'Father had a good idea about that today,' Françoise said. 'I spun him a tale about having a rich boyfriend who'd pay for the cruise, and he said Grandfather might agree if this imaginary rich boyfriend chartered the boat – just as long as one of the family were aboard.'

'Do you think he might?' Raoul said.

'We can only ask,' Françoise said. 'I'll tackle Stella first. Father's face lit up at the thought of getting rid of us for a while. Stella wouldn't be too displeased either. Maybe she'll talk Grandfather into it.'

'You two don't sound madly popular with your family,' McTaggart said.

Raoul grinned.

'We're not,' he said. 'Not at all.'

McTaggart was staring fixedly at the phoney ship's wheel that decorated the end wall of the bar.

'What else did he say?' he asked.

'Not much more than that he thought the plan was amateur. I told him that we weren't fools and we knew that he was hiring us because we *were* amateur, and that you'd discovered no pro would touch it at the moment. I think I convinced him that it had to look as if we were a bunch of kids having a cruise on daddy's yacht, and I told him that no way would you unload at Marseilles. He seemed to think that made sense, though he was a bit sarcastic about how we thought he was going to get that much hash to Tangier.'

'That's his problem,' McTaggart said.

'That's exactly what I told him.'

'So, what's the next move?' Raoul said.

'Getting the boat. The charter idea might work, though where I'm going to find this mysterious rich boyfriend who's footing the bill, God knows.'

'Knowing Grandfather,' Raoul said, 'he won't ask too many questions, just so long as he gets a fistful of the right currency.'

'It's getting too complicated,' McTaggart said. 'Just try to get permission in a straightforward way.'

'I suppose I couldn't just give you the order to go to sea,' Françoise said thoughtfully.

'Nothing doing,' said McTaggart. 'I'm not allowed to move that yacht out of harbour without either Philip de Courtenay's or his wife's permission, and if we're going to get away with this, everything must be done by the book. And talking of everything being done by the book, I ought to be back on board. Not much point getting the sack at this stage. You'd have to start working on the new skipper, wouldn't you, Françoise?'

She did not reply and he looked momentarily discomfited before he said:

'Are you coming with me?' His eyes were fixed on her mouth.

There was no question of that. She'd had quite enough of men and sex and messing about to last her for a good while.

'No thanks,' she said. 'I'll come down one evening later in the week.'

'Right.' He hesitated, looked as if he wanted to say more, but after a quick glance at Raoul decided against it. He gave them both a casual wave and moved out of the bar and back towards the harbour.

They watched him go through the open windows.

'Do you like him?' Raoul asked.

'He's not bad.' She sounded indifferent. 'With him I feel something, and I enjoy teasing him. It's better than the awful Achmid. I didn't get my little present today either. I don't

125

'think I will somehow,' she said thoughtfully. 'I've got a feeling he won't be wanting my services in that direction again. What a relief.'

'Why do you let him do it if you hate it so much,' Raoul said, his thin boy's face prurient and curious.

'Well, he doesn't actually do it,' Françoise said. 'It's only messing about, and I just think about my bank balance. We'll get away from here one of these days, Raoul.'

'Where shall we go?'

'Anywhere. We'll be free. We can have any adventures we want.' She was speaking dreamily, and Raoul said impatiently: 'But we ought to have a plan.'

'No plans. Just do what we like when we like.'

'You really don't know *what* you want to do,' he said.

'That's right,' she said. 'No plans.'

He looked at her, and Françoise could see he was exasperated. But it was true. There were no plans. There was just a knot of impatience in her all the time; a tense, expectant feeling that something, anything must happen soon. But she did not know exactly what she wanted to happen or where she wanted to be. The only certainties were that Les Hirondelles was not the place for her, and that enough money was essential to any kind of a future at all. Much more money than she would ever be able to screw out of her grandfather. She lived with a feeling of waiting, waiting to get money, waiting to get away, waiting for something to happen. And it was not a peaceful waiting; it was an urgent, impatient 'why doesn't life get on with it', sort of waiting. She had tried sometimes to explain this sense of impatience to Raoul, but he did not understand. His temperament was to plot and to know the next move, and in that way they made a good pair. Even though he was eighteen months younger than her, he was sometimes able to curb her leaps into the unknown.

'Anyway,' he said, breaking into her thoughts. 'We'd better have a plan about this bauxite.'

'You're right,' she said. 'We better had.'

Martine saw a red-headed girl walking to the house below the swimming pool from the shelter of the long ridge of cypresses that hid the tennis court. She dodged out of sight, not ready to meet any of the other inhabitants of Les Hirondelles just yet. Martine was exploring. She had sorted out how many houses there were on the estate, she had walked as far as her unsuitable shoes would permit down through the olives on the southern side of the mountain in front of the biggest of the houses, which she figured must be Philip's. Then she worked her way back eastwards to come out near the swimming pool. She had peeked at the pool and seen the good-looking man and the red-headed girl lying there, and wondered who they were. It was going to take a while to sort it all out but this time, she thought, it looked as if she had really struck lucky.

No one else was about. The estate slumbered in the heat of the afternoon sun, and she was hot and sweating as she set off down the courtyard, trying to keep out of sight.

Philip de Courtenay had left that morning about a quarter of an hour after drinking the tea she had made. He had said goodbye formally, calling her madame as she called him monsieur. He had not said a word about another encounter, but Martine was sure there would be one – and soon. He had liked what she had provided, that she could tell, and there was something about his extreme relief after he had come that made her sure he hadn't for a long time. She was going to be irresistible to him. He wasn't going to be able to stay away from her particular honeypot for very long.

She was in a state of suppressed excitement about the whole thing. The guest house was luxurious to a degree she had not expected. She felt as if someone had handed her a gold brick. The only cloud was that she was hungry. There was tinned food in the kitchen cupboards, but nothing perishable, and she wondered where one went for shopping. Would she be able to ask the family, or would she be expected to ask the servants? It was going to be a problem to know how to play it at first. The servants would be the most difficult. They'd spot their own kind and do their best to make her feel small.

In the kitchen there was everything anyone could possibly

need to hand except a bit of bread and butter. She opened a can of sardines and ate them with a fork straight from the tin, poking in the cupboards, learning about her new territory and mentally hugging herself for her good fortune as she polished off the oily fish.

She spotted a cherry tree in the garden behind the house and going out through the kitchen door helped herself to a fistful from the lower branches. That would do for dessert. She ate them, spitting out the stones, as she set about her tour of the estate.

The further she walked, the more impressed she became. Who would have imagined from those visits to the massage parlour that he was so rich? He had not even tipped enormously well at first, though the amount had grown in ratio to the amount she let the towels and her fingers slip as time went on. Now, having got him properly into bed and into her, and on his own territory, she was quite certain that she had him, the house and the run of the estate for quite a long time. Getting money out of him might be a problem. But perhaps not after the second time she had made him come and he had realized that he really could still do it. Then it would get easier.

Her feet were hurting and she got to the door of her – as she already thought of it – *her* house. Inside the hallway, on a carved wood chest, she spotted the telephone, and shutting the door behind her she picked it up and dialled a Nice number.

'Jacques?' she said very quietly so that no one could possibly overhear. 'Jacques, it's me. Yes, it's fantastic. *Formidable.* You're not going to believe it. But I think you're going to enjoy being my husband.'

Elisabeth had been about to take her afternoon nap in her bedroom overlooking the courtyard when she saw the girl walking past, keeping close to the walls of the houses, and almost scuttling back to the guest house.

That would be the new *locataire*. A funny little thin thing with her colourless hair in a ponytail, she wore a cheap jean-fabric skirt and a cotton blouse with the sleeves rolled up; Elisabeth's nose crinkled. Her father had found another peasant, of a different age to Pamela Whitton, whom Elisabeth considered also a peasant, and yet none of them had ever let her live down that one mistake of years ago.

Tomas's accusation had stung, and her only satisfaction was that she had not let him see it. In fact he was the one who had been discomfited. She had behaved with dignity, as she had always behaved with dignity in her life. What they did not know was that her affair had been one between two dignified people. But then no one had ever asked her what had really happened or even why it had happened.

She pulled the shutters across quietly once the girl was out of sight so that she should not know she had been observed and then, slipping off her dress and shoes, lay down on the bed, pulling a light coverlet over her to guard against any draughts.

Tomas's remarks had opened old wounds, and she had very neatly got her own back by presenting Stella with the news of what Tomas was up to, and putting Peter on his guard. In a way it no longer mattered to her what happened at Les Hirondelles; she did not care whether she stayed or went. In her fantasies, she would leave and make a spectacularly successful new life elsewhere, but she knew the possibilities of that happening in reality were slight.

Elisabeth had been cushioned and contained by Les Hirondelles all her life. Like the rest of the de Courtenay children she had been sent away to school, finishing in England, but in her case education had never taken. She spoke English reasonably well, but unlike her brothers and sisters was never at ease with it. Nor had she been a good student as the rest of them were. She had been the least bright of the family, and the plainest, and the one who was always left out of the mischief and the adventures when cousins from her mother's side came for the holidays.

She knew that she had never had the gift of making friends either. She had protected herself in childhood by adopting a superior manner, making others think she did not want to be involved in their stupid games and pastimes. It had worked so well that even the slightest effort to include her stopped and the superiority had become the strongest facet of her grown-up personality.

She had been just sixteen when she met Hassan, back from a British girls' boarding-school and lonely. Her own mother was dead and the estate neglected that summer. Her father's long-standing affair with Olivia Barton had ended; there were only the servants to show any interest in her, and Elisabeth had never been the servants' favourite. Tomas was spending the summer in England with a schoolfriend, and she had wandered around her father's house and walked in the grounds, not knowing what to do with herself. Philip had spent much of his time down at the coast, on *Les Hirondelles I*, and he was busily pursuing Stella Sanderson, who was then a slim, lively, intelligent girl with a great many American dollars and a mind of her own. He brought her to Les Hirondelles occasionally throughout the summer, and Stella was kind and pleasant to the awkward, sullen schoolgirl, but was not of a type to deliberately ingratiate herself with her lover's daughter. When her lover's daughter was offhand to the point of rudeness, Stella left her to her own devices.

And her own devices were Hassan – aged seventeen, with liquid brown eyes, perfect straight features, so much more attractive than her own hawked nose; Hassan with the sensuous mouth and a leaning towards poetry, whose job on the estate was to tend the peach trees, and who lived in one of the simple stone houses in the valley that had been provided for the agricultural workers.

His mother and father were also working on the estate, and it was as important to keep the secret of their romance from them as it was to keep it from Elisabeth's father. Not that that was difficult. Her father was too preoccupied in other directions. It was more difficult keeping it from the eagle eye of Claudine, and in retrospect Elisabeth had realized that she had never fooled Claudine, but that Claudine had decided it was best not to know, and if the child had nothing better to do or no one to take an interest in her, she could sharpen her teeth for life on the young Hassan without coming to too much harm. Claudine had been wrong.

130

But Hassan had been *gentle*, kind and loving and astonished at his good fortune in finding a friend in the daughter of the house. But he never abused the privilege. He had dreams, had Hassan, dreams of being someone; not working on the land, but getting an education and living in a house with a bathroom and a lavatory and being able to read books and converse with people who were educated too. And he really loved her.

A pair of children they had been, Elisabeth thought, and it had all begun when she had found Hassan trying to read a book she had left lying under one of his peach trees. He asked the meaning of a word, shyly and diffidently, and she explained, and then they met every day for a reading lesson in the time when he was allowed his lunch.

She had enjoyed being the guru and expanding his horizons, and had felt a puffed-up pride at seeing how quickly he learned under her tutelage. But then, eventually, she had learned quickly under his tutelage and she had become pregnant.

Claudine had spotted it first. Elisabeth's pregnancy took a classically boring direction with the humiliation of being sick in the morning, which was what made Claudine realize.

It was to Claudine, who seemed as old then as she did now, that she confessed, and Claudine who had decided that her father must be informed. He had come raging back to Les Hirondelles with an embarrassed Stella in tow. Stella had said that he ought to permit the child to have an abortion, and she knew a man in London, but Philip de Courtenay was far too good a Catholic for that, though not a good enough Christian to let Elisabeth keep her child after its birth. How would it be explained? What would such an occurrence do to the good name of the de Courtenays?

The boy, dark as he might well have been with two raven-haired parents, had immediately been put out for adoption. Elisabeth had seen him only for an instant after the birth. Hassan had been sacked, his parents too, and Philip, who had sent her back to Paris for the later stages of her pregnancy, said that the whole matter could now be forgotten.

But no one had forgotten, including Elisabeth. Nor had she forgotten Hassan. Even now she would find herself searching the features of Algerian men who could be of his age and feel her heart thump when a young Algerian with the classic looks of her childhood lover crossed her path in the street or came, as Hassan had come, to work on the estate.

It had been her first and last encounter with a man. Her punishment, mostly self-imposed, had been to stay at Les Hirondelles in a sort of purdah. At twenty-five she had been given her own home on the estate – the least attractive of the available houses – but her income had hardly been raised. She accepted her life and only occasionally wondered what her son's life was like.

But she despised them all, her brother more than anyone. No one ostracized him because he was sleeping with his half-sister. They just pretended it wasn't happening. It was sick.

Still, she thought, as her eyelids fluttered in the state between sleep and consciousness, I've cooked his goose today. He won't be father's favourite for much longer.

Chapter Eleven

Anne decided to forget work on a Friday morning after two weeks of fairly concentrated effort. She had found Les Hirondelles conducive to drawing and produced a prolific amount of work, despite the time off for swimming and getting to know Marion better again. She found her old friend more appealing at each fresh meeting.

Stella de Courtenay and Anne had also struck up a comfortable friendship begun by Anne drifting with Marion to the morning coffee sessions on the lawn behind the main house, finding she was welcome and arriving again. Stella was there every day, cat on lap, breath wheezing, controlling a conversation that had some point and purpose.

The older woman was well read and well informed, as, surprisingly, was Marion. Stella's daughter was not the lightweight bird-brain that she appeared to be. Her mother said drily that quite a lot of the very expensive education had stuck.

The other bonus had been that Peter, who obviously liked and respected his mother, also appeared most mornings. Daily, Anne found herself more and more attracted to him. This was something she was fairly sure that Stella's brilliant green eyes had not missed; and hopefully something of which the older woman did not disapprove.

She had made herself a light lunch from the supplies that someone always brought from the list she left. Everything had been carefully put in the fridge and the larder; the list had been left on the kitchen table with items ticked off, a price at the side, and exactly the correct change from her hundred-franc note. That was how marketing was conducted at Les Hirondelles. True luxury, thought Anne, someone to do the shopping, as pleasant as it was to potter in Provence markets.

The cicadas were screeching their heads off in the grass outside, and the afternoon sun was a haze in the sky. Looking from the front windows, the crouching lion mountain and the entrance to the gorge to the west were veiled with a light heat-mist, and only the faintest blue trace showed of the mountains behind.

It was very hot. Anne's heavy hair was sticking to the back of her neck, and a row of pearls of perspiration banded her upper lip. She decided to swim

She took a wrap this time, thinking she might lie out for longer on the reclining chairs that were scattered around the pool and build up the tan that already had hidden her London pallor. She tanned quickly and well; the long summers in the South as a child with her aunt had accustomed her skin to the sun.

The pool was marvellously inviting, and she dived neatly in at the deep end and swam underwater the full length, then turned, and with an elegant crawl completed ten more lengths before she stopped and floated gently on her back, staring into the blue mist of the sky above.

'May I join you?' a voice said – Peter de Courtenay's voice. Instinctively she flipped on to her stomach to hide the scars on the leg and, treading water, said: 'Of course. I'm just coming out. Shall I leave you in peace?'

'No,' he said. 'Don't get out. It's pleasant to have company.'

He casually tipped himself into the water and came up beside her.

'Let me do twenty lengths,' he said, 'then we'll chat. I want to talk to you.'

That's nice, Anne thought. He wants to talk to me. What about? But she just nodded, and keeping to one side of the pool swam with him. He was a powerful swimmer but he could only just outclass her, and it wasn't necessary for him to keep his pace down to hers, so they touched the pool's edge at the same moment, twisted and turned to face the other way with a powerful push and completed the twenty lengths in unison.

'That was good,' Peter said. He had heaved himself up on to the side of the pool and was dripping on to the terracotta tiles, his fair hair streaked back in thick strands. 'Can you get out all right with that leg, or do you want a hand?'

'I can manage,' Anne said, and using her arms lifted herself to sit a few feet away from him. He was extraordinarily affable. No doubt, she decided, he wants something.

He did. He settled them both in sunbathing chairs and then said: 'I wonder if I could ask you a favour?'.

She nodded.

'It's rather a big favour, I'm afraid. I think I mentioned that a friend of mine was coming from the States. Well, I was going to put her up at the guest house, but of course Father's rented it out, so that's impossible. I don't want to put her up in my place – it might embarrass her with the family around. Evelyn's known my mother since she was a child, you see. Without the guest house there's so little room, and I'd hate to inflict Elisabeth on her. She's about your age, fun and attractive, and she might even be company for you.'

Anne felt her heart sink and she hesitated. She was used to living alone and preferred it and she felt panicky that the

134

shadowy girlfriend was about to become reality. Evelyn was something, rather someone, she had been trying to push out of her mind.

Yet if she were a serious girlfriend, surely he would want her under his own roof? Anne couldn't believe that the de Courtenays were remotely prudish, and Peter was hardly a boy to be told he couldn't sleep with whoever he wanted in his own home.

She would rather have said no for all sorts of reasons – the strongest she realized being a solid sense of pure jealousy. What was Evelyn like? Beautiful? Rich? Tall, with beautiful legs? Someone who would eclipse her?

Yet it was impossible to refuse, so as warmly as possible she said: 'Of course. Just as long as she realizes that I do have to work rather a lot of the time – but then I don't expect she'll be relying on me for entertainment, will she?'

It was a question, and the answer was disappointing.

'Not at all,' he said. 'She's never been here before, so I'll be showing her the sights, such as they are.'

'That's fine then,' Anne said.

She closed her eyes against the brightness of the sun above and concentrated on enjoying its caress on her body, pushing the thought of dark Evelyn away. The warmth made her very aware of the man lying beside her, and she found to her amusement that her head was full of outrageous ideas for the exploits of Rhoda Rabbit. The sun, she decided, was dangerous in more ways than one.

'Another thing I've been meaning to ask you,' Peter was saying sleepily, though the lines of his body were those of a man very alert. 'How do you think your aunt would feel about Tomas's plan to get Father to sell Les Hirondelles? Would she be attracted by the idea of so much money? Some of it would be hers, of course.'

Anne thought about Olivia Barton and tried to answer the question honestly.

'I really can't speak for my aunt,' she said, 'but she's never struck me as being very interested in money, except to use it. I know she loves it here and I would think she'd rather have the pleasure of the place than the cash. She always seems to make enough for what she wants.'

'So she might not go along with Tomas?'

'Honestly, I don't know,' Anne said.

He had swung his legs over the side of the bed and was sitting up, staring at the pool.

'Had it occurred to you that your aunt is really the key to the whole thing?' he said. 'If Father's liking for money made him decide to go along with Tomas and this Arab, your aunt could still scupper the whole thing. She owns that cottage outright, and the land around it. And I'd guess her house is sitting on about the only spot where this Arab could build his golf course. Your aunt's home would be ideal for the nineteenth hole. If she said no, the whole thing would collapse.'

'I think, under the circumstances, my aunt would do exactly what your father wanted,' Anne said. 'She's not the sort of person to create a difficult situation. It would embarrass her.'

He grunted.

'Since you seem to be her heir, how do you feel about it?'

'Her heir!' Anne laughed. 'My aunt is about fifty-two years old. I don't think what I feel has anything to do with it.'

'Nevertheless, how do you feel?'

'What a question!' But she stopped and thought. 'I suppose I'd be tempted by all that money, but when it came to the point, if I had enough money to live as well as you all live, I think I'd prefer to keep the estate intact. I mean, it's not as if you're all on the breadline, is it?'

'Well, most of this family believe they are,' Peter said. 'Our father isn't very generous in handing out cash, and he has this paternalistic attitude of keeping us all here. He knows that with more money most of the family would be off elsewhere. So he keeps us to hand by keeping us short of ready cash, though we can all have as many *things* as we like.'

'You seem to have escaped.'

'That's Mother. She was determined I'd have some kind of career, and she was right, but ironically I'm the only one who really loves this estate and wants to keep it.'

'But what would you do if it were yours?'

'Ah,' he turned to look at her, pushing the fast-drying hair back from his forehead. 'This place, run properly, could be just as profitable as Tomas's Arab's millionaires' retreat. Well – nearly as profitable. Do you know we already have enough vines here to make a thousand litres of wine, and it's good wine – you drank it at table the other night. And that's without trying. We could make three times that amount.

'We neglect our olives – we only press enough for our own use and for friends and the servants. Yet the southern side of the mountain is one vast olive grove.

'If we were to terrace more of the land we could grow every kind of fruit you can think of. As it is we have an abundance of vegetables. We have our own fish in our own streams – and we could factory-farm trout and *écrevisse*. We have space enough to breed guinea fowl or more exotic forms of game to supply every restaurant for miles around. This estate could be more than the rich man's toy it is, believe me. And it could still be beautiful.'

'Your father seemed very proud that most of the meal I ate with your family that first night was from the estate.'

'True,' Peter said. 'He gets great pleasure out of feeding us all from the land, but that's only because he's mean. Nothing is done properly.'

'Yet he was very generous to give my aunt the cottage. He can't be entirely mean,' Anne said.

'Well, he adored your aunt. He wanted to marry her, in which case I wouldn't have been here. But she wasn't interested.'

Anne considered for a moment and then asked: 'Was she his mistress?'

Peter nodded. 'Didn't you know? She was – for years, on and off, after his first wife died. But she'd never stay with him for too long. She had her own life in England. According to my mother she said to him that she wasn't landing herself as the wife of a feudal *seigneur* who'd be laying the servant girls every time she turned her back – not that Papa has ever done that – and that she was perfectly happy to be his mistress *officielle*, thank you very much. And she was his mistress *officielle.* He took her everywhere with him, and the whole thing was perfectly open and accepted by all his *haut bourgeois* friends for years. Since then he's been having mistresses *cachées*, kept well tucked away and out of sight. Except for Pamela Whitton of course, and God only knows what she is.'

Anne was trying to imagine her aunt with Philip de Courtenay. It wasn't difficult. Her aunt was still a pretty, sexy woman. Thirty years ago she would have been stunning – tiny, hourglass figure, and a perky face with enormous brown eyes and a pixie cast of features. Philip de Courtenay was fanciable now. He must have been irresistible when young.

'I really didn't know,' Anne said, 'but I suppose it did occur to me that gentlemen don't give ladies houses in the South of France for hardly any reason at all. But since you tell me that about her, I would think she most certainly will be on your side. I mean, for a girl of that age, as she was then, to have turned down your father, his estate and all his money must have taken some character. Particularly as she obviously liked him.'

'I think she loved him,' Peter said, 'but she knew it wouldn't work permanently. Which is just as well for me.'

He laughed.

Anne was still digesting the new information, enjoying the intimacy and openness of their conversation. 'But doesn't your mother mind her still coming here and having the house?' she asked.

'My mother is a very sensible New England woman and takes most things in her stride,' Peter said. 'I think she likes your aunt and she's certainly very fond of you. She was always full of admiration when you were little. She said you had guts, and that was something that sometimes the de Courtenays were short on because they were all spoilt.'

'I like her,' Anne said. 'I like your father too. And I like Marion.'

He grinned at her. 'You've left out my niece and nephew, my half-brother and sister, and you've left out me.'

His eyes were challenging.

'I like you,' Anne said, knowing that this was a masterpiece of understatement, 'or I wouldn't be lying here listening to gossip with you. I find your half-brother, Tomas, quite fascinating; Elisabeth scares me a bit; and your niece and nephew, to be honest, I could never stand.'

He laughed out loud. 'Are you always so direct?'

She pulled a face. 'I'm afraid I am.'

'Well, at least we'll all know where we are with you.'

'I'll try to be more diplomatic if you'd prefer it,' she said, aware that she was flirting with him, and aware also that he had suddenly seen her sexually and was looking at her differently. He wasn't thinking of Evelyn Grenville now, she thought triumphantly.

'Don't bother,' he said. 'I'm used to it. My mother's much the same.'

She had a feeling that this was the right moment to leave – while he was intrigued by her. To linger could spoil things.

'Well,' she said. 'I'm off. Things to be done. Thanks for the company and see you soon.'

'Tonight I hope,' he said. 'I've instructions from mother to ask you to dinner. It seems that Tomas's Arab is to be with us. Will you come?' He paused, then added, 'I'd like it, too.'

She felt a surge of pleasure.

'I'd love to. What time?'

'Seven thirty,' he said. 'There will be other guests. Tomas's wife has arrived as well. See you then?'

'See you then,' she said.

That evening there was the same vaguely sinister quality about the light and the atmosphere of the de Courtenays' dining-room which Anne felt whenever she sat at their table. She could never decide exactly what caused her uneasiness unless it was that the entire family gathered together made for bad vibrations.

This was her third invitation to dine on a Friday evening. The week previously she had dined with them *en famille*, but on this sweltering early June evening the full feudal glory of the room was on display: candelabra burning, heavy silver marshalled on the long dark table, fine glass, and extra staff hovering to tend the de Courtenays' guests.

It appeared that Margaret de Courtenay, a thin, foxily pretty blonde woman, had arrived unexpectedly the evening before and Anne would have known instantly that she was the mother of Françoise; the likeness was unmistakable. When Tomas had presented her to Anne in the *salon*, the French woman had flickered her eyes over the English girl, pricing her dress, assessing her hair, skin and breasts before saying coldly, *'Enchantée, madame'*, and turning away. Anne felt she had been stripped.

And as promised by Peter the other guest was Achmid Fouezanne. Curious about the man who had loaned Tomas a million francs, Anne watched him covertly while drinks were served before dinner. He wore dark glasses, a hot-looking dark dinner jacket, unmistakably Savile Row, white frilled shirt and a deep blue, heavy silk bowtie. Had it not been for the Semitic features and yellow-brown skin he could have been any rich London businessman out to dine. A glass in his hand, he had been listening impassively to Philip de Courtenay who was explaining the self-supporting qualities of Les Hirondelles. Anne wondered if anyone had told Philip that the Arab at his hearth, drinking his whisky, planned not only to buy his home but could ruin his older son if he wished.

Tomas looked strained and anxious – as well he might, Anne thought. He seemed unable to concentrate on any conversation, even with Marion, who chattered away at his side, a brightly plumaged bird in a scarlet and pink splashed slender dress. His eyes kept straying to where Achmid Fouezanne and his father talked.

'I've put him between you and me,' Stella said quietly to Anne. 'Shall we try to find out a little more about him?' She looked up from the depth of her chair, whisky glass in hand, and grinned her surprising youthful grin. 'Poor Philip,' she said, expressing Anne's thought. 'If he only knew! I think I am going to have to enlighten him very soon. It's only just. I've put Peter on your left,' she went on, the eyes glinting, 'to make up for him—' nodding emphatically in Achmid's direction.

Peter led her into dinner. Philip escorted Margaret while Pamela Whitton, bizarre as ever in a long dirndl skirt and scoopneck blouse, sulked behind. And Achmid, looking ill at ease, held the arm of Stella. The others all moved in a group behind.

'It's something of an odd situation, no?' Peter murmured as he led her to the far end of the table. 'Really, someone should tell Papa.'

'I think your mother is going to,' Anne told him.

'Good,' he said, 'she's the right person to do it. Tomas is a fool.'

He stopped and shook his head abruptly and then, settling her in her seat said: 'You're looking very attractive tonight. That's a very pretty dress.'

It was a pretty dress. Anne had bought it on her shopping trip to Nice, urged on by Marion. It had cost more than any dress she had ever owned. In emerald green pure silk jersey, it plunged low, front and back, the tight waist emphasizing the neatness of her body, supple fabric clinging to slim arms, supple hips and then swaying to the ground. It made the most of her small stature and emphasized her full breasts; wearing it she felt confident and attractive.

'Thank you,' she said, smiling at him, deliberately looking straight into his eyes, and then suddenly dropping pale green painted lids over her own. She wore her aunt's seductive Opium scent, her skin was smooth and tanned, she knew her eyes were clear and bright. Notice me! she was willing him. Forget Evelyn whoever-her-name is.

'Yes,' he said, 'very pretty,' and it wasn't her imagination that his hand rested on her bare shoulder for a fraction longer than necessary to see she was comfortable in her seat.

Satisfied, she turned to Achmid Fouezanne, smiling into the dark glasses that pointed at her like black moons.

'Have you been to Les Hirondelles before, monsieur?' she asked politely.

'Once,' he said.

'You're a friend of Tomas, isn't that right?'

'You could say that.'

If his conversation was sparse, his English was perfect, totally without accent, which reinforced the City gent image. He seemed to be smiling, the mouth was stretched and the teeth were bared below the thin hooked nose, but without sight of the eyes there was no way of telling.

Stella turned to join the conversation.

'Where do you live, monsieur?' she asked.

'In Cannes. In an hotel.'

Anne opened her mouth to ask which hotel, but there was something about his guarded answer that made her realize he did not wish to volunteer any more information.

Instead, feeling she sounded inane, she said, 'I should hate to live in an hotel. I'm afraid I'm a nester – I need my own home.'

'We all need our own home,' he said, his voice deepening. 'I no longer have one. It was taken from me long ago.'

'Really?' Anne composed her features into suitably sad lines. 'And where was your home?'

'Palestine.' His voice was abrupt.

Stella de Courtenay looked at him, her face tipped sideways heavy on her neck. 'But you are too young,' she said, 'or did your family stay on?'

'After the Jewish occupation, you mean?'

Anne said, innocently: 'Occupation? But Palestine is surely the Jewish homeland?'

She realized she had made a mistake. The narrow mouth shut over his teeth and his body tensed, showing barely controlled anger. Anne felt herself recoil from him.

'My ancestors, the Canaanites, were in Palestine thousands of years before Abraham arrived with his wandering band of Jews,' he said, cold and precise. 'And when Israel was created it had been two thousand years since the Jews had laid any claim to our land. Imagine,' he said, turning to face Anne, 'it is as if the Italians decided that by right of their conquest of Britain in Hadrian's day they should reclaim your country as their own.'

'Well, yes,' Anne's composure had gone. 'I see what you mean, but I'm afraid I know very little about the history of the Middle East.'

'Few people do,' he said icily. 'And that is to the advantage of world-wide Jewry. When your country, Britain, handed my country to the Zionists there were more than six hundred thousand Arabs living in Palestine and only sixty thousand Jews. Where are all those Palestinians now? Scattered and homeless.'

Stella de Courtenay picked up her spoon to eat the pale green cold soup that had been put before her.

'I've always thought,' she said casually, 'that all those refugee Arabs have been splendid propaganda for the Arab cause. Deliberately kept homeless. Such a pity!'

Achmid's face suffused under his yellowish skin. He put down his spoon very carefully and said savagely: 'Then you are wrong, madame.' Anne hurriedly intervened.

'Tell me, monsieur, what happened to your family?'

'It is a long story,' he said. He hesitated as if not certain whether to go on or not, then, the decision made, his voice became resonant as if telling a story told many times before. 'My grandfather sold most of our lands to the Jews in 1926 when the first wave of migration came. He was wise enough to see what must eventually happen. Wiser than those who ran the country at that time who believed British promises. My own father took his share of the money and left to start a new life in Egypt. There we prospered, but my grandfather refused to leave. He was too old, he said, to start life in another country. Most of the family stayed with him.'

He hesitated, then continued:

'They lived in a small village called Deir Yassin – you have heard of it?' he asked, turning to Stella.

'I'm sorry, no,' she said.

'It was wiped out by the Zionists in 1948. The whole population was massacred, because the people of the village had fired on one of the Zionists' invading vehicles. My mother was visiting the family. She died too. No one was left. I was sixteen years old.' He paused. 'You see, the Jews understood terrorism before us and did not hesitate to use it. We only fight fire with fire.'

'I'm sorry,' Anne said, feeling inadequate.

'I, too, am sorry,' said Achmid. 'We were the chosen victims of a political expediency. But my people have long memories. Palestine has changed hands many times before. It will change hands again.'

'That's surely the whole crux of the argument, isn't it?' Stella said, her husky voice deliberately conciliatory, as was necessary to a guest. 'The number of times the land has changed hands. And the number of times that it was Jewish. When you speak of Abraham you're speaking of a thousand years before Christ. Were there boundaries in the Middle East then? I doubt it. And for generation upon generation we have lived in a world where conquest has been by the strongest. Last time round, the Jews won. And so they have their so-called homeland.'

'They won by trickery, treachery and the connivance of the western world,' Achmid said.

'Conquest has always been part trickery,' Stella said, 'from the Wooden Horse to New York being bought for a handful of trinkets, and,' she paused to think, 'what about say, Drake and his fire ships? You could be right though. In the fullness of time no doubt Israel will become Palestine again. *On sait jamais.* Every dog has his day.'

Anne could see that the Arab's anger was turning to interest in the debate.

'You believe trickery to be an ingredient?' he asked.

Stella shrugged. 'Trickery backed either by power or sheer nerve,' she said. 'Brute strength is important in the end, in spite of David and Goliath.'

'I believe in power,' he said flatly.

Tomas, who was sitting next to his stepmother and opposite Achmid, had been listening to the conversation uneasily, half-chatting with Françoise who was placed on his right, her brother next to her.

'Well, you fellows have all the power at the moment,' he said jovially. 'The oil—' He mopped at his forehead in the heat with a white handkerchief.

'Ah yes, the oil,' Stella de Courtenay said, her green eyes malicious. 'Don't you sometimes fear, Monsieur Fouezanne, that the policy over the oil – shall we say the greed of the sheikhs – will perhaps cause all the powers to declare war on the Arab states? And if that happened they – the western powers – would win, you know.'

'They?' Achmid said sarcastically. 'Do you not include yourself and your own country in this judgement, madame?'

Stella was signalling for the maid to remove plates.

'I don't include myself, monsieur,' she said, 'because I am no longer young, no longer fit and I care little what the world gets up to. I like my backwater here and I think it unlikely that I shall ever leave it.' She paused as if to let the remark sink in. 'But in my home country – now there is a different kettle of fish. In my country we are used to automobiles that are too big and too thirsty and homes that are too warm in winter and too cold in summer. These things we consider pretty much a way of life and ones we're not going to lose. The right to run a hot and cold home, a large and greedy car, plus the right to keep a gun under the pillow or in the pocket, are dubious Americanisms that most of my countrymen will fight to the death to keep. Would you believe that in USA *circa* 1979 a man with a gun in his pocket would shoot to kill for a tankful of gas in times of shortage? It happened. Forgive me if I sound detached. It is now many years since I have lived back home, and yet were I there I would probably defend these rights too. It is only with three thousand miles and the Atlantic Ocean between that the standards appear a little futile.'

She stopped while the maid served, drinking from the whisky glass at her elbow. Achmid was sitting very still, his head turned to her attentively.

'However,' she continued. 'I therefore think it is possible that if the Arab oil-producing countries' greed curbs the living standards of the western world – perhaps even the far east – the Arab states will be attacked. And Israel will be supported and encouraged to begin the job for the rest of the world and give us all a great excuse to join in.'

'I'm not sure you're right, Mother,' Peter said. 'I think in ten years time OPEC will be outplayed. We'll move on to nuclear energy. It makes sense. A pound of uranium costs about fifty American dollars and does the work of about forty barrels of crude oil which cost seven hundred dollars more, with the price going up all the time.'

'But is there that much uranium?' Anne asked.

'It's being heavily mined in Australia, the States and Canada. It's there to be used. The prejudices against nuclear energy will be broken down for just the reasons Mother has been stating,' Peter said, his voice positive. 'People don't want their comforts disturbed. The big oil companies don't see themselves as just producing oil any more. They're into energy. We're not going to need a war with the oil states. Another form of energy will be developed, though we may have a rough ten years till it gets going.'

'There's a twist,' Achmid said, leaning forward. 'Imagine if the Arab world controlled not only the oil we produce but your Oklahoma and your Texas oil as well. And the North Sea oil, and the oil being produced in Canada and anywhere else in the world where it is not actually nationalized; suppose as well as the oil the bulk of the uranium production was controlled by Arab money. What then?'

'Instant war, I should have thought,' said Tomas.

'No,' Fouezanne said. 'You don't understand. War is outdated. Power is now in commodities. The western world, as our hostess points out, will not give up its overheated homes, its greedy motorcars. Nor would it part happily with its refrigerators, the car itself, its central heating plant – and therefore all the tin, aluminium, copper, steel, the raw materials that harnessed to technology and turned into consumer goods have made the western world so soft. Suppose the Arab states controlled all those essential commodities – not by force, but with money?' He leaned back in his chair and stroked the side of his moustache with a long lean finger. 'Think about it,' he said.

Anne had been listening intently and was trying to decide in the light of her lack of knowledge on the subject if what he was saying made any sense at all. Stella, she could see, was

146

intrigued by the conversation. The green eyes were narrowed thinking, but they caught Anne's questioning gaze over Achmid's bent head as he began to tackle his food, and the eyes opened wide, the eyebrows flew upwards and the expression without speaking suggested that they were in the presence of a sort of madness.

'And how,' Stella was asking Achmid, 'would you manage that?'

'It's possible,' he said.

'How?'

'Do you realize that OPEC – which is under the thumb of the sheikhs could pay off the entire US foreign debt in two years or buy all the copper, tin and lead in the world, just as a start? Black gold is power,' Achmid said. 'And my own group already has the controlling interest in more commodities than you can imagine.'

'How fascinating.' Stella's breathlessness had become a purr. 'Which commodities interest you in particular? Gold?'

The dark glasses swung towards her and the thin mouth pursed. He pushed his wine glass further from his plate like a man who had suddenly realized he had drunk enough.

'No, not gold. My father dealt in gold. I am not interested. There are others.'

'And the point of it all?'

'How long do you think it will take before our vast revenues and our control of the world's natural wealth make the people of the west less sympathetic to the Jewish cause?' he said. 'Will the New York Jew or the London Jew care about his brethren in Israel if his family are cold or his creature comforts have become too expensive for his pocket?'

'You're saying,' Peter said, 'that if you can control the commodity markets you can blackmail the rest of the world into letting you take back Palestine?'

'Of course that is an oversimplification,' Achmid said. 'But in essence – yes.'

'Without bloodshed?'

'There will always be the hot-heads who believe in terrorism, and they will prove important in their way.'

147

'And what will happen to the Israelis?' Stella asked.

Achmid paused.

'Much of their expertise could be used. That would have to be decided. But they have always been a wandering tribe.'

Stella leaned back in her chair shaking her head.

'You alarm me, Monsieur Fouezanne,' she said. 'I don't think I wish to know more, but whatever happens remember I'm just a spectator, living out my days in this backwater of Provence. Where, incidentally, I propose to stay.'

Achmid took off his glasses and stared at her, and the black olives of eyes revealed made Anne wish he would replace them.

'As you say yourself, madame,' he said, smiling thinly, *'on sait jamais.'*

'Oh, but I do know, I do,' Stella said, her voice positive. 'More wine, monsieur?'

'Of course he was a bit drunk, wasn't he?' Anne said doubtfully as Peter walked her to her own home. He had offered to escort her, saying that perhaps they could discuss the arrival of Evelyn Grenville, which meant it was now-or-never time. She must register her presence quickly with Peter. After the American girl appeared on the scene it might be too late.

She did not really want to talk about Achmid Fouezanne either, but she sensed that Peter was anxious and uneasy about the dinner table conversation.

'I mean,' she went on, 'he has to be mad, doesn't he? But he's so creepy with it. Those glasses. And the eyes were worse. Your mother was baiting him. I think he said more than he meant to.'

Peter was holding her arm against the hot darkness. 'He's a fanatic,' he said. 'And my mother was making the points she wanted to. He knows he'll get no help from her in buying Les Hirondelles.'

She was very conscious of his closeness. His shoulder was just six inches above hers. She could tuck herself under his arm quite neatly and tidily, she decided, but keeping her tone conversational she said: 'What on earth does he want Les

Hirondelles for? Private villages don't seem to go with cornering a market in natural resources and the Arab cause.'

Peter shrugged.

'Headquarters for Operation-get-back-Palestine, maybe.'

They were both momentarily silent, quietened by the thought of Achmid and by the heavy atmosphere of the night around them. Darkness had brought no relief from the sweltering heat of the day. Lightning flickered somewhere behind the crouching lion to a background of a low rolling growl of thunder; the heat brought out tiny beads of sweat on Anne's temples. A thin moon was struggling through heavy scudding clouds, and the phallic row of cypress bordering the swimming pool were first deep purple and then silver against the sky. The first weighty drops of rain that announced a mountain downpour began to fall, each a separate stinging slap.

Peter put out a hand to catch the drops. 'Hell,' he said, 'do you want to run for it or shall we shelter at the pool?'

The sensible thing was to run for it. Anne's front door was no more than two minutes away. But something in the over-casualness of his tone gave her the assurance to say: 'Oh, let's shelter. It'll be cooler and we can watch the storm.'

'Right,' he said, and took her hand while they both ran for the terrace. Already the rain was heavier, beginning to drum on the surface of the pool, and Anne's shoulders were wet, the bodice of her dress starting to cling.

He led her into the deeper darkness of the covered terrace where the long garden chairs had been put for the night. He chose the one which swung and where they could sit side by side, asked if she was very wet, offered her a handkerchief to dry herself, which she accepted, then a cigarette, which she declined, and lit one himself. She could smell the lavender scent of his cologne, the persuasive smell of the pure tobacco he smoked, and she had found herself very aware of the fair hairs on his wrist below his white cuff as his gold cigarette lighter had flared into light. She was also aware that he was sitting a little closer to her than was absolutely necessary.

'I checked him out, you know,' he said abruptly.

Her mind had wandered completely towards how it would

be to make love to Peter de Courtenay. Would he undress her slowly? What would he taste like? Would he taste her? Would she enjoy him? His remark caught her off guard.

'Who?' she said.

'Fouezanne,' he said. 'And I don't like it.'

'What did you find?' She did not want to talk about Fouezanne any more, but Peter was leaning forward in the pose of a man thinking. His arms rested lightly on his thighs and he stared out over the pool where the rain, now falling in a torrent, bounced noisily on the water. It was suddenly cooler.

'That's just it,' he said. 'I found very little. He's something of a mystery. I used a financial journalist friend from the *Wall Street Journal*, and he tackled a friend of his who works on your *Financial Times*. Neither of them came up with anything much except that Achmid Fouezanne is incredibly rich. They think he has a number of different companies registered in practically every country in the world. They know he operates the world's stock exchanges and the commodity markets, but to what extent is uncertain.

'Other than that, nothing much is known about him. A lot of his companies are probably in the names of nominees. That means it's practically impossible to sort out what he owns and what he doesn't own. He must employ bloody good lawyers.' He stopped. 'Of course he employs bloody good lawyers!' he said, reprimanding himself. 'If I find out who—'

'But he can't get his hands on Les Hirondelles through stock exchange dealings,' Anne pointed out. 'If your father doesn't agree – that's that.'

'True,' he said. 'But he's bad news. Definitely bad news. Fanatics are always trouble.'

'But he seems to want big trouble. International trouble,' Anne said, noting how the faint glow of his cigarette as he drew on it briefly lit his face and fair hair. 'It is so odd that he should want Les Hirondelles.'

'That's what bothers me,' Peter said. 'I'm uneasy.' He sat quietly for a moment and then shrugged, a flash of lightning bringing his silhouette to temporary colour as he turned to her. 'Take no notice of me. It's the weather. One always thinks the worst when the elements are playing up.'

It was dark again and very silent except for the consistent drumming of water falling on water. He had turned away, the de Courtenay face in profile, dark and yet without colour in the moonlight. On an impulse Anne heard herself say: 'Why don't we swim? Wash your troubles away—' And for the second time that evening she felt herself inane, but his nearness was causing her problems of composure.

'In all this rain?' he said, his voice surprised.

'Well, we couldn't get wetter than running through it,' she said, and laughed.

His head had turned again and she caught the gleam of moonlight in his eyes. 'You're not afraid of the lightning?'

'It's miles away,' she pointed out.

'In that case, it's a very good idea,' he said. 'Do you mind swimming without a suit? More important, do you mind if I do?'

'It's very dark,' she said, 'and to tell you the truth I've always thought those two strips of bikini women wear quite ridiculous.'

Wondering if perhaps she was a little drunk and surprised at her own audacity, she was on her feet, moving a few paces away from him and pulling at the long zip at the back of her dress. It slid to her feet and she unhooked the lace bra, hesitated and then stripped off the small matching pants. Leaving her clothes discarded where they had fallen, the white of the underclothes faintly gleaming, naked she moved deliberately from under the terrace and alongside the pool to the deep end. She could only be a silhouette to him – the damage to her leg would not show. There quite consciously she stood posed while the rain beat down on her until another distant flash of lightning faintly lit the scene she had set. And then she dived into the pool.

The water was textured velvet and each thudding raindrop caused tiny shockwaves pounding on her body. Had she not already wanted Peter de Courtenay, the touch of the water and the rain would have aroused the hungers that she had kept controlled for too long. As she reached the shallow end, Peter was in the water, his shape indistinct against the terrace walls behind. Without speaking he started to swim alongside her as she flipped round to cover another length of the pool, and with only the distant thunder and the sound of the rain they swam, not speaking, side by side. Then Anne, hoping the moment was right, stopped at the shallow end and lifted herself on to the side with her arms where the warm rain stung as it fell on her body. She had chosen one corner of the pool, and he lifted himself on to the other; the distance between them in the darkness was more electric than the storm. She could sense that he was not sure enough of himself or the situation to come nearer.

'We do have one problem,' she said lightly. 'How to get dry.' She had decided she did not want to go to her home naked. It could prove undignified and the sensuality of the scene she had carefully created would be lost.

'No problem,' he said. He stood up and walked back under the terrace and, carefully feeling his way, went up the stairs to the floor above. She could hear his footsteps above then in a minute he was back down again, a blur in the darkness.

'Come here,' he said.

She got to her feet and moved towards him, trying not to limp. He was standing, a large towel around his waist and one outstretched between his two hands.

Two paces from him, she stopped. 'Lift up,' he said, and like an obedient child she lifted her arms. He moved forward and from his superior height dropped the towel behind her back, and then wrapped it around her body, under her arms, while being careful not to touch her.

'I'm always having to lend you towels,' he said and he sounded a little breathless.

He was very close. She stood on tiptoe, head tilted back to emphasize their height difference, said, 'Thank you,' and moved to kiss him on the cheek. It was the moment, she knew, when either he would accept the small caress as a genuine thank-you, or turn it into something more. And as her mouth touched his wet face, his arms went around her, he pulled her close to him, and the kiss became something quite different.

She had remained stretched against him as he held her close against him. Their bodies were cold, the water from their wet hair mingling as they kissed. His tongue was gently touching hers, and she twisted her own into his mouth and tasted him. Whisky, cigarettes and behind a clean warmth. The thickness of the wrapping of towels they both wore disguised any body excitements but she was sure, certain, that he wanted her.

The kiss lasted a long time, and eventually he released her and said quietly:

'You'll catch cold. Let me take you home now. It's time for bed.'

Anne had never wanted anything so much in her life as to go to bed with Peter de Courtenay. Every nerve-end felt exposed, and the heat in the pit of her stomach was demanding to be cooled. Gently he was pushing down the towel that he had wrapped around her, and then his head bent to take her nipple into his mouth and between his teeth. He seemed to be biting her and teasing her with his tongue at the same time. She shut her eyes and shivered, then somehow made herself think.

It wasn't easy; little gasps were escaping from her as his mouth shaped her nipples into a hard point. But she was sure it was necessary to keep her head. She wanted Peter in her life and her bed for a long time – not just this one night. She had made all the running, taken the initiative in all that had happened between them so far. Yet in the background was the shadow of the unknown Evelyn. Competition. Possibly serious competition. It seemed important to break away. She was not an easy lay to pass the time with before Evelyn took over. Better to leave him unsatisfied. Perhaps intrigued and truly wanting her.

Gently she pulled his head away from her.

'You're right,' she said. 'I must go to bed.'

She said it lightly and quickly, with the faintest of accents on the 'I'. He looked at her, his head on one side in the darkness, questioning her.

'I could manage alone from here, so you won't get any wetter,' she said.

'Can't I come with you?'

'If you'd like to, but it's not necessary,' deliberately misunderstanding.

He was silent for a moment.

'I would like to go to bed with you,' he said.

She hesitated. 'And I with you. But not now.'

'Why not?'

'Because.'

'Because of what?'

One hand was caressing her breast while the other pulled gently at her wet hair, smoothing it from her face.

'Because your girlfriend is coming to stay and will be living in my house. Because you will have to see me every day on your home territory when I am here. And because for those reasons you might regret it.'

'I wouldn't regret it.'

'Then I might regret it,' she said. 'Peter, it's ...' she hesitated, and then dropping pretence said with honesty she had not meant to reveal: 'I might not want it to be only once. And so it's too soon.'

There was a long silence and impulsively she stretched up and this time made sure her kiss was on his cheek.

'I like you, Peter,' she said. 'Very much—'

And pulling the towel to cover her breasts again, she turned and half-ran clumsily from the terrace across the sharp, springy wet grass to her own front door, because if she hadn't hurried from him, she knew she would have had to relent.

As she disappeared and became a blur in the night, Peter stood looking after her, more puzzled and exasperated than angry. He let the towel drop from his waist, revealing to the night a man aroused.

'Much good that'll do you,' he muttered to himself, and dived cleanly back into the pool, covering two fast lengths before climbing out again.

154

He dried himself in the shadow of the terrace, watching the night. The rain was falling more gently and the sky was clearing so that the cypresses looked softer and the water shone with little shafts of silver.

Dry, he pulled on his shirt and trousers and bent to pick up her clothes where she had left them. The dress felt as soft on his fingers as her skin had, and the tiny pants and bra were soft too, but with firmer areas where the flimsy lace was. Instinctively he put them to his nose to find a clean smell of sun-dried garments, scent, and just a touch of the persuasive musk of woman which came near to arousing him again.

He hesitated before deciding to leave both dress and underwear neatly placed on one of the chairs well back and in shelter. The temptation was to take them to her home. But he did not want to find her sending him away. Best to leave things for the time being.

But she was in his head as he walked back to his own home. She had been so pliant, melting into him right up until the moment she had drawn away. Her body had become fluid, arched and curved, something that never happened to Evelyn. Evelyn was somehow always angular. He could make her respond, but it was always a challenge – exciting in its way – but the eagerness in Anne Paradine's responses to his kissing and his touching was far more appealing.

And then she had stopped. For a moment he was angry. But then he remembered what she had said.

What had she meant, once would not be enough? For a moment warning bells rang. Was she suggesting something permanent? His mind skittered away from the thought, but if she was all she promised, once would probably not be enough for him either. The summer would end, he would be in New York, she would be in London, and any dreams she had would have to fade.

But for the time being he wanted to explore the soft, small body further. Remembering the way her nipples had stiffened and the hungry little cries she had made, he found himself aroused again. And as he opened his front door he made a decision. He would telephone her now see if she were safely

155

home and ask her out to dinner; first thing in the morning, he would gather up her clothes from the pool and return them.

After all, they still had Evelyn's visit to discuss.

Chapter Twelve

Philip found himself vaguely alarmed when his wife said in the sort of voice that he knew brooked no arguments that she wanted to talk to him before he went to bed.

The family and guests had all drifted away and the big drawing-room was quiet; cigar smoke hung in the air, and the maid was efficiently and silently cleaning ashtrays and removing glasses.

It was the only moment of the day when he and Stella were alone together. For years now they had lived their separate lives – he with his routine in the fields and his visits to Nice to see old friends and make, in the case of Martine, new ones; and she confined to her garden and her room, running the house like a great spider, he often thought. Her lunch she took in her room, but dinner was sacrosanct, and he was expected to attend and always did.

They had never discussed the rules of their particular game. In fact they rarely discussed anything. It was a very civilized separation. No quarrels, no shouting, just a calm indifference, one to the other.

He liked her enough, and he respected her. She had always been the cleverer. Her mind was sharper and her interests wider. He had been surprised and grateful all those years ago when she had agreed to marry him, and delighted that she had seemed to enjoy the *châtelaine* role and played the part so well. And she had been a good mother to the children, both pairs of them; though it seemed to him that her children were definitely pleasanter than those by his first wife. In spite of Marion— but his mind shied away from that.

The real trouble was that he could no longer bear the physical sight of Stella. Her huge bulk, her wheezing, her drinking, the thick coarseness of her unloved iron-grey hair, all repelled him. Under all that flesh was the girl he had married, but so deeply buried even the memory was suffocated. To look at her hurt him. Only if he concentrated on her unspoilt eyes could he persuade himself that this whistling hunk of flesh had once shared his bed and given him two children.

Normally when the family and guests were gone, he made his excuses and went to his room, leaving Stella in her armchair, a fresh nightcap at her elbow and Claudine to hand to put her mistress to bed. But this night Stella had asked him to sit, told the maid to bring him another brandy without so much as asking if he wanted one, and then told the maid to go. That in itself was alarming. The de Courtenays had always acted as if their servants were deaf, dumb and blind, and for one moment he thought she might have found out about Martine. But then, what if she had?

'Philip,' she was saying. 'There's something you must know.'

'What's that, my dear?' he asked, swirling the brandy in the bottom of the balloon glass. Another thought had struck him. Could she have found out about Marion? But even that, so long after – what of it?

'Tomas is in debt to that Arab. He owes him a million francs.'

'What!' Philip sat straight up in his chair. 'It can't be.'

'I'm afraid it can,' Stella said crisply.

'How on earth—?'

'Gambling. Fouezanne kept giving him loans.'

'Then Fouezanne is a fool,' Philip said flatly, 'and will have to whistle for his money.'

'You won't help?'

'Certainly not.'

'And if Fouezanne sues him. What about the de Courtenay name?'

Philip shifted uneasily in his chair.

'Let him sue,' he said eventually. 'Whatever possessed the man to loan money to Tomas? And that much money—' His voice was petulant and angry.

'Because Fouezanne wants to buy Les Hirondelles and has been using Tomas as his agent in the matter.'

'Buy Les Hirondelles? Whatever for?'

'Twenty million francs financially. To create a private village for the very rich – like Castelleras – in theory. A concentration camp for millionaires is what he seems to have in mind,' she said drily.

Philip was on his feet, staring down at her; she noted that in his agitation, his bowtie had gone askew. That would annoy him when he saw it.

'Twenty million francs – well, well!'

'It's a difficult choice for you, Philip,' Stella said softly. 'Which do you love most: money – or the estate?'

He stared at her, walked across to the window and pulled back the curtains. Outside, the courtyard was peaceful, each house softly lit with its own lamp. A dog barked somewhere, and the buzz of the cicadas vocalized the darkness. Only in the winter was it ever truly silent at night, he thought, watching the sky brighten from lightning somewhere that he could not see.

He turned back abruptly.

'You underestimate me, Stella,' he said. 'I would not sell Les Hirondelles for twenty million francs. We have enough money for all we could possibly need. Certainly all I need. The children are greedy. It does them good to be controlled financially. If they had their way, we would need to sell. They'd go through the lot in no time. But Les Hirondelles is ours. When we're dead they can do what they like with it. But not before.'

'And in the meantime, what about Tomas?' Her voice was kinder.

'Tomas is a grown man. He must find his own way out of his own dilemma.'

He was still standing, the brandy glass empty.

'There's one thing,' Stella said. 'If I were to pay Tomas's debt from my own money is there any way that the estate could go to Peter?' He started to speak and she put out her hand to silence him. 'No, let me explain first. It's not just because Peter is my son and I love him; it's more. He loves the estate as much as you do, and as much as I do, and it's his dream to own, run it, love it as much as, if not more than, we do. He's very much your son as well as mine, you know.'

Philip found himself deeply moved. 'You didn't have to explain,' he said. 'I know how Peter feels about Les Hirondelles, but the law here won't permit it. You knew that when you married me. What money I could leave Tomas would never satisfy him – the value is in this place, though twenty million francs—' he shook his head. 'That I don't understand.' He smiled at her. 'But there's time,' he said. 'I don't intend to leave you all for a long time, which may disappoint Tomas. Let's just wait and see what happens, shall we? But I'm glad you told me.'

She sounded almost shy as she said : 'I thought it was only fair that you should know. I wondered if you did know. Bringing in the *locataires* seemed as if it might have been done for a purpose.'

'Not at all,' he said hastily. 'But I shall be prepared now when he speaks to me. Thank you, my dear.' He wanted to kiss her, but the fat powdered cheek repelled him. Instead he moved to take the pudgy hand, seeing how his wedding ring was almost sunk in flesh, pressed it, then forced himself to kiss it lightly.

'Sleep well, my dear,' he said, and he could have sworn that there were tears enhancing the brilliance of her green eyes; he left the room hurriedly without looking back.

He was thoughtful as he walked up the stairs to his own bedroom. Tomas's debt to this Arab could cause all kinds of complications. He would have to see his lawyer in the morning. Run down to Nice and get the whole thing sorted out. He sighed. He hated disruptions, and just as life was going so well.

He opened his bedroom door and snapped on the light, then stopped dead in his tracks at the sight which confronted him. Martine was sitting up naked in his bed. Her small triangular breasts were pulled taut as she leaned with her elbows back on his pillows. Her fair hair was loose about her shoulder, and she looked very young and very innocent – which he knew she was not.

'Good evening, monsieur,' she said, chin tucked into her chest, eyes directed upwards at him. 'I came to see you because my husband comes tomorrow and I thought perhaps—' she stopped and tipped her head sideways. 'Did I think right?'

'You did!' he said. He had shut the door with one hand, releasing his trousers with the other. He undressed all the way to the bed, leaving his clothing trailed behind him. One hand pulled back the bedclothes, exposing her flat stomach with its comical duckling fluff of fair hair, and the other reached for her breast.

The surprise of finding her there and all the implications had given him the most enormous erection, and as his hand found her soft, secret parts, and his mouth sucked up her small breast, he felt her hand close over him, tugging, scratching and stroking in a most encouraging way.

He felt twenty-two years old, rampant as a bull. Her compliant young body under him encouraged the illusion. He was thrusting his fingers into her, feeling how the dark entrance opened and closed under his probing, and then he was certain he could wait no longer.

She had sensed his intention, and she fell back on to the pillows, twisting so she was flat on her back. She opened her legs very wide, her knees up, and with one hand around his shoulder she pulled him down on to her while the other hand guided his splendid erection inside her.

She gasped as he thrust in, a choking little sound. She wasn't ready for him, and he was pleased at the dry tightness surrounding him, and thrust harder, his head pressed into the pillows, his full weight flattening her into his bed.

He rode her triumphantly, and as she gasped beneath him while the climax neared and swelled he heard the door handle turning and the plaintive voice of Pamela Whitton whispering: 'Philip, darling, it's me.'

160

For a moment, he stopped in mid stroke. He could feel the girl underneath tense and tighten, and his excitement grew. She was trying to wriggle free of him, but he just rode her faster.

'Philip – oh, Philip—' he heard Pamela say. 'What are you doing!' The thought of her watching added to the excitement.

He was near to the end, and he pushed convulsively until release came, and then for a few seconds he flopped on to the girl beneath him so that her breath came out in a gasp.

Then leisurely he sat up, swinging himself to sit on the edge of the bed. His erstwhile mistress was standing in the doorway in her red woollen dressing gown, her hand over her mouth, her eyes wide with horror.

'Philip,' she said, 'how could you!'

He looked at her, his expression friendly. He could not find it in him to even resent her intrusion. And still amicably he said: 'Pamela – why don't you just fuck off?'

She gave an outraged little cry, turned and blundered from the room.

He turned back to Martine.

'First time that woman's done what I told her in years,' he said.

'I told him, Claudine.' Stella de Courtenay was in bed, her breath coming in slow bubbles, her mouth pursed into whistles, trying to force the air through to her lungs.

Claudine was quickly but carefully preparing the asthma pump, which she handed over to her mistress when the few drops of fluid were safe inside.

'And what did he say, madame?'

'He said he wouldn't sell Les Hirondelles for twenty million francs,' Stella said, when breath permitted. She was very, very tired.

'And Monsieur Tomas?'

'That he must get out of the mess himself.'

Claudine nodded impassively. 'Exactly as I would have thought,' she said. 'The estate has meant most in Monsieur Philip's life.'

'More than his wives and his children,' Stella said, with a half-smile, her breath beginning to ease.

'More than his wives and his children,' Claudine agreed, 'but also more than his money.'

Stella sighed.

'You've known him longer than any of us.'

'True,' Claudine said. 'He is not a bad man, madame. It is just that his appetites have always been too strong.'

Stella was surprised but too weary to question. In all the years, Claudine had never ventured an opinion about Philip. Why now? Was it that she had sensed the resurgence of Stella's old pain and hurt that dated back so long it had been numbed and forgotten for years? He had been kind tonight, and they had talked – the first time for so long. And he had kissed her hand, touched her. She no longer cared, but sometimes there was nostalgia. It was too late for anything to change now, but occasionally the old sadness and the old regrets reappeared. Had she been French perhaps she could have coped with his infidelities, but she was not French. She was from a place and a class and an age where husbands were faithful, and if they were not you divorced them.

She had never divorced Philip because she would have lost too much – Les Hirondelles, perhaps her children, and certainly him. At one time he had been the most necessary.

'Do you know what, Claudine?' she said. 'Tonight he said Les Hirondelles was ours – his and mine.'

'And so it is, madame,' Claudine said. 'Now sleep.'

'It is really insupportable that you've let that frightful man have the guest room.' Margaret de Courtenay's voice was querulous as she sat in front of the dressing-table in Tomas's bedroom, scowling at her own reflection in the mirror and removing mascara and make-up with quick angry strokes. She had hated every minute of dinner.

Tomas was already in bed. As a concession to his wife he had found some blue and white striped silk pyjamas and worn them. Now he was looking at a book without seeing the words.

'If you'd said you were arriving ...'

She bridled and flung a piece of soiled cottonwool into the waste basket. 'I hardly expect to find no room for me in my own home.'

'There is room for you,' he said wearily. 'Here – in what used to be our bedroom.'

'I prefer sleeping on my own, as you very well know.'

Tomas put down the book.

'There was nothing I could do. Achmid was invited and he came. What should I have done? Send him back to Cannes?'

'Put him in with Elisabeth,' Margaret said sourly. 'She's the one with the taste for Arabs. How long is he staying anyway?'

'Just one more night. He goes on Sunday. Besides,' he said, 'you could have stayed with Elisabeth if you'd asked.'

'I wouldn't ask her the time.'

'All right, one of the others.'

'I wouldn't give them the satisfaction.'

She swung round on the dressing-table stool and stared at him, her blue eyes unfriendly.

'You're looking very nervous. I suppose you're in some kind of trouble. As usual.' She paused then asked abruptly: 'Are the children all right?'

'I think so,' Tomas said. 'Françoise is up to something, but I can't control her. And Raoul is her devoted slave. They're far too much together. But what can I do? They need a mother.'

Margaret looked at him coldly. 'They're always welcome in Paris with me, as you well know. Anyway, Françoise is up to what?'

'I don't know. That's what worries me.'

'She's always been up to something,' Margaret said dismissively. 'Ever since she was about fourteen. At least she hasn't got pregnant. I really don't know what one does about children these days. They go their own way. No morals, no standards. Everyone in Paris complains about it. At least at the back of beyond here she shouldn't be able to get her hands on heroin, which is a blessing. My friend Tilly de Villebonne's daughter has practically ruined the family buying the stuff.'

163

She stopped and stared at him again. 'I presume you're still ruining yourself at the casinos?'

'I have my good days,' he said lightly. He lifted himself up on the pillows and picking up the book said: 'Why are you here, Margaret? What went wrong in Paris?'

'What do you mean what went wrong?'

He grinned at her amiably, knowing it would annoy her.

'Well, something went wrong, or you wouldn't be at the back of beyond here, now would you, three weeks too soon.'

'I wanted to see the children.'

'You did?' He raised his eyebrows. 'That's nice for them after so long.'

She was heading for the bathroom door.

'Well, you're hardly the perfect father,' she said, slamming it behind her.

She was a long time. Running taps, her own water hitting the water in the WC – why did women make so much noise when they peed? he wondered. The cistern flushing, more running water, and then she emerged an ice maiden in a white nightgown and négligé. She looked very beautiful, and he felt an old familiar disappointment at her remoteness.

'Now come on,' he said. 'What happened? Man trouble?'

'Certainly not,' she said, with such force that he added: 'Okay, how about woman trouble?'

'You never think of anything but sex,' she said, her voice disgusted. 'You never did. So I suppose I shouldn't expect anything to change.'

'Your trouble was you didn't think about it enough,' he said. 'And that's obviously not changed.'

She was approaching the bed with barely concealed reluctance, and delicately, with long white, red-tipped fingers, fastidiously lifted the sheets on her side.

'Sorry I haven't any tongs to lend you,' he said sarcastically. 'But the linen is clean. And I've showered.'

Her nostrils flared and she slid herself between the sheets as if they contained a tarantula. Suddenly he wanted to annoy her, and he made a sudden lunge for her across the width of the king-size bed. 'Come here, my darling—' he said theatrically, arms wide open, and she leapt out of the bed like a jack rabbit and stood staring down at him, quivering with fury in her opaque nightgown. He found himself laughing out loud at her outraged expression.

'Don't touch me!' she said. 'If you were a gentleman, you'd find a bed elsewhere.'

'Oh, come on, Margaret,' he said, still grinning. 'I think I can keep my hands off you after all these years. Do you want to put pillows down between us? Or will you trust me?'

She still hesitated, so to reassure her he heaved himself to the far side of the bed and turned his back on her. He could hear the light rustle of the sheets as she lifted them again, and feel the slight depression in the mattress as she climbed in, careful to keep to her side and presumably turning with her back towards him.

'This is really insupportable,' he heard her mutter, her voice full of injured dignity.

'Oh come on,' he said. 'It's not the first time we've shared a bed and with a bit of luck it will be the last. If it's proving so dreadful you could always go and stay in a hotel.'

'And how would that look to the children?'

'Pretty much the same as you sleeping in the guest room whenever you come here. They're old enough to notice things like that. They probably think that we're having a reconciliation tonight.'

'Heaven forbid,' she said, so fervently that he felt a touch of injured pride.

'Anyway, do you mind if I read for a bit?'

'As a matter of fact,' she said coldly. 'I do.'

'Very well then,' he said. 'We'll turn out the lights.'

Both leaned simultaneously to pull the switches on the tall bedside lamps.

'Goodnight, Margaret,' he said.

'Goodnight,' she replied.

She waited until she was absolutely certain that he was deeply asleep. She knew from the past how his breathing changed and the exact depth it reached, spiced with the occasional small whistling snore. Then nothing would wake him.

She could now permit herself the luxury of tears as she

had done on those other occasions when he slept leaving her feeling defiled and dirty. Slow hot tears that fell down the sides of her nose and into the corner of her mouth on to the pillow via her neck as she lay on her back staring at the ceiling.

'Oh, Tilly, Tilly,' she whispered out loud. 'Why did you have to end it?'

'Do you think they're having a reconciliation?' Raoul asked.

He was in Françoise's room, lying across the foot of her bed in a towelling robe while she in a long, bright pink nightshirt leaned on her pillows. A full box of after-dinner mints was between them, and they were eating greedily.

'No,' Françoise said, wrinkling her nose, her mouth full. 'Mama can't bear him. It's just that the awful Achmid's got the guest room.' She looked at him inquiringly. 'Would you like them to get together again then?'

Raoul shook his head. 'Oh, no,' he said. 'It's good having Paris to go to as well as here. I mean, one would go mad here all the time. Father's hardly ever around.' There was a wistful note in his voice.

'You sound like Mama,' she said flatly. 'Anyway, while they're separated they're both good for a touch. I wonder why she's here? One of her girlfriends let her down, I'll bet.'

Two hands simultaneously went for the chocolates and there was a brief silence as they chewed.

'Why's he here?' Raoul asked.

'Achmid? Papa invited him. I suppose he's come to look at his investment. Funny, isn't it, to think we're sitting on a fortune.'

'You're sitting on two fortunes,' Raoul said, and she giggled and said: 'Don't be crude.'

They were both silent again, Raoul staring into space, his eyes unfocused.

'It's a pity it'll spoil the mountain, though, isn't it,' he said.

'What?'

'Mining the bauxite.'

'Raoul, there are a million mountains. Think of all that lovely money. And, talking of money—' She paused, folding her thin pale hands over her stomach complacently. 'I've got good news. I asked Grandfather about the yacht tonight, and he didn't say no. In fact he said it seemed like a good idea and he'd think about it.'

Raoul looked suitably impressed. 'What did you say?' he asked.

'I said I'd got this boyfriend who wanted to take a crowd of us out and pay all the expenses. Grandfather was funny though – he said, "Never mind about the friend, do you and Raoul want to go?" So I told him how mad we were about yachting and foreign parts and how you'd never had a long trip and it seemed a shame to leave the boat in harbour like that all the time when we'd enjoy it so much, and he just grunted and said *d'accord* – he'd think about it.'

'The awful Achmid will be pleased,' Raoul said.

'Yes, won't he?' Françoise was thoughtful. 'But did you hear all that stuff about Palestine and his mother being killed and getting Israel back for the Arabs?'

'Only bits and I didn't understand much.'

'Nor me. It all happened years ago. But as I gather it, he's trying to get his hands on all the oil and natural materials, which I suppose explains why he's so keen on the bauxite. It's a natural material, isn't it? Heavens! He must be unbelievably rich.'

'He's gaga.' Raoul yawned.

'Of course he's gaga,' Françoise said impatiently. 'No one knows better than I do just how gaga. But where does the hash come in, I ask myself? Why does he want hash, and why is he going to all the trouble to persuade us to get it for him?'

'Maybe he smokes it. Heavily,' Raoul said, kicking his legs with pleasure at his own joke.

'Very funny!' she said caustically. 'I don't know. It's odd. I'll have to try to get him on his own tomorrow to tell him about the yacht. I'm not sorry he's here, really. I don't want to go to that hotel again. I think I'll give McTaggart his way and let him come with me next time. Funny, isn't it? He didn't look at me once all evening. God, he gives me the creeps.'

167

'He's also going to give us a lot of money, isn't he?' Raoul said. 'Just think about that.'

'Oh, I do,' she said. 'All the time. Here, have another chocolate.'

Achmid was wide awake. He had slept briefly immediately after climbing into the big bed in Tomas's guest room, but woken with a start to find two fifteen figured in the green glow of his bedside clock. Now the digital figures said three thirty and he was no nearer sleep. His ulcer burned; he wanted a glass of milk; he was hot and uncomfortable, but too cold when he threw back the covers.

He was philosophical about wakefulness. Achmid rarely slept easily and needed little sleep. His problem was to still his brain, which in the dark hours of the night seemed to him to become as fragmented as shattered glass and quite uncontrollable. In the daytime his concentration was unshakable, but at night while his body tried to rest his brain had its own way with him, flittering from thought to thought, one idea crowding out another while each fragment jostled chaotically for position.

He lay on his back, hands folded on his stomach, eyes tight shut, and endeavoured to relax the body that was always too taut.

He was trying not to think of the red earth of Les Hirondelles. Fidgeting in the bed, he brooded on Tomas. He was sure that Tomas had not approached the father yet, and a surge of irritation increased the burning in his gut. Tomas would have to be punished eventually for the delays his tardiness had caused with some small, but not inconsiderable, punishment. He would need to think about that. That gross old woman, Stella de Courtenay, was culpable too. She knew what he wanted. He was sure of it and she had meant him to be sure. He felt she was mocking him through her cat-green eyes, and he was not easily mocked.

He burned with impatience to get his hands on the land and what it would eventually yield in money for the cause, but the problem was that obviously the de Courtenays had no need of money. Maybe money was not their price. There might be another, more effective way to get the land. Tomorrow he would watch the family, size them up, find the weak link. The weak link had to be found in all dealings.

The thought of the cause crowded out Les Hirondelles. Had he said too much at the dinner table? The de Courtenay woman was no fool, nor was her son. Tomas, on the other hand, was a fool; the girl Anne, merely bewildered and embarrassed. He remembered uneasily that all through the conversations he had seen that Françoise's cold blue eyes were watching.

He twisted on to his side, angrily remembering their last meeting. The fury that motivated him in all the areas of his life raged as he remembered the lash she had given him, and her insolence at the hotel table afterwards.

Once she had persuaded her grandfather to let the de Courtenay yacht go to Morocco, she must be punished too. But how? What was her weak link? Brooding, he decided that her brother was the only person she appeared to care for. When it was all over, he would be beaten – with her watching – just as she had beaten him so that blood was drawn. His only regret was that he would not be there on the yacht to see it nor, better, to do it himself.

Still it was a pity she had gone too far on that last occasion, he thought. Someone else would now have to be found. He had known the moment he laid eyes on her on the first visit to Les Hirondelles that she would do. The faint traces of cruelty were obvious in her sharply pretty face, but he had believed that she was too young to be a fully developed, and therefore dangerous, sadist.

It was possible that she had now taken the step towards the real thing and he could no longer use her. He felt a momentary self-pity for himself that his sex life should be so barren. Somewhere there must be a woman who could make him react normally, but in nearly twenty-five years he had never found one. Miss Patterson, the English nanny in the hot Alexandrian days and nights of long ago, had imprinted her own peculiar perversion on to him.

His mind skittered back to the bauxite and Tangier – both so important. And he had to deal with this odd, arrogant and feudal family if either project was to come to fruition. It was an interesting exercise in its way.

Achmid thought how his life had been spent in manipulation of money, shares and people. And of how often he had won. Stella de Courtenay was right, he thought. Power and trickery did go together. If he could trick the de Courtenays into doing exactly what he planned, his power would be greater than ever.

It was a relaxing thought, and he rolled on to his back again, eyes to the ceiling, and contemplated the extremely satisfying and uncomplicated pleasures of playing God.

Chapter Thirteen

It was dawn and the air was clear and fresh from the storm of the night before. The sun shone thinly over a rain-washed Les Hirondelles. Two motorcycles, one without a silencer, roared into the parking area at the back of the houses. The noise disturbed three magpies, which flashed white, black and blue into the sky and down to the olive groves, sounding their displeasure.

Only in the guest house were the shutters back, showing signs of life. Martine, in a dark blue towelling tracksuit, slid through the front door, quietly closing it behind her, and ran to the parking area.

Two space-age figures in tight black leather trousers and zip-fronted jackets wearing heavy helmets were parking their bikes. Large black bikes, gleaming with silver. Both figures were medium height and bone slim, and from the back Martine could not tell which was her brother and which was her sister.

'My God,' she said. 'What a racket. Be quiet.'

'Ah, there you are, Martine.' The slightly taller of the two figures was removing the helmet, and her brother's dark-skinned face, thin, freckled and with oddly elongated black eyes, grinned wolfishly at her. 'What a dragon that old bird at the gate is. I thought she'd never let us in.'

'You're a fool arriving at this hour. I was going to be down there to explain. Anyway, she telephoned and I told her it was all right, but you're making enough noise to wake the dead.'

'It looks as if it could do with a big of wakening up—' Marie's helmet was off too, and she was looking around her with a supercilious air. 'How can you stand it up here?'

'I like it,' Martine said. 'Come on, let's get inside – and for God's sake be quiet, if you can.'

Brother and sister unstrapped baggage from the back of the bikes, and then Marie said suspiciously: 'It's all right leaving the bikes here? It's very open.'

Martine looked skywards. 'If you think anyone at Les Hirondelles is going to steal a couple of motorbikes, you're out of your mind,' she said. 'Now come *on.*'

She led them around the back of the houses on a rough path and then through to the courtyard where her own front door was.

'Quickly,' she said.

Jacques was grinning at her, his helmet under his arm, his thick black hair ruffled.

'Anyone would think you were ashamed of us,' he said.

'I just don't want you queering the pitch,' she said impatiently. 'Why couldn't you have borrowed a car?'

'I like my bike, thanks,' Marie said belligerently as she put her helmet on the hall table.

'All right, all right. Just watch it.'

She was leading them down to the big country kitchen where she put on the kettle. Jacques stripped off his leather jacket and trousers; underneath he was wearing a thin shirt and trousers. Marie swung a chair around with its back to the table and settled herself across it, arms leaning on the top rung. She made no move to remove the leathers.

'Not bad, not bad at all,' she said looking around the room.

There was little family likeness between the three of them, except that all were slender and small-boned. Jacques was dark with a wide full mouth and a non-European look. The girls both had fair, colourless hair, but while Martine's face was thin and sly with a jumble of teeth, her sister had broad Moroccan features.

'Is the rest of the house as expensive?' Marie asked her.

Martine nodded. 'I'll show you round after breakfast. It's quite something.'

'Can't wait,' her sister said sardonically.

In her way Marie was the best looking of the three. Her mouth was full and down-drooped sulkily, and her short cropped hair suited the good planes of her face. Her eyes spoilt her; they were constantly narrowed as if keeping out the smoke from an imaginary cigarette.

She had lit a cigarette now, leaving it in the corner of her mouth.

'So what pitch is it we mustn't queer?' she asked gruffly.

Martine was visibly excited as she made three cups of coffee and put out bread and *confiture*.

'I'm so pleased you've arrived,' she said. 'I've been dying to tell you. I think this time I've got it made. There are some snags, but you might have some ideas about those.'

'Tell us the good news first.'

'Well, for a start don't forget you're my husband. I'm wondering if that was a mistake now. I think I should have been a poor little alone-and-unprotected girl and not a married woman. But maybe it was right. He might not have fallen for it if he hadn't thought I had a husband in the background. Gave him something to tell his family. That's why you had to come this weekend, Jacques.'

'What's wrong about being married then?' Marie asked.

'Well, only money. I've got this place free, and he's always dropping in food and stuff, but not a *centime* so far, and he's fucked me about seven times. I suppose he thinks my husband is supporting me. But I reckon he's mean.'

172

'It's no good if you don't get paid for it,' Jacques said disapprovingly.

'I know. But I like it here and I wouldn't mind staying. The luxury ... And you two can come any time you like just as long as we're careful not to upset any of the others. But I've got to have money.'

'Who are the others?' Marie asked.

'There's dozens of them. They've all got different houses. This, apparently, was the guest house, and though he doesn't say much I gather he wasn't exactly popular for letting me have it. He treats me a bit like a servant – I call him monsieur and he calls me madame –' she giggled '– even when we're screwing.'

'Then he should definitely pay you,' Jacques said. 'Haven't you said anything?'

'Well, I did say I was short of cash the other day, but he just said surely I must be better off, living rent free. The mistake I made was that I asked him after I'd made him come. I should have done it while he was still randy.'

'I think I'm going to have to catch you both at it one day,' her brother said thoughtfully, 'and demand a price for my silence.'

'Fat chance you'll have catching us if you arrive on that motorbike,' Martine said. 'Couldn't you at least put the silencer back?'

'Mine's the one without the silencer,' Marie said stolidly.

Martine groaned. 'I might have guessed,' she said. 'Anyway if we put our minds to it there must be something here for all of us. He's got an ancient wife who looks as if she's about to croak any minute, and none of them seem to get on very well. They're mostly out, except the wife and a sort of elder daughter who never leaves her house. I haven't really got them all sorted out yet, and he doesn't tell me anything. The servants are no good. Toffee-nosed lot. They look down on me. I suppose they know he's screwing me.'

'Anything worth stealing?' Jacques asked.

'There must be. He's filthy rich, but I've never seen any of them wearing any jewellery. I got into Tomas's house when they were all out one day – I can tell by which cars are in the parking area whether they're in or not – and there wasn't a thing. Television set, of course, and a good radio. But they don't seem to go in much for things.'

'There's bound to be some silver somewhere.'

'Suppose there is? Who's going to be suspected instantly? Me! That Claudine – she's the housekeeper – watches me like a hawk. She's certain I'm up to something. No – I've got to get money out of him. That's the answer. Honestly, Jacques, it's the best place I've ever found. You know I like the country and you know I hate working. How would I ever afford this sort of luxury? I even use the pool when most of the cars have gone. You can hear them coming up the mountain on their way back, so I've never been caught yet. I'm brown all over. Right down to the pubes.'

'And all you have to do is fuck monsieur,' Marie said.

'That's the worst bit. Getting him up takes *ages* and it's harder work making him come. Be all right if I fancied him, but he's so old. Admittedly not bad looking for his age, which is a blessing. Still, at twenty-three I can afford a little time with him – just as long as I get something out of it. I'm just worried how long I can keep him going before he gets used to me. Which reminds me, did you bring those poppers, Jacques?'

'I got a dozen – will that do?'

'Great – I'll give him one, and if he likes it, charge him a hundred francs a sniff for the others.'

'Make it five hundred,' Marie said.

Martine grimaced. 'I'm not sure what I can get away with. He's definitely mean. Mind you, I think he's hooked. Last night I got into his house while they were having a grand dinner party and waited in his bed. I got it all worked out – after the light went out in his room I knew the maid had been, so I nipped in the front door while they were all in the dining-room and got upstairs and into his room. No one saw me. His face when he came in the door! Talk about aston- ished! I think the shock really got him going – or maybe it was doing it in his own bed, with his wife downstairs. You

174

know how some of them like it dangerous. Anyway before I crept out again he told me that he was fixing to send as many of the family as would agree to go off on a cruise on the yacht he owns. So, as he put it, we can be together more.' She gave a long theatrical sigh.

'One funny thing happened though. There's this weird old bird who hangs around the house. I think she must live there, but she's English and quite hideous. Anyway, just as he was getting into bed with me, she started trying the door handle and calling him.'

'What did he do?' Marie asked, interested.

'Told her to fuck off.'

'And did she?'

'Yeah, eventually. But he treated her to an exhibition first. Still, I wonder why she was trying to get into his room. He couldn't be screwing her, could he?'

'Who knows,' said Jacques, 'but there seem to be all sorts of possibilities here.'

'Blackmail?' Martine shook her head. 'I don't think so. I might be wrong but I don't think he'd care. He's so—' She paused and sipped her coffee. 'It's hard to describe. Maybe independent is the word but it's something more than that. I suppose when you're that rich and self-sufficient you can get away with murder. I don't think he gives a damn for anyone. I don't think ordinary blackmail would work.'

'We'll think of something,' he said. 'But show us the place and then we'll think.'

Marie endured the guided tour of the house, barely able to conceal her contempt. It was certainly luxurious, but it would have to be a lot more luxurious before she, personally, could endure screwing some old man she didn't even fancy in order to live in it.

It amused her to think that Martine would be superbly, self-righteously indignant if told she was nothing but a whore. Because when it came right down to it, that's exactly what she was – a whore.

And, she thought critically, Jacques wouldn't make a bad pimp either.

She felt restless and closed in, and couldn't think why she'd succumbed to curiosity and let Jacques persuade her to come up here. She found the estate with its cluster of houses and the heavy mountains behind claustrophobic. She resented Martine's strictures to be quiet, to behave. There was no freedom living like that. It was better to be your own person in your own place even if the life was hard.

Normally she would have been on the beach by now in the special spot where all her friends met on precious weekends. Saturday and Sunday she moved in a flock, a shoal – drifting with a group that changed all the time, picking and choosing who she wanted to be with – if, of course, they wanted to be with her. That was sometimes the rub. It was hard to find someone special, but at least she was always with her own kind. Up here she felt isolated.

'I'm just going out to the bike,' she said abruptly when they were back in the kitchen again.

'You and that damn bike,' Jacques said. 'Can't you get something better between your legs?'

She looked at him coldly without replying. 'I'll be back,' she said to Martine.

'OK. But mind where you go. Stay away from the pool. They have early-morning swims.'

Fuck them and their early morning swims! she thought as she strode back towards the parking area, her heavily shod feet pounding the damp earth. She felt better out of the house, with the sky over her head. Perhaps she'd go back to Nice after lunch. A whole weekend here would be too much.

The bike was where she had left it and, using the soft chamois she kept specially for the purpose, she wiped off the red dust that had settled on the black paintwork and gave the chrome a bit of a polish. Then she checked the oil and the tyres and bounced experimentally on the saddle, yearning to switch on the starter motor, pull out the throttle and roar off back down the mountain. Without Jacques she could do the journey in half the time, sweeping round mountain bends, leaning on air, faster than anything else on the road.

'It was you making all that noise, was it?'

The voice from behind her back made her jump. She turned

to see a woman standing, arms lightly folded, looking at her and frowning.

'If you mean the bike – yes.'

'You woke me,' the woman said accusingly. She was very pretty with soft blonde hair and blue eyes; doll-like, and her white silk pyjama suit enhanced the impression. Marie stared at her stupidly.

'I'm sorry.'

The woman stepped forward and smiled, showing white even teeth.

'Oh, you're a girl. I thought you were a boy at first.'

'Everybody does.'

'Aren't you hot in all that leather?'

'Not at the moment.'

The woman stepped back as if to get her better in focus and then she smiled again.

'By the way, I suppose I should ask who you are, shouldn't I? I'm Margaret de Courtenay.'

'My name is Marie. I'm the sister of the *locataire*.'

'Ah, the one they're all so angry about. They'll be angrier now you've woken the entire household.'

The woman was looking at her almost mischievously, and Marie was uncertain how to respond. A growing suspicion, almost a hope, was in her mind, but – one of the de Courtenays? It wasn't possible. But then, why wasn't it possible?

'Actually,' Margaret de Courtenay was saying, her voice confidential, 'you didn't really wake me. I've hardly slept a wink. I was just about to escape this place for a while.'

'Oh?' Marie made her voice noncommittal.

'Were you doing the same?'

'No. I just wanted to get out of the house. But I was thinking of going.'

'That's your motorbike?'

Marie nodded.

'It's very big.'

'It's not big enough.'

The woman raised her eyebrows. 'It looks very big to me,' she said.

'Do you want to ride it?' Marie said casually.

The woman laughed a trilling little laugh. 'Now can you see me on that great thing? No, I prefer my car.'

The parking area was full of large and expensive cars.

'Which one is yours?' Marie asked.

'That one.' An elegant finger was pointing out a huge black Mercedes. Marie climbed off her bike and walked over to it. Solemnly she circled it, peering through the windows at the white leather upholstery before giving her verdict.

'It's a beautiful car,' she said. 'I wouldn't mind driving that.'

'Wouldn't you?' The de Courtenay woman had her head to one side as if she were deciding something. 'Can you drive?' she asked.

'Yes.'

'Well?'

'Yes.'

'I believe you.' There was a silence, and a small breeze raised a tendril of blonde hair on Margaret's forehead. She pushed it away. 'You know, I hate driving. I was thinking of going down to St Trop, but it's such a long way. What I need is a chauffeur.'

Almost holding her breath, Marie nodded. She could feel her pulse pounding in her throat.

'Would you like to go to St Trop for the day? Drive the car?' The slightly husky voice had deepened.

Marie nodded again.

'We might have fun. Listen, keep your leather gear and we can pretend you're the chauffeur. But you'll need something for the beach.'

'We could go to the nude one.'

Margaret's mouth opened and her teeth came down to bite her lower lip.

'I suppose we could.'

'I've got a teeshirt and shorts underneath all this.'

'I suppose that would do. And anyway there's lots of lovely shops in St Trop. I love shopping, don't you?'

It seemed to be an important moment, the silence between them was a question mark.

'Only with my own money,' Marie said finally and firmly.

She moved towards the garden exit of the area. 'I'll just go and tell Martine I'm off. And maybe I'll get some things.'

'Don't be long,' the woman called after her, and there was something in her voice that made Marie turn back and say gently: 'I won't. I promise.'

Peter awoke at eight o'clock. The early sun streamed through the window, bringing out the peacock hues of Anne's brilliant green dress where he had hung it over a chair in his bedroom. The lacy bra lay across it with the small white pants and her shoes were neat beneath the chair.

The sight created an instant arousal, and he groaned, then grinned and climbed out of bed to walk rampant across the room and into a cold shower.

'God damn her,' he muttered, but there was no malice in it.

By nine thirty he was knocking at her door, her clothing over his arm, her shoes in his hand. She opened the door wearing a short wrap-around velvet robe in dark green, her hair tousled and her eyes still sleepy.

'Oh, hello,' she said, fingers trying to arrange her hair.

'Did I wake you?' he asked.

'No. No. Come in. I just got up,' she said. 'You've brought my clothes back. Thanks. That was kind of you.'

Very formally she took them from him and he noticed how she hid the white underthings beneath the dress as she laid the clothing down on the hall chest. She was shy, he realized, and perhaps even a little embarrassed.

'Are you going to give me a cup of coffee?' he asked. 'I had my breakfast an hour ago and I'm ready to start again.'

'Of course,' she said. 'Come into the kitchen.'

It seemed she had found her composure as she busied herself with kettle, filters and coffee-pot. She looked very young without make-up and with the slight bloom of sleep shining on her cheeks; he could see that she was trying not to limp as she walked.

'Why do you worry about your limp?' he heard himself say abruptly.

She flushed and then went pale.

'I don't worry about it.'

'Oh, yes you do. You're trying your hardest to hide it right now. Relax. Forget it. Nobody cares.'

'I am glad about that,' she said stiffly.

He saw he had wounded her and felt immediate contrition. 'Listen – I'm sorry. It's none of my business. But all I was thinking was nobody's going to notice one unfortunate leg when there's a body and a face like yours above it.'

It wasn't entirely true, he thought as he said it. Her body was beautiful, as he had discovered – her face just ordinary, but the kind of tranquil face that grew on you. She had flushed again.

'That was a nice thing to say,' she said, ignoring the sexual connotation. 'Thank you. And coffee's ready.'

As he took it from her she looked him full in the face, her eyes very bright and challenging. 'Tell me,' she said, 'when is your girlfriend arriving?'

He looked at her sharply, but the challenge had gone. Her expression was bland. It was just an ordinary question. Or was it? He felt sure she was getting at him and not too subtly.

'Not this week but the week after,' he said. 'Are you sure it's still OK with you for her to stay?'

He was remembering how Evelyn had been one of the reasons for her running the night before.

'Of course,' she said. 'I'm really looking forward to meeting her.'

It occurred to him at that moment that he wasn't too sure whether he was looking forward to seeing Evelyn or not. The young woman demure in her dressing gown sitting across the table from him was becoming something of a challenge and an enigma. The way she watched and listened to the family, rarely saying much but very positively of the group, intrigued him. As quiet as she could be, her personality was strong and in no way to be dismissed or ignored. And he had been decidedly startled by her response and her ardour the night before until she had switched off. But then, he thought, the quiet ones were often the sexiest.

He found her attractive, but she was not really of his

world. Not in the way that Evelyn was. Evelyn had to be given a fair chance, he thought, and then mentally chided himself for his own conceit.

'What does she look like?' Anne was asking, eyes down, stirring her coffee.

What did Evelyn look like?

'Elegant, I suppose is the word,' he said. 'She's tall – nearly as tall as I am. Dresses beautifully.'

'Does she work?'

'The only work Evelyn does is shopping and giving parties,' he said and laughed. 'She's always threatening to get a job, but it never seems to happen.'

She made a sort of noncommittal sound, and Peter grinned at her.

'I bet you disapprove of that,' he said.

'I'd be bored if I didn't work,' she said, parrying the question.

'Me too,' he said. 'But I've never been too sure about dedicated career women.'

'Well, I suppose you can make a career of always looking good,' she said lightly, but he detected the faintest touch of bitch, which rather amused him.

He had wanted to mention the night before. He had even thought about kissing her. But her introduction of Evelyn into the conversation had made both impossible. She seemed cool and withdrawn now, the kitchen table firmly separating them, and the electricity that had echoed the storm was not there. He found himself wanting it back. Perhaps if they swam together it would return.

'Feel like a swim?' he said abruptly.

She considered.

'Bit later maybe,' she said. 'I thought I'd go just before I went to see your mother.'

'What time were you thinking of?' he heard himself persisting.

'About ten fifteen.'

He was irritated with himself for letting her control the situation, and finished his coffee almost angrily.

'OK,' he said. 'See you then. We'll go over to Mother's together.'

'If you like,' she said, her voice indifferent.

As he walked back to his own home he said out loud: 'I'll get you into bed, madam, if it's the last thing I do.'

'Stella, I really must speak to you.'

It was eleven thirty a.m., and Claudine had just helped her mistress into the garden and was settling her in the big upright chair in the shade of the oak tree when Pamela Whitton appeared, practically trotting, as she crossed the lawn from the terrace.

'Sit down, Pamela, relax,' Stella said. 'Get your breath.'

Pamela was shaking her head and wringing her hands, behaving like a bad actress portraying agitation.

'There's something I think you ought to hear,' she said, her voice rising uncontrollably.

Stella sighed. 'Whenever anyone says there is something I ought to hear I know it's going to be something I don't *wish* to hear,' she said. 'Are you certain you should tell me?'

'Yes.' Pamela lowered her voice to a whisper. 'It's Philip.' She paused to wring her hands again. 'He's having an affair with the *locataire*.'

'Really?' Stella regarded her with interest. 'How do you know?'

A faint flush of purple appeared on Pamela's already mottled cheek.

'Well.' She hesitated. 'I saw her coming out of his bedroom.'

'Oh, really. When?'

'At four o'clock this morning,' Pamela said triumphantly.

'Oh,' Stella nodded her head several times and stroked Suki, who had jumped on to her lap. 'And what were you doing up at four o'clock in the morning?'

'Really, Stella,' Pamela said irritably, 'anyone would think it was I coming out of his bedroom the way you're interrogating me.'

Stella did not reply and, made frantic by the silence, Pamela said: 'I wanted a drink of water. I got up, and there was a noise, so I looked in the hallway and there she was sneaking off.'

'You'd make a terrible witness, Pamela,' Stella said. 'Your geography's all over the place. But I believe you. Philip's having an affair with the *locataire*. What do you expect me to do about it?'

'Well – stop it of course.'

'I've never managed to do that in the past. Why should I be successful now?'

'Don't you care?'

'Not a great deal. As long as he doesn't make a fool of himself yet again.'

The flush of purple reappeared.

'What do you mean, *yet again*?'

'Just that,' Stella said casually. 'But I reckon he'll control that situation without too much trouble.' She looked away from where Pamela stood in front of her and said: 'Ah, look – two nice people coming to join us,' and the inflection on the word 'nice' was positive enough to send Pamela Whitton flouncing back into the house without greeting Peter and Anne as she passed them.

'What's the matter with her?' Peter said as he bent to kiss his mother's cheek.

'I've no idea.' Stella smiled at them both. 'You're well met, you two.'

'I had to take something back of Anne's,' he said, 'so I brought her with me.'

Stella waved them into garden chairs.

'Settle down,' she said. 'Claudine's arranging for more chairs to be brought out. I've a feeling we'll have a full house this morning.'

'Oh yeah? Why?' Peter asked.

'There's a lot of fish about to be fried,' Stella said, nodding her head heavily. 'You'll see.'

'Do you think Fouezanne will come?' Anne asked.

'Certainly. And with Tomas, because Tomas won't know what to do with him.'

'Mother, you're a witch,' Peter said. 'They're coming now.'

Tomas and Achmid were indeed crossing the lawn, walking not quite side by side. The Arab looked ill at ease and out of place in the open air. His dark glasses were heavy on his nose, a straw trilby on his head, his mouth a hard line under the heavy moustache. He picked his path across the damp grass in a pernickety way, a man trying to keep white suede shoes dry and unsullied.

'Good morning, madame,' he said and bent to take Stella's hand and kiss it.

'Morning, Stella,' Tomas said. 'How are you?'

'Better,' Stella said. 'This cooler weather suits me. You've probably noticed I'm asthmatic, Monsieur Fouezanne. But some rain followed by a small breeze makes all the difference to me. My lungs and my wits are very clear this morning.'

'I would have thought, madame,' he said, 'that your wits were always very clear.'

'As your own are, eh? Well, sit down by me here.'

Achmid gave her a suspicious look and settled himself cautiously into the garden chair. Without a word of thanks he took the cup of coffee that Claudine offered.

'Will your husband join us?' he asked casually.

'He doesn't usually, but I think he will this morning.'

Achmid nodded and sipped his coffee thoughtfully, with the air of a man prepared to wait.

He had a long wait; but then so did everyone else. Marion drifted in some ten minutes after Tomas and Achmid, and settled herself on a huge cushion on the grass, not far from Tomas's feet. They were speaking in undertones, while Peter and Anne had split slightly from the main group and were standing together looking out at the view. Françoise and Raoul appeared near to midday and sprawled on the grass, careless of the damp.

There was an expectant atmosphere in the garden. Everyone spoke in quieter voices than necessary, and Stella, with Achmid at her side, was silent and watchful, waiting for something to happen. Her mood communicated itself to the group; when Philip appeared through the terrace doors they were all silent as, smiling broadly, he made his way over the lawn to the big oak tree.

'Good morning,' he said, beaming benevolently on his family and their guests. He was neatly dressed in expensive slacks and a shirt, his peasant image discarded, which was unusual in itself. He looked what he was – a rich and aristocratic landowner. He sniffed the crisp air appreciatively, looked at the expectant faces turned to him and felt a surge of power. He was about to conduct an orchestra in a symphony of his own composition. He was going to enjoy himself.

'What a splendid morning,' he said as he settled in a chair and took a cup of coffee from his wife's hand.

'And what a surprise to see you here,' Stella said, her tone faintly malicious.

Her malice could not irritate him this morning. Ignoring the remark, he turned to beam at his grandchildren.

'Well, Françoise,' he said, 'I have done as you wish. I have rung McTaggart this morning and instructed him to have *Les Hirondelles* ready for sea tomorrow. Your cruise is agreed. But –' he smiled around the group '– I have arranged for all of you to go, as it would be stupid to send the yacht out half-empty. Marion, Peter, Tomas – and you are invited too, my dear,' he said, nodding at Anne. 'McTaggart advises Tangier. He says a trip there and back would take just over a fortnight, and you will be able to take in the coast of Spain *en route*. It's time you youngsters saw a bit more of the world.'

There was a silence when he stopped speaking. Philip, whose squirrel eyes had been darting from face to face, noted a little curl of something that looked like satisfaction around the corners of Achmid Fouezanne's hard mouth. Peter looked glum, and Tomas and Marion had exchanged a fleeting look which confirmed the suspicions that Philip had felt for some time. But they would go. All of them would go. His children knew the side their bread was buttered on and rarely thwarted him when it came to the crunch.

'You don't expect me to go?' Stella asked drily. 'Though I realize it would be convenient . . .'

His wife's eyes were like green glaciers, and she stared at

him as unblinkingly as her cat. She knows, he thought. How? It had to be something to do with Pamela Whitton. But he did not care that she knew. The excitement and pleasure – the actual rejuvenation – that Martine offered was not to be lost at any price. This morning he felt twenty again. Stella had put up with his infidelities in the past. She would have to put up with them again.

'Convenient?' he said. 'It's never convenient to have you away, my dear. After all, I am staying here on the estate with you. This is a cruise for the young. Not for us old fogies.'

'I don't think I'll be able to come,' Tomas said slowly, his eyes on Marion. 'Margaret hates the sea. She'll never agree, and I can hardly leave her here alone.'

'Persuade her, persuade her,' Philip said jovially. 'After all, there's no point in going unless you're all aboard.'

'Oh, please, Papa,' Françoise said, a note of alarm in her voice. 'Do come. Raoul and I have so been looking forward to going. Surely Mama will agree? We see so little of her.'

The last sentence had been on a plaintive note. Philip saw how Tomas looked at his daughter with obvious surprise and he wondered exactly what were his cunning little grand-daughter's reasons for desiring this cruise so strongly. Not that it mattered much. Her unknown need and his coincided very nicely.

He knew Stella would never leave the estate, nor Elisabeth, nor Pamela Whitton. But none of these three women were any great threat. None liked the outdoors. Elisabeth never left her own home. Stella could barely move herself to the lawn without assistance, and Pamela Whitton rarely tottered beyond the courtyard on her arthritic feet. With the old confined to quarters and all the young gone he could indulge in his own youthful fantasies. He would lie with the girl under the olives, in the back of the Rolls, at the pool. He liked exotic surroundings when he took a woman. He wanted the coast to be clear.

'Well, I don't know,' Tomas was saying doubtfully, his glance sliding back to Marion again.

'Where is Mama?' Raoul said. The boy was sitting with his

back to the tree, his thin face watchful, his eyes on his father.

'I think she went to the coast,' Tomas said. 'She was up very early.'

'Well, we shall persuade her when she comes back,' Françoise said theatrically. 'Somehow we will persuade her.'

Tomas still hesitated, and Philip felt a surge of sympathy for him. That frosty bitch of a wife on board would curb Tomas's style with Marion. And Philip still remembered with only the faintest trace of guilt the charming eagerness of his daughter, and reflected briefly how right he had been to see her potential while she was still young and thus guide her into an awareness of her own sexuality. Some other man might have spoilt all that promise. No, there was nothing to be guilty about; only regret that he would never touch Marion in that way again.

'I have a problem too,' Peter was saying. 'Evelyn isn't expected for another week, and I must be here when she comes.'

Philip noticed how his son's eyes flickered towards Anne. It seemed there was something there. Peter dallying with Olivia's niece? How charming to keep it in the family.

'Simple,' he told his son. 'Meet Evelyn in Tangier. It will be very romantic.'

Peter looked thoughtful. The girl Anne was watching him, her face quiet but with some small flicker of anxiety in the eyes. His son turned to her and asked abruptly: 'Will you go?'

She nodded slowly.

'I would like to,' she said, and Marion gave a little squeal of pleasure. 'That's a help,' she said.

Peter seemed to have made up his mind. 'I'll ring Evelyn and see,' he said.

Philip regarded them all, slowly shaking his head from side to side.

'There I was, thinking to give you all a treat, and none of you seem at all pleased.'

He set his features into mock-sad lines, and Marion jumped to her feet to kiss him. 'Oh, we are, Papa, we are,' she said. 'But it is rather short notice.'

'The best happenings are always spontaneous,' he told them. 'Now it is settled. You will all go.'

There was a reluctant murmur of assent, and feeling extremely pleased with himself Philip beamed at his family. They were not difficult to handle; even as adults they never forgot that he was head of the household and what he wanted was not to be disregarded.

'I have told McTaggart to provision the yacht today,' he said. 'I suggest you all leave tomorrow, after lunch.'

'It really is too short notice, Papa,' Peter was saying, his voice firm. 'I think that if everything can be arranged we should leave on Monday afternoon. You seem to forget Tomas has a weekend guest. We need time to get things organized. Monday would be more sensible.'

'Of course it would be more sensible,' Stella said. She had been lying back in her chair, relaxed, stroking the white cat on her lap. 'You must curb your impatience to –' she hesitated fractionally '– give the children this treat.'

'It would be better, Papa,' Marion wheedled. 'Why don't we all leave after lunch, Monday? You can come and see us off.'

'I would have come to see you off *tomorrow*,' he said and sighed, knowing nothing would drag him from Les Hirondelles. 'But Monday is not possible. And you, monsieur,' he said, turning to Achmid, 'must excuse my bad manners. I was not aware that you were staying for the weekend.' He turned to Tomas. 'Really, Tomas, you should have told me, and yes – there is something else. You should also have told me of Monsieur Fouezanne's interest in Les Hirondelles.'

The group turned into a tableau; so silent that Suki's purr as her mistress's hand still stroked sounded as a loud throbbing in the morning air.

Tomas had gone very pale; Peter stiffened and waited, wary. Achmid's mouth pursed under his moustache, but he said nothing.

'Monsieur Fouezanne's interest ...' Tomas echoed. 'But Father ...'

The orchestra was responding well, Philip thought. The big

drum was about to play and crash into the finale.

'I understand, Monsieur Fouezanne, that you wish to purchase Les Hirondelles. For twenty million francs, it is not?' He laughed lightly. 'I am flattered that you should think my home worth so much, but unfortunately for your ambitions it means considerably more to me than twenty million francs. It is also unfortunate that you should have decided to use my son as your emissary, for had you come to me direct I could have told you that Les Hirondelles is not for sale. And you would have saved yourself considerable money and effort.'

Achmid remained in his chair, his dark glasses pointing at Philip. Only the unnatural stillness of his body showed the tension. He was, Philip decided, holding himself in very close check.

Achmid chose to ignore the reference to Tomas. He said: 'Worth considerably more than twenty million francs, monsieur? What price do you ask?'

Philip, still smiling, shook his head slowly from side to side and then he nodded just once, a nod that said Achmid had responded exactly as he, Philip, would have predicted.

'I did not say *worth* more than twenty million francs, monsieur. I said that Les Hirondelles *means* more than twenty million francs to me. In other words, the estate is not for sale and never will be in the lifetime of myself and my wife.'

'Father—' Tomas's voice was too loud. 'Must we discuss this now?'

Philip turned to face his son. 'But there is nothing to discuss,' he said gently. 'The estate is not for sale. That is the end of it.'

'But, Father—'

Philip held up his left hand, the palm facing Tomas. 'There is no more to say,' he said again, and looked at his wrist-watch. 'So late! I had not realized ... forgive me, Monsieur Fouezanne ... an engagement in Nice with my lawyers ...' He moved to put the untouched cup of coffee on the table in front of his wife and smiled at the faces surrounding him. Tomas was white with shock, Peter relaxed, his wife inscrutable, Marion anxious, the English girl frankly curious, and his two grandchildren somehow triumphant. The only face that showed no emotion at all was that of Achmid Fouezanne, but his body language – tense shoulders, hands tight-knuckled – gave away his anger.

'We shall meet at dinner,' Philip said blandly. 'I must go to Nice and then finish the arrangements for your cruise, my children. Monday afternoon it shall be. *À bientôt.*'

He ambled back to the terrace and through the glass doors into the morning-room of his home, congratulating himself on the way he had handled two difficult situations. Oh, he thought, oh to be a bird in the oak tree and hear what was happening now.

In fact little was happening other than an embarrassed silence that lasted far too long. Tomas spoke first, saying in a strangled voice that he would go and speak to his father.

'You will be wasting your time, Tomas,' Stella had said quietly, her voice not unsympathetic, but he had given his stepmother a haunted look and hurried off in the same direction Philip had taken.

'I am sorry for your disappointment, monsieur,' Stella said to Achmid. 'I'm afraid that my stepson may have unintentionally misled you. There is no possibility that Les Hirondelles will be sold.'

Achmid had not spoken but risen to his feet, smoothing the legs of his white trousers as if he had been wearing a robe. Then, still in control, he had looked around, then stood hesitant, the light breeze tugging at the brim of his trilby.

'Madame,' he said slowly. 'I would recommend to you an expression that I learned at my English public school. A very expressive race, the English.'

He paused, and Stella said politely: 'Yes?'

'The English say that there are more ways than one of killing the cat,' he said, and there was just the faintest stress on the word 'killing'.

Stella's hands tightened on Suki's white fur, but she said calmly: 'Yes, we Americans use that expression also.' She turned her head away from him. 'Françoise – why don't you show Monsieur Fouezanne back to your father's house. I'm sure he would like some time to himself before lunch.'

190

'Yes, Grandmother,' Françoise said, raising herself from the grass and presenting herself to Achmid, head bent meekly, very much the dutiful granddaughter. She turned, he moved to her side, and together they walked through the garden past the side of the house and to the courtyard.

Once out of sight of the others he had said abruptly: 'There is no need to come any further. I know the way. In the morning I shall leave here. There is no point in staying on. Not at this time. However, I shall expect to see you tomorrow on the yacht. You will be there with McTaggart at three thirty precisely, I will arrive at three forty and give you the final instructions. Make sure no one else is there.' His voice was cold. 'Is that understood?'

'What about the crew?' she said.

'They won't matter. But no one else.'

'I understand,' she said.

He nodded, and the thin mouth curled upwards.

'I congratulate you,' he said. 'But then I have always had more faith in your ability to manipulate situations than I had in your father. You can tell him that while he is enjoying the sea air he would be wise to consider how the original objective can be achieved, and to consider also the matter of a million francs. You should perhaps warn him and your family that I am not a good person to cross.'

'I'll tell them,' Françoise said and shivered even though the sun was warm on her back.

'I think I would like another cup of coffee.' Stella was sitting upright in her chair, leaning just slightly forward in the way that Anne had come to know meant an asthma attack was near.

Marion hurried to pour from the big earthenware pot, and Anne asked quietly if Stella would like her to fetch Claudine.

'No, it's not necessary.' She smiled. 'I'm sorry, Anne,' she said, 'but you always seem to get embroiled in our family dramas. We're not usually as theatrical as all this. Normally nothing much ever happens.' She sighed. 'I don't think we've heard the last of the gentleman, do you?'

'I'm afraid not,' Anne said.

'What worried me,' Peter said slowly, 'was that he never mentioned the money that Tomas owes him. Now that could be because he's a gentleman. But somehow I don't think he is.'

'It leaves him with another hold over Tomas, that's why,' Marion said, her voice higher than usual.

Anne tried to think of something comforting to say but could think of nothing helpful. The morning sun was high and hot, but a cool breeze stirred the grass and the dusty green oak leaves. The view was spectacular, and yet Achmid Fouezanne had left behind him a very definite sense of menace.

She shivered a little and felt herself move closer to Peter, who put his arm around her shoulders and then led her to Marion where he did the same thing. The three of them stood linked, looking down at Stella.

'Don't worry, Mother,' Peter said. 'You know and we all know that there is really nothing to worry about. The worst he can do is to sue Tomas for the money, and between us we might be able to sort that out if Father would come around a little.'

Stella sighed; her hands were still protectively around Suki. 'Of course you're absolutely right,' she said. 'It's just imagination giving us the jitters. Come along and help me back to my room.'

'I'll do it,' Marion said quickly. 'You look after Anne, Peter.'

Marion was matchmaking, Anne thought with gratitude, and she was pleased to note that Peter seemed to have no objections to being left alone with her again.

'I'm sorry about changing the time of our date,' he said when they were alone. 'Is it OK? You didn't mind Sunday instead of tonight? It gave everyone breathing space.'

Anne had minded when he had made the announcement. It was longer to wait to be with him, but now she said: 'Not at all. It was wise. No one could have been ready to leave so quickly.'

'Umm.' Peter brooded at the view. 'I wonder why Papa wants us all out of the way so suddenly. It must be a new mistress – but who? He said quite definitely that he was staying here.'

'The *locataire*?' Anne suggested.

'Impossible! Have you seen her? Father's always gone for elegant, intelligent women. Even Pamela Whitton was good-looking ten years ago.'

Anne was not so sure. There was something furtive about the *locataire*. An air of decadence in spite of the thin body and colourless hair. There was something about the way she moved and something in the eyes ... but she decided to say no more.

'I'm going to take you to the Colombe d'Or, because as an artist the place will fascinate you,' he was saying. 'It has the most incredible collection of paintings which the old proprietor had given to him back in the days when he used to feed starving artists. Matisse, Picasso, Léger – the restaurant is like an art gallery. You'll enjoy it. And St Paul de Vence is the most chic of the hill villages.'

'Is the food good?' Anne asked mischievously.

He looked at her and laughed: 'Excellent,' he said. 'There are better restaurants for cuisine, and if you are a gourmet I shall take you to those on another occasion.'

'I shall hold you to it,' she said.

'Done. Now, tomorrow: I think we should have coffee with Mama as she is going to be deprived of all our company for two weeks. But we must be at the restaurant by one at the latest. You know how the French are when it comes to Sunday lunch. American brunch seems more relaxing, but still ... It's a long drive, so I suggest we join Mother sharp at eleven o'clock. OK?'

'OK,' Anne said.

He left her at her door and hesitated for a second, then gave her the traditional kiss on each cheek; she gave him no encouragement to do more.

'Have a good day,' he said.

'You too,' she said, and as she shut the door behind him she said out loud: 'But tomorrow will be better.'

*

Raoul stayed sitting with his back to the oak tree, listening and saying nothing, so that the others were unaware of his presence. No one ever took much notice of him. He was quite the least forceful member of the household – regarded as Françoise's shadow with little personality of his own.

It was the first time that Raoul had been at close quarters with the Arab, and the man had made the hairs on the back of his neck tingle. The concealed and yet somehow obvious anger was so potentially dangerous that Raoul was frightened. He felt sure that the Arab was quite capable of anything. And he and Françoise were totally committed to this mad escapade, to get the hash.

Raoul's bravery wilted when Françoise was not there to boost it. But there was something more. Secretly the boy hero-worshipped his father for his charm, good looks and ease of manner. And he grieved that Tomas took so little notice of his children, seeming almost not to like them very much. For many years it had been Raoul's fantasy that he and his father would be friends, and that maybe he could do something so brave and spectacular that his father would be proud of his only son.

Now he felt strongly that his father was in danger and that he must do something. Maybe this was the opportunity to make himself regarded. He was still brooding, his back to the tree, when he saw Tomas come back through the doors of the house and on to the terrace; on seeing that the coffee party had broken up, his father stood hesitant.

Suddenly Raoul made a decision. He leapt to his feet and ran across the lawn.

'Papa, Papa,' he was calling. 'I must talk to you.'

Tomas turned to face him and said impatiently: 'What is it, Raoul?' His face was grey and he seemed to have aged in the past hour. Raoul felt his heart burst.

'Papa – I must tell you. I know why that man wants to buy Les Hirondelles.'

It was out, and Raoul stood appalled at what he had begun, wondering what Françoise would say. She would be angry, of that he was certain.

His father looked at him sharply then back at the house, and taking the boy's arm led him out on to the lawn.

'Now what do you mean?' he said. 'Explain.'

Raoul realized his impulsiveness had put him in a difficult situation. How could he tell how he had come by this knowledge? But it was too late to prevaricate now.

'Les Hirondelles is all bauxite,' he blurted out. 'Worth millions and millions of francs. He's trying to cheat you, Papa.'

His father was as dangerously still as the Arab had been.

'How do you know this?' he asked softly.

Raoul stared at him dumbly. No lie would come to mind, and how could he explain the circumstances under which Françoise had seen the papers? He shifted from one foot to the other, hung his head and said: 'Please don't ask me, Papa, because I can't tell you. It's not my secret. But I wanted you to know, and if you tell Grandfather ...'

'No.' The interruption came like a small explosion. 'No.' Tomas turned abruptly and stood staring out over the mountains. 'All right, I won't ask you questions, and you won't speak of this to anyone again. Not anyone at all. Even Françoise. You could be in great danger and—'

'But Papa.' Raoul's voice was anguished. 'I told you because I thought you might be in danger.'

'No.' Tomas tried to smile. 'I'm not in danger, and neither are you. Not unless you speak of this. Forget all about it.'

'I'll try,' Raoul said doubtfully. 'But it does explain all sorts of things, doesn't it?'

Tomas seemed to be trying to pull himself together.

'If you're right,' he said, 'it does. Perhaps we should get a team of geologists in once this is all over. But for now – forget it. Don't even tell Françoise you've told me. Promise?'

'I promise,' Raoul said.

'Good lad.' His father leaned and kissed him on both cheeks. 'And thank you for telling me, my son. You have done me a great service.'

That had made it all worth while; full of pride, and relieved he had had to promise not to tell Françoise what he had done, Raoul watched his father hurry away. It was not until later that he wondered at Tomas's lack of curiosity and, even more extraordinary, his lack of surprise.

If it hadn't been impossible under the circumstances, he would have sworn that his father already knew.

Chapter Fourteen

The roar of the motorcycles arriving up the mountain and growing in volume until they silenced in the parking lot had disturbed Elisabeth from her sleep. Wide awake, an hour and a half earlier than necessary, she lay in her wide bed fuming. It had to be that common little *locataire*. No one else at Les Hirondelles would know anyone who rode or owned a motorbike. The noise had been excruciating, at an hour when no one but agricultural labourers would normally be up. And the labourers employed by the de Courtenays had more sense than to make such a din on the estate.

Awake, she grimly stayed in bed until her usual time and then rang for her maid to run her bath and lay out her clothes, telling the girl she would breakfast in her chamber. Elisabeth was angry and resentful that her routine had been upset, and by the time she had bathed, dressed and eaten she decided that she would most definitely complain. There was no point in approaching her father – with his peasant habits he had probably already been up when the motorbikes arrived and therefore would not have been disturbed.

She would make her own protests and go in person to do so. She looked out of the window at the morning. It seemed not as warm as it might have been, and the leaves on the lemon trees in her own area of garden were trembling, showing that there must be some slight and possibly harmful breeze. The fact that the weather was inclement and she would have to brave it annoyed her even more. Resolute with irritation she took her warmest shawl from the collection in the big dark oak chest in her bedroom and wrapped it around her shoulders before setting out from her own front door, across the court-yard and down the hundred or so yards to where the guest house stood.

The front door was firmly shut and locked, a fact that annoyed her all the more because this house had always been common ground for the entire de Courtenay family, and used only by their friends and relatives.

She rapped on the heavy dark wood of the door, and nothing happened. She rapped again, harder, hurting her hand; she was sucking the skin on her knuckles in a way that she would never have done with anyone observing when the door flew open, and a thin boy with black hair, elongated eyes and a full mouth was standing grinning at her.

She snatched her hand from her mouth and thrust it protectively under the shawl, opened her mouth to demand to see the girl who was the *locataire*, and then stopped short.

The inquiring face of the boy brought back a flood of memories. The Asiatic cast of the eyes, the dark skin and the smoothed-back black hair were echoes of Hassan lost so long ago. The strange boy tipped his head sideways questioningly and said: 'Can I help you?' Elisabeth remembered how Hassan used to bend his head in just the same manner when he could not quite understand something she was trying to explain to him.

She stared. She could not speak. Her throat seemed to have closed, and if years of self-discipline had not dried up her tear ducts long ago she knew her eyes would have been wet. Instead they just ached, and somehow she managed to pull herself together sufficiently to say stiffly: 'Where is madame?'

'You are—?' he was asking politely, and it seemed to Elisa-beth that even the accent was that of Hassan.

'I am Elisabeth de Courtenay,' she was able to say, knowing that it was her prerogative to demand to know his identity, 'and I wish to speak to the madame who is *locataire* here.'

'Ah,' he said, 'my wife, certainly.' And then turning behind

197

him he shouted: 'Martine, there is someone to see you.'

'She won't be a moment, madame,' he said with a smile that pierced Elisabeth's heart. 'Please come in.'

'There is no need,' she said. 'Would you please tell your wife that she should ask her guests not to arrive at such an early hour in future, and that if they must, would she please ensure that they do not disturb the repose of those of us who live on this estate.'

She found herself unable to say another word, and snatching the shawl about her shoulders she turned and walked back to her own home, trying to walk slowly and desperately holding on to her dignity.

Jacques shut the door, his face thoughtful, as Martine came down the stairs from her bedroom, her hair in curlers, lipstick in one hand, cigarettes in the other. 'Who the hell was that?' she asked.

'That's just what I was going to ask you,' Jacques said. 'Middle-aged woman. Greying hair, sharp features, wrapped in a shawl as if it was a freezing day.'

'Sounds like his eldest daughter,' Martine said. 'The one who lives in the first of the houses on this side. What did she want?'

'She said I was to tell you that your guests weren't to make such a racket when they arrived, or words to that effect,' Jacques said, 'and then she bolted. She was embarrassed – or something else.'

'Her embarrassed!' Martine said. 'You've got to be joking. She's the haughtiest old cow I've ever come across. She stares at me from her front window and manages to look at me as if I didn't exist.'

'Well,' Jacques said thoughtfully, 'she was very aware that I existed. Very aware indeed.' His long eyes sparkled as he turned to grin at his sister. 'I think I've got a chance there. Definitely a chance.'

'Well,' Martine said, 'rather you than me.'

He laughed out loud.

'Oh, come on little sister,' he said. 'We all have our crosses to bear. Who knows what it may be worth?'

His sister stared at him suspiciously.

'Listen,' she said. 'I don't give a damn what you do – but Christ help you if you queer my pitch!'

At high noon the face of the day had changed. The sun was a golden ball high in the sky, and the reflection from the sea danced in prisms of light in the tall grass by Marie's head. Behind were fir trees, and all around the fresh smell of pine. There was quiet – only the soft lapping of the sea on soft white sand and beside her the even breathing of Margaret, who slept.

Marie leaned up on one elbow to look at the slumbering woman. The blonde hair was just slightly disarranged, and the pale skin faintly tinged with pink at the cheeks. The mouth with its defiant streak of lipstick had fallen open just very slightly to show very white even teeth. Marie found herself fleetingly wishing that someone had cared for her teeth when she was young.

She still wasn't sure why Margaret had come to the cove with her without question. Marie had driven the big car to the clifftop well outside of St Tropez and parked it just off the road in a safe place among the trees; she had led the older woman down the narrow, dipping, pine-fringed path to the tiny stretch of sunny beach which she had discovered a long time ago when there had been someone a little special who lived on this part of the coast. The path was not easy but Margaret had followed her with reasonable confidence, putting out a hand for support at the steeper parts but giving no signs of whether she was in agreement with Marie's decision to come here – a decision Marie had made with hopes she did not expect to be fulfilled.

When they reached the cove, red cliffs enveloping them, Margaret had looked around, nodded and said: 'Now, you really must take off all that leather. You must be very hot.'

Marie was very hot. Mute, she had unzipped the heavy one-piece suit, letting it drop on to the sand. Underneath she wore thin white shorts and a teeshirt.

'And the rest,' Margaret had said. 'Or isn't this the nude beach?'

'It's not the nude beach,' Marie had told her. 'But no one much comes here. Particularly this early in the season.'

'Well then,' Margaret had said lightly, and begun to un-button the top of her white pyjama suit. Still uncertain, Marie had turned her back and taken off her shorts before pulling the long teeshirt over her head. She wore no bra and no pants on her lean angular body but suddenly shy and uncertain she dropped on the sand and lay face upwards, careful not to look at what Margaret was doing. There was a rustle of silk and a light laugh, and the older woman's drawling, cultured voice said: 'I haven't done this for years.'

Quickly Marie turned her head. The naked body beside her was very white, with a narrow waist and full breasts that had slightly dropped. Their faint slackness and the darkened nipples gave Marie a pang of deep sadness for all women, for their loss of youth, for the damage of childbearing and for their basic loneliness. She quickly turned her head back to stare into the blue of the sky above, watching one small cottonwool cloud that sailed alone away from the sun, waiting to see what would happen next.

They had hardly spoken on the drive to the coast. Marie had been intent on conquering the mountain road and then ne-gotiating the curves and ups and downs of the *autoroute* until they had reached Le Luc. She had streaked her way to the coast and along the cliff road to where she remembered this most private of little beaches was hidden.

She had been very aware of the woman beside her and of the faint, light scent of roses that seemed to come from her, and she had felt hot, heavy and ugly in the leather clothing but at the same time strong enough to safely drive someone so delicate. She had been too shy to make much conversation, conscious of her provincial accent and plain face, leaving the other woman to make the moves. After all – she was playing chauffeur.

And all the time she was asking herself why Margaret de Courtenay had chosen to ask her to come to St Tropez.

Now with the faintly blue-veined eyelids closed over the blue eyes, Marie felt she could look properly at the body beside her, and her own grey eyes searched from the manicured toe-nails to the soft blonde hair. The whole effect was very feminine. The breasts full, the stomach curving gently upwards, and the waist narrowing in. The legs were long, smooth and hairless, very white, as was all the skin. The only areas of colour were the dark red of nipples, the bright red of the mouth and the soft pink of the cheeks.

Unable to stop herself, Marie put out a tentative finger and gently traced the perfect circle of red on the full soft breast nearest to her, and then, bringing her thumb to the task, took the point of the nipple between her fingers and rubbed.

The blue eyes flew open, and hastily Marie withdrew her hand.

'I'm sorry,' she stammered.

The blue eyes regarded her steadily. 'It was nice – don't stop.'

Still she hesitated, and then Margaret de Courtenay smiled and said: 'Come here.' The very white hairless arms were lifting, and she had turned just enough to be able to put her hands on Marie's waist and pull her down. As the girl came nearer, the hands slid higher until they were on her shoulders and then her neck, and Marie found her face being pulled towards the slightly opened brightness of the older woman's mouth.

It was a chaste kiss at first. Still uncertain, Marie let her mouth go soft and nuzzled at the lips below hers, but then she felt the pointed tip of Margaret's tongue stroking at the inside of her mouth and then darting deeper below and above her tongue. With a little groan, Marie stretched herself out and wrapped her arms around the other woman, pulling her close as they both lay on their sides in the soft sand.

First she only kissed Margaret, busy little kisses over her face and neck interspersed with deeper searchings into the open, waiting mouth. She held her very close, rubbing her body against the other softer, more rounded body, breast to breast, nipple to nipple. Margaret's legs were first twining around hers and one was edging its way very insistently, knee pressing between knees, until there was a thigh rubbing between her legs, up and down, opening the lips and moving until Marie could not control her breath with the pleasure of it.

But she was too conscious that she wanted to please this woman who had come so unexpectedly into her life to let herself be seduced into enjoying what was happening. She twisted her body so that she too could rub against Margaret's moist open lips and soft hairs, and then, pulling herself away, gently opened the white legs wide and with fingers and tongue parted the silky blonde hair, rubbed, kissed and stroked, crooning endearments until the arching of Margaret's body and the soft gasps told her she had achieved her objective to please.

Throughout it all, Margaret had not spoken. As Marie pulled away, she lay back on the sand, her blonde hair tangled behind her head, a down of sweat on her upper lip, breathing fast, her eyes closed against the sun.

'Are you all right?' Marie asked.

The blue eyes opened, and it seemed to Marie that the faint lines around Margaret's eyes had been erased and she suddenly looked younger.

'Very all right,' Margaret said huskily. 'But you are not.'

What happened next left Marie aware that she had never really known lovemaking before and she would never smell the fresh scent of pine again without remembering. Margaret de Courtenay first kissed her, and as she kissed her hands were running up and down the skin of Marie's back, cupping her buttocks, squeezing. Then, holding her own breasts so that the nipples stood free, she rubbed herself against Marie's nipples while her hips rotated, mound of Venus against mound of Venus, and mouth licking eyelids, blowing softly into ears, biting gently at the neck.

It was total pleasure. Almost too much pleasure. Marie wanted to respond, but could only lie, revelling in every touch, unaware of the grittiness of the sand, unaware of anything except the warmth of the sun on the areas of her body Margaret had left uncovered, and the feel of soft hands, lightly scratching fingernails, wet mouth and tongue and constant rubbing of flesh against flesh. The ending was a surging of what she could only have described as ecstasy, though the word would have been an embarrassment to use.

Somehow Margaret had manoeuvred her body so that as Marie lay on her back, drunkenly accepting the pleasure she was given, Margaret was on her side, one leg folded under the girl's back, the other folded on her stomach so that the dark pubic hair mingled with pale blonde, and the deep red of hidden flesh rubbed against the youthful rose of Marie.

This time they both came-together, Margaret's free hand plucking at Marie's breasts, her husky voice saying: 'I love your body. I love your tiny breasts, your little nipples, your soft cunt ...' as Marie heard herself saying: 'Oh, yes – oh yes – oh yes.'

And then it was over, and they were both still and sleepy in the sunshine, Marie clutching the older woman's hand.

They must have both dozed, and then Margaret said: 'Was that good?'

'Oh yes. The best ever. I didn't know.'

Margaret was smiling.

'Well you are very young ...'

'I've had lovers,' Marie said defensively and then added, 'but not like you.'

'You will have more,' Margaret said, and her voice was sad.

'I can't imagine anyone being better.' Marie's body was still languorous, the sun heightening the impression of total sexual fulfilment.

'When you love someone it will be even better.'

There was a long silence; Marie rolled on her side, and leaned on one elbow, her other hand cupping one full breast to lift it to its lost youthful contour.

'I think I could love you,' she said, 'but you wouldn't want me to.'

'Why wouldn't I?'

'Well, we're different. You're rich and beautiful. I'm less than ordinary.'

'Why do you say that?' The older woman had closed her eyes against the sun again.

'Because I'm not educated – nothing. If you can imagine poor *pieds nois*, that's what we are. My family couldn't even make it in North Africa. And when we had to come home, we couldn't even make it here. My brother and sister live by their wits. I can't even do that. I sort of despise them for it, yet maybe I only despise them because I haven't any wits to live by. You see, I know I'm not very pretty but I've always dreamed of finding someone to love. Someone I can look after because I'm strong and I'm capable even if I'm not clever. Someone beautiful. Someone like you.' Her voice trailed away.

The blue eyes were open, and the head with tumbled blonde hair was turned to look up at Marie.

'You'd leave me in the end. Everyone does.'

'Why would I leave *you*?' Marie's voice was startled.

'Because I'm an arrogant bitch. Because I want too much. They all leave me.'

'Is that why you're so sad?'

'Does it show? Yes, I'm sad. My lover just left me. That's why I'm here. Would you believe she went back to her husband. She said she'd rather have him – a *man* – than put up with me.'

'How awful. She must be mad.' Marie leaned over and gently kissed the white forehead and then with her index finger smoothed the three faint runnels that lined it. She felt very confident now and sure that something important was happening to her.

'No, she was right. I do demand too much. I've always had my own way. Always. I've always been able to pay for what I want.'

'I'm not for sale,' Marie said. 'Not like the rest of my family. But I'll be your servant ...' She hesitated, wanting to explain herself. 'I've been lonely. I tried men but I hated it. And in our world so few are faithful. I want to be faithful to someone.'

'I understand,' Margaret said. 'I understand entirely.' She paused, then asked: 'When did you first know?'

Marie considered the question.

'I think I've always known. There was a little girl when I was five and we found how nice it was to touch each other. But then when I told one of the boyfriends I had when I was trying to explain why it wouldn't work with him he told me everyone does that. I never wanted to play with little boys. And I never fell in love with a boy.'

'You were lucky.' Margaret's voice was bitter. 'They never left me alone with anyone but my nanny and my governess. I didn't know the first thing about sex when I married. Tomas was very handsome and very charming, and I thought I loved him, but then when he put his great hairy hands on me and fucked me – it was disgusting. I hated it. I hated it for years. But I thought I had to put up with it. Then after Raoul was born I knew I couldn't stand him on me, pawing me, a minute longer. I'd had two children, I'd done my duty. I wanted to be free.'

'Did he mind?' Marie was stroking the blonde hair away from Margaret's face.

'I don't know. I never asked him. And then I found a woman. So much more gentle. So much more civilized. We know what we like. I knew how to please you. You knew how to please me. We weren't crude. We didn't hurt each other. It was lyrical.'

'Lyrical.' Marie tried the word softly. 'Yes, it was. That's just what it was.'

'Shall we do it again? Tonight. In a bed?'

Marie nodded.

'But where?'

'We'll stay here in St Tropez. We won't go back.' Margaret's voice had become authoritative. 'We'll stay at the most luxurious room that the Byblos can provide, and you'll make me forget about Tilly.'

'Was that her name?'

Margaret nodded. 'Marie will make me forget Tilly and Margaret will teach Marie how not to be lonely.'

'What will you tell them at Les Hirondelles?' Suddenly Marie was doubtful.

'I shall tell them I've decided to stay at St Tropez. That I have friends here.'

'I've left my motorbike back there,' Marie said slowly.

Margaret laughed her trilling little laugh.

'Darling, really – the motorbike! When you have a Merc. And you have me.'

'You're right,' Marie said humbly. She sighed. 'It won't last.' Her voice was sad. 'But maybe we'll be happy for a little while.'

'Of course we will,' Margaret said. 'Now put on your clothes and drive me back to St Tropez. I'll have to buy you some-thing decent to wear and maybe get your hair done. The Byblos is very smart.'

Marie hesitated. It was a moment of decision, and she knew it. To say no and keep her freedom or to say yes and lose her loneliness?

'Yes, Margaret,' she said.

Chapter Fifteen

What did one wear for lunch at a smart South of France res-taurant on a Sunday, Anne wondered, looking critically at the clothes in her wardrobe. Certainly not trousers or jeans, and somehow a long skirt didn't feel right either. A dress seemed to be the answer, but then there was the probem of her leg.

She hadn't been worrying overmuch about the leg for the past two weeks. The pain had lessened, and though she still limped as she always would getting about was easier.

Today she wanted to wear a short dress – one with a full swirling skirt in soft strawberry pink silk and with a decep-tively simple shirtwaister top; the bodice buttoned just a little lower than demureness demanded and clung to accentuate her

pointed nipples. It was another dress that Marion had persuaded her to buy, insisting she worried too much about her
leg.

'All you need is a pair of sun-tan coloured tights that aren't
too sheer, and no one will ever notice the scars,' Marion had
said. So dutifully Anne had bought six pairs of Dior sandal-
foot tights in the darkish shade that Marion recommended, but
as yet had never worn them.

Her leg was nowhere near as red, she thought peering at it,
and the skin seemed to be smoother – less flaky and blistered
looking than it had been at first. She could have almost had
nothing more wrong than a severe case of sunburn, and she
decided to wear both her new dress and her new tights.

'Nothing ventured ...' she muttered to herself.

Marion had been right. The scar hardly showed at all once
her legs were covered with the shiny nylon, and she decided to
go the whole hog and wear brand-new slender-heeled pink
sandals, hoping that walking would be possible in them.

The girl who looked at her from the long gilt mirror once
she had finished dressing was almost a stranger – a girl whose
auburn hair had been highlighted by the sun, whose face was
smooth and rested, whose skin was honey-tanned, whose eyes
were bright with glistening white around violet pupils. She
looked at herself in surprise. This was a vastly different someone from the pain-wracked young woman who had arrived
only a month ago. And there was something else – a suppressed excitement, a kind of electricity. She felt as if someone had burnished her.

Maybe this is love, she thought, and laughed.

And maybe it is love, she thought again as she left her house
at least ten minutes too early for the meeting with Peter on
Stella's lawn. There was the thought that maybe he would be
early too, and she felt she could not wait another minute to
see him. The night before she had been restless. It had been
difficult to work because she had been so looking forward to
their evening out. Now she was glad it had been postponed. If
it had not been, what would she have had to look forward to
this morning?

There was no one under the big oak tree, though the chairs were set out. The table was also there, but Claudine had not arrived with the tablecloth or the coffee, and the big house behind seemed still asleep. She settled herself carefully in her usual place arranging her skirts with care and lay back, a heat of impatience somewhere in her stomach, trying to look as if she were merely enjoying the view.

And then she heard the noise. It was a strange, half-strangled, peculiarly muffled cry on a high wailing note. It came at brief intervals and seemed to be getting fainter. The sound had desperation in it and was so eerie that Anne felt as if the hairs on her arms and the back of her neck were rising.

Cautiously she got to her feet and cocked her head to listen. The sound was coming from above, from the tree. She stepped back to see better and then realized exactly what the noise was: Suki; Suki high among the leaves and swinging from her jewelled collar, hanging from a thin branch, slowly strangling, and from the look of her, with not much longer to go. Somehow the cat had managed to get her back legs on to a lower branch that was giving some support from the throttling collar – but not sufficient to save her.

Without stopping to think, Anne kicked off her shoes. The table was exactly underneath where the cat hung, and frantically she climbed on to it, stretching to reach the animal, but the height was not sufficient.

'Suki! Suki!' she was saying. 'Hold on! Oh, please don't die.'

Then she screamed at the top of her lungs, astonished that she could make so much noise: 'Peter! Peter!' She jumped from the table to the ground. Her leg gave way, flinging her on to the rough turf, but she scrambled back on her feet and screamed again: 'Peter! Peter!'

The cat was silent now, but the green Persian eyes still rolled frantically, and with one last shout for help Anne grimly began to try to climb the tree. If she could get to the first strong branch, she would make it. The pain from her leg was excruciating, and she could feel the wetness of blood running over her foot as she scraped her way up the trunk.

Then, just as she had almost been able to grasp out and reach the branch, hands grabbed her around the waist, pulled her down, dumped her unceremoniously on to the ground, and Peter was climbing the tree.

It only took a second and he was down again, holding the cat firmly and breathing into its open mouth. After a minute Suki began to recover enough to scratch and claw. She then let out a croaking outraged cry from her damaged throat, wrenched herself from Peter's hands and, tail stiff in the air, bounded across the lawn and into the house.

Anne had stayed where he had put her and to her annoyance she found she was crying.

'Oh Peter,' she said. 'I thought it was dead, and Stella – she loves her so. My leg – my leg wouldn't let me get there fast enough ...'

'It's all right now. Cats have nine lives.' He was kneeling beside her. 'More important, are *you* all right?'

He saw the blood on her leg and he whistled quietly between his teeth.

'Let's have a look at your leg,' he said. 'Does it hurt?'

Anne took a deep breath.

'I'm afraid it does,' she said.

He was gently moving the torn tights away from where the blood seemed to be escaping.

'You'll have to take these tights off,' he said. 'Or shall I get some scissors?'

'No,' she said. 'I'll take them off.'

He helped her to her feet, tactfully turning his head while she peeled off the torn and bloodied tights. She then settled back into the chair and closed her eyes tightly while he looked at her leg, holding her bare foot in his hand. She was not yet ready to face whatever damage she had inflicted on herself.

'It's not bad,' he said. 'You've just torn the skin in one place and it's bleeding like mad, but the graze is only a small one. It's just as well you were wearing those tights. They seem to have been some protection.'

He looked up and grinned at her.

'Come on, cheer up,' he said as she cautiously opened her

eyes. 'You'll be all right. But we'd better clean you up.'

Without saying any more he lifted her up from the chair and swung her into his arms and was heading towards the big house. Anne put her arm around his neck and let her head fall on his shoulder, thinking that whatever damage there was it was almost worth it.

'You'll get blood all over you,' she said.

'So what? You've already got it all over you.'

'Oh, no,' she said. 'My new dress!'

He laughed.

'Typical woman,' he said.

They met Stella, who was being helped by Claudine on her way out to the lawn, as they reached the terrace, and Stella, taking in the blood with one look and without asking any questions, said: 'Take her to my bathroom, Peter. Claudine – get bandages and disinfectant. Do we need a doctor?'

'I don't think so,' Peter said. 'But if Claudine can clean up the wound we'll decide then.'

In two minutes she was sitting on the bathroom chair, wincing, as Claudine on her knees, the stern grey bun belying gentle hands, dabbed disinfectant on the graze and bandaged her shin.

'It will be all right, madame,' Claudine said. 'It's only bleeding so badly because the skin is so thin. Let us see how it looks tomorrow, and if you're at all concerned you must go to the doctor. But I am certain it is not serious.' She got to her feet and began to wash her hands. 'Do you wish Peter to carry you out again?' she asked.

Anne very much wished Peter to carry her out again but she said she would walk, and moving with caution went through the house and back on to the terrace where she could see Stella, Peter and Marion waiting – plus Suki, who was in her usual place on Stella's lap looking no worse for her narrow escape.

'I hear from Peter that you have been very brave,' Stella said, as she reached the shade of the tree. 'You saved my Suki's life.'

'I didn't, I'm afraid,' Anne said. 'It was Peter. I'd never have climbed to her in time.'

'But you tried, and Peter says he heard you calling.'

'I must say you have a fine pair of lungs,' he said. 'I heard you from my own front room.'

She grimaced. 'I didn't realize that I could yell so loudly.'

'It was fortunate for Suki that you did,' Stella said. 'But what exactly happened?'

'I don't know,' Anne said. 'The lucky thing was that I got here early, because Suki was still able to make a noise. I tried to get her by climbing on the table, but that didn't work, and then I started yelling and tried to climb the tree. She was hanging by her collar but she'd slipped far enough along the branch to support herself a bit.'

Stella was nodding slowly as she spoke, her hands stroking the cat's smooth white fur.

'But how did she get there?' Stella asked. 'That is the question.'

'Climbed and caught her collar, I suppose,' Anne suggested.

'Suki has never bothered to climb a tree in her life,' Stella said, then added quietly: 'But – there are more ways of killing a cat . . .'

The group fell silent.

'Do you think, Mother, that he—' Marion broke off short, shaking her head.

'He left without saying goodbye a quarter of an hour ago,' Stella said. 'Claudine saw him leave. He could just have done it, on impulse and quickly. He's a tall man. Was the table right under where Suki was hanging, or did you pull it there, Anne?'

'It was there,' Anne said.

'Well, maybe he did and maybe he didn't. It seems a petty revenge, but we'll never know; Suki is safe, and that is all that matters.'

'He's a bad man,' Marion said positively. 'I'd put nothing past him.'

They had not heard Tomas approaching them across the lawn, but he caught the tail end of the conversation as he reached the group and he said: 'What wouldn't you put past who?' And taking in the bloodied clothes of Anne and Peter – 'What happened to you two?'

'Your bloody disreputable friends—' Peter started to say, glaring at his half-brother.

Tomas looked bewildered. 'What disreputable friends?'

'That sodding Arab—'

'Oh, hang on, Peter,' Marion was saying, her colour heightened. 'You can't blame Tomas.'

'Will somebody please explain what's going on here?' Tomas said angrily.

'Suki was caught up the oak tree, strangling by her collar,' Marion said. 'Anne and Peter got her down just in time.'

'And we think your friend hung her there,' Peter said.

'We don't know,' Stella said. She heaved her body upright in the chair, her breath whistling. 'And it's all history now.' She made a dismissive gesture with her left hand while the other lay lightly on the cat's head. The subject was closed. 'Your father wants to know if you've made your arrangements for the yacht tomorrow.'

Tomas looked as if he did not want to abandon the subject of the cat, but he said: 'Margaret's not coming.' His voice was flat. 'She rang last night and said she's staying with friends at St Tropez. She wants her luggage packed and Dupré to drive it to the Byblos.'

Anne noticed how Marion's head lifted sharply, her eyes brightened and how she waited and caught Tomas's eye before she too composed her expression.

'And Evelyn's meeting us in Tangier,' Peter said. 'She's getting her travel agent to book her into the El Minzeh. I'll pick her up from there. But I need to know from McTaggart exactly when we will get there. Evelyn doesn't want to be alone in the town more than one night.'

His voice was expressionless, and Anne felt her spirits drop. She had held on to the idea that Evelyn might reject the idea of Tangier. But would you, she asked herself, if he were at the other end?

'Just ring the yacht,' Stella said, and added: 'Ah, here's Claudine with coffee. What we all need.' Claudine was coming across the lawn with the laden tray. 'How about you, Anne? Don't feel you have to stay. Why don't you and Peter change

212

and get off for your lunch? Leave your clothes for Claudine to collect and clean and don't think any more about this.' She was making shooing motions with her hands, and as Claudine put down her burden Peter said: 'Well, if you don't mind. Time is getting on.'

He went to kiss his mother on both cheeks and with a last hostile look at his half-brother took Anne's arm and led her around the side of the house and into the courtyard.

'I don't know about coffee,' Anne said. 'I reckon I need a stiff drink.' She could have added: 'And for more reasons than one.' She was still shaking slightly, and her leg smarted, but the bleeding seemed to have stopped. The thought of Evelyn arriving in Tangier was more disturbing.

'Change your dress and pour yourself one,' Peter told her. 'I'm going to change too, and then I'll come across and get you. Are you OK to walk?'

'Perfectly all right now,' Anne said. She hesitated. 'Sorry to have cried as well as bleed all over you. It was frustration really – not being able to get at Suki. I was so afraid she'd die. Stella would have been heartbroken.'

'Well, all's well that ends well—' He paused. 'But what made you yell for me?'

He was looking down at her quizzically, and Anne felt her innards turn over.

'You just seemed the most dependable, I suppose,' she said. 'But I didn't stop to think. I just yelled.'

He looked pleased and patted her bottom. 'Go on,' he said. 'Off you go. I'll come and fetch you in ten minutes. Try to get your appetite back, eh?'

'I'll try,' she said, thinking that if anything would take her appetite away it wouldn't be the morning's drama, but the nearness of Peter de Courtenay.

As it happened, Anne's appetite was totally unimpaired by the time Peter had driven her over the mountains and into St Paul de Vence. If anything, she was hungry. They had just a quarter of an hour before the time of the table booking, and Peter said he would show her the village, making her take off her

213

shoes and walk in stockinged feet to cope with the abrupt steepness of the streets.

'I'm not having you falling again,' he said, 'and the alleys of this place are far too precipitous for those shoes.'

So, shoes in one hand, her other on his arm, Anne explored St Paul de Vence. The place was pretty, if somewhat artificial. The shops were for the rich, the houses beautified, and even the cobbles were arranged in patterns of different colours.

'Does anyone actually live behind all those elegant shutters and façades?' she asked Peter.

'I'll show you,' he said and, leading her back down to where the town windened out from under an arch, he took her into a big café beside a large *boules* court where ordinary men in blue *blousons* and trousers, dedicated to winning, played on the sandy pitch. Peter ordered Pernod, and they watched the game until he said: 'The restaurant is just across the road, and I think we should go now.'

'Right,' she said and downed the remainder of her drink.

They ate on a beautiful terrace with a view across a wide valley. The *maître d'* seemed to know Peter well and personally escorted Anne on a guided tour of the Colombe d'Or's art treasures. They drank champagne, followed by a great deal of rich red Burgundy; Anne ate from a bewildering assortment of *saucissons* served on a huge wooden tray, and followed it by chicken cooked with *écrevisse* and a *sauce Americaine*. Peter insisted she must have the speciality of the *masion* – a Grand Mariner soufflé. She found herself watching him as she swallowed the food; far too much of a sybarite not to enjoy it, but eating faster than normal, and wondering what would happen when they returned to Les Hirondelles.

They talked of the Arab as they ate.

'I know it's absurd,' Peter said, 'but I have a great sense of unease. I could murder Tomas. I think he's started something that we may not be able to control.'

'Oh, you'll control it,' Anne said blithely, spooning up the liqueur that the waiter had poured over her soufflé. 'Of course, you will.'

Peter laughed out loud.

214

'I think you're a little bit zig-zag,' he said.

Anne found herself regarding him solemnly, and it seemed that she needed to shut one eye just a fraction to get him quite into perspective.

'You may well be right,' she said. 'I had the most enormous gin while I was changing. Now I come to think of it, I had another one before you arrived. I change very quickly,' she said nodding her head. 'I am not,' she said severely, 'one of those women who mess about at the dressing table. So there I was with time to pour another drink. And I did. I must say that second gin settled all my wobbles. Because you see I was wobbling quite a bit. I thought I'd done my leg in again, and if you knew the trouble I've had with this bloody leg ... more trouble than you can possibly imagine. I don't want to go through all that again anyway. I really don't. It is,' she said carefully, lifting the remains of her Burgundy in a toasting gesture, 'a pain in the proverbial arse, and to hell with it, I say.'

He was still laughing at her.

'What happened to the cool, controlled English lady?' he asked.

She drew herself up in mock hauteur.

'Who said I was cool and controlled? You!' she said. 'That's who. You. You de Courtenays are all the same. None of you are interested in anyone but yourselves. You're all spoilt. And I have to tell you that I am not *really* cool and controlled. Not in the slightest. Oh dear me no. If you knew what was bubbling away underneath all this British phlegm ...'

'I caught a faint glimpse the other night,' he said, 'but you ran away.'

'Hah-hah,' she said triumphantly, 'I knew you'd bring that up. Of course I ran away. And I bet it's the first time it's happened to one of the aristocratic de Courtenays in years. But I'm me and nobody else. I have to admit that I fancy you rotten, but on the other hand I'm not there sitting on a plate. I'm not even sitting waiting to be served up if you'll pardon the mixed-up metaphors and oh dear me I think we ought to go home.'

She stopped and stared at him, something at the back of her head, where she was still in control, telling her that she must look positively ridiculous. But she didn't seem to be sufficiently in control to behave like her normal self.

'What a fantastic meal,' she said, unable to resist the urge to chatter on. 'I've eaten too much and I've most certainly drunk too much.' With some concentration, she counted her day's intake off on her fingers. 'Gin: two, very large. Pernod: one, not so large. Champagne: half a bottle. Burgundy: lost count. Grand Marnier: all over the pudding. Result: pissed.' She stopped and looked at him appealingly. 'Can we go home?'

The waiter had brought a glass of Strega on the house, served in a tall thin liqueur glass, and she had not touched it, but now she cupped her hands around it and with her speckled hazel eyes looking into his she ran her carefully manicured red-tipped fingers up and down the smoothness of the glass.

'I don't think I want any coffee,' she said, watching how his eyes were watching her stroking fingers. 'Do you?'

'No,' he said abruptly, and signalled for the waiter.

'Great!' she said.

Later she couldn't remember getting into his Lancia or the drive back to Les Hirondelles. She must have slept. But when he woke her in the parking area, her eyes opened with a snap, she had no hangover and she felt remarkably alert.

He was sitting in the driver's seat, his hands light on the wheel, smiling down at her.

'I think you had better have your coffee now,' he said. 'Will my place do?'

'Why not?' she said and made an experimental tasting of her mouth and found it wasn't as bad as it should have been.

She still felt light-headed as well as light-hearted as he finished parking the car and she followed him, two paces behind like a Moslem woman, in through the garden windows of his own home, next door to that of his father. She noted that the grounds were deserted, the coffee things cleared from under the big oak. Everyone was sleeping, she thought, it was siesta time, time for bed.

She hardly took in the living-room of his home except to

notice that it was full of big comfortable furniture and in particular an enormous sofa that must have been seven feet long and three feet wide. She settled herself primly in the centre of it, perched on the edge because her feet would have dangled if she'd sat back, folded her hands on her lap, and waited quietly while he vanished into the kitchen.

'Black or white?' he shouted through.

'Black,' she said.

'Sugar?'

'Never.'

She was wearing one of her long skirts, to hide the bandaging on her leg, topped by a plain silk shirt. Thoughtfully she unbuttoned one more button and kicked off her shoes. She noted her tights were very dirty from walking through St Paul barefoot, but what the hell!

He came back in with a tray with coffee-pot, cups and saucers and a small jug.

'Do you mind coffee in the mid-afternoon?' he asked. 'Wouldn't you rather have tea?'

She looked at him dreamily, deciding the die was cast.

'No,' she said, 'but how do you feel about love in the mid-afternoon?'

He stood quite still, as she rose to her feet and smiled at him. Then, very deliberately, he put down the tray on a large glass coffee table and advanced towards her.

'I've always liked love in the afternoon,' he said.

'And I've always wanted to try it,' she told him.

First he kissed her, and then his expert fingers undid the remaining buttons on her blouse, revealing bare breasts, and he slid down the zip at the side of her skirt so that it fell in a soft heap around her feet.

'Here we go,' she said and stepped out of it, and then held out her arms while he took off her blouse. He stood back and looked at her.

'Tights,' he said with a frown, 'I cannot cope with.'

'I'll do it,' she said cheerfully and slid them down over her hips, gaily kicking them off her toes and then lifting them with one foot and dumping them in a chair.

'There,' she said, naked except for the white bandage around her shin, and glad of the Dutch courage from the alcohol she had drunk. She knew that the semblance of tipsiness was allowing her to lose any inhibitions she might have, and she knew also that she wasn't as tipsy as she was pretending to be.

'Your turn,' she said cheerfully and with deft fingers unaffected by the drinking unbuttoned his shirt, carefully removed his gold cufflinks, and with exaggerated care placed them on the coffee table. He had unloosened the band of his trousers by the time she turned back to him, and she unzipped the zip. 'Ah,' she said as his erection sprang free, and she knelt before him to take it in her mouth.

'Wait,' he said quietly, 'wouldn't you like to go to the bedroom?'

She looked up at him, leaning back on her heels, her hands cupping him.

'Why waste the time walking when that beautiful sofa is right behind you?' she said. 'If you were to sit – I wouldn't have to stretch. And,' she added, 'you do look silly with your trousers around your ankles.'

He laughed, stepped out of his trousers, slipped off his shirt, shoes and socks, and bent to lift her up.

'Come here,' he said, 'cool and distant English girl, who watches us all and dissects us – come and lie on this beautiful sofa with me.'

'*Avec plaisir, monsieur,*' she said, leaning to kiss his chest. '*Voulez vous coucher avec moi—?*'

'You are very forward,' he said as he arranged her on the sofa and lay alongside her, his hands on her shoulders, his hardness pushed between her thighs.

'You were complaining I was very backward on Friday,' she said plaintively, her face buried in the bend of his shoulder, lips plucking at his skin.

'I prefer this,' he said, pulling her head to close his mouth over hers.

He preferred a lot of things, Anne decided as he made love to her. He seemed to want the pleasure to be hers, and he explored her body, testing every crevice and every curve, watching her response, giving soft little grunts when he found the touches and the places that made her gasp and lift her hips, thrusting them towards him.

She felt as if desire had heightened all her senses. The velvet of the sofa under her head seemed deeper and softer than velvet should, and the hairs on his arms were like small wires, stinging her. His skin was very tanned and soft but there was a lean, tough feel to his body. His nipples were tight, neat and flat, and she discovered that they responded just as hers did when she touched them, hardening into positive points, and that he liked it when she bit, plucked and sucked at them.

Their lovemaking was leisurely and without urgency. She never opened her eyes as he held her and turned her, but she was aware of the hard muscles of his forearms, the smell of him, the scents of lemony aftershave and French tobacco, and the growing smell of her own sexuality. She had the picture of his face between her closed eyes, and it was only when his exploring tongue and fingers had reduced her to a damp panting hunger that she opened her eyes.

She looked into his face and said, 'Now – please, now,' and he rolled her on to her back and mounted her, kneeling above her, his hands on her breasts. As he looked down at her, their eyes were as locked as their bodies were one second later.

She sobbed as he thrust himself into her and then gasped with pleasure as he rode her, turning her sideways so that he could get even deeper into her.

'Oh, beautiful, beautiful, beautiful,' she was saying. 'Deeper, deeper—'

She watched his face as his loins thrust and then he was pulling her breasts to the same rhythm, and finally his tongue was flickering in and out of her mouth, duplicating the strokes of his hips.

'Now,' he said. 'Now—' His voice was strangled and his eyes intensely blue. She would have known that he was about to come without his warning.

'And me,' she said. 'And me.'

They strained together, she clinging to him, her head and

face again hidden in his shoulder, and then both were quiet, their arms tight about each other. Neither moved or spoke until she felt him diminish and slip from inside her, leaving a warmth and wetness behind.

'Ummm,' she said sleepily.

He pulled away from her, and the bright blue eyes below tousled fair hair looked at her questioningly.

'And what does that mean?'

'What?'

'The "ummm".'

'It means I'm contented. If I were Suki, I'd be purring.'

'It wasn't too quick for you?'

'No. It was just right. The best. Love in the afternoon is to be recommended.'

He sat up and reached for his cigarettes; she lay beside him, her head on one of the big velvet cushions, and almost shyly traced her fingers down his spine as he turned away from her to find his gold lighter from the coffee table.

'We never did drink the coffee,' she said.

'Do you want some now?'

'No. Anything would be an anti-climax.' She looked at him anxiously. 'Was it all right for you?'

'It was exceptional,' he said. 'I haven't hurt your leg?'

'I'd forgotten all about it.'

He had lit his cigarette and was puffing smoke gently into the air as they lay side by side on their backs. She wanted to turn to rest her head on his shoulder, but felt shy, and then he pushed his free arm behind her and turned her so that she was lying just as she wished, as if he had guessed her thought.

'Is that really your first experience of love in the afternoon?' Peter asked.

'Umm,' she said.

'How extraordinary.'

'It's not really,' she said slowly. 'For a start there haven't been that many, well – encounters, and only one that lasted any length of time. And I've always preferred the dark because—' she stopped.

'Because of your leg, I suppose.'

'That's right.'

'And you didn't mind with me?'

'Well, I was a little bit drunk.'

'Was that all?'

She laughed and buried her face in his neck. 'No, not really, I wanted to.'

'And so why did you run away the other night?' His hand had found her breast and was stroking it softly.

'That's nice,' she said dreamily. 'Why did I run away? Well, for all the reasons that I told you: Evelyn; proximity; liking you.'

'And why did you change your mind today?'

'Because Evelyn's not going to be in my house now and because I couldn't wait any longer, oh – and other complicated reasons.' She stopped and then said abruptly: 'You've never said if it's really serious with Evelyn.'

There was a small silence that seemed long.

'Evelyn and her family like to think so.'

'And what does that mean?' She kept her tone light.

'It means they are thinking of marriage and I am not.'

She nodded, not entirely satisfied, but deliberately letting her eyelashes tickle his cheek.

'And you?' he said. 'What were the encounters?'

'Three kind, nice middle-aged gentlemen who weren't put off by my leg and who treated me like porcelain because of it. Very straightforward and simple sex it was. No frills like today.'

'And the one who lasted?' he persisted.

She moved uneasily against him.

'That was a long time ago.'

'What happened?'

'I don't like to talk about it.'

He sat up and looked down at her.

'That's probably a very good reason why you should.'

'No.'

'Who was he?'

She hesitated and then shrugged. 'Just a man. I met him when I was twenty. He actually picked me up. I was going to

221

see some friends in the country and I was struggling along the platform at Victoria Station with a huge suitcase, and he took it from me. I couldn't find a porter. He said that someone with such a bad limp ought not to be carrying heavy things, and he came on the train with me, got off it with me and found me a taxi at the other end. I was terribly impressed.'

'Then?'

'Well, I agreed to meet him, and one thing led to another. I was mad about him. He taught me all about lovemaking.' She tried to make her voice sound as if that was the end of the conversation.

'Then?' he pressed again.

'Oh—' She rolled away from him, burying her face in the sofa. 'It went wrong.'

'How?'

She sat bolt upright and stared at him.

'If you must know, he was a kink, and I was too idiotic to spot it, even when he said things like how much more comfortable I'd be in a surgical boot.'

To her astonishment Peter let out a hoot of laughter, and she stared at him unbelievingly and then found herself pummelling his chest.

'It is not funny,' she said.

He grasped her hands and held them, pulling her close to him.

'Of course it's funny, you silly goose,' he said. 'Stop and think about it. It's hysterically funny – a girl like you in a surgical boot, him suggesting it and you not realizing. It *is* funny, darling. It's nothing to get hung up about.'

'Well,' she said sulkily, appeased a little by his use of the word darling, 'it wasn't funny at the time; what happened after wasn't funny either.'

'OK. What did happen after?'

'You'll laugh again.'

'I won't. I promise.'

She looked at him suspiciously.

'Well, he was into cripples. One day at his flat I found a drawerful of letters from disabled women, all with photographs. Grotesque. Awful. He'd actually advertised. And when I accused him he was quite calm about it and said sex had been marvellous with me but he really preferred someone with a more serious affliction. That was why he'd advertised, and perhaps it was time we said goodbye.'

'And you were hurt?'

'Terribly. It gave me more of a complex about my leg. But I told my aunt and she reacted just like you. She said that one day I'd see the funny side of it, and that the world was full of peculiar people and that I wasn't to let it put me off. But it did.'

'Until now?' he asked.

She shifted uneasily under his soothing hands.

'I think what happened was that with him I realized that sex was absolutely marvellous, and that left me confused. You see, I decided it was far too good to waste on strangers, so I didn't want to get myself into a series of one-night stands. I mean, I simply couldn't go down on a stranger, and I wouldn't want a stranger to go down on me – but I love it, as you might have noticed. Also I didn't want to be used as someone's horrid old perversion, so that made me pretty cautious too. So I just stopped doing anything.'

'What a terrible waste of time for such a sensual lady,' he said and ran his hand over her stomach to slide his fingers between her legs, gently stroking until she arched with pleasure. 'And aren't you afraid that I only fancy you for your poor old leg?'

'No,' she said, 'you forget. I saw the look of absolute distaste you gave it that first morning at the swimming-pool.'

He frowned. 'I don't think that was distaste. More surprise.'

'Well, anyway, you didn't look at it all gloatingly like he did.'

'Well, I'm not into cripples.'

'Then what are you doing in bed with me?' she said stiffly.

He laughed out loud again. 'A, we're not in bed, and B, I don't regard you as a cripple. I think you're a very beautiful, sexy young woman. And seeing as how you like gentlemen going down on you so much, I think I'll do just that.'

'Why don't you,' she said a little breathlessly, 'and then later, I'll return the compliment.'

Chapter Sixteen

Françoise decided to skip lunch at Les Hirondelles on the Sunday morning and get herself down to Antibes and the yacht. She was too nervous to eat, generally jumpy and thanking her lucky stars that Achmid had decided to come to the boat and would finally meet McTaggart. She had no wish to be alone with Fouezanne, nor had she any doubt at all that it was he who had hung Suki from the oak tree.

To keep herself up to date with all that was going on at Les Hirondelles she had forced herself to go to Stella's coffee morning, an event that left her yawning with boredom. She had just missed Peter and Anne, but the visit was worth while. She had learned that her mother was not coming on the cruise and also that Peter's Evelyn was to be met at Tangier. She was pretty sure that both Achmid and McTaggart would want to know exactly who was to be on board and as many details of the trip as she could possibly supply.

She drove almost dangerously down the mountain, through Antibes to the Marina and picked her way along the walkways to where *Les Hirondelles* was moored – a big, slender, old-fashioned boat, gleaming with brass and polish. She clattered on board and went aft, straight down to the captain's cabin where McTaggart was lying on his back on his bunk, a thin cigar in his mouth pointing at the ceiling.

'Welcome,' he said, sitting up as she came in through the door. 'You're early.'

She did not reply. She unzipped her jeans, impatiently kicked them off and pulled her thin teeshirt over her head. She wore nothing underneath. Still without speaking she climbed on to the bunk.

'Fuck me,' she instructed him.

He leaned over her to put the cigar in an ashtray.

'Your servant, ma'am,' he said.

It was over very quickly. She was too impatient for preliminaries. Afterwards she leaned to take the still burning cigar from the ashtray and puff at it before passing it on to McTaggart.

He was still fully dressed, only the zip of his jeans undone.

'What was all that about?' he asked. 'Why no games today?'

'There's no time,' she said. 'He's coming at three forty and he wants to see you.'

'*He* being Achmid Fouezanne, I presume.' McTaggart sounded irritable. 'And it's only three o'clock.'

'I was nervous. I needed it.'

'You got it. And there's time to have it again.'

'You'd never get it up,' she scoffed. 'No. Now we've got to concentrate. Did you get the crew?'

'Yes. The ones he recommended, though I don't like the look of them too much. Still, their papers are all in order and they seem to know what they're doing.'

'And the cook?'

'An Indian. Doesn't speak French.'

'I hope he's good. You know what the de Courtenays are like.'

'Only one de Courtenay, and I've never noticed that her mind has been too much on food.'

Françoise ignored him. 'When do they all come on board?'

'I said five this evening and told them they'd get paid for today. I thought it was better to keep the place clear after your phonecall.'

'Right,' she said. 'Now all we've got to do is wait.'

He put one hand on her small breast and pulled her nearer with the other. 'Why don't I get undressed and then do it properly?' he whispered in her ear.

She shook herself away from him impatienlty.

'Oh, get lost!' she said. 'I want to think.'

He pulled back from her. 'So think,' he said curtly, zipping up his jeans. 'I've got things to do. I'll see you when your boyfriend arrives.'

Achmid arrived at exactly three forty p.m., as he had said he would. He greeted McTaggart coldly, making no effort to shake his hand – looking him up and down as if to assess what type of man he was dealing with. He gave a sharp, brief satisfied nod and still standing at the head of the gangway said to Françoise: 'Now I wish to see the yacht.'

Françoise noted how McTaggart made absolutely no attempt to treat Achmid as he would an owner. The Scotsman was curt to the point of rudeness, his accent becoming increasingly tough Glaswegian.

'She's eighty feet,' he told the Arab. 'There are six cabins; three doubles and three singles, all with their own bathrooms and heads. Forward are the crew's quarters – four cabins, all doubles, one of which I have to myself. The galley's there, and on deck the stateroom plus an open dining and drinking area. The prow's done up as a sunbathing area. Why don't you go round on your own? There's no one aboard.'

'And the engine rooms and the stores?' Achmid asked.

'Below,' McTaggart said briefly. 'Nothing's locked. You'll find them.'

He turned his back abruptly. 'Damned wog,' he said under his breath once he was out of the Arab's hearing.

'Do you want me to come with you?' Françoise asked Achmid.

He looked at her coldly, took off the straw hat he was wearing and placed it on one of the tables on the deck.

'No,' he said. 'You and McTaggart can wait for me in the main saloon.'

'Nasty looking, isn't he?' McTaggart said, his blue eyes fierce, once they were alone. He pushed a hand through his mop of sandy-blond hair and added: 'It'll be a pleasure to take money off him.'

Françoise only grunted. She was still nervous. She had thought the fuck might settle her down, but it hadn't. Perhaps she should have let him have another go, she thought, but it was too late now and she was decidedly uneasy.

They sat in silence until Achmid came in through the glass doors of the saloon and settled himself in the big armchair. Both of them had left it vacant and, as to the manner born, he settled himself in the expensive leather and leaned back.

'She's a little old. I'd have preferred something more modern.'

'Don't be put off by the wood and the polish. Just because she's not a floating gin palace it doesn't mean she hasn't got the guts and the heart of a newer boat,' McTaggart said, again belligerent.

'How many will you have on board?'

'Six from here,' Françoise told him. 'Raoul and I, my father and uncle, my aunt Marion and that English girl.'

Achmid grunted. 'Good – not too many,' he said. 'What's her speed?'

'Twenty knots,' McTaggart said. 'We'll reach Tangier in a week without looking as if we're in too much of a hurry.'

'You could be there on Sunday evening?'

'Late Sunday,' McTaggart said. 'You can never get the rich like this lot to leave exactly when they say they're going to.'

'We'll take no chances then. I shall expect you to be there by Monday night. Now, have you a pencil and paper? You're to write down your instructions, learn them and then dispose of them.'

McTaggart pulled a face as if all this cloak-and-dagger stuff was not to his taste, but Achmid ignored it.

'You will arrive off the coast of Morocco by nightfall on Monday evening. You will not go into Tangier harbour. Anchor for the night off the beach near Cape Spartel lighthouse. You must make some excuse not to go into Tangier.'

'Correction,' McTaggart said laconically. 'I've already promised the owner to be in Tangier harbour Sunday evening. His son's girlfriend will be staying at the El Minzeh and she's to be taken aboard Sunday evening. It seems she doesn't want to spend a night alone in wicked Tangier.'

'Which son's girlfriend?' Achmid asked sharply.

'My uncle, Peter's,' Françoise put in. 'She's an American, and

227

we're to meet her in Tangier. She was coming to the estate until Grandfather set up the cruise and insisted we all go.'

Achmid was silent, his mouth pursed, thinking.

'Correction,' he said ironically, echoing McTaggart's phrase. He thought a moment longer and then said: 'Yes, that will do very well. Very well indeed. Go to Tangier on Sunday night but get there without fail. Better be sure your engines are in tiptop condition.'

McTaggart bristled. 'The engines of any boat of mine are always in tiptop condition.'

'I'm glad to hear of it,' Achmid said drily. 'Now on the Sunday evening you pick up this girl. What is her name?'

'Evelyn Grenville,' Françoise said, adding the explanation: 'Her mother is an old friend of my step-grandmother.'

'Evelyn Grenville.' Achmid wrote it down in a small notebook he had before him where Françoise could see he had scribbled a plan of the yacht. 'And she's staying at the El Minzeh?'

'That's the intention,' Françoise said.

'Good. Once you have the lady aboard, you must have some convenient trouble with your perfect engines, Captain McTaggart, and it will become imperative to go to sea instantly for testing.'

'Wait a minute,' McTaggart said. 'Boats don't operate like that ...'

Achmid stopped him, putting up a thin yellow hand.

'I am not interested in details of that kind,' he said. 'I'm not a seaman. These details are for you to manage and what I am paying you for. Once Miss Grenville is aboard, you will sail down the coast towards Cape Spartel lighthouse. About two miles from the lighthouse you will see a white house on the clifftop, a path coming from it down to the beach, and on the beach a small jetty. It is the only point at which the beach is accessible along that stretch of coast.

'You will anchor a few hundred yards outside that jetty, and then you will give all your passengers time to get themselves safely to bed and asleep. Should you wish anything to assist them in this, something perhaps added to their nightcaps can be arranged. One of your new crew has an interesting medicine chest. He sees himself as a medical man.

'Once the passengers are securely asleep, you will take a dinghy to the shore. The crew will assist you, and I suggest that mademoiselle here and her brother also lend a hand. On shore at precisely four a.m. one ton of marijuana, split into eight separate blocks, will be waiting for you to load on the beach. The elderly woman who owns the house will be sleeping peacefully – with a little assistance from us. But she will wake most refreshed in the morning.'

'One ton!' Françoise said. 'How can we cope with that much weight?'

'One ton, worth one and a quarter million English pounds, in bulk exactly five English feet by three English feet by two and a half English feet,' Achmid said. 'About the size of that—' he pointed across at a writing-desk.

'Nevertheless,' McTaggart said, 'even in eight parts it's still bloody heavy.'

Achmid ignored the interruption.

'On the beach you will find four donkeys laden with the resin, and in charge of them a frogman. He will by then have assembled eight *dragueurs*.'

McTaggart started and then nodded approvingly.

'I see you are with me,' Achmid said. 'For your information, mademoiselle, a *dragueur* resembles a very large inflated condom. Condoms are known as French letters in England, *capotes anglais* here. Odd that, don't you think? However, in the normal way, *dragueurs* are used by the navy to carry extra stores, generally extra oil. They are towed behind a ship, but because of their buoyancy can be towed behind something as small as a row-boat. Or an inflatable dinghy.

'These eight oversized condoms will be joined by a tow rope, and the frogman will load them and then adjust them to neutral buoyancy so that they float just below the surface. You will tow them to the yacht and then attach them from the stern of your yacht. They will then be towed and dropped off, one by one, at your various ports of call. Naturally you will not go too far inshore. And we will discuss exactly which ports you plan to visit and exactly when you will arrive so that there will be someone there to greet you and to take away the – shall we call them spoils?'

'It's not a bad idea,' McTaggart was saying softly. 'It could work. As long as your frogman knows his business. If you get positive buoyancy they'll show, and if it's negative they'll drag. They've got to be balanced right. And there is one snag. The line could foul the propellers.'

'That's your problem. Attach the tow rope somewhere where that can't happen,' Achmid said impatiently.

'That's OK,' McTaggart said. 'It might be better to tie up below the waterline anyway. One thing, though.' He looked at Achmid searchingly. 'How do we get paid?'

'The three of you will be paid a quarter of a million pounds,' Achmid said. 'How you divide it is your own affair. It will be paid in ten parts. One part I shall give you today – in Deutschmarks. You will be handed the second part in French francs by the frogman on the beach at Tangier; I suggest you take a torch ashore if you wish to count it, as I see you do not trust me. The remainder will be paid every time you unleash one of the *dragueurs*, in various currencies of your choice. Does that meet with your approval?'

McTaggart grunted.

'A hundred thousand each for you and me,' Françoise said, her eyes shining, 'and fifty thousand for Raoul.'

'Sounds a lot for a kid who's done nothing,' McTaggart grumbled.

Achmid smiled thinly. 'Oh,' he said, 'I have no doubts that you will quarrel over the distribution. But, mademoiselle, the money will be given to him—' and he pointed a thin thrusting finger at McTaggart.

'You said you'd pay it to me.' Her voice was a squeak of indignation.

'Since last week I have changed my mind. A small lesson, shall we say. Now, perhaps you would be kind enough, Captain McTaggart, to work out exactly when and where you will be stopping on your cruise, and I will see to it that information is fed to you daily by your telephone or radio as to exactly where on the coast my men will be waiting to remove your precious cargo.'

'Give me about an hour,' McTaggart said.

'I have plenty of time,' the Arab said, 'and this is a very comfortable chair. Now before you go, are there any more questions?'

'I'd like a map reference for this place near Cape Spartel. After all, it's going to be dark.'

Achmid smiled, pleased with himself.

'You will find it already marked on your charts. We took the liberty of placing a small red cross exactly where you should anchor.'

'And what happens if the owners get wind of something while we're loading?'

'I rely on you to see that they don't,' Achmid said. 'But that is not something that's unduly worrying me. I don't think you will have a problem.'

McTaggart looked at him suspiciously.

'Why do you think that?'

'Call it intuition, Captain. Simply intuition,' Achmid said. 'And now perhaps you had better get to work.'

It was very early on Sunday morning when Jacques stole out of the guest house while the ground was still wet with early morning dew and the sun struggled through watery clouds and crept into Philip's garden.

He had noticed that under the windows close to the house, where he could not be seen from the inside, there was a bed of roses. With Martine's kitchen scissors to speed the task and avoid the thorns, he quickly picked a dozen of the best blooms, robbing the red bushes and leaving the white and yellow untouched.

He hurried back to the guest house, sure no one had seen him, and arranged the flowers into a fairly professional-looking bunch, wrapped in the tissue paper that lined the drawers in his bedroom. After looking at them critically he placed them in the bottom of the refrigerator.

Then he went back to bed.

At eleven thirty sharp he was knocking on Elisabeth's door. He wore a pair of his sister's jeans because they were cleaner than his own, and he had persuaded her to iron the shirt he had been wearing under the leathers when he had arrived. His hair was slicked back, his shoes shined, and he smelt of his sister's toilet water. In his hand he carried the bunch of stolen roses.

The maid answered the door.

'Yes?' she said, her expression surprised. It looked as if no one called on Elisabeth de Courtenay, Jacques thought.

'Is madame at home?' he asked politely.

'I'll see,' said the maid. 'Who shall I say has called?'

Jacques hesitated.

'Someone with an apology,' he said.

The maid nodded briefly and went back into the house, closing the door behind her and pointedly leaving Jacques on the doorstep. Bitch, he thought. She knows exactly who I am. He cooled his heels for about three minutes until the door opened again.

'You may come in,' the maid said, staying close to him as she led him towards the back of the house. 'In there—' She had opened a heavy carved wooden door into the drawing-room.

Elisabeth was sitting with her head turned towards him, and Jacques's darting eyes took in the antiques, the silver, the clutter of rubbish and the things of great value. A log fire was blazing in the large open fireplace, and as before the woman was wearing a shawl around her thin shoulders. Her eyes were wide and startled as he moved towards her; she stared at him without speaking for a full thirty seconds. Her voice was husky when she said: 'Yes? What is it you want?'

'I came to apologize for waking you,' he said humbly, his eyes down – and without looking at her he thrust the roses in her direction, making sure he was sufficiently close for her to have to take them from his hand.

Once she held them, he looked up and smiled at her in the way he knew always worked with older women – a shy boyish grin, his head to one side. He had a trick of just slightly

232

narrowing his eyes when he smiled so that they sparkled and looked lighter in colour than they were.

Elisabeth de Courtenay was holding the flowers awkwardly. She bent her head to smell them, looked up at him and said: 'Thank you. Won't you sit down and have some coffee?'

'Oh – I don't want to presume,' he said with an apologetic flutter of the hands. 'I just came to assure you that we would be much quieter in future.'

She hadn't taken her eyes off him, he noted with satisfaction. She was definitely interested. He let her persuade him into a chair on the other side of the fire while she rang for the maid, and he watched covertly as she bent to move the logs to a higher flame with a large brass poker.

'Are you warm enough?' she asked. He felt as if he was about to sweat heavily but he smiled and assured her that he was just right. He was mesmerized by the poker. It seemed symbolic in her hand. He'd come to poke the old trout and he wondered if her use of it was a discreet invitation. God knew, laying her wasn't going to be a labour of love, but it was possible that the heat from the fire would help to get him interested. The question was – was it going to be worth the effort? What would he get out of her? There was no doubt that she fancied him. She couldn't keep her eyes off him, and that always meant they couldn't keep their hands off either. The only thing he had to do was to work out his approach. However, if he'd guessed right about the poker, the approach might come from her. It was a pity about the maid. He'd have preferred the house to be empty.

But that problem was easily solved. As the girl came to answer the bell, Elisabeth ordered coffee and then told her that after she had served it she should go to the big house and help out, as Monsieur de Courtenay had a luncheon party.

Jacques mentally congratulated himself on his judgement. She was clearing the decks for him.

'I appreciate your coming, monsieur—' She hesitated.

'Jacques,' he said quickly. 'Jacques Borrel.'

'I appreciate your coming, Monsieur Borrel. One does not expect such courtesy from the young these days.'

He made a deprecating little gesture.

'I gather the young woman at the house is your wife?'

Jacques thought fast.

'Well,' he said, hesitant. 'Yes, but—'

'But?' She raised her heavy dark eyebrows over the black eyes.

'I am afraid that we are thinking of divorce.'

'Oh? And why is that?'

'Well, she—' He looked down at his hand and then up at her, with the nearest to a tragic expression that he could manage. 'Well, shall we say that her loyalty is not entirely for me.'

'I know exactly what you mean,' Elisabeth said, and her face was grim. Ah-hah, thought Jacques. She knows what her old papa is up to and into.

'You are a croupier, am I not correct in thinking?' she asked after a small silence.

'Trainee,' Jacques said quickly. 'My ambition is to go into hotel management. Soon I shall be leaving the casino. I do not like the atmosphere,' he said, his tone self-righteous, while wondering where the hell the girl was with the bloody coffee.

On cue there was a knock at the door, and the maid came in pushing a trolley. Without speaking she laid out the cups and saucers on a heavy wood coffee table set before the fire and put out English biscuits.

'I will pour, Janine,' Elisabeth said, 'and you may go.'

'Very well, madame,' the maid said, directing one last suspicious look at Jacques before she quietly left the room. Bitch, he thought again.

Elisabeth poured the coffee, letting the shawl fall back from her thin arms. Thin white arms covered with dark hair, Jacques noted; the light from the fire on her bent head caught the dark line of hair on her upper lip and a sprinkling of coarse hair on her chin.

He made a small bet with himself that she had hairy tits.

He politely accepted milk, declined sugar and sat with his cup in hand, one finger elegantly crooked. He waited for her to make the next move.

'You remind me very much of someone I used to know,' she

said abruptly. She was staring into the fire, and the scent of the roses, still in their tissue paper and lying on the small table beside her armchair, was suddenly overpowering.

'Oh yes?' he said, recognizing a common ploy. He was going to be the spit and image of a long-lost love. He probably *was* the spit and image of a long-lost love, judging by her reaction on seeing him when he had opened the door to her.

'You could be his son,' she said, and then added, almost as if speaking to herself, 'you could be our son.'

Jacques was suddenly alert. He had a strong feeling that things were taking a different turn and that maybe he would not have to fuck this stringy old hen after all.

'Your son?' he said. 'Surely not, madame. You are too young ...'

'I was seventeen. My son would be twenty-five now.'

'Extraordinary,' he said. 'Just my age. You say he *would* be twenty-five, madame. Have you been bereaved?'

'No—' She was still staring into the fire and then she looked up, her eyes very bright. 'Not exactly bereaved. My son was adopted when he was just three days old. I have never seen him since.'

Jacques's heart was beating very fast. He had to control his excitement. He had to keep his head.

'Do you know who adopted him, madame?'

She shook her head. 'It was done through an agency by the nursing home.'

'And which nursing home would that be?'

'In Paris.' She looked at him again, a look of surprise on her face. 'But why am I telling you all this?'

He took a deep breath and his voice became very solemn.

'Perhaps it was ordained because you see I –' he looked at her with his frank and truthful expression '– I was adopted.'

'In Paris?'

'In Paris, twenty-five years ago.'

'Your birthday? Is it 5 May?'

She's talking herself into it, he thought triumphantly, but cautiously he said: 'I have always believed my birthday to be 6 May.'

Her face was alight with excitement, and he could suddenly see that maybe she was only forty-three.

'They could have got it wrong by one day. Do you know who your parents really were?'

I know all right, he thought, thinking of Monsieur and Madame Borrel, failing at everything they tried; grey and drab, piss poor, life's losers.

'My mother was someone rich from the South of France.' He took a wild guess, a guess he figured had to be right. 'Her father would not permit her to keep me. That was all we were told.'

She was sitting forward on the edge of her chair now, the shawl thrown off her shoulders.

'And the father? Did they tell you who the father was?'

It was a moment for caution. 'Alas, no,' he said sadly. 'I have always longed to know.'

'Jacques.' She leaned forward to take his hands in her dry, bony ones. 'This may hurt you. He was a young Algerian. Only a gardener. But he was the kindest, sweetest, most gentle of boys. We truly loved each other, there was a child of our love and I have never loved again.'

'An Algerian,' he said slowly, 'I have always wondered about my looks.' That, he thought, was certainly true. He had speculated on many occasions what his colourless mother married to his ginger-headed Gallic father had got up to to produce him. Martine and Marie looked much more like their parents.

'Do you mind?' she was saying anxiously. 'You must not mind, because he was one of the special people.'

'If you loved him, he must have been,' he said solemnly.

She had released his hands and was looking at him, her black eyes glowing.

'It does sound as if—' She hesitated.

'As if I might be your son?' he finished. 'Oh, it's not possible.'

'But it is. Don't you see? You are so like him. We must ask your parents what else they know.'

He shook his head, his expression grave.

'It is not possible, madame. My parents are dead. They died in the last of the troubles in Algeria. Our home was burned with all we owned. I was fortunate. As a child, I was spared.' He was improvising wildly now. 'Would you believe that the authorities brought me back to France and that I was put for a while into a Harki camp with the Algerian refugees until the mistake was realized. And then, for the second time I was adopted by another *pied noir* family who had known my parents.' He sighed. 'My life has not been easy, madame.'

'Oh, Jacques.' Her eyes were full of tears now. 'What a legacy we gave you, Hassan and I. But we had no choice. You were the most beautiful little black-haired baby, so like your father, but they took you away from me. Yet I have never forgotten you, or Hassan. My life has been dry and sere since the day I lost you both. I know in my heart I will never see Hassan again, but it is almost as if the good God has led you back to me. The sins of my father have been visited on me in the most miraculous of ways.'

'It is true,' Jacques said, his head bowed, thinking how the sins of Elisabeth's father were being visited in exactly the age-old way.

'Madame,' he said, pretty sure he was home and dry, but wanting to clinch the situation, 'there is nothing in the world I would like more than to believe I have found my true mother – so long lost to me. But we cannot be sure. We have no proof. I cannot let myself hope that I have found my home again. Somehow I must find some way of proving what you believe, but how? Our tragedy may be that there is no way, and I could not accept your love and your affection if it did not rightly belong to me.'

Elisabeth was clasping her hands together, and the tears were spilling down her cheeks.

'Oh, you are truly Hassan's son,' she said. 'Those would have been his sentiments. You have his delicacy, his honesty and his purity of purpose.'

'You flatter me,' he said sadly, 'but were what you say true, we still can never know for sure.'

She paused. He waited, holding his breath. What a drama queen the silly old cow was!

'Jacques,' she finally said, sitting upright in her chair and lifting her coffee cup. She had recovered her dignity and was suddenly authoritative again. 'Where are these second, adopted parents of yours?'

'I never see them,' he said. 'Unfortunately they did not approve of my marriage to Martine. I realize now that they were right, but at the time I was very much in love; she seemed like everything a man could want. Now I know better.'

'They were quite right,' Elisabeth said firmly. 'She is a common little slut, I'm afraid. More so than you know.' A wave of her hand dismissed Martine. 'But where are your parents?'

'In Lille,' he said. It was the furthest place in France he could think of. 'My adopted father is a surface worker at the mines.'

Elisabeth made tut-tutting noises.

'It is most definitely time that you received your heritage,' she said. 'To think that a son of mine ...'

She was sold, totally sold. Mentally Jacques applauded his own performance. He'd pulled it off. And now, he asked himself, what?

'Where are you living?' She was bossy in tone now.

'I have a simple little room in Nice,' he said. 'Of course it has little in the way of amenities, but the neighbourhood is good ...'

'You must move here.'

'But I could not do that,' he protested. 'You are too kind. My work ...'

'Your work is not suitable,' she said firmly. 'The de Courtenays do not work. You must busy yourself with studies. I shall teach you. We shall travel. Would you like to travel?'

'I have always wanted to see the United States,' he said, 'but it is a dream of course.'

'We shall go to the United States if you wish. I am hopeful that I shall be receiving my portion of this estate very soon, and I have always wanted to travel. But not alone. Now ...' she smiled at him. 'We shall travel together.'

Jacques felt a cold hand squeeze his heart, freezing his elation. He had won. He had his meal ticket. But would the price be too great? This woman was convinced he was her son ecause she wanted to be convinced and wanted an end to oneliness. But her end to loneliness would be his end to free-lom. Was it worth it? Without knowing, he had reached the ame crossroads as his sister had the day before; he looked t the log fire, the polished silver, the fine paintings and took . deep breath. 'Madame,' he asked humbly, 'would you permit hat I call you *Maman*?'

Chapter Seventeen

They could have been going to the Crusades, Anne thought, as he de Courtenay retinue set out for Antibes and the cruise on *Les Hirondelles III*. Their departure had a positively medieval quality. Every maid had been pressed into service to pack clothing, an estate car had been laid on, merely to carry the passengers' luggage, a small van was crammed with extra ood, drink and general comforts in spite of the fact that the acht was already provisioned. When it came to 'things' Philip le Courtenay was always generous. The whole exercise had been supervised by Claudine, bun in place, severe in her black dress, keys at her waist, very much the *châtelaine* and ery much in charge.

They set off in procession at ten thirty a.m., more or less he time they had intended to leave. Dupré was driving the Rolls, with Marion, Peter, Tomas and Anne as his passengers. Peter's Lancia, the second most comfortable car owned by the amily, followed behind, driven by one of the gardeners and carrying Raoul and Françoise. Then behind came the estate car and the small van; the four vehicles moved in convoy down he mountains and finally on to the coast road and into Antibes.

Anne was very quiet as they travelled, listening to the others talk and thinking with some amusement that Peter would again accuse her of assessing them, once they were alone. There was some truth in it. Her aunt Olivia had accused her of being a typical Virgo, and perhaps she was. She did watch and listen. She liked to store people in her head, remember their expressions, their speech patterns, and she had to admit that she enjoyed spotting their weaknesses; the little give-aways revealing conceit, greed or dishonesty. The only weakness she had found in Peter was a slight touch of arrogance – but then with the possible exception of Marion all the de Courtenays suffered from that.

The yacht came as something of a shock. Anne was not quite sure what she had been expecting, but it most certainly was not a boat of the size and beauty of *Les Hirondelles III*. She lay at anchor on the far side of the marina where the bigger boats were berthed, a long, lean, white, elegant lady, but very big.

There seemed to be radar equipment from the mast that protruded from the bridge. There was a big speedboat resting on its own platform at the stern. The ship – for it seemed too big to call a boat – was fluttering with bright awnings and flags: dressed, as Peter explained, for their arrival.

A big sandy-haired man with very bright blue eyes and a skipper's cap, floppy jeans and a shirt was waiting at the top of the gangway; he half-saluted as Tomas reached the deck. Anne had the feeling that the cap would be the only concession the man would make to any kind of uniform, and he looked capable and strong. His voice when he spoke was strongly Scots.

He shook hands with Tomas and said: 'Welcome aboard, sir. You'll find everything ready. Josef will show you to your quarters.'

A dark-skinned man standing slightly behind him came forward and half-bowed, half-salaamed; Tomas gave him a curt nod, before turning back to the skipper.

'I think you know most of the family, McTaggart,' he said. 'But you may not have met Miss Paradine, who is our guest on this trip. We'll be picking up another guest in Tangier and we have promised to be there by Sunday when she is expecting us.'

240

McTaggart nodded. 'No problem, sir,' he said; then, turning to Anne, 'Good morning, Miss Paradine. I hope you'll enjoy the trip.'

'I'm sure I will,' Anne murmured.

He greeted Peter and Marion, nodded briefly at Raoul and Françoise, then said he'd leave them with Josef while he gave instructions for the engines to be started. Anne, standing on the polished deck, was slightly stunned by this fresh evidence of the de Courtenay wealth. They constantly surprised her. She knew they were rich, but they did not behave like very rich people, and the size and luxury of the yacht had come as a bit of a shock.

The gangway had led on to a wide open deck, furnished with comfortable garden furniture and bamboo tables. A large table was set with drinks in the centre. Behind she could see a long, elegant saloon, the front of which was laid out as a dining-area and beyond a sitting-room. Neither room looked as if it belonged on a boat. The effect was of a home.

Josef first led the three women to their quarters; the below-deck cabin to which he took Anne and Marion was a luxurious bedroom with a small bathroom *en suite*. The only sign of shipboard life was that the daylight and sprinkling of sun came from three portholes and not windows.

'I didn't think you'd mind sharing with me,' Marion said. 'This boat is awfully short of cabins. There are only six – three doubles and three singles. Father decided he'd rather have large cabins for a few people than small cabins for a lot of people. I think he was right really, but as we've got to leave one cabin for this Evelyn woman, I thought you and I might share.'

'I don't mind a bit,' Anne said. 'In fact it'll be fun.'

'I knew you wouldn't,' Marion said. 'Of course Tomas and Peter have the main cabins. Personally I think they ought to have offered them to us, but the de Courtenay men are all male chauvinist pigs at heart and terribly spoilt.'

'You're *all* terribly spoilt,' Anne said, looking at the soft pale blue carpeting, the *toile de joie* blue and white curtains and bedcovers and the Louis XIV dressing-table and chaiselongue. 'Honestly, all this on a boat! It's almost immoral.'

Marion looked surprised. 'Do you think so?' she said. 'I've never thought about it.'

Anne burst out laughing. 'That's exactly what I mean.'

As it turned out, Marion was in error with her assessment of why Peter and Tomas had taken the main cabins.

'Listen,' Peter said to Anne as they sat on the sun deck, drinks being served by the impeccable Josef, 'I wish you weren't sharing with Marion.'

It was just after midday, *Les Hirondelles* had left harbour and the Fort Carré and ramparts of Antibes were receding slowly into the background.

'Why ever not?' Anne asked.

'Because I deliberately took one of the main cabins so we could share it. There's the best of the single cabins next door which I was hoping McTaggart would allocate to you, and then no one would have been any the wiser.'

'But what about Evelyn?' She made her tone deliberately casual.

'McTaggart's left that cabin for her, which complicates everything.'

Anne felt a rush of something like relief. He didn't want to sleep with Evelyn so he couldn't be that interested in Evelyn.

She thought for a moment and then said: 'Would you mind if Marion knew I was sleeping with you?'

'No. But you would, wouldn't you?'

'Not in the least.'

He looked at her in surprise. 'You are a funny girl. After all that running away and everything else I thought you'd be embarrassed.'

'Not at all,' she said firmly. 'Look, I've made a decision about you and I'm not in the least ashamed of it. Why should I be? We're both free – aren't we?'

It was a direct question, and she held her breath waiting for the answer. He hesitated, then said: 'I guess so. So what do you propose?'

She would have preferred a stronger answer but said: 'I shall just tell Marion that I'm sleeping with you – if you don't mind, that is.'

The ball was in his court.

'I don't mind Marion knowing,' he said slowly. 'But I'd rather McTaggart wasn't aware.'

'Not in front of the servants?' she mocked. 'When most of the time you treat them as if they didn't even exist!'

'You're confusing me with Tomas and his part of the family,' he said, his voice indignant. 'Marion and I never act as if the servants aren't there. My mother does sometimes, perhaps, but then she's old school. No, I don't want McTaggart to know because—' He hesitated. 'Well, it would appear discourteous to Evelyn and actually discourteous to you as well.'

She brooded about that, not caring for the mention of Evelyn. The threat was still there. Then reluctantly she nodded. 'I understand.'

'Good.' There was affection in the grin he gave her. 'Come and join the party.'

The day was idyllic. *Les Hirondelles III* moved swiftly and surely through untroubled waters, her sharp bows parting the blue seas, raising a soft white spray. The coast lay hazily to their left, mountains and pine forests clear in the sunlight, like a continuous graphic painting, after they had passed the glistening white façade of Cannes.

Lunch was served on the deck under a blue and white striped awning, and afterwards Anne and Marion sunbathed on the open deck at the bows, dozing to the faint background hiss of water and the continuous throb of the engines. Raoul and Françoise had asked for the speedboat to be lowered into the water and were streaking ahead of the yacht, and then speeding in circles until the boat caught up.

'Noisy little horrors,' Marion muttered as a close pass cut across the yacht's bows, causing a heavy wash that disturbed the stately tranquillity of their passage. She sat up and lit a cigarette, clasping her knees with one hand and staring out over the open sea.

'Listen,' she said abruptly, 'would you mind if I snuck off and left you tonight?' She hesitated. 'I want to go with Tomas.'

Anne rolled over on to her side and squinted through the

sun at the other girl, whose tan had noticeably deepened in the hour they had been sunbathing.

'Funny you should say that,' she said. 'I was going to ask if you minded if I snuck off to be with Peter.'

Marion let out a little squeal.

'No!' she said. 'Honestly, what a dark horse ... I didn't know. That's marvellous. I told you you ought to try him. What's he like?'

'None of your business,' Anne said crisply.

'I see.' Marion was grinning. 'That means it's serious. Is it?'

Anne rolled over on to her back and stared up into the sky.

'I don't know,' she said. 'But let's say I wouldn't mind if it were. But there's Evelyn what's-her-name to think about. She's lurking in the background all the time.'

'Forget her!' Marion said. 'Do you love him?'

'How do I know!' Anne said. 'I fancy him rotten. I think he's gorgeous and he's nice. And I can't forget Evelyn – not for a moment. Though it'll be better when I've actually seen the competition.'

'You love him,' Marion said authoritatively. She was silent, and Anne, turning to look at her, saw that her head was bowed and her shoulders dejected as she stared at the smoke from her cigarette.

'What's the matter, Marion?' she asked.

The other girl sighed.

'You are lucky,' she said. 'There's a chance for you. But for me—' She flicked the cigarette overboard with a practised wrist movement. 'You see—' She stopped and then said in a rush: 'It's no good, but I've fallen in love with Tomas, Anne. I can't get him out of my mind. I want to be with him all the time. And the worst – or the best – of it is, he feels the same way about me.' She was silent again and then said: 'Whatever are we going to do?'

Anne sat up. 'Oh dear,' she said softly. 'Oh dear.'

'Oh dear indeed!' Marion said. 'The only hope is to get away from Les Hirondelles. If we could go somewhere where no one knew us, we could live together and it wouldn't matter.

But we need money for that. And Tomas is in such a financial mess, and I know Father won't help him. Father might give me money – but not if he knew about Tomas and me. He'd go mad.'

Anne considered and then decided to say exactly what she thought.

'You know, he probably does know,' she said. 'Everyone at Les Hirondelles seems to, and no one seems to be taking much notice. Why don't you just go on the way you are?'

'Do you really think people know?' Marion looked startled. 'No one's said a word. Oh, Christ – you don't think Mother knows?'

'I'd be astonished if she didn't,' Anne said. 'Your mother doesn't miss a trick.'

'That's true.' Marion thought again and then said: 'But Tomas and I can't just go on like we are. It's not enough. All the sneaking about—'

'But you said you liked the element of danger,' Anne reminded her.

'I didn't know I was in love then.'

'Marion, listen.' Anne put her hand on Marion's tanned arm. 'Just let things go on as they are for a while. Anything can happen. It'll sort itself out. Things do. But it would be better if *you* could go away alone – and try to forget him. You can come and stay with me in London if you like while you sort yourself out. You have to think of the future. With Tomas there'll be no kids, no marriage – if you want either of them. You'd have to lie all the time. And he's so much older than you.'

'Do you think that we both haven't talked about those things?' Marion said. 'We have. And it doesn't alter the fact we love each other.' She reached for another cigarette. 'Oh, Christ, what a mess.'

'Yes, it's a mess,' Anne said thoughtfully, and trying to find something comforting to say she added: 'But love, however it appears in one's life, has to be worth having, doesn't it?'

'Oh yes!' Marion said, her face alight though her eyes were

moist. 'Imagine if I didn't have him! Whatever would I do?'

Find someone else, Anne wanted to say. But even she knew it wasn't always that simple.

That night, after they had made love, she told Peter about the conversation. She had not intended to do so, but the subject came up at a moment when they were too close for secrets.

They were half asleep, her head on his shoulder, his arm around her holding her breast, while she held the firm mass of his scrotum in her hand, her leg curled over him.

'Did you tell Marion?' he asked.

'Ummm.'

'What did she say?'

'Not much.'

'No problem?'

'No problem.'

They were quiet for a moment, and then he said: 'I suppose she's in bed with Tomas.'

Anne did not reply.

'She is! Tomas is really impossible.'

'He loves her,' Anne said.

'Who says so?'

'Well, Marion, I suppose, but she loves him as well. She's terribly unhappy, Peter.'

'Oh, God,' Peter groaned. 'The complications of this damn family!'

'Are they so bad?'

He was lighting himself a cigarette, trying not to disturb her.

'Well, Tomas has got us involved with Achmid Fouezanne. He's in debt to the tune of a million francs. My father is laying the *locataire*—'

'Do you know, I thought so—' Anne broke in.

'Mother confirmed your suspicions. Pamela Whitton decided to enlighten her. But then, Father's always been laying someone or other.'

'Including my aunt.'

'Your aunt was different.'

246

'And now,' she said sleepily, stroking him, 'you're laying her niece.'

'Her niece is different.' He leaned over to kiss her. 'And Marion's in love and laying her half-brother. You know, I sometimes suspect that she and Father ...'

Anne sat up, genuinely shocked.

'You don't!'

'I do. Just from things she said years ago, and the way she used to look at him. There's something between them that's always been different. Oh, hell – I'm probably wrong.'

'I'm sure you are,' Anne said. 'My aunt wouldn't be involved with anyone who'd do that.'

'Sometimes you're very young,' he said.

'I'm twenty-three,' she said indignantly.

'You *are* very young.' He squeezed her breast and ran his hand over her flat stomach and into the soft growth of hair below. 'I still have this premonition that something is badly wrong. No family should be as lucky as we are. You know, when I'm in my office in Boston the life here seems like a dream. It's something so few people can have any more. It's not so much that we're rich, it's the way the estate is, the way Father is, the way the whole place is run. It's archaic really.'

'I know what you mean,' she said. 'I felt as if we were going to the Crusades this morning when we set out.'

He laughed. 'You're right,' he said. 'Nevertheless I'd like it to go on. I can see myself as Father—'

'What? Laying the *locataire*?'

'No – being the *seigneur*. Being in charge. Being the head of my own family. I'd like it.' He stopped and asked abruptly: 'Are you into women's lib?'

'Never had to bother with it,' she said. 'I've never found being a woman the slightest handicap.'

'That's because you're individually talented,' he said. 'But would you fancy a man who liked to be boss?'

She considered the question.

'I don't mind anybody being boss in their own domain,' she said lightly. 'Someone has to be or confusion sets in. But

I'd be furious with anyone who bossed me in my own kitchen.'

'I promise not to enter the kitchen,' he said, and she longed to ask him exactly what he meant by that but decided it was best to let the moment pass.

'That was nice.' Marion's voice was drowsy, her head on Tomas's shoulder, as he lay on his back and she curled against him.

'I thought so,' he said. 'Why is it better every time?' His hand was entwined in her hair, the other lay on her stomach.

'I don't know,' she said. 'But aren't we lucky?'

They were quiet, dozing, the rhythm of the moving boat lulling them as they lay together on the big bed in the master cabin.

He awoke to find her gently licking his shoulder, while her fingers gently scratched at his back and his thighs.

'I do love you,' she whispered as she blew gently, little warm breaths on his neck, and then her tongue was exploring the curls and curves of his ear.

He turned to hold her tightly, pulling her so that he could feel her breasts flattening against him. He felt a great surge of genuine love and affection. He wanted to cherish her and he needed to talk and explain himself.

'Marion,' he said abruptly. 'Would you come away with me?'

She was wrapping herself around him now as tightly as she could, and he could feel her damp mouth pressed into his shoulder.

'Of course,' she said. 'But what would we do for money?'

'Would you take a chance without money?'

She must have sensed the challenge in his voice, because she pulled away from him, leaning back so she could see his face properly.

'Yes,' she said. 'I would.'

'Supposing I told you that there could be money? A great deal of it?'

'You're talking about the sale. But, Thomas, Father will never agree to it.'

248

'We've got to persuade him,' he said and he knew he sounded desperate. 'It's my only chance. *Our* only chance.'

Marion was sitting up now and she leaned over him to pick up the cigarettes and lighter from the side of the bed. She put one between his lips before lighting another for herself.

'Darling,' she said, 'even if it did come off it would only just pay your gambling debts.'

He puffed out smoke in a long slow stream, one arm still around her, stroking her waist.

'No. Much more,' he said. 'If Father sells I get ten million francs for myself on top of the deal. It's on a banker's draft, waiting to be picked up the minute the sale goes through.'

'You get *what*!' Marion's voice was disbelieving.

'Ten million francs.'

'It's nonsense.'

'You don't believe me?'

'Well, if you say so – but I can't think why—'

'Because I conned him, that's why,' Tomas said abruptly.

'You conned him? How?' She still sounded unconvinced.

'It's a bit of a long story,' Tomas said. He too was sitting up, and all physical contact between them had gone. 'It started when I went to that stag dinner at the Baumanière at Les Baux-de-Provence about nine months ago. I drove there, and because it was a lousy wet day I decided not to take the *autoroute* and went on the old N8.

'I drove through St Maximin La Sainte-Baume' and noticed the red mud all over the road without taking too much notice because we're so used to it at Les Hirondelles. Then I saw the signs saying to beware of bauxite on the road. Apparently it gets dangerously slippery when it's wet.

'It was Roger Reybaud's stag night. You don't know him, but we were at school in Paris together. He was into his third wife and the evening was a bit heavy. Anyway I stayed the night at Les Baux mainly because I was in no fit state to start on a three-hour drive, and the next morning in daylight it struck me how similar the terrain was to Les Hirondelles. And Les Baux is where bauxite was first discovered.' He stopped to stub out the cigarette.

'I was worrying myself sick about finance driving back,' he went on, 'because I already owed the Cannes casino a packet and Achmid a small sum at that point. I was even more fed up because Roger's so stinking rich it makes you sick. Imagine taking twenty people to the Baumanière and not giving the bank manager apoplexy.'

'Well, certainly, Father apoplexy,' Marion put in.

Tomas laughed without mirth. 'Yes, well, that was when the idea suddenly struck me ...'

'Tomas – what have you done?' Marion's voice was frightened. 'You didn't give Achmid the idea that there was bauxite at Les Hirondelles.'

He nodded and took the cigarettes from the bedside table, putting one in his mouth and leaving it there without lighting it.

'That's exactly what I did. I told him I was sure that there was a deposit of stuff on the mountain and that I was hiring two geologists to check. Then I really honed up on the subject. I found out how it's mined, how it outcrops, what it's worth, where there are other deposits. I'm pretty much an authority on the subject now.' He lit the cigarette and stared into space and grimaced. 'My geologists were two con-men, one French, one German. I got hold of them through one of my less reputable acquaintances at the Monte Carlo casino. They cost a packet, but they did the job brilliantly. I'd written a report which they presented to Achmid and they sold him – hook, line and sinker. Once he'd read it and talked to them, he even paid them a bomb to keep their mouths shut. They're the only ones who've made anything out of it at the moment, which is maddening.

'Anyway, he told me he was going to check it out for himself, and I got the most terrible cold feet then but I don't think he ever did, thank God. My report must have convinced him. It was full of nice little authoritative touches like how easy the stuff would be to ship with Marseilles so near and how the land wasn't a swamp like in Guyana where a lot of bauxite comes from; and how the ownership wouldn't be complicated politically as it had been when someone dis-

250

covered bauxite in Jamaica. It was pretty good. And Achmid fell for it.'

He stopped. Marion was very still and she said quietly:

'He's not a man to cross, my darling. I'm frightened.'

'Well, that's it. If somehow Father agreed to sell, the minute we laid hands on that money we'd have to disappear. And quickly. I had to make a separate deal for myself because no one would be mad enough to give that kind of secret away for twenty million francs, but he'd only settle for ten million cash to me and a share deal. I couldn't argue. I sold him the line that Father would never agree to Les Hirondelles being ruined by open-cast mining, and that if he was going to get his hands on the estate we'd have to persuade Father to sell for something that might just appeal to him. We dreamed up the millionaires' paradise between us.

'The so-called geologists' report said that the yield of the mine would be something like a quarter of a million million, and Achmid's eyes were practically gleaming behind those sodding glasses he never takes off. I could see he wanted it so bad he could hardly contain himself.

'But now Father won't sell, and I can't get my hands on that ten million let alone my own share of the estate.' He stopped and turned to gently stroke her bare breast. 'But if you were to ask him—'

'Me?'

'Yes.' The fingers were still stroking, and her nipples became pink and tall under the slow caresses. 'If you threatened him with exposure about what happened when you were a kid ...'

Marion pushed his hand away and looked at him, her eyes glistening.

'Tomas,' she said. 'I do love you. I can't help it. But, oh boy, are you a shit.'

Chapter Eighteen

Martine had spent the Saturday and Sunday burning with resentment. First there had been the telephone call from Marie saying briefly that she was staying in St Tropez with, of all people, Margaret de Courtenay, and then her wretched brother had vanished to explore his chance and had not reappeared. That seemed to indicate that he'd been correct in thinking that Elisabeth de Courtenay fancied him.

When he did come back it was late on Sunday evening, and he had a grin as wide as the Mont Blanc tunnel all over his face. As he explained what had happened between him and Elisabeth, Martine's anger turned to resentment. He and Marie were going to fuck up everything between the pair of them if they weren't careful – and it was her pitch. She'd found Les Hirondelles and the pluckable de Courtenays and she was furious with herself for ever letting any of her family near the place.

Philip had not been in touch with her, but she reasoned that was because the whole lot of them were packing up to go off, and as far as he knew her so-called husband, Jacques, was still on the scene.

'You've got to get out of here,' she said, glaring at Jacques. 'He'll never come near me again if he thinks you're around.'

He just laughed at her.

'Not on your life,' he said. 'You've got five days' grace to decide what lies you're going to tell this time. I'm going down to Nice to pack up my room and my things, give in my notice and make the travel arrangements for my mother and myself to visit the United States. I'll be back at the weekend.' He strutted around the room, thumbs in his leather waistcoat, as he gave her the information.

'Your mother!' Martine hissed. 'She's no more your mother than I'm the Virgin Mary—'

'You can say that again,' said Jacques.

'And I'm going to tell Philip what you're up to.'

'In which case I shall tell him that I'm really your brother and what you're up to.'

She stared at him helplessly.

'Checkmate, little sister,' he said softly.

When Philip appeared on the Monday morning he found her in tears. He was not particularly patient; the intention of his visit had not been to comfort a crying girl. She was aware of this, so as she sobbed on his shoulder she kept her hand on the fork of his trousers and stroked gently. It made him a lot more sympathetic.

'It's Jacques, my husband,' she said. 'He's leaving me.'

She felt him stiffen and not where her hand was.

'Oh,' he said cautiously.

'Oh, monsieur, it's so embarrassing—'

'Embarrassing?' She could feel him pulling away from her and she said quickly:

'You see, Jacques was adopted when he was a baby. And the strangest thing has happened. Your daughter – the eldest one – is convinced he's her son, and Jacques thinks it's true. He's leaving me and going off with her to the United States.'

'Wait a minute,' Philip said. 'You're saying your husband is Elisabeth's son? Impossible!'

'That's what I said – impossible – but he swears the birthdays are the same and that everything fits.'

He was walking around the room now and he said thoughtfully: 'I suppose anything could be possible. Stranger things have happened. But it couldn't be ... What does he look like, this husband of yours?'

'Very dark. Slim. Twenty-five years old. He's good-looking and very charming when he wants to be.'

Philip burst out laughing.

'So she's found herself a young lover, has she? What a complicated excuse to get herself laid. Well, I suppose it's about time. But if she thinks I'm paying for their gallivantings around the United States—'

He had moved back to where she was sitting and was undoing the buttons of her blouse, thrusting his hand inside the small bra she wore. He pushed her off the sofa and on to her knees and then sat down himself, his legs apart, undid the zip of his trousers, and thrust what there was of an erection into her waiting mouth.

She closed her lips over him, began to move her tongue up and down the length of him and felt him growing; she had to control the urge to sink her teeth into the damn thing. She was boiling with rage. The bastard, she thought, the arrogant bastard. He doesn't see either of us as people – just things for fucking.

But she lifted her head from him and looked up, her eyes melting: 'Is that good, monsieur? Do you like it?'

'Very much,' he said and pushed her head down again.

On the Tuesday they had been through the massage routine again, and on the Wednesday it had been difficult to make him come. She began to be frightened that he was getting bored with her, and if that happened she might lose the roof over her head and her meal ticket before she'd even established it properly. She had to keep him interested.

It was on Thursday that she gave him the first of the poppers. He had decided he wanted to make love on the floor, and they were lying on a black fur rug in front of the empty fireplace. The fur was tickling her skin, and she had a terrible need to scratch but she kept up the little moans, the small cries of excitement, and her fingers and mouth were busy titillating him. His penis remained infuriatingly slack.

She had put the popper on the mantelpiece and she whispered into his ear: 'I have a present for you, monsieur. Don't move. Just stay where you are.' She pressed him back into the rug and got to her feet, having a quick surreptitious scratch on her left buttock before she lay down again.

'Lie still,' she whispered and put her head very close to his, breaking the glass ampoule under their noses. It made a sharp little crack, and suddenly the room was full of the heavy acrid odour of amyl nitrate.

'What the—' he started to say.

'Breathe it, breathe it,' she whispered, her own heart already beginning to move in strong loud beats and her head starting to float. 'Breathe it.'

They were clinging together, breathing very slowly and deeply, and everything seemed long and dreamlike. She was very aware of his body. He felt hard and muscular and his

254

heart was beating in exact rhythm against hers. They were close in a way they had never been before. They could have been in love, she was so conscious of him holding her, his hands moving up and down her back. She could feel him growing against her stomach as they held on to each other; kissing, hands moving leisurely over the other's body, and then, in slow motion, he was rolling her over, and pinning her shoulders to the rug, lifting himself to push in between her open and waiting legs. Then with long, easy, slow strokes he was riding her with skill and confidence, and she was accepting every thrust, her breath coming deeply, and muttering: 'More. More. More—' She had the feeling that the world had slowed right down, and then came the swell and the final deep delving into her. She was juddering, her insides contracting in the most marvellous way, and she could hardly breathe at all as he exploded into her, and they lay, while she narrowed to keep him inside her with muscles that tightened on him like a vice.

They slept, and when she awoke he was still on top of her, their legs entwined, his shoulder pressing into her mouth. She felt hot and sticky. She pushed him off, and he sat up and stared down at her.

'What was that thing?' he asked.

'A popper.'

'A what?'

'An ampoule of amyl nitrate.'

'Do you have any more?'

'I can get them from a friend in Nice. But they're ever so expensive. I could only afford the one – as a present for you.'

'How much?'

She took a chance: 'Two hundred francs each.'

He got to his feet and walked naked across the room to where he had flung his clothes. He picked up his trousers and from an inside pocket took out two thousand-franc notes.

'Get some more,' he said, putting the notes down on the coffee table before walking into the small downstairs cloakroom to wash.

She picked up the money lovingly. Income at last, and there were enough poppers to keep him happy for the cash he had given her plus the added bonus that the amyl nitrate made the whole thing more bearable for her. She'd really quite enjoyed it.

'You'd better meet me tomorrow in the olive press behind the grove below Tomas's house,' he said. 'Your husband will be back, won't he?'

'I think so,' Martine said, adding self-righteously, 'but he won't be here. He's going to stay at your daughter's. It's bad enough to lose one's husband to another woman, but when the other woman is—'

'Oh, he'll be back,' Philip had said, shutting her up. 'He'll soon get fed up with Elisabeth. Right then, four o'clock at the olive press. And bring one of those things.'

Dutifully Martine was there on time and saw there was a rough bed in the small stone building that housed an old circular stone olive press. Philip had put a clean blanket over it and he led her in, leaving the door open. The air inside was stale and damp smelling.

'If it gives you any satisfaction,' he told her, 'this is one of the places where Elisabeth used to screw her Algerian gardener. Who knows, maybe your husband was conceived right here.'

Martine thought it a joke in rather poor taste but she managed a little laugh. He was kicking off his clothes in his usual enthusiastic manner and he sat on the narrow wobbly bed and watched while she undressed more slowly.

'Where's that thing?' he asked, holding out his hand.

After it was over she lay still looking out of the door of the hut into the olive grove and up the mountainside, narrowing her eyes to watch the sun dancing in motes across the trees, waiting for him to wake.

Philip was breathing deeply and evenly, and she looked at him dispassionately, thinking things could have been worse. He was a good-looking man for his age. She knew now that there was no possibility that he would ever love her any more than she would love him. That was a pity, but only because had he loved her he would have been so much more pliable.

His light brown eyes snapped open as she moved slightly, and he ran a hand over his moustache and his hair and then looked at his watch.

'I must go,' he said. He was on his feet with the extra-ordinary quickness that characterized all his movements, pulling on his trousers, slinging his shirt over his shoulders. 'Wait until I'm out of sight, then you can go home yourself. I'll telephone you about tomorrow.'

She was feeling exceedingly bad tempered when he telephoned her that night long after she had gone to bed and told her that she was to drive her Volkswagen down the mountain as if she were going to the coast. He described in detail a small turn-off on the left that went higher into the mountains and came to a dead end in a valley.

'I'll meet you there,' he told her, 'at four o'clock.'

Not even Sunday off! she thought as she put down the phone. And where were they going to fuck this time? Philip de Courtenay quickly became bored with bed and seemed to be turned on by places that were definitely not comfortable. It was all right for him as he was generally on top of her in the old-fashioned way, or making her kneel on all fours. She noticed he picked a bed when he wanted her to massage him like the first time. Only then did she get to be on top. Also, servicing him once a day was getting to be too much of a good thing. It had been better when his family were around. There was no affection, no gifts, no money – just the roof he provided. She had a nasty feeling he'd present her with the electricity bill if she wasn't careful. The situation wasn't moving as it should.

What had annoyed her more was that she had seen her brother moving about Les Hirondelles as if it belonged to him. He'd arrived on his motorbike over the weekend – she'd heard that – and he hadn't come near her. She had seen him in Elisabeth's garden and he seemed to have acquired some very smart clothes. His hair was well cut and already he had a new-found look of prosperity. Also she'd spotted him coming up the courtyard, having obviously used the pool, which she didn't dare do unless no one was about. It wasn't fair.

257

Her temper had not improved as she set off in the Volkswagen, thinking that she'd like to leave Philip de Courtenay up his alley, valley or creek, whatever it was, and not turn up. But prudence prevailed.

She drove out past Berthe, who gave her a hostile look, and set off down the mountain road. She had previously noticed the turn-off that Philip had told her to take and had wondered exactly where it went. It was about a mile and a half down the road, still on Les Hirondelles property, narrow, no more than a dirt track, and her little car bounced over the rutted surface complaining all the way.

It was hardly a valley it led to. The road petered out in an opening where someone at some time had tried some quarrying. The surface of the exposed rock was deep red, and red mud lay in patches like rusty blood. There was a tumble-down wooden hut leaning drunkenly near a pile of rock; Martine looked at it and shuddered. Please, not there, she thought.

She had a short wait, and then a cloud of red dust on the road gave the signal that someone was arriving. It was the Rolls with Philip at the wheel. She gave a little giggle – that would be it. He'd fuck her on the back seat of the Rolls, and it might even be quite fun. She'd never had it in a Rolls.

'You found it all right?' he said as he got out of the car.

'Obviously,' she said drily.

He was looking around him with an expression she could not read.

'I haven't been here for years,' he said slowly. 'I've tried to persuade myself it didn't exist.'

'Why should you do that?' she said, puzzled.

He bent and picked up a handful of the red mud, and rubbing it into dust he let it trickle through his fingers.

'It was a decision I made.' He seemed abstracted. 'I was never sure whether or not it was the right one.'

'What sort of decision?'

He ignored the question. 'Have you brought the thing?' He could never bring himself to say popper, or even amyl nitrate.

'Of course.'

'Let's get in the car then.'

It looked as if it were going to be one of those occasions when he wouldn't undress completely. He did that sometimes when they were in offbeat places. And, logically, had they been screwing in a car where they might have been seen he would have kept his clothes on. He liked to be logical.

She herself had worn a light cotton dress with nothing underneath. He wasn't into sexy underwear; in fact, she had a strong feeling that if pressed he'd be hard put to describe what she looked like. He was only interested in what she did to him and what he finally did to her.

He was walking towards her Volkswagen, and she couldn't believe it when the Rolls was also sitting there! He opened the door, tipped both seats forward and said: 'Get in. I've always wanted to see if it was possible.'

Martine could have told him from experience that it was – but only just and it wasn't much fun. Trying to hide her long face she climbed into her car and stretched out on the back seat. She had to raise her knees at right angles to get in at all, then she placed her hands behind her neck using the edge of the window for a headrest and smiled provocatively at him, deciding to make the best of it. He was still standing in the red dust, the door open, and as he watched her she slowly lifted her skirt until it folded back on her waist; the feel of the fresh air between her naked and opened raised legs was oddly exciting.

He never spoke. He just dropped his trousers where he stood and bending low got into the car, closing the door behind him, his shirt-tails concealing him down past his thighs.

Surprisingly he squashed himself beside the seat and pushed his head between her legs, while his hands slid up under her dress to pull and twist at her breasts, hurting her. Normally he did not attempt oral sex.

'Don't hurt me,' she said, and he immediately climbed over her, folding himself in a jumble of arms and legs so that she could take his languid penis into her mouth. They were jammed into the seat, head to tail, and much more *soixante dix*

259

sept than *soixante neuf* she thought, resisting the urge to giggle with her mouth full.

It was too uncomfortable to stay long in the position, and he sat up and turned her to half-sit, half-lie alongside him, her bottom hanging off the seat. Then he asked: 'Where is it?'

She had the ampoule in her hand and cracked it with a sharp movement of her fingers right under his nose. He breathed it in deeply, and she felt her heart begin to beat in long slow thuds. He had rolled her over on to her face and lifted her so she was on her knees on the seat, her forehead pressed into the window, and then kneeling behind her, his hands still pulling at her breasts, he took her with the slow motions that the popper created.

She was uncomfortable, the metal edge of the window hurt her, and his fingers pulling at her nipples were not gentle. The car was shut up tight, and the smell of the amyl nitrate was overpowering. Her heart felt as if it would burst. He was gasping behind her and erect enough to push into her painfully. She just wanted it to be over. Why couldn't he have chosen the Rolls?

He came without her, collapsing when he did, so that her face was pushed down into the upholstery and she could hardly breathe. She tried to push him off her, but he was still panting; his weight was too much for her to shift. She was beginning to panic and fight for breath, but he still stayed above her and now he was groaning.

'Monsieur,' she mumbled into the seat, desperately trying to twist her head. 'Get off me, please. I can't breathe. Please.'

The weight seemed to be increasing, and he had started to moan out loud. Something was terribly wrong, and she gathered together all her muscles and all her strength to make one effort to heave him from her before she suffocated.

It was not necessary. As she made the push, he toppled off her naturally, so that her body sprang into the air as he fell, shirt-tails open to show his heavy scrotum and, astonishingly, an erect penis. He was on his back, jammed between the tipped-forward front seats and the floor, his face grey, his eyes rolling in his face.

'My heart,' he said. 'Get help—'

Then his head jerked and fell. His chin was on his chest and he was very still.

'Oh, God,' Martine said to the one she prayed to only out of superstition. 'He's dead. Oh, God – please help me.'

She thought afterwards that she must have passed out for a while. It wouldn't have been surprising, what with the stench of the amyl nitrate in the totally closed car, the terror of near suffocation and then the realization that Philip de Courtenay was dead.

When she opened her eyes the light was going from the small clearing, and the red earth looked more than ever like dried blood. Philip was where he had fallen, undignified in death as he had never been in life – exposed, his mouth and eyes both open, legs sprawled, and crammed into the sardine can of the car like a parcel with the wrapping coming off. She shuddered and tried not to look at him, but the eyes seemed to be following her wherever she went.

Her immediate problem was to get out of the car. The air was fetid and heavy; she pushed back the flap of the window beside her as far as it would go. His body was jammed against the tipped-forward driving seat and she could not get at the door handle on that side. Kneeling on the seat, she was able to pull his legs up beside her on the passenger side, and leaning over him, again with a shudder, she could pull the seat back sufficiently to open the car door. The worst bit was climbing over him to get out.

Once in the open air she stood breathing in great gulps. She felt sick and dizzy and her heart was still thumping too fast. She would have given the earth for a glass of cold water. Philip's trousers lay in a useless heap outside the car door, and looking at them she started to laugh hysterically until the extent of her situation suddenly began to dawn on her.

She had a good two miles to get to the entrance to Les Hirondelles with a half-naked dead man in her own car and not the slightest possibility of being able to get him out. Equally there was no possibility of getting into the driver's seat and driving the car anywhere. She was tough, but she was small in stature; her hands were strong, but pulling a six-foot-two-inch corpse from where it was jammed in the back seat of a tiny car with only two doors was totally beyond her.

Her first thought was to abandon the whole lot – Volkswagen, Rolls, everything. Her second thought was that if she did, the car would instantly be recognized as hers. Without explanation the circumstances of Philip's death would look remarkably suspicious.

Whichever way she looked at it, she was going to find herself in a highly embarrassing situation, but if a little embarrassment, she reasoned, she could cope with.

Sitting on the red earth in the darkening valley, she began to plot again. Maybe here was a chance to earn a little on the side. Madame de Courtenay surely would not want the details of her husband's death too well known. Perhaps she could capitalize in some way. She *must* capitalize in some way because, as sure as eggs were eggs, she'd lost her roof. And with a profit of only two thousand francs.

'I'll have to drive the Rolls back,' she said, her voice loud in the silence of the clearing. She approached the big black car cautiously and found to her enormous relief that he had left the keys in the ignition. She did not fancy disturbing those crumpled ownerless trousers. Without a backward look at her own car she climbed into the driver's seat, experimented until she found how to pull it forward so that her feet would reach the pedals, and then started the engine. An appointment with Madame de Courtenay was indicated, she decided, as she set off down the rough track back to Les Hirondelles, discovering that the Rolls despite its size was a pleasure to drive – so much so that she speculated briefly on the idea of taking the car as the price of silence.

'Don't be stupid, Martine,' she said to herself as she turned into the main road. 'You can't eat Rolls-Royces.'

The first snag hit her at the entrance to the estate. The gateway was closed and the *gardienne*'s hut dark.

'Silly old cunt,' she said out loud. 'Where the hell is she?'

Impatient, she got out of the Rolls and slid behind the barrier, hoping that perhaps she could lift it and drive through without Berthe spotting her. Berthe had made it clear from the outset that she did not approve of Martine or of any of Martine's family.

She had no luck. She had her hand on the steel bar of the barrier, trying to raise it, when the light sprang on inside the little house and the hatch flew open, Berthe's suspicious old face peered at her, and the black eyes darted to the interior of the Rolls.

'Where is monsieur?' she demanded.

Martine had had enough for one day.

'Mind your own fucking business,' she snarled, 'and let me through.'

'Where is monsieur?'

'Oh, piss off and open the barrier, for Christ's sake,' Martine said, 'or I'll ram the fucking thing and that won't do monsieur's Rolls the slightest bit of good.'

Berthe's face through the opening was absolutely outraged. '*Sale pute*,' she hissed, and the bar flew upwards.

Martine was back in the car like a flash, and the engine smoothly caught as she rolled through and past the hut. Then she put her foot down and drove as fast as she could to the parking lot.

Again she had no luck. She had just finished parking the car and was climbing out when the slightly breathless austere figure of Claudine appeared standing at the exit into the courtyard.

Martine began to feel a sense of mounting hysteria. Claudine was standing, arms folded, looking like the Angel of Death, which seemed highly appropriate.

'Where is monsieur?' she said.

Martine looked at her and shrieked with laughter.

'Dead,' she shouted. 'Dead as a doornail.'

Chapter Nineteen

McTaggart had never enjoyed a cruise less. The sea had been calm and the yacht had made perfect time, never dropping below twelve knots, but he had continually watched the sky, worrying that a break in the weather would delay them and they'd arrive late at Tangier.

He disliked the crew. McTaggart had always picked his own crew, and he preferred to work with Scots if possible, though he'd settle for English at a pinch. These men were all of indeterminate origin though probably Eastern Mediterranean. They were certainly Moslems.

To add to his frustrations, Françoise had decided that it was better if they acted as skipper and owner's daughter for the duration of the cruise, and altogether the only thing that cheered him was the neat parcel of German banknotes he had taped behind a bulwark in his cabin. Françoise had clamoured for her cut, but he had told her the share-out would come after the last of the marijuana was dumped. He didn't trust her to see the whole thing through once she had her hands on a sizeable amount of money, and he wanted her almost as much as he wanted the money.

The few stops that Tomas had insisted they make for swims and lunches ashore had made him uneasy enough to sail on through the night, and by the time the outline of the Rock of Gibraltar stood clear in a perfect blue sky it was Saturday morning and McTaggart was grey with fatigue. Also, he was in a situation where he had to reduce speed or arrive too early, and Achmid had made it clear that that was as culpable as arriving too late.

He suggested an offshore swim and lunch at Estapona; then after he had heard the speedboat roar away, he flung himself on his bunk for two hours' solid sleep.

But not all his passengers went ashore. Anne and Peter had stayed sunbathing on the deck.

'Well,' she said to him. 'It's nearly the moment of truth. By tomorrow you'll have two women on your hands.'

She spoke lightly but she was suffering considerable jealousy. So far they had not discussed what would happen when Evelyn finally arrived. She was uncertain what his choice would be, but natural reticence and pride had not allowed her to bring the subject up.

He frowned.

'I suppose I'll have to explain to her eventually,' he said. 'But it doesn't seem right to do it while you're around. It's not going to make for a comfortable cruise. It was madness to have invited her, but things were a little different at that point, weren't they?'

He grinned at her, and his hand went to rest on her bare flat stomach. She felt an enormous sense of relief but she still needed to be absolutely sure.

'What do you have to explain?' she asked, staring into the sky where one small white cloud sailed above.

He sounded surprised, and his hand stroked her, lightly exploring her navel. 'Well, I don't have to explain anything, I guess,' he said. 'Hopefully she'll get the idea there's nothing doing without any actual discussion. But the rest of the trip is going to have to be celibate for both of us, darling. I can't sleep with you while she's in the next cabin. And that won't be easy. And would you believe that I have the most overwhelming urge to make love to you right now?'

The sun seemed to be penetrating the thin fabric of her white bikini, and she felt languid and sensuous. He lay beside her in nothing but small blue briefs. She turned on one elbow to look down at him and said in a demure voice: 'So I see.'

'Bitch!' he said and laughed.

'Well, why don't we?' she said.

He looked at her, his expression suddenly serious.

'Want to go to the cabin?'

'Not really,' she said, 'I fancy the open air, but there's too many people about all the time.' She felt superbly happy and confident. 'I'm sure those creepy Arabs would love to watch, but I've never thought sex was a spectator sport, have you?'

She had let one hand fall over the small white cup of her bikini and she put the tip of her tongue out at him, narrowing her eyes and stretching her throat as she did so.

'Not just a bitch,' he said. 'A sexy bitch!' His mood seemed as light as her own, and he regarded her for a moment, then said: 'Open air, eh? All right. Follow me.'

He walked the length of the yacht to the stern where a rubber dinghy was suspended over the side from two davits. Deftly he untied the ropes holding it and it flopped down neatly into the water, glistening black, a rolypoly whale that pulled gently away from the yacht and sat bobbing on the faintly choppy surface of the sea. He let down a line from the stern while she stood watching him.

Without saying anything he dived over the side, swam to the dinghy, pulled it to the drifting line and tied up. Then he looked up at her, grinned and shouted: 'Come on in. The water's fine.'

He had climbed into the dinghy and was moving the inflated seats, one to make a headrest and the other put somewhere in the middle of the wooden planks that formed the flat bottom.

A growing warmth filling her, she flipped neatly over the side, down into the blue depths of the water, itself a cool caress, and then up again, hair flattened against her head as Peter waited to help her on board.

He had swung the outboard between the two torpedoes of the dinghy to leave the bottom completely clear, and as she came aboard, streaming water, he pushed her down so that her head lay on one inflated roll and her thighs were over the other. Then he kissed her, his hands around her back unfastening her bra, his mouth nuzzling at hers. He rolled over to lie beside her and asked: 'This private enough?'

The dinghy floated in the shadow of the side of the yacht, bobbing gently.

'As long as no one hangs right over the rails,' she said, looking up at where the rope ladder descended from the stern.

'No one will,' he said confidently, his hands peeling the strip of bikini from her breasts. 'Look what the sea did.' He was leaning to take her nipple in his mouth. 'Standing up straight already.'

266

She shivered with pleasure and said: 'It's the cold.'

'Then you must have this wet bathing suit off,' he said and began to roll the damp mass of her bikini bottom down over her thighs. 'But let's mind your leg ...'

When the two scraps of white were discarded she said: 'For God's sake don't let them go overboard – I'll never be able to get back on the yacht.' The thought made her laugh. 'I feel giggly,' she said.

'Just as long as you don't feel seasick.' He was kissing her, licking the salt water from her breasts and belly. 'Clothed in the Mediterranean, you are,' he said, 'and very nice too.'

'Well, take your drawers off,' she said, putting out a hand to help him. 'I'm at a disadvantage.' As he began to pull off the briefs she said, 'The cold doesn't bother you, does it,' and moved quickly to close her mouth over him, making the dinghy rock alarmingly.

She lifted her head. 'And we'd better not fall overboard either,' she said. 'But what a way to drown ...'

The hot sun was already drying their bodies, leaving soft white traces of salt which they tasted from each other. The dinghy swayed and rocked with their movements, and every now and then a small wave tossed them closer making them cling to each other and laugh. They made love very slowly, lying flat, pressed tight, her face between his thighs, his between hers. She said plaintively that the boarding was hard, so he rolled and turned her so she lay on top of him, cushioned by him, his erection throbbing between her legs, his hands clasped on her buttocks, her tongue in his mouth, the sun hot on her back.

They lay very still like this for some time, letting the movement of the dinghy enhance the pleasure, and then very gently he pushed her from him, turning her again, resting her head on one seat and lifting her buttocks on to the other so that he could penetrate deeply into her, his hands supporting her back from the boards beneath her.

She gasped as he entered and tightened her arms around him so that his breath caught for a moment, and then he was riding her very fast, gasping himself, muttering endearments while she said, her voice harsh, 'Tell me when you're coming, tell me!'

'Now!' he half-shouted, and their combined excitement caused the dinghy to rock so wildly that for one moment it seemed it would overturn. He was still inside her, and they held each other very tightly until it righted.

'That was a near thing,' he said into her wet hair.

'That was a lovely thing,' she said throatily.

'Lovely what?'

'Lovely fuck, of course!'

'You are a lovely fuck.'

'So are you.'

'Better than Evelyn?'

'Oh, fuck Evelyn!' he said.

'I'd rather you didn't,' she told him.

It was Josef who woke McTaggart. The Arab was close-faced and obsequious, saying there was a phonecall for the skipper. McTaggart ran his hands through his hair and pulled on jeans. His passengers, he figured, were all ashore, so barefooted and shirtless he hurried to the bridge.

'Captain McTaggart ...' The English voice on the phone through the electronic waves of sound was unmistakably Achmid's.

'Speaking.'

'How far are you from your destination?'

'Less than a day's sailing, but I'm slowing down. Letting them play.'

'Good. You will be there by six tomorrow evening?'

'Easily.'

'You will see that no one, no one at all except Josef and Hassan, leave the ship. You must say that you do not have landing authority from the port officials and you are forced to wait. Josef and Hassan have Moroccan papers and therefore they can go ashore.'

'You do realize that I've another passenger to pick up?' McTaggart said.

'I realize it very well. There will be nothing to stop your

passenger coming aboard, and Josef and Hassan will deliver her. But you must keep your other passengers on the yacht until they return. Is that clear?'

'It's clear, but it's easier said than done,' McTaggart said. 'What's it all about anyway?'

Achmid had hung up, and McTaggart was left with the electronic waves hissing in his ear.

'Fuck you,' he said into the mouthpiece and then hung up himself.

That afternoon he reported a touch of engine trouble to Tomas and Peter, suggesting they stayed anchored where they were for the night.

'You could take dinner ashore, sir,' he suggested.

'Great idea,' Peter said enthusiastically. 'Nice little town, Estapona.'

Nice little bird you're laying too, McTaggart thought cynically. He wouldn't have any problems with Peter panicking to pick up the other girl, that was for sure. He had a feeling Peter couldn't have cared less whether they picked her up or not.

The next morning he reported solemnly to Tomas that the engine trouble was temporarily held at bay and asked for permission to sail.

'Of course,' Tomas said, 'but get the thing fixed properly when we get to Tangier. What's the matter with it anyway?'

'Oh, nothing serious, sir,' McTaggart said.

'Right then,' Tomas said and hurried back to his cabin.

What a family! McTaggart thought. Tomas screwing his half-sister, Peter screwing the English girl when there was another bird waiting to be plucked in Tangier, and Françoise, who at seventeen years old had the sexual habits of an alley-cat. They all thought no one noticed what they were up to. Arrogant bastards, McTaggart decided as he tramped back to the bridge.

By mid-morning on the Sunday, *Les Hirondelles III* was sailing serenely past the Rock of Gibraltar.

'Can we stop here on the way back?' McTaggart heard Marion ask as his passengers leaned on the rails to look at

269

the huge ugly mass with its rocky sides levelled into water catchments.

'If you like,' Tomas said, 'but it's the arsehole of the world.'

Marion thought it looked quite pretty once they were able to see the town, and exclaimed at the American destroyers in the harbour. McTaggart thought uneasily that Gib with the US Sixth Fleet in force was not a place where he cared to stop with eight great floating turds containing a ton of marijuana hanging behind him. If he thought he had problems now, what was it going to be like once that little lot was loaded?

With Gib receding, they entered the straits; Africa and the Pillars of Hercules appeared misty in the distance. He reduced speed until they were rounding the African coast and Tangier was ahead, glistening and white, the *casbah* climbing the hill, the big hotels of the European part of the city square against the sky. He was at the wheel when Françoise came up on the bridge and stood with him.

'Is it going to be all right?' she asked.

He looked at her searchingly. Her small, pointed face was pinched and she looked very young and frightened.

'Getting cold feet?' he asked, but kindly.

'A bit,' she said. 'It's that loading bit that worries me. Suppose Tomas and Peter wake up. How will we explain?'

'I got some powder from Josef,' McTaggart said. 'Do you think you and Raoul could get it into their brandies?'

She shivered. 'Oh, it's all too ridiculous for words.'

'I told you that right back at the beginning. Just keep thinking of the money.'

She gave him a foxy look. 'Where are the Deutschmarks he gave us?'

He laughed at her.

'Never you mind. They're safe – all £25,000 worth of them – and when it's all over, we'll go away and spend them, OK?'

'Where?'

'Where do you want to go?'

Her eyes looked into the middle distance.

'South Pacific?' she suggested.

270

'Anywhere you like.' He looked at her affectionately. 'Go on, baby – off you go. It'll all be all right.'

The arrival at Tangier went smoothly. He pulled into the private yacht marina, a scruffy area near the main port where the *Mons Calpe*, the ferry that ran between Tangier and Gib, was pulling out, swarming with Moroccans with huge straw baskets full of produce to sell in rocky Gibraltar. As soon as he had given the order for the engines to be stopped and the gangway to be lowered he went to where Tomas was leaning on the rails with Marion, Peter and Anne, watching the confusion of the harbour.

'Sir,' he said.

'What is it, McTaggart?'

'I'm afraid I shall have to ask you all to stay aboard until I get landing permission.'

Tomas seemed unconcerned, but Peter said immediately:

'But I have to collect Miss Grenville.'

'It's under control, sir,' McTaggart said. 'I've already made arrangements by ship-to-shore telephone. Josef and Hassan have Moroccan papers. They can go ashore, and I've arranged for them to fetch Miss Grenville. The Moroccans say they have no objections to anyone coming aboard, but I have to present our ship's papers before any of us can leave.'

'Is that all right, Peter?' Tomas asked.

'I suppose it will have to be,' Peter said. 'But I must telephone her and warn her what's happening.'

'That's perfectly possible, sir,' McTaggart said smoothly. 'Would you like to make the call from the stateroom or the bridge?'

'Which is easier?'

'The stateroom is more comfortable, sir. I'll put the call through and switch to that extension.'

McTaggart went back to the bridge, made the call and switched it through to Peter, then he sent for Josef and Hassan. Hassan, who had been employed as a deck hand, spoke no English and only a little French. Josef was fluent in both languages. Both men were wearing bright red and white striped *jellabas*, ready to go ashore.

'We have our orders,' Josef said. 'We pick up Miss Grenville from the El Minzeh and bring her back here.'

'Well, you'll bloody well take them again from me,' McTaggart said, knowing he was being childish; but Josef's obsequiousness covering dumb insolence had irritated him all week. 'You pick up Miss Grenville from the El Minzeh hotel, and her luggage, and you get her back here as quickly as possible.'

His face expressionless, Josef said: 'We pick up Miss Grenville from the El Minzeh hotel, plus her luggage, and get her back here as quickly as possible.'

'Right,' McTaggart said. 'Now get on with it.'

The two men gave exaggerated salutes and left the bridge to McTaggart again. He debated what to do next. Peter de Courtenay and Anne Paradine were both sitting reading under the forward deck awning. Marion and Tomas had disappeared, no doubt gone back to bed; McTaggart wished he could do the same. Raoul was on the sun deck aft, Françoise beside him in a bikini which appeared to consist of a few pieces of string. McTaggart felt good old-fashioned lust rising, and there wasn't a damn thing he could do about it.

He was also nervous, and not having anything positive to do made it worse. He tried to busy himself with charts but he felt out of control. Something was wrong. Why was Achmid so insistent that none of them should go ashore? He felt distinctly uneasy.

It was about three-quarters of an hour later when he saw two red and white striped *jellaba*-clad figures, a European woman between them, coming through the police post at the entrance to the harbour. No one seemed to take much notice of them, and then the three figures were walking leisurely to the yacht. As they came nearer McTaggart could see that one of the men was holding the girl's arm. There was no sign of any luggage except a small striped bundle.

Something about the way the girl was moving troubled him, and he called down to Peter: 'I think Miss Grenville's arriving, sir.'

Peter put down his book and went to the head of the gangway, and on impulse McTaggart ran down to the deck to join him.

As the girl stepped on board McTaggart saw she had an expression of sheer terror on her face. And he also noticed in the same moment that the faces under the hoods of the *jellabas* were not those of Hassan and Josef. The men escorting the girl were complete strangers.

'Wait a minute,' he started to say, when he realized the reason for the girl's terror. The taller of the two men was not just holding her arm. He had a gun at her ribs.

'McTaggart?' the man with the gun snapped. He spoke in English.

'Yes.'

'Right. Get this ship out of harbour. Now.'

'What the—' Peter had stepped forward.

'Just shut up and you won't get hurt,' the man said to him, and turning to McTaggart, 'get a move on!'

'For God's sake do as they say,' Evelyn Grenville whimpered.

McTaggart had never believed in arguing with guns. Without speaking he went back to the bridge, signalling down to the engineer to start the engines. But what the hell was going on he had no idea, except that it seemed highly likely that Evelyn Grenville had been used as a decoy to get the two men on board. The distinctive striped *jellaba* had obviously fooled the men at the police post, just as they had fooled him until he had seen the strange faces and the gun.

The Lebanese engineer must have been waiting for his signal. Instantly the engines began to thud and he was able to start moving the boat out of its berth. The crew were all in place, and the other, shorter man of the two strangers was acting as deck hand in Hassan's place, casting off ropes in an expert manner.

What the hell was up? McTaggart asked himself again, his attention on moving his ship without colliding with anything in the harbour.

From his place on the bridge he could see what was happening on the forward deck. Anne had put her book down and risen as if to greet the new arrival and then she too stopped dead in her tracks as the man casually motioned with the gun that she should sit down again. Raoul and Françoise had not yet realized that anything was amiss unless, McTaggart wondered, they had prior knowledge of what was going to happen.

But no. The shorter man, who had also produced a gun from the folds of the *jellaba* had gone round to the sun deck and was shepherding the pair of them to join the others, Raoul looking petrified, Françoise furious, her nose in the air, totally dignified in spite of her near-nudity. McTaggart felt a rush of admiration for her. She had guts.

The scene on the deck below him was like a tableau. No one moved. Françoise, ignoring the men, had stretched herself out to sunbathe again, and he noticed that the Paradine girl had picked her book up and was reading as if nothing had happened. Peter had sat down again, very still and watchful, and the American girl in her elegant white trouser-suit, highly suitable for a cruise on the Med, seemed to be whimpering quietly. Raoul had seated himself on the deck by Françoise, and the two men, totally relaxed, had slipped off their *jellabas* and were lounging against the rails, their guns barely concealed.

The yacht was nearly out of harbour, the open sea ahead, when the shorter of the two men, moving springily on the balls of his feet, came along the deck and made his way on to the bridge.

'I'll take over now,' he said. 'But stick around. We'll just get out to sea and ride out until it's dark.'

He seemed curt but almost friendly, and McTaggart realized that he was acting as if they were on the same side. Perhaps they *were* on the same side, but he wished someone would tell him what was going on.

'OK, so what then?' he asked.

The man looked round from the wheel.

'We pick up the hash,' he said.

'And then?'

'We head for Palestine.'

274

'Palestine!'

The man grinned, his teeth very white in the dark Semitic face.

'Yeah. You've been hijacked. How about that!'

McTaggart felt an urgent need to sit down.

They were moving fast now and well away from harbour when Tomas appeared on to the forward deck. The movement of the boat had probably interrupted his screwing, McTaggart thought. Marion was behind him, looking pink and flushed.

McTaggart had to watch what happened next in dumb show; he was too far away to hear conversation. It seemed to him that Tomas, angry and stiff-necked, was demanding to know what was going on, and the tall man waved the gun at him and indicated that he was to sit down and shut up. Tomas, red with anger, strode across the deck, his hand out, probably saying 'Give me that gun' like the damn arrogant fool he was. And then it was all over very quickly. Quite casually, as if he had been picking off bears in a shooting gallery, the man shot Tomas, neatly and tidily through the heart.

Claudine repeated the question. She could not bring herself to believe the answer she had received.

'Where is monsieur?'

'Dead!' Martine shouted again, 'Dead, dead, dead, dead, dead!' Then she sank to the ground, wailing and sobbing hysterically.

Claudine stared at her implacably, making no move to touch her or lift her. She was beginning to fear that the slut might be telling the truth.

'Where?' she asked.

'If you want to know,' the girl shrieked, 'in my car. In the back seat. His trousers in the dust. In that clearing off the road. That's where. And you can bloody well try to get him out – I can't!'

The light was going fast, and a dark shape came hurrying into the parking area where Marie's bike still stood, abandoned and incongruous among the expensive cars; Berthe's twanging Provençal accent said: 'Claudine – where is he?'

'She says he's dead.'

'Dead?' The old woman crossed herself. 'Where?'

'In her car. In the red valley.'

The two old women looked at each other.

'It killed him in the end,' Claudine said softly, then squared her shoulders. 'Madame mustn't know how.'

She was thinking carefully, her mouth pursed; finally, a decision made, she turned to the girl and said:

'Get up and stop making that row. You'll drive us back to where you left him.'

The girl had scrambled to her feet, shaking, her teeth chattering.

'I can't go back there—'

Claudine deliberately moved towards her, drew back her arm, and her hand landed across the girl's face with a loud crack, knocking her to the ground again, where she lay whimpering.

'Now get up and get into the car,' Claudine said.

She knew there would be no need to tell Berthe what she had in mind. Berthe would know immediately what had to be done.

The pair of them moved on Martine, grabbed an arm each and with surprising strength for women of their ages dragged her to her feet and towards the car. They bundled her in the driving seat and then both squashed into the front beside her.

'Drive,' Claudine said grimly.

The girl started the engine. The slap had ended her hysteria, and Claudine observed that her common little mind had already started to work again. She knew the type. The girl would try to capitalize on the situation, but she, Claudine, would make sure that she never got the chance.

The girl drove without speaking, and when they reached the red clearing she parked the Rolls so that the headlights shone on her car where it sat, the passenger door hanging drunkenly open.

The two old women got out of the Rolls, the headlamps

elongating their shadows to grotesque stick-like proportions, and peered into the Volkswagen. Martine remained slumped in the driving seat until Claudine returned, and taking her arm, pulled her out into the clearing.

'*Sale pute!*' she said. 'Come and help—'

'No,' Martine said, putting her hands up in front of her face.

Claudine's arm whipped back again and her hand landed heavily over the girl's ear. 'Do as you're told, *vache*,' she said.

With a reluctant Martine hardly helping, the three women somehow got the body from the Volkswagen. Claudine did not trust Martine and was careful to remove the keys before doing anything, putting them into her apron pocket, in case the girl tried to drive off and leave them in the clearing. Then Berthe pushed from the far side of the car, while she and Martine heaved; eventually the stiffening body tumbled out into the dust. Then with grim concentration Berthe and Claudine somehow managed to drag on the trousers, tucking in and buttoning up the shirt that had still flapped open as they pulled and pushed him from the car.

Sobbing and gasping, the three of them dragged Philip's body across the dust and heaved until he was on the back seat of the Rolls. Berthe had to sit on the running-board to get her breath back, and when she had recovered Claudine hustled Martine back into the driving seat. 'Take us back to Les Hirondelles,' she said. 'Get moving.'

She was thoughtful as she sat beside Martine with Berthe crammed in next to her. She had noticed the weird, acrid smell in the car, and she had in her pocket along with the keys to the other car two halves of a broken glass capsule. She had an idea it could be important.

She instructed the girl to drive into the courtyard and to turn the engine off and glide to a halt before the front door of the main house.

'If we can get him in quietly and into his room without madame hearing, she need never know,' she whispered to Berthe. 'Get Dupré.'

She made the girl help them with the body as far as the front door and then said: 'Take the car around to the back, *sale pute*, and then make yourself scarce.'

She noted how the girl needed no urging. She jumped into the car, backed it, and disappeared up the narrow road that led into the parking area.

Dupré had been in the middle of his supper and he came wiping his mouth with a large white napkin.

'What is it?' he said. 'What's happened?'

'Monsieur has been taken ill. We must get him to his room,' Claudine told him.

Dupré bent down to look at his master where he lay on the red tiles of the courtyard and looked up again, his face shocked.

'Ill?' he said. 'He's dead.'

'I know,' Claudine said impatiently. 'Just help us get him to his room. And don't disturb madame.'

With Dupré it became simpler. He took Philip de Courtenay's rigid shoulders, while the two old women took a leg each. They had the body inside the house and as quietly as possible were carrying it down the hallway towards the stairs when the door of Stella's room opened.

All three stopped dead and stared at her, the body held vertically in their grasp. She stood leaning on her stick, her breath whistling in her chest, her brilliant eyes taking in the scene and the line of red dust that had dropped from her husband's body. Then without speaking she turned and quietly closed the door behind her.

When they had laid him out decently on his bed, Claudine went in to see her mistress. Stella was on her bed staring at the ceiling and she turned her head to see Claudine's austere figure, hands folded in front, standing waiting, her black skirt dappled with red dust.

'You may as well tell me the truth, Claudine,' she said quietly.

Claudine hesitated.

'Come now. What happened? He's dead, isn't he?'

'Yes, madame.'

'Have you sent for a doctor?'

'Yes, madame.'

'And now tell me what happened.'

'He died in the red clearing.' Claudine stopped again.

'Had he been with the girl?'

'Yes.'

Stella sighed and stared back up at the ceiling again.

'Do you know what happened?'

'Not really. He was in her Volkswagen. I found this—'

She took the two pieces of glass from her pocket, and Stella sat up to take them, weigh them in her hand and then sniff them.

'Amyl nitrate,' she said softly. 'The fool . . .' She stopped and thought for a moment, then said : 'Try to persuade the doctor that he died in his room, will you?'

Without speaking, Claudine left the room, and for ten minutes Stella lay totally still while silent tears slid down her cheeks. She got up and sat at her small writing-desk. First she wrote out two cheques and then she made a telephone call. Afterwards she settled herself in a big armchair and rang for Claudine.

'I never thanked you for all you did,' she said abruptly as the woman came back into the room. 'How did you manage it?'

'Berthe came to the clearing with me; and Dupré, as you saw, was helping when we got back here. We made the girl help too.'

Stella nodded. She had no need to ask if her servants would keep their mouths shut.

'I'll thank Berthe and Dupré afterwards,' she said. 'For now, can you ask Pamela Whitton to come in? Then when I have finished with her, ask Dupré to fetch the *locataire*, and tell him to get ready to drive into Nice.'

Claudine nodded and left again.

Stella found she felt very calm as she waited for Pamela Whitton to arrive. Suki had come into the room and was on her lap, and she lightly stroked the white fur until she heard a light knock at the door.

Pamela Whitton sidled in.

'Whatever's going on?' she said. 'No supper being served, everyone acting so oddly and no sign of Philip anywhere.'

'He's in his room,' Stella told her.

'But it's locked, and no one answers.'

'That's hardly surprising,' Stella said. 'Philip is dead.'

Pamela Whitton gave a shriek, and her large eyes opened wider, showing a roll of white around the iris. Her hand came up to cover her mouth, and she said: 'Dead? Oh, no! Oh, no!'

'I'm afraid it's oh yes,' Stella said calmly, 'and therefore the end of the road for you here.' She picked up an envelope from the table beside her. 'There is a cheque for two thousand dollars. It should cover your expenses until you get yourself settled again. There is an airplane ticket waiting for you at Nice Airport. Your plane leaves at eleven o'clock. Tonight. I would suggest you only take what is absolutely necessary, and Claudine will pack and send on your things. Such a bore, travelling with a lot of luggage.'

Pamela Whitton was standing with her mouth wide open, hands clenching and unclenching.

'But you can't do this to me!' she said. 'I won't go!'

'I can do it, and you will go,' Stella said. 'Please let's not have any undignified scenes. You have had a very good run. Now it's finished.'

'He loved me!' Pamela Whitton shouted, tearing at her permed red curls. 'This should all be mine.'

'He loved a great many women,' Stella said calmly. 'But he married me.'

'For your money!'

She shook her head.

'No, Pamela – not for my money. Not at the beginning. There were others with more money.'

While the woman seemed to struggle for breath, Stella rang her bell again. Claudine must have been right outside, she appeared so quickly, and there was the faintest vestige of what could only have been called a triumphant smirk on the old woman's face.

'Take Mrs Whitton to her room, Claudine,' Stella said. 'She may need help packing.'

Pamela Whitton stared at the two implacable faces which stared back at her.

Suddenly she shrieked again, a long low wail.

'Oh, you bitch, you bitch, you bitch,' she said, as she turned and hobbled from the room. 'You'll be punished for this.'

The two women looked at each other, expressionless.

'Well, that was fairly simple,' Stella said matter-of-factly. 'And now the *locataire*. I think I'd like you to stay with me while I deal with this.'

'With pleasure, madame,' Claudine said.

'Sit down then,' Stella suggested. 'You must be very tired.'

'Oh, no, madame. I'd rather stand,' Claudine said, folding her arms over her bony chest. 'For this I'd much rather stand.'

The girl looked defiant and yet still faintly pleased with herself as she came into the room with Dupré hovering behind.

'Don't go, Dupré,' Stella said. 'It occurs to me that you can drop Madame Borrel at her car when you take Mrs Whitton to the airport.' She turned to the girl. 'Your car is still in the clearing, I presume?'

'Yes.' The *locataire* suddenly seemed slightly less sure of herself.

'I would say that you have about half an hour to get your things together,' Stella said chattily. 'Dupré has to be in Nice for the eleven o'clock plane. Perhaps you'd like to start packing right away. There is a cheque in this envelope –' she handed it to the girl, who automatically took it '– repaying the week's advance rent that you gave my husband—'

'What advance—?' Martine started to say and then stopped. Glaring at Stella, she tore open the envelope and snatched the cheque from inside. 'Five hundred francs! It's an insult!' she said. 'You've got to be joking.'

'Joking?' Stella raised her eyebrows.

'When I start telling the newspapers how your husband died...'

'And when I start telling the doctor that you gave him amyl nitrate, you may have to answer to a charge of murder, madame,' Stella said crisply. 'Did you not know that amyl nitrate is used to control heart attacks but that it can create the condition it cures? Morally, and possibly also criminally, you are responsible for the death of my husband. Perhaps we should ring the police now and find out.'

She put out her hand and rested it lightly on the receiver of the telephone. Martine started forward.

'No, don't,' she said. 'Anyway, he bought the amyl nitrate. Not me.'

Stella looked at her consideringly, certain the girl was lying. 'Then why is the rest of it in your room?'

'It's not in my room, it's in—' Again she stopped dead.

'It doesn't matter where it is,' Stella said. 'Nor does it really matter if you tell the newspapers how my husband died. It can no longer hurt him and it most certainly would not hurt me. But as I say, you could find yourself in deep waters. It is very difficult to fight people with as much money as we have. Therefore I would suggest that you go, as they say in my country, quietly.'

The room was silent, and then Dupré who stood in the open doorway coughed and said: 'I wonder if I could hurry you, madame. I must leave in no more than half an hour.'

'Listen,' Martine was saying desperately, 'you can't just chuck me out. My brother's your stepdaughter's son. He's staying with her. And my sister's gone off with Margaret de Courtenay. I'll make a scandal.'

Stella's face was implacable. 'My stepchildren lead their own lives,' she said. 'Claudine, see madame out.'

The girl looked at Claudine, who smiled at her with bared yellow teeth and said:

'Would you like some help with your packing?'

Martine hesitated, shrugged her shoulders, and without speaking marched from the room, Claudine close behind her.

'You'll enjoy your drive with Mrs Whitton,' Stella heard her say. 'The two of you can compare notes.' And she closed her eyes against the thought.

She was standing staring out of the window when Claudine returned.

'Would you like some supper now, *chère madame*?' Claudine asked.

282

Stella shook her head and moved back to her chair. She stared into the empty fireplace and said:

'Well, that's that. Both of them disposed of. Now I can mourn my husband with some dignity.' Her face crumpled, and Claudine hurried to the whisky decanter. But Stella put out a restraining hand.

'No,' she said. 'No, Claudine. I don't believe I'm going to be needing that any more.'

Chapter Twenty

McTaggart had instinctively left the bridge and, moving as fast as he could, went down on the deck after the shot was fired. The man at the wheel had made no attempt to stop him. Evelyn Grenville appeared to have fainted. She was collapsed in a heap on the polished boards of the deck, and for a moment he thought she too had been shot.

Marion and Peter were both kneeling by Tomas's body, Marion with bright splashes of blood splattered over her bare legs.

'He's dead,' she said as McTaggart knelt with them. 'Oh, Christ, he's dead.' She dropped her face into her hands and wept, and Peter stared at McTaggart over his brother's body.

'What's going on, for God's sake?' he said. 'What is this all about?'

'We've been hijacked,' McTaggart answered briefly. 'It's as well to do as you're told.'

'That's very good advice,' the man with the gun said. 'Very good advice indeed. Now I suggest that you all get into the main saloon and make yourselves comfortable. Nothing will happen to any of you if you keep quiet. If you don't –' he pointed to Tomas's body and the blood running over the deck '– well, let that discourage you.'

Dazed with shock, Marion got to her feet. Anne took her arm and led her towards the saloon. Peter bodily picked up Evelyn who was laying inert, moaning, and followed them.

'You kids can stay out,' the man with the gun said, nodding at Françoise and Raoul. 'I gather you're in on it, and we may want your help later.'

The other man had left the wheel and come down on to the deck. Using his gun as a persuader he was herding Peter with his burden and the two women along the deck. McTaggart was cold with shock and he could see naked terror in Raoul's eyes, though the boy was biting his lip and trying not to cry. Françoise's face was set like a stone.

'God almighty!' he thought. 'What have we got ourselves into!'

He had to keep his head and he said calmly: 'What do you want done about this?' He indicated the body with his feet.

'Get one of the crew to cover it with a tarpaulin,' the man who had fired the shot said. 'Later we'll weight it and chuck it overboard.'

He might have been talking about disposing of some kitchen garbage, his tone was so casual, and he turned to his companion and said: 'Lock that lot in where they can't get in the way, OK?'

McTaggart stood staring down at the body and thinking of the suddenness of death.

'This is all a bit unexpected,' he said. 'I gather we're changing our plans.'

'Not a lot. You're just getting me back to Palestine.'

'You're the cargo, are you?' McTaggart said. 'What about the hash?'

'That's cargo too. Achmid wants the whole lot delivered outside Tripoli.'

'You mean we've got to tow it all the way to bloody Libya?'

'That's right.'

The other man had come back.

'They're locked in, Lefrère,' he said. 'And all quiet.'

'Lefrère—!' McTaggart started, involuntarily repeating the name, and looked hard at the man with the gun, unable to control his alarm. Was this Lefrère, the Palestinian terrorist who had taken over where the infamous Carlos had left off? A murderer who had hijacked two El Al jumbo jets, had been responsible for the death of dozens of Israelis, had been wanted by Interpol for three years and never been caught. The man had barely been seen sufficiently to give the police a decent description of him.

The man grinned, took off his sunglasses and bowed.

'That's it,' he said. 'You've got it in one. Good way to get back home, don't you think? Who's going to suspect a rich man's nice elegant yacht on a Mediterranean cruise?'

'It should work,' McTaggart agreed. But his mind was racing ahead to what would happen once Lefrère was delivered back to Palestine. He was pretty sure he knew. *Les Hirondelles III* would be scuttled or blown up with all aboard. If he could ingratiate himself sufficiently with Lefrère, make him believe he was no more than a sailor of fortune motivated according to whoever paid the most, he might get out of it with Françoise and maybe even Raoul. Even that was pretty unlikely, as he'd be able to identify the man. He wasn't at all happy about the casualness with which the terrorist identified himself. It smelt of someone who knew he was perfectly safe. There wasn't going to be a damn thing he could do about Peter, Marion, Anne Paradine and the American girl, all of whom had been dragged into this willy-nilly; the de Courtenays might be arrogant but they didn't deserve the sort of death that was probably waiting for them.

'And where do you come in?' he asked the other man, still keeping his voice casual.

'Me? I'm Benjie, a professional like yourself. Sailor – and frogman. You're going to be needing me later when we pick up that hash.'

He grinned too, and McTaggart thought how cheerful they were for a couple of murdering bastards.

'Well, I'll get myself back to the bridge,' he said.

'Don't worry,' Benjie said. 'I can cope.'

'I'm sure you can,' McTaggart said, his professional pride taking over. 'But as a pro, you'll understand she's my ship.

285

Though you're welcome on the bridge anytime.' He wanted control of the boat. It might be their only hope.

Benjie's grin faded and then returned. 'Right, skipper,' he said. 'I'm with you.'

Anne and Marion were sitting side by side on the big settee in the stateroom. Marion, her eyes now dry, was staring blindly into space but she had hold of Anne's hand in a grip that hurt. Peter was pacing up and down.

'I don't understand what the hell's going on,' he said. 'Christ, Tomas! Dead! I can't take it in. And what are Raoul and Françoise up to? Nothing makes sense.'

'We know it's a hijack,' Anne said. She was still trembling inside but managing to keep calm on the surface.

Evelyn had been laid out on the other large sofa and was quietly crying. Anne could have hit her. Why couldn't she shut up? She was contemptible, with her elegant white suit, her perfect hair, nails and make-up, which even the grizzling hadn't disturbed. All that and total panic.

Outside, it was dark, and the yacht was cruising smoothly. They could see a few, but very few, shore lights; all was quiet on deck.

'But a hijack for what?' Peter said.

They had been locked up for at least an hour and now were beginning to ask questions for which there weren't any answers.

'They're Arabs,' Anne said thoughtfully. 'Remember Achmid's conversation at dinner that night? It must be something to do with the Palestinian terrorists. And it must be something to do with him. It's the only explanation.'

Peter stopped pacing. 'That man with the gun – the one who killed Tomas – could he be Lefrère?'

'It seems too far fetched for words,' Anne said. 'But the truth is that he could. Do you remember Achmid said something about terrorists having their place in the struggle?'

'That's true,' Peter said, 'but if it is Lefrère, we're in trouble.'

'Yes,' Anne said drily, 'we are. Is there any chance of getting through the windows?'

Peter shook his head. 'Father had them permanently locked when he put the air conditioning in.'

They could see a lighthouse now sending out its beams in a regular pattern some distance ahead, and suddenly there was the grinding noise of the anchor dropping.

'Now what?' said Peter.

'Oh, God!' Evelyn suddenly sat up and stared around the stateroom, her eyes wild. 'Why did I ever come here? This can't be happening to me!'

Anne stared at her and wondered that this woman had caused her so much anguish. If, she thought, Peter preferred Evelyn Grenville then Peter could not be worth worrying about.

'Oh – do shut up,' Marion was saying.

'Yes, be quiet, Evelyn,' Peter said abstractedly. 'I'm trying to think. That's got to be Cape Spartel lighthouse, but where are they heading? Do you think McTaggart's in on whatever's going on?'

'Françoise was always very thick with him,' Marion said suddenly. 'I always thought they were having a thing.'

'Right, so we have Achmid involved with Tomas. We have a couple of Arab terrorists aboard. We have McTaggart probably in with them and Raoul and Françoise definitely in with them, and we appear to be anchoring a couple of miles off Cape Spartel lighthouse. What does all that add up to?'

There was silence in the saloon, and then Anne said: 'Not much.'

'In fact,' Peter said, 'fuck all.'

They looked at each other helplessly; instinctively Peter took Anne's hand in his, and her head fell to his shoulder.

Suddenly Evelyn stopped snivelling. She sat upright, her long elegant legs swinging to the floor. As she smoothed back her short, springy fair hair her voice had become authoritative.

'Peter – what is going on here? With you, I mean? Who is this girl?'

'Me?' Marion said with studied rudeness. 'I'm his sister.'

'I gathered that,' Evelyn said.

Before she could say more, Peter said in a drawing-room

287

voice, 'Evelyn, I'm so sorry. It just didn't seem the moment for formal introductions. This is Anne Paradine. Anne, Evelyn Grenville.'

Both women nodded curtly, and Anne took the opportunity for a close look at Evelyn Grenville. She was so perfectly featured that it seemed as if both sides of her face were identical in boring symmetry. She had very clear pale blue eyes, a neat little nose with sharply defined nostrils, and a rather small cupid-bow mouth. She was very pretty, but the blue eyes were frosted.

'Well, Peter,' she said sharply. 'What is the situation?'

'Situation?' he said. 'Pretty unclear, I'm afraid, Evelyn. What these men want—'

'It's perfectly obvious what these men want. They've kidnapped me. They obviously know who I am. And you've landed me in this situation when it appears blindingly obvious that you and this girl—'

'Evelyn, really,' Peter said impatiently. 'This is no time for—'

'Oh, yes it is,' she said. 'You fetch me all the way to Tangier when I could have been at Malibu; you made it clear originally that the intention was for me to see your home, suddenly you change the arrangements, subject me to this God-awful danger – even letting those two murdering thugs snatch me from the hotel – and then I find that you have another girl on board this floating—' She spluttered, lost for words, and then turned to Anne and demanded: 'Are you sleeping with him?'

Anne found herself speechless. She had despised Evelyn Grenville when she was panicking and frightened. But she found herself totally detesting this uppercrust *grande dame*. On the other hand she knew Evelyn had cause for complaint. She and Peter had not behaved well.

'Oh, for God's sake,' Marion said suddenly from her seat on the sofa. 'What fucking business is it of yours? And who the hell are you that anyone would want to kidnap you?' Evelyn's mouth opened and shut again as Marion, teetering on the verge of hysteria, screamed: 'There's a dead man out there and you're going on about who's sleeping with who? For

Christ's sake ... you've been a bloody nuisance ever since you got on board. You came because you're after my brother, so don't blame him.'

'Marion, lay off,' Peter said firmly. 'Evelyn, take it easy—'

'Take it easy!' Evelyn's flat Bostonian voice had risen in indignation. 'What an elegant sister you have—'

'Not piss-elegant like you,' Marion chipped in.

'Please!' Anne was finding the situation surrealistic in its extravagance. 'Marion's upset. You must understand, they've murdered her brother. She's right. It's not the moment for personal recriminations. We have to think how to get out of here before they murder us too.'

For the moment that seemed to be of little interest to Evelyn. Quivering with rage she stared at Anne and repeated her original question: 'Are you sleeping with him?'

Anne hesitated, and then said: 'I love him.'

'So do I. Do you think I'd have come all this way—?'

'Oh, my God,' Peter said. 'Now stop it. Just stop it.'

'Hearts and bloody flowers – that's all we need. I loved *him*. And he's dead,' Marion shouted, pointing out to the deck, and burst into a storm of weeping.

Peter dropped down on the sofa beside her and took her in his arms, rocking and soothing her, stroking her dishevelled black hair. 'Go on, cry,' he was saying, 'Cry it all out.' He looked over her head to Evelyn and said in tones that allowed for no argument: 'We'll talk later.'

She stared at him and abruptly turned and walked to stare out of the window at the darkness outside. Anne realized she was crying too.

Raoul was absolutely terrified, but along with his terror there was anger. He kept seeing the man with the gun shoot his father so casually and without second thought. He could see the fall, the blood appearing in a tight and then spreading circle on his father's white shirt, and he could see Marion kneeling beside him, her legs splattered with his father's blood. He had wanted to kneel beside him too and mourn but he had been too afraid. He was still afraid but he had made a decision. He had never had the opportunity to make his father proud of him in life. He would do something that his father, watching from wherever he was, would understand and realize that he had a son to be reckoned with.

When the anchor went down he figured he had the opportunity. The man called Lefrère was in the bows, staring at the land. The other man had taken a wet-suit from the striped bundle he had left on the deck and was pulling it on. McTaggart was on the bridge; Françoise was with him. And the other crew members were assembling the rubber dinghy, fixing the outboard motor between the two stabilizing torpedoes.

He knew where the spare keys to all the cabins were kept – on a ledge at the back of the bridge behind the wheel. He slipped up quietly, neither McTaggart or Françoise heard him arriving, and he swept up the keys on the ledge and put them in his pocket. The jangle, fortunately, was infinitesimal. There was no time to sort out one key from another. He had just hidden them when Françoise turned round. Her face was very pale, and he sensed that she was as frightened as he was.

'What are you doing, Raoul?' she asked, and he was afraid for the moment that she had seen him scoop up the keys.

'I was looking for you,' he said. 'Are you all right?'

'Yes. Are you?'

They stared at each other, a genuine fraternal concern sparking between them. He knew now that she had seen him take the keys, but that she wouldn't say anything.

He stayed with them on the bridge for a minute or two to make things look normal. No one was speaking. There didn't seem to be anything to say. And after a while he crept away again. The Arabs were still at the bows, and he wriggled on his stomach to the door of the stateroom, desperately afraid but aware that everyone had forgotten his presence. He had a very good chance of getting away with it.

He tried several keys before he found the right one, and he could see Peter's anxious face motioning the others to keep quiet as he tried each one in the lock. His breath was coming in quick sharp bursts, and he was scared out of his wits; finally, miraculously, a key turned. He pulled the door open as little as possible and slid through, still on his stomach.

'Don't get off the floor,' Peter said. The lights in the state-room were full on, and had he stood up he could have been visible to anyone outside. By now he was sobbing with fear. He knew they'd kill him if they discovered what he was doing.

'Here's the key,' he said and flung it into the middle of the room; fear propelled him as he scuttled back towards the door.

'Wait!' Peter said, his voice urgent. 'What's happening, Raoul? What's going on?'

The boy was almost sobbing with terror.

'I can't stay,' he said. 'You've got the key. You can get out. I can't do any more.'

Peter's voice betrayed his anxiety: 'Raoul, wait – why have they stopped?'

'It's for the hash, that's all.'

'Raoul—' Anne was speaking. 'Can you persuade McTaggart get as near to Gibraltar as possible?'

The boy lay still, and three pairs of eyes turned to look at the key where it lay on the large Spanish carpet.

'I'll try,' he whispered and with one last wriggle was through the door, closing it gently behind him.

No one seemed to have missed him, and trembling he went down on the deck, where Benjie had finished pulling on the wet-suit and made a sinister figure in shiny black, holding a pair of flippers. The body of Raoul's father was still on the deck, a tarpaulin flung over it. Raoul shuddered.

'Ah, there you are, boy,' Benjie said. 'Can you steer that?' He nodded to the rubber dinghy.

'Yes,' Raoul said.

'Right, then you're elected as skipper. I need the lightest one of you. Get in. We might as well lower away with you aboard. Just take these—' He thrust the flippers into Raoul's hand and then tipped himself over the side.

He never bothered to get back into the dinghy once the rest of the crew had launched it with Raoul hanging grimly on to the sides. He gripped one side and floated while the boy started the outboard.

'Keep it quiet as possible,' he said. 'We've got all the time in the world. There's no hurry.'

'Where do I go?' Raoul asked. He was still terrified, but the man hanging on the side was whistling unconcernedly through his teeth, so some of the terror was evaporating.

'How good are your eyes?'

'Good,' Raoul told him.

'So they should be at your age. See straight ahead? When the lighthouse comes round, you'll see a white house on top of the cliff.'

Raoul peered through the night.

'I see it,' he said.

'Right – just steer for there. And take it easy. Keep the engine quiet, eh?'

The man had taken hold of the tow rope and was floating behind.

'Yes, sir,' Raoul said.

It was Peter who picked up the key. He dropped out of sight of the windows into an armchair and, copying Raoul, slid on his belly along the floor to reach up and lock the door again. Then he crawled back to the chair.

'We could swim,' Anne said.

'I could swim,' he said firmly.

'No. *We*,' she said. 'At night it's better with two, and I'm just as strong a swimmer as you are. I might even have more stamina –' she managed a small joke '– I don't smoke.'

'Out of the question,' he said.

'How would you stop me? But it's academic unless Mc-Taggart gets near Gib.'

'Spain would do,' Peter said thoughtfully. 'But Gib would be better.'

Marion, who had been listening quietly, still holding Anne's hand, said: 'What did Raoul mean about the hash?'

'God knows,' Peter said. 'Hash, hijacking – it gets madder by the minute.'

'And murder,' Marion said and bit her lip to hold back tears.

'You realize they'll murder us all.' Evelyn's voice was high and she sat up trembling violently. 'Don't try anything stupid, for God's sake. Do what they say.'

'Relax, Evelyn, there's a good girl,' Peter said. 'We've got to keep our wits about us. That's all.'

It was at that moment that the telephone on the table by Peter's chair rang.

'Christ!' Peter said. 'It's still switched through.' His hand had shot out to pick up the receiver.

'Hello,' he said.

'Peter?' Through the hissing of the electronic sea sounds it was unmistakably his mother's voice.

'Mother – thank God—'

He silenced abruptly. Someone on the bridge had come on to the line.

'Achmid?' The voice was eager as if taking an expected phonecall.

'Peter?' he heard his mother say. 'I want to speak to Peter de Courtenay.'

There was a silence, and then the voice said: 'I'm afraid Monsieur de Courtenay is ashore and not expected back until tomorrow night.'

'Then is Tomas de Courtenay available?'

'All the family have gone ashore.'

'And McTaggart?'

'Ashore. May I take a message?'

'Do you have any idea where they are staying?'

'None, madame.'

Peter heard his mother sigh.

'Will you please ask either monsieur to ring their mother as soon as they return. There is some family news—'

'Certainly, madame.'

Both his mother and the gunman – Peter was sure it was his voice – hung up. And then, very carefully he hung up too.

'It was Mother,' he said. 'There's some family news. I don't know what. Someone cut in.'

Marion said eagerly: 'Did she hear you?'

'I don't know. I think so, but more important I don't think whoever answered the phone realized I was on the line.'

'That's very good news indeed,' Anne said softly. 'Your mother misses nothing. That's what I'd call fire insurance.'

'But why was she calling?' Peter said. 'Something must be wrong at home.'

'It never rains . . .' said Marion. 'And, oh God, it's raining in torrents right now.'

'And you all keep asking for trouble,' Evelyn said. 'Why can't you just—?'

'Why can't you just shut up,' Marion interrupted fiercely. 'Just – shut – up.'

The rocking of the yacht at anchor had made Marion faintly queasy and after a while she slept. Evelyn slept too, probably out of sheer exhaustion, Anne thought. No one could go on being that dramatic indefinitely. It was gone ten o'clock, and she and Peter were the only ones left awake in the stateroom.

'Well?' Anne asked. 'Now what?' She spoke very softly.

Peter had been trying to see what was happening ashore, but apart from the odd flicker of light he could see nothing; there was movement on the bridge directly above them.

'But who's up there?' he said. 'McTaggart? The gunman? Who?'

Anne had begun to find herself calmer. The original terror and the shock of what had happened to Tomas was beginning to fade, and a spirit of self-preservation was asserting itself. She didn't want to die. She didn't want Marion to die and she certainly didn't want Peter to die. If pressed she would have had to admit that she wasn't too concerned about Françoise, but now because of his last action she was faintly concerned for Raoul. Though she had a very strong feeling that those two had led them into this dangerous situation.

'Let's talk it out,' she said. 'What are the possibilities?'

'Right,' said Peter. 'Possibility one is that if we have terrorists aboard our chances are pretty slight. I didn't say anything before because I didn't want to answer questions, but whoever answered the phone asked if Achmid was there. Our first guess that this is something to do with Tomas's little friend was correct.'

'So what have we been hijacked for? What's the purpose? Kidnapping? Ransom?'

Peter shook his head.

'I doubt if it's for money somehow. It doesn't seem to fit with Achmid. I think he wants the yacht for something else.'

'Do you remember how keen Françoise was on this cruise?' Anne said slowly. 'It was she who really engineered the whole thing, if you think back to that morning in the garden. And she was so keen to get the whole family aboard. Doesn't that point to kidnapping?'

'I don't think she wanted the family aboard,' Peter said. They were almost whispering now. 'I think that was Father. He wanted to be left in peace with the *locataire*. I'm sure of that. Françoise was probably helping persuade us because she knew Father wouldn't agree to the cruise unless we all went.'

'So why did Françoise want the cruise so badly?'

'Beats me,' Peter said. 'I just don't know, unless she was getting paid for engineering it. But I'm sure it's not kidnapping. They had the perfect opportunity to make their demands when Mother rang.'

'No they didn't. We're too close to Tangier, where someone might have seen us. It would have been too soon. I think it's kidnapping.'

But Peter wasn't convinced.

'The hash is confusing,' he said. 'But my guess is that we're no more than transportation to get those men to somewhere in the Middle East. Probably Palestine. And if that's the case—'

'They'll kill us because we know too much,' Anne said, astonished to find her voice was matter-of-fact, but she could not control a little shiver.

He got up from the chair where he was sitting, came and lifted her and held her very tightly.

'Darling,' he said, 'what have we got you into? I'm so terribly sorry. But don't be frightened. I'll get us all out of it.'

'Well, we won't go quietly,' she said lightly. It all felt much more bearable with his arms around her. 'But what do we do?'

'I'm going to swim for it,' he said. 'Try to get help.'

'And I'm coming with you.'

'Anne, you are not.' He pulled back and looked down into her face. 'It's far too dangerous.'

295

'So it's a Sunday-school outing around here?' she said.
'Listen, I'd rather drown nice and cleanly than end up like
Tomas. And I'd rather be doing something positive than wait-
ing for them to bump us off in their own good time.'

She could see she had convinced him.

'And I think I'd rather have you with me than left here,
come to think of it,' he said.

'Right,' she said. 'Now when do we go?'

'Not from here,' he said. 'It's too far from habitation. There
are too many of them out there. And they're doing something
ashore. But wait a minute,' he said slowly, 'I've got it – I know
what we'll do . . .'

The frogman had left Raoul sitting in the dinghy anchored
about a hundred yards off shore. The water was still very
shallow, only up to the man's waist, as he waded in, and there
was a strong swell which kept the little dinghy rocking. Raoul
was too frightened to feel seasick and was straining his eyes
through the darkness of the night to see what was going on
ashore.

He could hear much more than he could see. Oddly he
heard the braying of a donkey a couple of times, the murmur
of voices with the guttural, throaty sound of Arabic, and
dragging sounds, grunts and the odd splash from something
heavy landing in water.

He must have been rocking in the dinghy for more than
half an hour when Benjie came back, this time with the helmet
of his frogman's suit pulled over his head and two cylinders
of oxygen on his back, the mask dangling round his neck. He
seemed to be hauling something; standing waist deep in water
Raoul saw that he was tying a line around his own waist.

'Right then,' he said. 'Get the anchor up and get going.'

Raoul hurriedly did as he was told, and again Benjie found
the tow rope and let himself be pulled along. But this time
there was more resistance, a lot of resistance, and behind him
Raoul could see what looked like a string of enormous bobbing
sausages. The hash, he thought. They were towing the hash
in some sort of floating container.

As they got back to the yacht Benjie told him to stay where he was, and he dived down below the hull. When he surfaced it seemed as if the rope was longer around his waist. Then he swam along the length of the 'sausages', submerging beside each one and using a small torch to do something that Raoul couldn't work out, except that one by one the long shapes sank gently below the surface of the water.

Having made the last one disappear Benjie swam back to the dinghy.

'Right,' he said. 'All done. Back on board now.'

Raoul took the dinghy amidships, and the pair of them scrambled up the rope ladder which hung there, while the crew lifted the dinghy back to its place on deck.

No one was taking any notice of him now he was no longer needed, so Raoul went back to the bridge. McTaggart was at the wheel, Françoise sleeping on the long banquette behind him.

'Are you all right, laddie?' McTaggart asked.

'I think so.'

'I'm sorry we got you into this,' McTaggart said, his voice so solemn that Raoul was more afraid than he'd been before.

'McTaggart—' he said and then stopped, uncertain.

'What is it lad?'

'I gave the key of the saloon to Peter.'

McTaggart looked at him sharply.

'And they said can you get as near to Gib as possible.'

The skipper did not reply. He wiped his hand over his forehead, shook his head and finally said: 'Go and sleep somewhere and don't try anything else. It's too dangerous.'

But Raoul had the definite feeling that McTaggart was not displeased with what he had done.

Chapter Twenty-one

The yacht engines had started again, and as far as Peter could see they were leaving the coast of Morocco behind them. About a quarter of an hour later Benjie came to peer in through the saloon windows, presumably to check they were all present and correct.

Peter made frantic signals, and the man stopped and looked inquiringly. Peter then mimed feeling cold and mouthed, 'Can we have some blankets?'

Benjie grinned, made a thumbs-up sign and disappeared. He was back in about five minutes with one arm full of blankets, a gun and the key in his other hand.

He unlocked the door, flung in the blankets and said, 'OK?'

'OK,' Peter said. 'We're going to sleep now.'

'Do as you like,' Benjie said, shutting the door again quickly. He grinned through the glass and walked off.

'I must say he's remarkably amiable for a terrorist,' Peter said. Very carefully he covered Marion with a blanket and put another over Evelyn, who stirred and whimpered.

'Now,' he said to Anne, 'it's time for lights-out.'

Even with the lights out it wasn't totally dark in the saloon – the light from the companionway outside filtered through, and on one of the sofas where the light fell most strongly Peter piled up cushions from the chairs in the darker corners and covered them with blankets.

'Does that look like two people curled up together?' he whispered.

'It'll do,' Anne said.

Then they both settled themselves in the darkness where they could look from the windows out to sea.

'Do you think Raoul will tell McTaggart? And do you think McTaggart will help?' Anne whispered. She was close to him for warmth, and he had his arm around her.

'No way of knowing,' Peter said. 'But there's not much point in going overboard unless we can see land. And in swimmable distance.'

They sat silently and he could feel Anne dropping into a doze against him every now and then, and he held her tighter. He had positioned them so they could see from the windows on both sides of the saloon, but there was only blackness outside and her warmth against him. He felt enormous tenderness for her as well as gratitude for her courage. Marion was totally shocked and therefore of no help, and two Evelyns would have been too much of a burden. He also felt a tremendous sense of responsibility that his family had led both Anne and Evelyn into so much danger. He shivered slightly at the thought of what lay ahead. Anne, sensing his anxiety said sleepily: 'Don't worry. We'll get out of it somehow.'

The night and the darkness seemed interminable. He could hear little sobbing noises coming from Marion. She was crying in her sleep. Evelyn was very quiet, and the ship seemed silent as if the crew might be sleeping too. There was no movement from the bridge above. He looked at the time, and the greenish hands of his watch said three o'clock. Only three o'clock! But it was then he saw the flashing light high in the sky. A steady, regular beam of red and gold. He thought at first it was an airplane, but the light stayed exactly in the same place. Then he realized: it was the clifftop warning light at Gibraltar. McTaggart was steering through the straits and letting the boat veer to the European side.

Peter was suddenly excited, exhaustion gone.

'Anne, look—' He shook her gently. 'Look – the Rock.'

Now he had realized what the light was, his eyes could see the dark mass of Gibraltar against the only just paler sky, and as they chugged on at thirteen knots, lights began to appear. Anne had not spoken but was clinging to his hand, peering with him; beacons of hope, the shore lights became clearer.

'It's still a hell of a long way off,' he said doubtfully.

'And we're not getting any nearer,' she said. 'I suppose McTaggart, if he is trying to help, can't get in any closer without someone noticing.'

'What are you two doing?' It was Marion's voice. She had woken up and come up quietly behind them.

'We're going to try to swim for it,' Anne said, still looking out at the shore lights.

'Oh, darlings, you can't,' Marion said. 'It's miles!'

'About eight,' Peter said. 'Not too bad.'

'It looks a damn sight further than that to me,' Marion said. 'Look, leave it. Chance what will happen here. I mean, they can't kill us all.'

Having said it, all fell silent, the picture too sharp and clear in their memories of the casual way the gunman had felled Tomas.

'Come on, Marion,' Peter said, 'I don't think these people are too much into life preservation. It's worth a try. You hang on here. Keep her quiet—' He jerked his head in Evelyn's direction. 'Don't let her say what we're doing if anyone disturbs you before morning.'

Marion's voice was steady, but Anne could see in the faint light that her eyes were too bright.

'I'll hold the fort,' she said, then added as casually as possible: 'Are you going now?'

Peter nodded. The lights were not getting any nearer; if anything, they were receding. He was stripping off shirt, trousers and shoes. Anne, followed his example by stripping down to pants and bra.

'We've got it all planned,' he said. 'All you have to do is to lock the door behind us and hide our clothes under the blankets. That's us sleeping there.'

'It's as good as done,' Marion said. Her voice was shaking. 'Goodbye and good luck, brother – and sister.'

She kissed them both, and then picking out the shadowed parts of the saloon they crossed to the door, which Peter opened; he handed Marion the key.

'Be careful,' he said. 'Try to sleep. You don't know a thing.'

'I always was dumb.'

The ship was still quiet, and they crawled on their bellies to where the companionway began amidships; the rope ladder normally used for nothing more sinister than cooling dips, hung there. It was absurdly easy slipping over the side and creeping down the ladder, entering the sea inch by inch so that the silence was undisturbed. It took Anne longer once on the ladder. Her leg slowed her down, but they reached the water without incident. Then in unison they started swimming, though

Peter was appalled to realize that the shore lights were much harder to see now they were at sea level.

By using a hard, fast crawl they were able to get themselves out of the wash of *Les Hirondelles III* and into calmer waters, Anne tight at his side. Peter asked if she was all right.

'Fine,' she said. 'But it's bloody cold.'

It was bloody cold. 'Only until we get going and warm up,' he said encouragingly.

'Can you see the shore lights?'

'Oh yes,' he said, lying in his teeth. 'But it's also bloody dark. Where the hell's the moon?'

It seemed like a ridiculous conversation under the circumstances, but what else was there to say? They were embarked now. *Les Hirondelles III* was rapidly sailing down the middle of the straits. They had no other choice than to swim or drown. He could feel the tide pulling them; a strong current appeared, at least, to be going in the right direction, though whether or not into Gibraltar harbour it was impossible to assess.

He knew that what they were attempting was madness. The night was black, the sea freezing, the shore miles away – even if they could ever find enough light to swim in the right direction. It was sink or swim, both metaphorically and literally.

'OK,' he said. 'Now we swim. Take it easy. We mustn't wear ourselves out. Just a good steady crawl in the right direction.'

'I think the tide's with us,' she said, 'but it seems to be pulling us to the left.'

'Then we'll just have to correct,' he said. 'Come on, my darling, swim for your life.'

'And Marion's,' she said, puffing out water as they set off again.

Stella could not sleep. Grief had been the strongest element in keeping her awake. She grieved that things had not been different between her and Philip and she questioned herself as to whether their estrangement had been her fault or his. Had she not let herself get so fat, had she not been so neglectful of her body and health, would things have been any different?

But then, had he not been so neglectful of her . . .

It was a question that could only go around in circles.

Now there was something else worrying her too. Earlier that night she had been too concerned with her own distress to puzzle deeply that she had not been able to contact any of her children on the yacht. Exhausted by her dismissal of Pamela Whitton and the *locataire*, she had been too tired to question whoever answered the phone any further and had put down the receiver thinking that the morning would have to do. The boys could have one more night of the cruise before the problems of the funeral and all the details of death had to be dealt with.

But lying awake in the darkness she was troubled. She could have sworn she had heard Peter's voice through the static on the phone and could have sworn he had said: 'Mother – thank God!' And then there was just the voice saying eagerly, 'Achmid,' after which she had been told that no one, not even McTaggart, was aboard.

It didn't make sense. Why wouldn't McTaggart be aboard?

She lay and pondered for a while, and then sitting up in bed reached for her telephone and dialled international information.

She had a long wait before anyone answered but she lay with her head on the pillow, with the receiver to her ear, waiting for the response. When it came she asked for the telephone number of the El Minzeh hotel in Tangier. She had remembered that this was where Evelyn Grenville was staying, and therefore if her children were off the yacht for the night the chances were that they would be there too.

The operator gave her the number, explaining she had to dial nineteen, then two-one-two for Morocco and nine for Tangier. She followed the instructions and got through at the first attempt. It was four in the morning.

The night concierge sounded intelligent enough and spoke good French. She explained she did not wish to disturb anyone, but were three members of her family guests at the hotel? Marion, Tomas and Peter de Courtenay.

The concierge went to check.

'No, madame,' he said when he returned. 'They are not staying here.'

'Could they have checked out?' Stella asked.

'No, madame,' the man said. 'They have never been registered.'

'I'm sorry to trouble you,' Stella said, 'but would you see if a Miss Evelyn Grenville of Boston, Massachusetts, is still with you.'

He seemed quite happy to have something to do and left her holding on. When he spoke again he said that Miss Grenville had departed that afternoon, but as yet her luggage had not been collected.

'Did she say she was returning?' Stella asked.

'I'm sorry, madame, I have no idea. Perhaps if you were to telephone in the morning.'

'I'll do that,' she said. 'And thank you for your help.'

'*Je vous en prie,*' the man said.

Stella put down the phone puzzled. A conviction that all was not well was growing. Where were her family? Why was someone on *Les Hirondelles III* expecting a call from Achmid – she had to accept that the Arab world was littered with Achmids, but even so it was a coincidence. Why had Evelyn left all her luggage behind? From what Stella remembered of careful, prim and proper Evelyn, she wouldn't leave her luggage in Fort Knox let alone a Tangier hotel.

Stella deliberated and then, a decision made, picked up the telephone once again and dialled.

When it was answered she said: 'John – this is a terrible hour to call you. You know I'm not an imaginative woman, but I think I need help.'

They must have been in the water well over an hour when Peter knew he was going to have to slow his stroke to keep with Anne. She was tiring and swam on grimly in the darkness at his side. Neither spoke – there was no breath for words, and he wasn't even sure if they were all that much nearer their hoped-for landfall. The night was pitch black, and the small choppy waves totally blocked out any chance of seeing shore lights. It was about four thirty he reckoned, and a long time till dawn. For all he knew they could be swimming straight down the middle of the straits, into the ocean and afterwards God knew where.

'Let's rest,' he said, breaking his stroke to touch her arm. She turned her head, lifting it from the water and nodded silently, flipping over on to her back and floating.

He did the same, taking her hand, and they lay staring into the sky, letting the water rock them while tired muscles relaxed and breath came back.

'We mustn't stay too long like this or we'll get cramp,' he said.

'I almost don't mind,' she said dreamily. 'I'm so tired ... Do you realize that there's about seven miles of nothing but water and fish underneath us? Isn't it strange? All that blackness. All that nothing. It's scary.'

'Don't think about it,' he said. 'We've got to keep going.'

'Oh, I know,' she said, matter-of-fact again. 'It's only one of my little flights of fancy. If only we could fly,' she added inconsequentially.

He was worried about her state of mind. 'Five minutes,' he said, 'and then we go on.' He was anxious that he might lose what sense of direction he had left and focused on a small cloud, only too aware that small clouds moved. But there wasn't a star to be seen.

'We'll count out the time,' he said. And two voices counted 'one, two, three ...' in second spacing, speaking softly into the darkness, until the five minutes passed. 'Now back to work,' he said.

She squeezed his hand very tightly before letting go and then she said: 'I'm glad I'm with you, Peter.'

He felt his throat contract.

'And I'm glad I'm with you,' he said. He wanted to kiss her but didn't know how to begin. He even wanted to make love to her, for maybe the last time ever for them both. And he heard himself saying: 'I'm sorry. It was our problem. A de Courtenay problem. Not yours. How it happened ...'

'It just happened,' she said. 'Come on – swim.' And she added: 'I do love you.'

'And I you,' he said, knowing this time it was true for the only time in his life.

304

He turned, and heaved himself up out of the water in an attempt to try again to see the shore lights. And, astonishingly, over to his left was not one light but many; dozens of little glow worms in the darkness and not very far away. His sense of despair had been so acute that for a moment he thought he was imagining things. And then he knew what they were.

'Anne,' he said. 'We're OK. We're going to be all right. Quick, swim with me.'

Marion tried to sleep after Peter and Anne had left, but her grief was so intense that she lay dry-eyed and motionless on the long sofa until the dawn began to edge its way into the saloon. She had heard the other girl tossing and turning throughout the night and felt no sympathy for her fear, for she herself did not care what happened. The shock of losing Tomas so violently had numbed her to the situation.

It was about eight o'clock when Evelyn finally woke. She sat up, stared about her and said frantically: 'Peter – where are you?'

'He's not here,' Marion said, not moving.

The other girl had thrown the blanket off her and was swinging her legs over the side of the sofa.

'Not here? Where is he?'

'He went for a swim,' Marion said flippantly. She had disliked Evelyn on sight.

'A swim? In this dreadful situation he's gone for a swim!'

'He felt in need of exercise,' Marion said.

'What a disgraceful way to behave.' Evelyn was standing up, her cheeks pink with anger, her hands clenched. 'I can't imagine why I came here. He's barely spoken to me since I arrived. Sending those frightful Arabs to collect me. Putting me in danger like that. I really—'

'Oh, piss off,' Marion said.

'I beg your pardon!' Evelyn's face was such a caricature of outrage that, had she not been so desperately miserable, Marion would have laughed. Instead she repeated: 'Piss off.'

'Really!' Evelyn said.

It was just then that the door of the saloon was unlocked and Raoul, carrying a tray with a coffee-pot, cups and saucers, bread and a pot of *confiture*, came through the door. Close behind him was Benjie, still grinning amiably and still holding the gun.

'Good morning,' Raoul said nervously, putting down the tray on the coffee table. Evelyn stared at him with hostility and Marion barely acknowledged him – she had laid herself flat on the sofa again. Benjie went across to the other blanket-covered sofa and whipped back the covers saying: 'Up you get—'

His grin faded when he saw nothing but a pile of cushions and he turned around, his grip tightening on the gun.

'Where is he?' he asked.

'I don't know,' Marion said, her voice indifferent. 'I've just woken up.'

He made a threatening move forward, and Evelyn said quickly: 'She just said he'd gone for a swim.'

Marion looked at her with hatred, regretting the feeble little joke.

'A swim, eh? And the girl?'

'I don't know,' Evelyn said.

'And how did they get out of here?' The gun was being lifted now, and Evelyn, total panic in her voice, said: 'He –' thrusting an accusing finger in Raoul's direction '– gave them the key.'

Raoul shrank back against the wall, and Benjie moved quietly towards him, grasping his arm and twisting it behind his back.

'You gave them the key, did you son?'

'No! No! I didn't,' Raoul said, whimpering with pain.

'He did,' Evelyn said indignantly. 'He's lying. I saw him do it with my own eyes. I told them not to do anything stupid—'

'That was good advice,' Benjie said. 'But now I think you'd better all come with me.'

He shooed them out of the saloon and up on to the bridge, where Lefrère was sitting staring at the yellow coastline of Africa with the towering mountains behind; a mug of coffee was in his hand. McTaggart was at the wheel, Françoise still lying on the banquette. It was very silent except for the throb of the engines and the small creaking noises that came from the wood panelling.

'What are you bringing them here for?' Lefrère said, his eyes black over the rim of the coffee cup.

'There's two missing. The man and the girl with the limp.'

'Where are they then?'

'She —' Benjie indicated Evelyn '— says that this one says they went for a swim, but this one says she doesn't know where they are. Also this one —' the cocked thumb went back to Evelyn '— says that he —' pointing out Raoul '— gave them the key, and that's how they got out.'

'Did you?' Lefrère's voice was dangerously soft.

'No—' Raoul was shaking with terror, and Françoise had suddenly sat bolt upright, alert to what was happening.

'Did he?' he asked Evelyn.

Her eyes were on the guns, and she looked from the big man to the thin shaking boy and said: 'I thought so. Maybe was wrong.'

'I don't think you were wrong at all,' he said. He turned back to Raoul. 'It was your father on deck yesterday, wasn't it?'

Raoul nodded dumbly. He had gone a pale green colour.

The man nodded back and very deliberately lifted his gun and aimed it at Raoul. 'We'll find your friends,' he said, 'but first we'll settle accounts with you.'

Before he could pull the trigger, Françoise had leapt on him, a small shrieking virago, all fists and teeth and flying feet.

'You killed my father. You won't kill my brother,' she screamed. 'You murdering bastard – killing kids! I'll kill you first!'

Off guard for the instant, the bullet from Lefrère's gun landed in the wood panelling, and as Benjie tried to take aim at the flaying figure of Françoise who had attached herself to Lefrère like a limpet mine, McTaggart got him from behind with a rabbit-chop on the back of the neck.

For once the de Courtenays were united. Marion shook off her apathy and joined in the fray. She had picked up a sextant and was repeatedly bringing it down on Lefrère's head. And Raoul, fighting for his life, sprang on his back, his legs clenched around the terrorist's thighs, his fingers gorging at his eyes.

Crew came running from all directions. Two men jumped McTaggart, while another snatched up Benjie's gun from where it had fallen. He levelled it at Raoul's back, when suddenly Benjie who was standing groggily shaking his head shouted and pointed out to sea: 'What the—!'

Coming up fast fore and aft of the yacht were two sleek gunboats flying the Stars and Stripes. There was a puff of smoke, a plume of water and a loud crump just ahead, and *Les Hirondelles III* rocked violently.

For a moment they were like children playing statues. Everyone on the bridge was frozen into immobility.

The gunboats were converging like marauding sharks. Another puff of smoke, plume of water and crump just in front of the bows of *Les Hirondelles* rocked the yacht even more wildly. Benjie fell heavily. On the deck of the nearer gunboat a sailor in spanking white ducks was shouting something through a loudhailer, and the man who held Benjie's gun took aim and fired. The rocking of the yacht deflected his aim, but the sailor dropped hastily under cover.

Lefrère started to snap out orders in Arabic, and the crew were dispersing in all directions. The staccato chatter of a machine-gun barked from the nearest gunboat, and Lefrère and Benjie, who was back on his feet, ran down to the deck, ducking and weaving, to position themselves with their own guns behind the rails, one each side of the deck. The rest of the crew had disappeared below, only one, holding a third gun, reappeared.

On the bridge the de Courtenays stood dazed.

'Get down,' McTaggart shouted. Evelyn was already prone, her face buried in the polished floor of the deck, her arms around her head. Raoul was busy being sick in the corner, Françoise holding his head, but he too finally collapsed and she fell with him. Marion was just standing staring through the glass at the boat that was being lowered from the gunboat astern, her face impassive.

'Get *down*,' McTaggart said, catching her behind the knees so that she fell.

He squirmed over to Françoise.

'Listen,' he said. 'I've got to get rid of that hash. If I can do it, we may get away with the whole thing.'

308

She was lying with her arms around Raoul and she did not seem to have taken in what he said. She was making a small whimpering noise, like a frightened puppy. He had no time to stop and comfort her.

There was more gunfire outside, and someone was shouting through the loudhailer again. The boarding party seemed to be well launched, and he hadn't much time. The yacht would be swarming with US Navy any minute now.

The gunboats were hemming them in port and starboard, and flat on his stomach McTaggart inched his way to the aft deck, his seaman's knife in his hand. He knew exactly where he had tied up the line that was stringing the hash behind them. He knew that without a wet-suit he'd never be able to sink the *dragueurs* but he could at least cut them free of the boat.

He swung himself over the side and dropped down into the water; clinging to the anchor chain he took a great breath before turning his body to dive down. The water was very clear, and he could see the line and its burden stringing out behind. With his lungs bursting he hacked at the rope until breath ran out. Then he surfaced, breathed and dived again. On the third attempt the line parted, and he came back into the sunshine, his head aching and his eyes smarting. Then he let the knife drop and set off to swim towards the gunboat's cutter, where one sailor sat at the tiller.

'Thank God you got here,' he said, as he climbed aboard.

Chapter Twenty-two

'Of course all our heroics were for nothing in the end,' Anne said and laughed out loud. 'There we were swimming about in a great black sea and getting nowhere fast, both convinced we'd had our chips and not admitting it, when suddenly we were bobbing about in the middle of a fleet of sardine fishermen who were quite happy to pull us on board but who weren't going to stop fishing until they were good and ready.'

'And all the action was going on back at the ranch – or rather, the yacht,' Marion said. 'The gunboats had everything under control in about ten minutes flat.'

'Nevertheless I think we should drink a toast to your niece, Olivia,' Stella said. 'She was quite remarkably brave. What a girl!'

'Hear, hear!' said Peter.

They all turned to her raising their glasses where she sat beside Peter, her aunt opposite at the de Courtenays' dining-table in the formal dining-room. Peter was at the foot, his mother at the head, beside her the young man Jacques, his hair and eyes gleaming oilily in the candlelight. Raoul sat at his grandmother's left, and Marion and Elisabeth were in the centre of the table facing each other. Anne noticed with a sharp pang that one leaf had been removed from the huge table, and yet still the survivors seemed to have too much room about them.

'To Anne,' Stella said, and they all echoed the toast.

Stella had insisted that they give this welcome dinner party for Anne's Aunt Olivia who had arrived from New York that morning, and in spite of the past tragedies it seemed that somehow the atmosphere of the room was lighter. The sinister undercurrents had gone, the candles seemed brighter, the log fire warmer, the guests more relaxed. Even Elisabeth, busy bossing her improbable son, had listened with interest to the saga of *Les Hirondelles III*'s voyage and actually made an occasional comment or a shocked exclamation.

Two weeks had passed since the end of the affair, but the story had to be told again for Olivia who was anxious for all the details, and Stella encouraged the telling.

Already she seemed different, Anne thought, her weight had dropped, her breathing improved. She was very much head of the household, presiding over her dining-table, the green eyes sparkling, cheekbones faintly appearing in her still, heavy face. There were moments when she was quiet and seemed in a reverie, but her spirits were generally good.

'What happened then?' Olivia asked. They had finished dessert, coffees and brandies had been served, and she sat with both elbows leaned on the table, her hands supporting her small head, listening intently.

'Well, Peter kept saying, "Police, *civil guardia* and *presto, presto*",' Anne said, 'but we couldn't rustle up enough Spanish between us to make them grasp the urgency of the situation. They weren't interested in the urgency of the situation – only their lousy sardines. So we sat going frantic, wrapped in stinking fishy blankets until they decided to take us back to Tarifa, from whence they'd come.

'We were miles from Gibraltar where we'd meant to be – the current had pulled us steadily back to Tangier and into the Atlantic. If Marion and the others had had to rely on us—' She stopped and shivered. 'Well, that doesn't bear thinking about.'

Marion had signalled the maid for another brandy. She was drinking just a little too much, Anne thought, but perhaps only sufficient to hold herself together until grief subsided. Marion's grief must have been hardest to bear because she could not tell the truth of it. She could mourn a brother, but not a lover.

'It was Stella who saved us really,' Marion was saying. 'Her quick thinking. She was puzzled about the telephone call she made to the yacht where no one seemed to be able to talk to her. And when they mentioned the awful Achmid's name she got suspicious. If she hadn't been so smart, none of us would be here now.'

'What did you do?' Olivia asked Stella.

'Well, it was rather fortunate that the American Consul in Marseilles is an old friend of my family,' Stella said. 'Another Bostonian, and thank God, he knew me well enough to know I wouldn't be panicking unnecessarily. He telephoned the American Consul in Tangier who checked with the port authorities and found that *Les Hirondelles III* had come in and gone out without anyone except two seamen landing and that they had brought back an American girl with them.'

'Those seamen were wearing very distinctive red and white striped *jellabas*,' Peter explained, 'and they made a big thing of

311

the fact they were returning with an American. The harbour police had checked Evelyn's papers when they came back, but hardly bothered to look at the men. They saw the same *jellabas*, so they thought they'd seen the same men. It was a neat trick to get Lefrère and his sidekick out of Morocco, and then to the Middle East – via us.'

'That's one thing about being American,' Stella said. 'We do look after our own! Everyone was thoroughly alarmed by now, and as I do know the odd influential person—'

'Like half of Congress!' Peter put in.

'And as the American Sixth Fleet was in Gib,' she went on, giving her son a reproving look, 'they just whistled up a couple of gunboats to go and check. All rather old-fashioned British style it was. The commander said afterwards it was good practice. Gave them something to do. And the Navy were beside themselves when they realized they'd netted Lefrère.'

Raoul gave a little shudder at the mention of Lefrère and Stella put her hand on his and patted it, as Anne took up the story.

'Our worst bit was after we got back to Tarifa, and we managed to get to the police station, still only wrapped in those awful smelly blankets. We tried and tried to get help, but no one took much notice. And I couldn't stop sneezing. I caught the most awful cold.

'The policeman wouldn't take us seriously until we managed to make him understand that hash was being smuggled. Then he moved. He was on to the Moroccan police, his own police in Algeciras, and they had helicopters up instantly; everything that moved was out.'

'Did they get the stuff?' Olivia asked.

'Not until later,' Raoul answered as the others looked to him. 'McTaggart managed to get overboard without being seen and cut the line holding it free. He was really very brave.'

'The Moroccans found it eventually,' Peter said, 'and commandeered it because it was in their waters lurking about like a great string of submerged sausages. No one did anything more, as the Moroccans weren't too keen on it being known they'd had Lefrère under their noses and never caught him.

'So the matter of the hash was quietly dropped in all the excitement of catching Lefrère and company – which was extremely fortunate for Raoul, Françoise and McTaggart.'

Olivia turned to Raoul. 'How come you were involved?' she asked.

There was an uncomfortable silence, and then Marion said: 'It seems he and Françoise had plotted with Achmid to bring the stuff out on the yacht. They were going to get a quarter of a million pounds sterling for smuggling it. And they did actually get a fifth of the money, paid in Deuschmarks.'

'We didn't really,' Raoul said. 'McTaggart disappeared with it. Even Françoise never got her share.'

'Just as well,' Stella said briskly. 'We thought it sensible to send her to stay with some relatives in Boston for a while. Just until everything dies down.'

'But how did she ever get involved?' Olivia asked.

'It was really only boredom,' Raoul said hastily. 'She only wanted some excitement. You know how restless she is. McTaggart was in it for the money. He wanted his own boat. I expect he's got one now.' He sounded sad, and again Stella patted his hand.

'It's the awful Achmid, as you all call him, who interests me,' Olivia said. 'He sounds mad as a hatter.'

'Madder. But he got away with it,' Peter said. 'With Françoise and Raoul having been so involved we thought it better not to shop him. Not very public-spirited of us, but without us spilling the beans he had no connection with any of it, and Lefrère wasn't talking. If we'd shopped Achmid he'd have shopped the kids and McTaggart. He was very vengeful. We had a bit of trouble persuading an old girlfriend of mine who was on board to keep quiet.'

'She wanted everyone involved shot immediately,' Anne put in.

'Ah, well, we calmed her down and sent her home by Concorde, which seemed to make her feel better. But it does mean that Fouezanne has lived to fight another day, which I must say enrages me. But I guess we had no choice.'

Olivia pushed a hand through her short dark hair. 'The

instigators of this world always seem to survive,' she said.

'He was a most unpleasant man,' Elisabeth said suddenly. 'Most unpleasant. A very bad advertisement for the Arab world, I would say.' She nodded gravely. 'However, if you will excuse me, Stella, I think I shall make my way home. Jacques, my dear boy, get my shawl, will you?'

'Of course, *Maman*.' The young man was instantly on his feet, a little too elegant in a midnight-blue dinner jacket and frilled shirt. 'Come, take my arm.'

He hurried round to help Elisabeth from her seat, his heavy gold cufflinks catching the light from the candles.

'My son and I are leaving for New York tomorrow,' Elisabeth said to Olivia. 'We had intended to go earlier, but Papa's death—' She stopped. 'We may not see you again on this visit, madame, but next year, no doubt ...'

'Certainly next year,' Olivia said. 'After all, it seems we are to be nearly related.'

'Yes.' Elisabeth permitted herself a stiff smile. 'I must say I think Peter has chosen very well. Your niece is a charming girl.'

'Thank you,' Anne murmured.

'And that,' said Peter, when his half-sister had left, 'is praise indeed.'

'She's right though,' said Stella. 'I was always uneasy about Evelyn and I must say from what I hear she was as I feared, as stuffy as the rest of her family.'

'Stuffy!' Marion's voice was bitter. 'She was downright lethal.'

'True,' Peter said. 'But then no one behaved well towards her.'

'It's a family failing – not behaving well,' said Stella. 'And on those lines, what do you think of Elisabeth's long lost son, Olivia?'

'Very attentive,' Olivia said cautiously.

'A nice little lapdog – if expensive – and very much one of the family.' Stella's green eyes were glinting amusement. 'Did you know his little sister-in-law has even become Margaret's secretary, so we shall all be one happy family.' She shook her head. 'It's sad in a way and yet not sad. He's no more her son than he's the man in the moon. It's a charade, and Elisabeth knows it. But she's finally found someone to love. And he's a nice enough imposter. He gives value for money – very much the dutiful son. Here's to them. Her life's been pretty barren up until now, and happiness takes many forms.'

She finished her brandy and put her napkin on the table.

'Would you mind if I left you to finish your coffee?' she asked and sighed. 'I find it keeps me awake, though I tire easily these days. There's some adjusting to life still to be done—' She broke off, and her children moved to kiss her goodnight.

'I shall come with you, Grandmother,' Raoul said. 'I think I too am ready for bed.'

'As you wish,' she said. 'But we shall all meet for coffee in the morning – plus Suki, courtesy of my future daughter-in-law.'

With Raoul holding her arm, she left, and after a contemplative moment Peter suggested they move to the drawing-room.

'Don't let's bother,' Olivia said. 'It's late, and all I want to know now is when you two are getting married?'

Peter pulled a long face.

'Ask her,' he said, pointing at Anne. 'She's stalling. She wants to live in sin for a while, but it's really not my style. Persuade her for me, will you?'

'I'll try,' Olivia said lightly. 'But you've only known each other a month. She could be right. More important, how about her leg? I've a vested interest in that.'

'It's not more important,' Anne said, 'because I honestly think it's better. That last plastic surgeon you found was a miracle-worker.'

Olivia looked at her sharply. 'You're still limping.'

'I'll always limp. But Peter doesn't mind. He says it's the only thing he can feel protective about.'

'She's so darned independent,' he said.

'Your fault,' Anne said to her aunt. 'You taught me to be.'

315

'I suppose I did.' Olivia was thoughtful. 'But it seemed necessary.'

'And if you hadn't made me learn to swim—'

'You'd have been safe on board that boat and not risking drowning.'

'Ah, but we didn't know what was going to happen.' Suddenly Anne was serious. 'I owe you a lot,' she said. 'My leg is all right. Even the scars are beginning to fade. And I've got Peter.'

'Yet she won't marry me,' he grumbled.

'Give her time.' Olivia was silent for a moment, twisting the bowl of the brandy glass in her hands. 'I was sorry to hear of your father's death,' she said. 'I was fond of him.'

'I know,' Peter said.

'But your mother seems fine.'

'Funnily,' he said, 'she's better than she's been for years. She's stopped drinking so much. She's lost some weight. She's very much in control. She loved Father, but he made her very unhappy.'

'His trouble was that he could never settle for one woman,' Olivia said. 'Which wasn't surprising with all that charm.'

Peter shook his head.

'His philandering killed him in the end. I don't see why you shouldn't know as you're one of the family, but he was making love to a girl he'd let the guest house to, Jacques's wife – the one Mother said will never come back again, though it seems we're pretty lumbered with the rest of that lot. Papa and the girl were in a car in that clearing off the road, the one we used to call the Red Valley as kids. He had a heart attack and died.'

'In the Red Valley! How strange,' Olivia said, sitting upright and alert.

'Well, not a pretty place to die in,' Peter said. 'And a waste. He had so much life in him.'

Olivia was still unrelaxed, Anne noticed, but her aunt said: 'What puzzles me is that a nice respectable, elegant family like the de Courtenays ever got themselves mixed up in such a series of dramas. When I got your cable I really thought you were making it all up.'

'I wish we had been,' Marion sa[i]
still be alive.'

'Well, it might make a plot fo[r]
Peter said. 'You could call it [....]
really caused it all. As you [....]
kept us very short of cash [....]
with Fouezanne, who loaned h[im....]
Tomas had sold Fouezanne on the [....]
was a mountain of bauxite. Absolute [....]
Fouezanne fell for it. Tomas was to get ten [....]
if Papa could be persuaded to sell, and Achmid w[....]
pay twenty million.'

'Bauxite?' Olivia said, taking a cigarette from the bo[x....]
the table. 'I wonder what made him think of that?'

'He thought our land looked much the same as that of Les
Baux,' Marion said. 'It gave him the idea. Fouezanne had
offered him a big share of the deal as well as the money, but
Tomas knew he'd never get that as he was going to have to
disappear quickly once Achmid realized there wasn't any
bauxite.' Her voice was expressionless. 'His problem was asking
enough money from Fouezanne to make it seem believable, and
he got stuck with the share offer when he'd much rather have
had cash and vanished. But all the time he was juggling.
Achmid couldn't possibly offer Papa the amount he believed
the place to be worth – Papa would have smelt a rat immediately. And the awful Achmid wanted it as cheaply as possible.'

'Thank God he never got it,' Peter said.

'Yes, thank God—' Olivia's voice was abstracted. 'Listen,'
she said. 'I think I'll follow Stella's example – jet lag is setting
in. Will you walk back to the cottage with me, Anne?'

Peter finished his coffee and got to his feet. 'I'll take you,'
he said. 'It is late. How long are you going to be staying?'

'Just a month,' Olivia said. She still seemed far away and
jumpy, and Anne wondered if her aunt had cared for Philip
more than she had said. Something was wrong.

'I want to take Anne and Marion back to New York with
me in about three weeks' time,' Peter was saying. 'Will you
be back there?'

Olivia said. 'Maybe London. Maybe Paris. wherever you have the wedding. And listen, I want my niece to myself for just a moment.'

something so positive in her voice that Peter sat

he said, 'send her back home though, won't you?'

promised she would, but her mind seemed not to be subject, and walking across the brightly lit courtyard down past the pool she was still silent. Then suddenly she pped walking and looked out towards the dark shapes of the ountains against the light sky.

'Is anything wrong?' Anne asked.

'Not wrong, just strange,' Olivia said. She began to walk again, taking Anne's arm. 'Look, you must make up your own mind whether to tell Peter what I'm about to tell you. And if you do decide to tell him he can make up his mind as to whether or not he should tell Stella—' She stopped abruptly. 'So strange Philip should die there,' she said.

'What is it?' Anne asked. She realized something important was about to be said.

'The bauxite. It wasn't a load of rubbish. Les Hirondelles is a mountain of the stuff. And the Red Valley, where Philip died, is the place where the geologists first found it and where they were beginning to mine until he decided against it.'

Anne stopped in her tracks. 'What!' she said. Patiently her aunt repeated what she had said.

'He couldn't have decided against it! If that's true, Les Hirondelles is really worth a fortune.'

'Indeed,' Olivia said drily.

'My God!' Anne said. She looked at her aunt in the moonlight. 'It explains an awful lot about why Achmid was so keen to get his hands on the place. And his willingness to pay what seemed a ridiculous sum.'

'Exactly.' They walked on in silence until they reached the cottage door. Olivia took the key in her hand. 'What puzzles me is how Tomas knew,' she said. 'He'd have been about fourteen and was away at school when it was all going on. I knew because I was living with Philip at the time, and Philip swore me to secrecy. He decided he wanted to leave Les Hirondelles as it was – and still is. I don't think he ever told another soul. Not even Stella. I can only think that Tomas overheard some conversation and never forgot. Unless his father confided in him, and that we'll never know now.'

'But Tomas didn't know,' Anne said, excited. 'He told Marion he made the whole thing up. The geologists he used to convince Achmid were a couple of con-men, and the one thing that was terrifying him was that Achmid might check. Maybe Achmid did check. Maybe that's why Tomas believed he'd been able to convince him.' She sighed. 'It's all so bizarre. Poor Tomas, if he'd known the bauxite was really there I wonder if he'd still be alive?'

Olivia considered and then said positively: 'It wouldn't have changed a thing. Except that he would have felt he could have demanded even more. He'd have just felt a lot safer. Remember, he was a gambler. But how incredible he should have hit on the truth without knowing it.'

She shook her head and then said quietly: 'And will you tell Peter?'

'Oh, yes,' Anne said. 'I'll tell him because it's quite safe to do so. In that he's like his father. He believes Les Hirondelles is far too beautiful to spoil, not for all the money in the world.'

'And you?' her aunt asked, putting the key in the door. 'Would you choose to mine the bauxite?'

Anne looked at her, grinned and turned to go back to Peter. 'What bauxite?' she said.

Bestselling Fiction and Non-Fiction

☐	**The Amityville Horror**	Jay Anson	80p
☐	**Shadow of the Wolf**	James Barwick	95p
☐	**The Island**	Peter Benchley	£1.25p
☐	**Castle Raven**	Laura Black	£1.25p
☐	**Smart-Aleck Kill**	Raymond Chandler	95p
☐	**Sphinx**	Robin Cook	£1.25p
☐	**The Entity**	Frank De Felitta	£1.25p
☐	**Trial Run**	Dick Francis	95p
☐	**The Rich are Different**	Susan Howatch	£1.95p
☐	**Moviola**	Garson Kanin	£1.50p
☐	**Tinker Tailor Soldier Spy**	John le Carré	£1.50p
☐	**The Empty Copper Sea**	John D. MacDonald	90p
☐	**Where There's Smoke**	Ed McBain	80p
☐	**The Master Mariner**		
	Book 1: Running Proud	Nicholas Monsarrat	£1.50p
☐	**Bad Blood**	Richard Neville and	
		Julie Clarke	£1.50p
☐	**Victoria in the Wings**	Jean Plaidy	£1.25p
☐	**Fools Die**	Mario Puzo	£1.50p
☐	**Sunflower**	Marilyn Sharp	95p
☐	**The Throwback**	Tom Sharpe	95p
☐	**Wild Justice**	Wilbur Smith	£1.50p
☐	**That Old Gang of Mine**	Leslie Thomas	£1.25p
☐	**Caldo Largo**	Earl Thompson	£1.50p
☐	**Harvest of the Sun**	E. V. Thompson	£1.25p
☐	**Future Shock**	Alvin Toffler	£1.95p

All these books are available at your local bookshop or newsagent, or can be ordered direct from the publisher. Indicate the number of copies required and fill in the form below

Name_____
(block letters please)

Address_____

_____

Send to Pan Books (CS Department), Cavaye Place, London SW10 9PG
Please enclose remittance to the value of the cover price plus:

25p for the first book plus 10p per copy for each additional book ordered to a maximum charge of £1.05 to cover postage and packing
Applicable only in the UK

While every effort is made to keep prices low, it is sometimes necessary to increase prices at short notice. Pan Books reserve the right to show on covers and charge new retail prices which may differ from those advertised in the text or elsewhere